PILGRIMS

PILGRIMS

GERARD MAC

St. Martin's Press
New York

Library of Congress Cataloging-in-Publication Data

Mac, Gerard.
Pilgrims / Gerard Mac.
p.   cm.
ISBN 0-312-11551-2
1. Massachusetts—History—New Plymouth, 1620–1691–Fiction.
2. Pilgrims (New Plymouth colony)—Fiction.   3. Young women—
Massachusetts—Fiction.   4. Mayflower (Ship)—Fiction.   I. Title.
PS3563.A2275P55   1994
813'.54—dc20   94-19661   CIP

First published in Great Britain by Robert Hale Ltd.

First U.S. Edition: November 1994
10 9 8 7 6 5 4 3 2 1

To Liz
and Kate

'It was properly the beginning of America. There were struggling settlers in America before ... but the soul of it was this.'
Thomas Carlyle
(1795–1881)

1

There was a large bread-knife on the table, the handle towards her hand. Daisy snatched it up and pointed it at his midriff. 'I am not going,' she told him. 'I am staying here – with the Duchess.'

'Ach!' Bates spat into the dying embers in the sagging grate. 'The Duchess'll be dead when yer gets back. Now you do as I say ...' – Slowly, menacingly, he unbuckled his worn leather belt and slid it from about his thin waist – 'or it'll be the worse for you.'

With the long-bladed knife she lunged at him, taking him by surprise, and he jumped back in astonishment, suddenly realizing she was serious. This waif, this slavey really intended to challenge his authority.

'Why, you ...' he began, but before he could make his move she had thrown down the knife and run out into the muddy, unmade street and out of sight along a narrow, rat-infested passage.

Later, when Bates was with his cronies in the Crown tavern, she crept back into the crumbling hovel where she had lived and worked for the past five years. Please, please let her live, she prayed, if only for another hour or so.

Hoping and praying, Daisy waited in the dark doorway of the communal wash-house. The Duchess was the one and only person in the whole world who had ever cared for her and now the Duchess was dying. Oh, God! Don't let her die. Please! She wanted to be there, with her, when the end came. There were things she wanted to say.

The Duchess had the pox, the dreaded disease that in time struck down most of the city's street women. Not that the Duchess was a street woman. The Duchess had never walked the streets or stood on street corners tarting for business in her life. But she had many patrons – 'gentlemen friends' – and she preferred to call herself a courtesan. She thought it sounded nicer and somehow more respectable.

'But whatever you call yourself and however careful you might be,' she would say in her more sober moments, 'the pox will get you in the end. It starts slowly; doesn't stop you working at first.

7

Then it spreads and it shows and it's obvious you've got it. You can't work any more. The doctor can't do anything for you. Most of 'em won't even see you. And so there's only one way out: feet first in a sack. Or, if yer lucky, in a box with a lid on.'

It was a caution, a warning to her young protégé, delivered at regular intervals and the message had not been lost. But Daisy had never really believed the terminal disease would one day claim her lovely Duchess. And now it had and the Duchess was sinking fast. Life was seeping out of her ravaged body and draining from her once serene and beautiful face.

In the early days, with her golden hair and clear blue eyes, the Duchess was a real beauty. She had told Daisy so and Daisy had believed her. But coming from a lowly background, the Duchess had explained, the only way she could get the most out of life was the way she had – through her 'gentlemen friends'. A great many men had wanted her and many had paid for the privilege.

She had known some very high-ranking gentlemen in her time, the highest in the land. Lords, some of them. And judges. And confidants of the King. She'd even had a visit, she sometimes hinted, from royalty itself. Oh yes, she'd had some wonderful times. Nice clothes. The best restaurants. Money in her purse. But nothing lasts forever, inevitably standards drop. The Duchess was past her best and towards the end she had been visited by men she would not previously have entertained.

'Don't let it 'appen to you, darlin',' she warned Daisy. 'Don't ever be tempted to go lookin' for men. Stay away from 'em. They're all the same in the end. They'll tell you they love you and they'll give you money. Then when they've 'ad what they came for they'll go 'ome to their wives and their families and their big 'ouses. Stay away from 'em, Daisy. That's my advice. Yer too good for that. And besides, yer got brains.'

When she was not calling her 'darling', the Duchess called her 'Daisy'. But Daisy was not her name. Bates called her 'girl'. 'Do this, girl, do that. Get this, girl, get that.' Nobody had ever asked her true name. And it was just as well. Because if she had one, she didn't know it.

At the convent they had called her Little Sister Teresa. But Teresa was not her name, either. It just happened that they took her in at a time when the work and example of the Carmelite nun, Teresa of Avila, figured prominently in church affairs. The nuns had taken her in as a baby and kept her to work for them in the kitchens and domestic quarters of their convent near Bath until she was old enough to be guided towards a vocation. But she didn't have a vocation and she didn't want to be a nun.

As a child she grew to hate the closed confines of the convent, the sweet cloying smell of burning incense, the musty pews in darkened chapels, the bell that tolled every three hours from matins to compline. She wanted to feel on her skin the clear, bright glow of the sun. But the sun appeared to be veiled in a permanent light mist above the blue meadow she sometimes glimpsed from the slit windows of the convent walls.

To be fair to the nuns they had given her one great asset: they had taught her to read. Every day she read her Bible and her Book of Common Prayer. And that was something. That was truly something. A genuine, worthwhile gift. As far as she knew, nobody around here could read. Not even the Duchess and certainly not Bates.

Silently she crept up the creaking wooden stairway. Perhaps she was too late. Perhaps the Duchess was already dead. She paused on the landing, held her breath at the door to the tiny bedroom, then slowly eased it inwards. A shaft of late sunlight from the small crooked window lay across the narrow bed. It was always clean in here. The only really clean room in the house. Daisy saw to that. The Duchess had never cleaned a room in her life, even before she fell ill. But Daisy had kept it neat and dusted and scented with violets and sprigs of lavender from the flower sellers at Spitalfields.

Ravaged by pain, the wasted face above the white sheet was the colour of old parchment. The Duchess, at twenty-eight years of age, looked like an elderly lady who, after a harsh and gruelling lifetime, had finally arrived at death's door. Her once smooth blonde hair had thinned until her naked scalp showed through. The skin of her face and neck had wrinkled and sagged and with her pale blue, translucent eyelids closed, she looked as though she was already dead. But when she opened her eyes and saw Daisy at her bedside a glimmer of fond recognition brought the life back to her face.

'Oh, Duchess! I thought....' Daisy bit her lip.

'I know,' the Duchess murmured. 'I know what you thought. But I haven't gone yet. I've bin waitin', 'angin' on. Jus' fer you. I 'ave somethin' ... somethin' I want you to 'ave.'

She patted the bed with her skeletal, vein-lined hand, inviting Daisy to sit down. Daisy sat down and took the hand in hers.

'You are goin' to 'ave to leave 'ere, darlin',' the Duchess said. 'You can't stay with Bates. Bates would jus' want to use you. As 'e used me once. Yer know that – an' yer mus' promise me you will not let that 'appen.'

'You needn't worry,' Daisy assured her. 'There's no chance of that. But try not to talk. I know it hurts when you speak and I can't bear to see you in so much pain.'

'I 'ave ter talk,' the Duchess said. 'I bin talkin' all me life an' if I stop now it'll be fer good. An' besides, there are things I mus' tell you.'

A tear ran down Daisy's cheek.

'An' we'll 'ave none o' that,' the Duchess went on. 'Don't you dare cry. Not fer me, anyway. I'm goin' to a better place. A far, far better place, I 'ope.' She tried to squeeze Daisy's hand but she hadn't the strength. 'It couldn't be much worse than this, eh? Wherever it is.' She started to laugh, heard herself and stopped abruptly, not liking what she heard. 'Now listen. The way things are 'ere, when I go it sort of puts you on the spot....'

The Duchess had lived in Bates's house since she was fifteen. She was the eldest child of a large family with a feckless father and a harassed, careworn mother. Her mother had died, worn out in her early thirties. The family had been split up, the children sent to various institutions or put into service and the father had disappeared. The Duchess had been sent to a country house near Hampton Court but had soon found her way back to her former home, now derelict, in Bow. A friend of her dead mother had then put her in touch with Alfred Bates who was said to be in need of domestic help.

As a pantry maid at the house in the country the Duchess had become involved with the boot boy who had promptly made her pregnant. Her employer had dismissed her, forcing her to confess her condition at the first hint of morning sickness. Bates's answer was to help her by arranging an abortion. But the unqualified butcher of an old hag who had performed the operation on a kitchen table in a back street slum had made a dreadful mess of it. The 'operation' had gone horribly wrong and the Duchess had almost died. But dazed as she was and barely conscious she had always suspected that the baby was well developed and alive when aborted. Though in a haze at the time she later recalled hearing the old hag refer to the child as a 'girl bastard'. The Duchess had been racked with guilt ever since and frequently pined for the daughter who had been so cruelly torn from her.

For weeks the Duchess had been ill yet she had recovered to the point where she could smile happily and assume an air of gaiety at will, only occasionally lapsing into a kind of self-reproaching melancholia. Within a year she had blossomed into a blue-eyed, blonde-haired beauty, much in demand by the gentlemen of the city. Bates had put her to work mainly at superior social functions and at first she willingly filled the role of escort on the strict understanding that she was not for bedding. But as her clientele became more elevated their demands became more difficult to refuse and their ability to pay more marked.

Her clients at that time were exclusively from the upper reaches of society. Dukes, senior members of the clergy, ministers of state – her name was known to them all. An intelligent girl, she had swiftly gained an understanding of the ways of the world and acquired an air of discreet sophistication. When the situation warranted she could put on the airs and graces and an exaggerated upper crust accent, reverting to her Cockney idiom with its dropped 'aitches' and mild obscenities when relaxing at home – or sometimes, to the delight of an elevated client, in the privacy of a bedroom.

But early on she had innocently fallen for just one client, a Duke no less, and for a time had taken no others. The Duke was a darkly handsome young man who seemed genuinely fond of her and when he took her to bed one night at a coach house near Banbury she went willingly and would have done it for nothing. In fact, in her own way, she did do it for nothing, unaware that the Duke had paid Bates.

When she discovered this some weeks later – it came out in a row they had about what she called her love affair with the Duke – she forbade Bates to accept any more money from him. She then informed the Duke she was not a common whore and would only continue to see him on equal terms. The Duke, who was touched by her reaction, told her he had never regarded her in that light and felt something special, something akin to love for her. He had no wish to end their relationship.

He was a married man, he told her, which she already knew. He had a high-born wife, three young children and had inherited a large estate in the country. Their relationship, he said frankly, could only end in regret, especially for her. If she wanted to end it now he would understand. Tearfully, after one final ecstatic night at the coach house, she decided not to see him again. But less than a month later they came across each other at a ball at Stationers' Hall. The Duchess promptly dumped the elderly priest she was escorting and the relationship was resumed.

Often, after a night spent together, the Duke would be gone early in the morning, long before she awoke. And always he would leave a little something for her – a sovereign perhaps or some expensive trinket. Though he could never be hers completely she

knew he was the love of her life and to her and to those who knew
her well he became 'her Duke'. It was an open secret that they had
this special relationship and that all her other contacts were of
secondary importance. So often did she refer to 'my Duke' that
Bates and others took to calling her 'the Duchess' and the
sobriquet had stuck.

Her true name was Dolly Mason but few, apart from Bates,
knew it. As a child she didn't like her name Dolly and, after seeing
a poster of a dancer called Daisy outside a theatre in the
Haymarket, she wanted to be called 'Daisy'. Had her baby lived
she would certainly have christened her Daisy. And so, when
Bates brought home a nameless fifteen year old with the slim
figure and the trim ankles of a dancer and all of the wide-eyed
innocence the Duchess felt she herself had lost that was the name
she gave her.

Bates had taken the girl in with a promise to feed and clothe her
and provide her with a home in return for domestic work. The
Duchess knew, of course, that Bates's plans for the girl were far
from domestic. She would be carefully groomed and nurtured until
she was ready to be smart-talked, coaxed, cajoled or, if necessary,
coerced into servicing clients, Bates's clients, and she would work
for Bates for as long as men would pay for her services. But the
Duchess had other plans.

The sudden appearance of the vulnerable fifteen year old had
revived all the deprived and suppressed maternal instincts that
surfaced from time to time to torment the Duchess. The girl
replaced the daughter the Duchess had lost, the daughter she had
been forced by circumstances to discard. The lost child would have
been thirteen now, nearly fourteen. This new girl would get all the
warmth and protection a young girl needed, the Duchess had
promised herself. And so she had.

Daisy was almost twenty now and, but for the Duchess's furious
interventions, might well have been out entertaining gentlemen, a
harlot in the making. Or so the Duchess believed. In truth Daisy
was far too intelligent to allow that to happen. She had only
remained in the Bates household because of the Duchess's
increasing dependence upon her. But the Duchess didn't know this
and was anxious for Daisy to move on.

For years Bates had threatened to inform the authorities that
the Duchess had undergone an illegal abortion. The baby had died
and been disposed of and, as Bates did not hesitate to point out,
the Duchess was, therefore, guilty of murder. She could be
hanged, strung up at Tyburn. She would not, she said, put it past

Bates to attempt to get a similar hold over Daisy. He might try to make her pregnant himself then force her to have an abortion. That was the way he worked.

'But I can show you a way out, darlin',' the Duchess croaked in a hoarse whisper.

The talking had tired her. Barely able to raise her hand she indicated that Daisy should look under her pillow. Daisy put a hand under the pillow and touched a package. Slowly she drew it out and handed it to her.

'It's for you, darlin',' the Duchess murmured. 'I want you to have it.'

It was a slim calfskin wallet, creased now from its hiding place under the pillow. On the outside in a long sloping hand was written the name Miss D. Mason. In the top left-hand corner were printed the words: The Company of Merchant Adventurers, London, 1619.

The Duchess nodded her encouragement and Daisy drew a clutch of documents from the wallet. The first item appeared to be a ship's warrant but the name of the ship and the name of the passenger had not been entered. The second was a copy of an agreement between 'the Company of Adventurers' and a group of people referred to as 'Planters'. A covering letter declared that the enclosed warrant entitled a Miss D. Mason to take passage of herself and her personal baggage, subject to space available, on a proposed voyage to the new and uncharted territories to the north of Virginia and now known to all, with the assent of His Majesty the King, as New England. The passage had been reserved and paid for on behalf of the said Miss Mason by the private secretary to His Grace the Duke of Buckingham. As an authorized 'Planter', the said Miss Mason was to benefit in full from all of the terms of the joint agreement. There was also a promissory note in the sum of twenty-five pounds.

It occurred to Daisy that unless someone had read and explained the details to the Duchess, who couldn't read, she would have only a vague idea of what was entailed.

'There's a warrant for you to travel across the ocean and become a planter or something, in what people are calling the New World.'

'It's for people who want to settle there an' make a new start,' the Duchess said. 'An' it's for a Miss D. Mason. Well, that's you now, darlin'. Miss Daisy Mason. I want you to take it an' go in my place. I'm goin' on a much bigger journey.'

Daisy read the letter again. It was from the office of a Mr Thomas Weston, Merchant, Ludgate Hill. London.

2

'The Duke is a lovely man,' the Duchess said, 'an' a good friend.'

Daisy took the word friend to mean client, but the Duchess went on, ' 'e really loved me, you know, an' I loved 'im. We were seein' each other for nearly seven years. Then a few months ago 'e told me 'e'd bin called to take up a position at court. It was a royal command, somethin' 'e couldn't refuse. It was 'is duty to accept. An' it meant our relationship would 'ave to end. I was 'eart-broke an' so was 'e.

' 'e really did love me, you know, an' 'e wanted to make sure I'd be all right. 'e asked if there was anythin' 'e could do for me. 'e was very sweet. I told 'im I would like to change my whole way of life before it was too late an' I was too old. 'e said that in 'is 'eart I would never grow old. Then one afternoon 'e called. 'e came 'ere out o' the blue. Bates was down the Crown an' you were at the wash.

'I didn't know 'e knew where I lived and I was ashamed when I saw 'im, ashamed o' this place. But 'e didn't seem to notice. I brought 'im up 'ere to my bedroom 'cos – thanks to you, darlin' – it's the nicest room in the 'ouse.' A hint of her old shameless smile crossed her wizened features. 'We couldn't resist it. We loved each other again, right 'ere in this room – for one last time. Then I cried an' 'e, too, was near to tears.

' 'e said 'e'd bin worryin' about my future an' 'e thought I might be interested in a new project that was jus' takin' shape in the City. 'e said that if I really wanted to take up a new way of life I might like to try my luck in this New World. I was still young, 'e said. An entire new world across the ocean was openin' up for young people. There was nothin' to keep me 'ere, 'e said. I could put the past behind me and start all over again. An' what's more, 'e would pay for my passage. It was jus' what I wanted, my chance to escape.'

Daisy couldn't help thinking it was probably just what the Duke wanted, too, an opportunity to end the affair gracefully and permanently. The Duchess would be many miles away and no longer a danger to his career. But Daisy's cynicism shamed her and she squeezed the Duchess's hand. If the Duchess was willing to believe her Duke had acted purely out of his love for her then Daisy had no wish to cast a doubt on so noble a motive. And if, in her heart, the Duchess didn't entirely believe it, it was clearly what she wanted to believe.

The voyage to the new territory across the Atlantic had been proposed and organized on behalf of a group of religious exiles, English families living in Holland. There would be other passengers, of course, but the people from Holland would make up the majority. They were living in exile, the Duke had explained, because they did not and would not accept the preachings of the Church of England. But they were God-fearing people, men and women of high principle and a high moral order.

'The Duke was 'appy for me to go,' the Duchess said, ' 'cos 'e believed I'd be safe with them. Of course, they would know nothing of my life 'ere. They'd treat me with respect an' I'd 'ave my entitlement just as they 'ad. It would 'ave bin a whole new beginnin' for me an' I really considered goin'. To tell you the truth, I planned to take you with me. Then I found I 'ad the pox. I knew no ship would take me. The ship's doctor would take one look an' I'd be banned from boardin'.

'Naturally, I didn't want the Duke to know. I didn't want to spoil what we'd 'ad between us. I 'ad some pride left, darlin', an' I wanted 'im to remember me always as I was when we first met. I didn't want 'im ever to see me or even think of me with these ugly black teeth an' 'orrible blue gums an' sunken eyes an' dead skin an'....'

'Stop it! Please!' Daisy begged her. 'Don't talk like that. Not to me.'

'That last time,' the Duchess went on, 'right 'ere, in this room, 'e urged me to go an' make a fresh start in this New World. An' one day, 'e said, though we might be old an' grey, 'e could visit me. We could meet again, 'e said, an' who knows what changes life can bring. I might be an 'ighly respected married lady with a family of my own. 'e might 'ave fallen out of favour at the palace. Anythin' can 'appen, 'e said. But no matter what or where or when, we'd always be lovers – if only in our 'earts. 'e would always love me, 'e said. 'e's such a lovely man an' so romantic. But 'e will never know, 'e must never know that I went like this.'

She urged the documents on Daisy. 'These are yours now. I want you to 'ave them an' think about them. I don't know if you want to cross the ocean, darlin'. Maybe you don't.' She laughed though the movement pained her. 'But it's one place where Bates would never find you.' Then she was serious again. 'But if you do go an' the Duke was ever to check the list of passengers on the ship commissioned by this Mr Weston 'e would believe 'e'd 'elped me to escape. An' that was what 'e wanted. 'e'd see the name Miss D. Mason and 'e'd think it was me. But it wouldn't be me. It would be you. Miss *Daisy* Mason. From this day forward, darlin', that's your name.'

The feeble hand dropped to the bedcover and the Duchess looked towards the window. It was a late evening in July. Darkness was creeping over the huddle of tightly packed dwellings and the warren of narrow alleyways that ran between them. There were no fields, no trees, no distant hills for the Duchess to rest her tired and weakening eyes on. Only the backs of dark hovels, the grimy windows and the sagging roofs and down below the domain of countless arrogant rats where cats watched warily as stray dogs scavenged in discarded rubbish.

Gazing out at the darkening sky Daisy remembered how, as a wide-eyed innocent, she loved to sit quietly in a corner of the small bedroom and watch as the Duchess dressed and prepared herself for an evening out with a gentleman friend. It was a long process beginning always with the tin bath which she and the Duchess would carry up the narrow stairway and fill with jugs of hot water from the cauldron settled on the living-room fire. They would test the water with their elbows, cooling it with cold water from a cask in the kitchen. And when it seemed about right Daisy would delight in sprinkling in lotions from the Orient, blue and green crystals from slim little phials marked 'E. India Co.', a company in which the Duke had an interest.

Daisy would watch admiringly as the Duchess luxuriated in the scented water and, conscious of the girl's presence, the Duchess would preen herself and pose naked when she stood upright in the tin bath to towel herself dry. Mentally Daisy would measure herself against her mentor, comparing her own breasts and thighs and trimness of waist against the only yardstick she knew, the uncommonly graceful figure of the Duchess.

The Duchess would take her bath before and after all of her engagements and Bates was regularly scornful of such waste. Most people are lucky if they bathe once a month, he would chide. The Duchess would reply that in his case it was more like once a year. Daisy could not recall any time in the last *five* years when Bates took a bath. If he did she had no knowledge of when or where. In her own case, with the Duchess's permission, Daisy would use the tin bath whenever the time seemed right and always when Bates was out. And sometimes, if the Duchess was present, she would tease Daisy until she blushed by drawing attention to Daisy's steadily burgeoning beauty.

Brushing her long blonde hair until it shone the Duchess would talk in those happier days of where she was going and with whom and who were the glittering guests who would grace the occasion. Ready to hold a dress for the Duchess to step into, Daisy would listen entranced. Then, as Daisy grew older, some of the stories the Duchess told grew progressively more improper and together they would dissolve into fits of laughter at the strange and often ludicrous behaviour of men. But also, as she grew older, Daisy began to see the picture more clearly, how in many ways the Duchess was used, exploited even, by her gentlemen friends and how she preferred to delude herself rather than face this simple truth.

Yet she would remember the Duchess with the greatest affection. They had spent many hours in this small bedroom, just sitting and talking, mostly discussing the Duchess's clothes or cosmetics or, perhaps, styling each other's hair. More than once, with the aid of her Book of Common Prayer and at the Duchess's insistence, Daisy had tried to teach her to read. The missal had seemed oddly out of place in the hands of a lady of the Duchess's occupation, but it was the only book in the house and Daisy had used it to point out simple words. Always the lesson would end in hilarious failure with the two of them falling about in despairing laughter at the Duchess's inability to learn.

Daisy would remember, too, the bustle of anticipation at the clip-clop of the horse's hooves in the cobbled square at the end of the street and the quietly crunching sound of the wheels on the unmade roadway. The lurch of the carriage settling to a halt would bring forth Bates and he would scurry in and out of the front door with his obsequious apologies as the Duchess grandly made them wait. Then, at last, the Duchess would raise her skirts, daintily descend the narrow stairway and sweep out to where a footman with pursed lips held open the carriage door. A shake of the reins and the paired horses would pull away. The carriage would trundle down to the end of the street and turn the corner and for a little while the Duchess would be gone and a shadow would appear to fall on the drab household as if a cloud had suddenly obscured the sun.

She had often wondered what it was that bound the Duchess to Bates. He was not an attractive man. He was long and thin with sparse, greying hair. His face was gaunt and sallow with hollow cheeks and thin lips that were twisted in an almost permanent grimace of disdain, as if he believed in nothing and trusted no one. Perhaps, thought Daisy, it was the uncertainty of his way of life – living, as he did, off young women – that made him so mean and joyless.

Bates had no friends. He had only acquaintances and these were mainly the scurrilous reprobates he drank with at the Crown. Professionally he had a fawning relationship with a number of gentlemen who could afford to pay for the girls he procured. He was not, Daisy was certain, and never had been the Duchess's lover. Not in any sense. Obviously, in the physical sense, the Duchess had known many men but Daisy believed she had loved only one.

Daisy had seen the Duke only once; a handsome man, kind, courteous, and so decent-looking. He looked like a man who could never do anything dishonourable. Then one Sunday, when she was taking a walk with the Duchess in St James's Park, they had paused to watch a party of elegant ladies and their children setting out a picnic by the lake. The Duchess had pointed out a quite beautiful Spanish-looking woman with two lovely dark-eyed girls. They were the family of her Duke, the Duchess had announced proudly as if this in some way confirmed her own good taste.

'Why?' Daisy had asked as they continued their stroll. 'Why do men do it? Why do they have other women?' Unaware at the time that the Duchess considered her affair with the Duke to be a genuine love match, she had blundered innocently on. 'Surely the Duke has everything he could possibly wish for.'

The Duchess had merely laughed and answered, 'A man must 'ave a mistress.'

'So all we hear of true love is false?' the girl asked.

'It 'appens,' the Duchess conceded, 'but it's different for a man. You can never ever trust 'em. They will tell you they love you an' would die for you an' maybe they would. But you can never be sure. I once 'ad a friend who spent a wild, passionate night in my bed, tellin' me 'e loved me, swearin' 'e would love me 'til the day 'e died an' only draggin' himself away at dawn. An' that same day I watched 'im arrive at church to be married. No, my love, the only man you can really trust, I'm sorry to say, is a dead man.'

Now, in the darkening window, Daisy pictured a reflection of the Duchess as she once was: a glowing pink in her off-the-shoulder dress, her hair falling in tresses of gold to frame her lovely animated face, her blue eyes wide and frank. Flushed with anticipation she was ready and eager to live and enjoy her life to the full. Daisy could almost hear her singing and laughing as she prepared herself for the evening.

For an instant, too, there was a hint of the scent with which she sprayed herself. It was almost tangible, filling the room, evoking the very essence of those times past. But like the reflection in the glass it was an illusion and Daisy couldn't hold it. The images faded and darkness returned. Outside there was only the blackness of a starless night. The bedside candle flickered low and Daisy felt a chill.

She looked at the Duchess. The worn, haggard face had dropped against the pillow. The once blue eyes were grey and vacant. The Duchess had gone and Daisy had missed the moment. She had slipped away unnoticed and Daisy was desolated. Her thoughts had been elsewhere. She was so close, only inches away, yet she had missed that last breath, the final beat of that warm and tender heart. Tears streamed down the girl's face. Oh, Duchess! She was so sorry, so very sorry. But then she had been thinking of the Duchess at her best, remembering her as she once was. The Duchess would not have minded that. She would surely have preferred it. For that was the real Duchess, the lovely face, the smile in the darkening glass, not this poor wretched remnant.

Daisy took the Duchess's limp hand and put it under the covers. Already it was cold, the fingers stiff. She straightened the Duchess's head on the pillow and, as she had often seen the nuns do in the hospital wing at the convent, she gently closed the Duchess's eyes with the tips of her fingers. She had never been afraid of the dead, of touching death or administering to the needs of the dying. Death was a fact of life, the nursing sisters had told her. We all have to go through it in the end and if we have lived a good and honest life the gates of Heaven will not be closed to us.

She wondered about the Duchess. Would the gates of Heaven be closed to her? Despite her profession she was a good and honest person. She didn't deserve to go to hell. Daisy's lips moved in a silent prayer with words of her own choosing: 'Please, please, please, Holy Father, open your gates to my dear and lovely friend, Miss Dolly Mason. Please don't let the Devil have her. She was kind and true and....' Tears blurred her eyes and coursed down her cheeks and she was unable to go on.

The convent hospital had often been the only refuge for lepers and the similarly afflicted. The nuns were convinced they could not contract the disease by bodily contact and if they did and they died they would go to Heaven anyway. Daisy, too, had become immune to any such fears and her genuine lack of concern for herself had endeared her even more to the Duchess. The pox, by which name the street girls knew the disease, was to many as repellant and as frightening as leprosy. But this had not deterred Daisy and she had nursed the Duchess through her worst days and nights with a love and a generosity that almost broke the Duchess's heart.

Nobody else would go near her. As soon as her condition had become obvious even Bates had kept his distance. In the early stages he had still wanted her to work, though he had lowered his sights to the less elevated spheres of society, and she had still brought home money of which he took, as he had always taken, a share. But it was plain, even to the Duchess, that he had mentally disowned her, written her off as an asset, and only the girl had the love and compassion to stay with her till the end.

Taking a last lingering look, Daisy slowly covered the face that was now at rest. It was over. The Duchess was dead. Daisy stood up and the calfskin wallet fell to the floor. She picked it up and clutched it to her. It was hers now. The Duchess had wanted her to have it. She lifted her skirts to her waist and slid the wallet inside her drawers for safe keeping. Then she caught her breath, suddenly aware of an elongated shadow thrown by the flickering candle up the wall and across the low ceiling. Blushing at her own immodesty she smoothed her dress and backed away. Bates was standing by the door.

3

The thin lips twisted. 'Thievin' from a dead woman, eh?'

'I'm not thieving,' Daisy protested.

Bates approached, his hand outstretched. 'Thank you.'

Daisy backed away. 'It's mine,' she said. 'The Duchess gave it to me.'

The wallet belonged to her now. It had been given to her, no one else, and no one was going to take it from her. It was her means of escape, her ticket to a new life. Even if she didn't use it, it was hers. And so was the money. The Duchess had wanted her to have it.

Bates grabbed her by the shoulders and she could smell the drink on his stale breath. 'Give it to me,' he said, 'or, by God, I'll take it!'

She struggled to break free but he caught her raised arms, pinned them to her side and forced her down to the bare wooden floor. Daisy screamed but he covered her face with a clammy hand and forced her head back, using his long gangling body to hold her down as his free hand pulled up her skirts and began feeling for the hidden wallet. Then at last, though she fought to throw him off, he found it. In triumph he drew out the wallet, laughing coarsely and waving it aloft. But he was not satisfied. The proximity of the girl's body and the intimacy of his search had aroused him. With a different aim in view he began to pull and tug at Daisy's clothing.

'No!' she screamed.

'Why not?' he panted feverishly. 'The Duchess is dead and gone.' He forced her down. 'You are going to be our little breadwinner from now on.' One side of her body was pinned beneath his weight. 'And you can put those airs and graces of yours to good use. I'm going to show you what to expect from all those fine City gents.'

Finding her left hand suddenly freed, Daisy brought it up and hit him hard on the side of his head. But he was not deterred. With his left he grasped her free hand, forced it back against the floor and held it there, his body heavy across her, trapping her right hand. Bates had the free hand now and, with his determination mounting, he began to prise her legs apart.

Again she tried to shake him off but without success and, in desperation, she let out a piercing scream. His long narrow face was flushed, his eyes wild, as his hand went to stifle the sound. Daisy turned her head away, opened her mouth and sank her teeth into his repugnantly damp hand. Bates drew back in pain and surprise and she rolled away from under him. She ran for the door, almost fell down the stairs and the door to the street was open. But she wanted the wallet.

Already Bates was at the top of the stairs. Daisy had to make her decision. She remembered the knife on the table in the tiny living-room and, as he appeared in the doorway behind her, she turned to face him, the sharpened blade pointing at his heart. He stepped back, recalling her previous lunge with the knife.

'And what do you plan to do with that?' he asked, eager to show his contempt.

'I want my papers,' she told him, her hand trembling.

'*Your* papers?' Bates held up the wallet. 'Is this what you
mean?'

He drew out the travel warrant, examined it, his lips moving
slowly though she knew he couldn't read it. He made a pretence,
too, of reading the contract and was none the wiser. But he had no
difficulty in recognizing what was left inside the wallet. Almost
purring with pleasure he drew it out and held it up. It was the
promissory note, signed and sealed by the Duke.

'A lot of money, eh?' Bates said, well able to identify the figures
and the signature. 'I suppose this is yours?'

'The Duchess gave it to me,' Daisy said.

'We'll see about that.' Bates folded the note and slid it into his
breeches pocket. The warrant and the contract he slotted back into
the wallet. He knew how he could dispose of the note for cash at
not much less than its face value, but he wanted advice on these
other items. Might be deeds to a property or some such. 'We'll see
what the constable makes of all this,' he told Daisy. 'The Duchess
dismissed you as she lay dying and as soon as she was dead you
crept upstairs and robbed her.'

'That's not true! That's not what happened!'

'That's what I'll say happened. And who do you think they'll
believe? Me? Or a little thief like you? This is my house. Not
yours. And you have no business being here. Your mistress
dismissed you.'

'She did not! It's not true.'

'I have friends in the sheriff's office.'

Daisy knew that Bates was friendly with the sheriff's man. She
didn't know exactly what the man's powers and duties were, but he
always seemed to be treated as someone important. Most people
were wary of him, even the law-abiding ones, but Bates would
boast he had him 'in his pocket'. Sometimes when the man came
by at night Bates would send a girl to see him and the Duchess
would warn Bates he was asking for trouble. If the sheriff's office
found the man was consorting with a street woman when he was
supposed to be on duty Bates could be charged with him. Bates
evidently believed it was worth the risk.

A word from Bates, Daisy realized, could probably get someone
put away and that was a terrifying thought. Once, when there was
a disturbance at the Crown and a man lay dying in the street
outside, it was the sheriff's man who came, hand-chained the
person responsible and led him away. They would take him, it was
said, to the prison at Newgate where once inside very few, if any,
came out – unless it was to be hanged at a public execution.

Obviously the constable would believe Bates. To the constable there would be no reason for the Duchess to give Daisy so much money, certainly not as much as twenty-five pounds. Bates's story was far more plausible. The knife was no longer pointing at Bates's heart. He could see she was wavering.

'Think, little thief,' he said with quiet confidence. 'They'd probably throw you into Newgate. Stealing from the dead indeed!'

'I'll go,' Daisy said. 'I'll just get my things.'

'Oh no!' Bates laughed. 'Not as easy as that you don't.'

'What do you mean?'

'You and I must come to an arrangement.'

'What arrangement?'

'Well,' he said reasonably, 'the Duchess may be gone but I still have many excellent contacts in the City.' He stepped closer to her. 'Gentlemen who will pay well to get to know a pretty girl like you.' He put out a hand, held her chin as if appraising her value in the market place. 'We can dress you up in the Duchess's clothes, make you look nice. You have a good body.' He touched her breast and she stepped back. 'No need to get alarmed.'

Daisy levelled the knife at him.

'You will have to get used to that sort of thing, my dear,' he said in the unctuous tone she had heard him use in dealing with clients. 'With a little co-operation you can enjoy a very pleasant and lucrative way of life. I can introduce you to influential people.' He lowered his voice. 'With a little luck you could marry above your station. I mean, after all, you have nowhere to go and life can be very hard for a girl with nowhere to go. Especially in London. London can be a dreadful place. The Duchess would tell you so if she was still with us, God rest her soul.'

Bates invoking God! She had heard it all now.

'The Duchess came to me,' he went on, 'when she had nowhere else. She was young and she was in trouble. She was sick and I helped her. I gave her a roof over her head. I fed her. I clothed her. I nursed her back to health and when she was well again I introduced her to a world she had never known. A world filled with beautiful ladies and elegant gentlemen.' His smile made Daisy cringe. 'And I can do the same for you.'

'You turned the Duchess into a whore.'

His lip curled. 'The Duchess was born a whore. She came to me pregnant, at her wit's end. I helped her to find a new life for herself.'

'And just look how she ended up. Dead of the pox before her thirtieth birthday.'

Bates was angry, his patience running out. 'It's either work for me, little thief,' he told her, 'or spend the rest of your days in Newgate. So what's it to be?'

'I would never work for you – and I want what the Duchess gave me. The Duchess loved me. She told me so. I was like a daughter to her.'

He was close again, his gaunt features reflecting his intent. 'I bet you never did it before, did you, girl? That what you're afraid of? It's nothing. Doesn't hurt. And you'll probably get to like it. The Duchess did. Come on, I'll show you.' He unfastened the leather belt that held up his breeches, then put both hands on her waist. 'It won't hurt. I promise.'

'Get back!' Daisy warned him. 'Get away from me!'

'You'll enjoy it,' he coaxed with his oily smirk.

Then suddenly he closed in on her, put his arms around her shoulders and lowered his face to kiss her on the lips. But his expression changed to one of shock and surprise for as he stepped forward Daisy involuntarily brought up the knife. She had intended only to warn him off but he had impaled himself on the long blade. His hand went to his side and he staggered and almost fell into the dead ashes in the fireplace. Then he went down on his knees.

With both hands he tried to pull out the knife but it was in deep. Blood gushed from the wound, oozing through his shirt and staining his cuffs and the long narrow face turned a ghastly pale, appearing for a moment to lose its outer cover. Watching in horror, Daisy imagined she saw only the head of a skeleton, an image that would haunt her often in the days to come.

Bates writhed in agony on the living-room floor. He gasped and spluttered, shook his head like a drowning man coming up for air for a third and final time, then lay still. Daisy had no idea how long she stood there, looking down fearfully at the inert body. Steeling herself, trying not to look at the popping eyes and the distorted purplish face, she at last knelt down and eased the wallet from his grasp.

There was also the Duke's promissory note. Her surety. Daisy thought fast. She had to have it. If she was to escape to this new world she would not go penniless. And there was little option now. She had not intended to kill Bates but who would believe her? His body would be found. A hue and cry would ensue. If she gave herself up, explained to the authorities what happened she could not be sure of a fair hearing. She was just a maid, a servant girl. The people's appetite for despatching murderers was insatiable and if the accused was a female the interest was even more malevolent. She could be carried off to the gallows with only the barest pretence of a trial.

Daisy held her breath, eased Bates's body on to its side and, careful to avoid the blood pooled on the floor, she forced herself to put a hand in his breeches pocket and retrieve the note. For an instant, touching the cold limb through the thin lining, she felt sick. She put her free hand to her mouth, her eyes closed. Then turning away she drew herself up and stepped over the body.

With both the wallet and the note in her possession Daisy suddenly felt calmer. This was her way out and she knew she must take it. She thought, briefly, of dragging Bates's body to the cellar steps and pushing it down there out of sight. But there was too much blood about and she didn't have time to clean up the mess. At any moment someone might come to the door. It would be better if no one saw her. Several people, neighbours and traders, knew she lived there but few knew her name and, as far as she knew, none knew anything of her background.

She blew out the candles in the living-room, closed the door and ran back up the stairs. The Duchess had told her to take what clothing she wanted. She took an emerald green dress she knew would fit her well, some frilly blouses she had always admired and a colourful neckerchief. Adding these few items to her own scant wardrobe she pushed them into a travelling bag and pulled on a dark blue topcoat the Duchess had given her. Then she drew back the sheet that covered the shrivelled face of the dead Duchess and kissed her forehead. It was cold to her lips, like kissing a statue.

'Goodbye, Duchess,' she said softly. 'I shall always love and remember you.'

It was midnight when Daisy left Bates's house in St Giles. The street was dark and the moon threw many shadows. On each side of the street narrow alleyways made black gaping holes that suggested unknown lurking terrors. She had never been out so late before, not even in the company of others, and she resolved to stay near the lights such as they were. But even this had its hazards.

The splashes of yellow light came from the windows of a tavern where groups of drunken men, long since ejected by the victualler, still lingered, singing snatches of bawdy and maudlin songs and swaying together in muddled conversations. Inevitably, as Daisy passed by, they made coarse and ribald comments and suggestive invitations as if she was a street girl. Further along, one such girl mistook her for unwelcome competition and rounded on her, hissing and snarling like an alley cat.

Daisy knew of a hostelry where she might stay for what remained of the night. But it turned out to be not so near as she thought and she had walked well over a mile when she saw it. The Turnpike Coach House at the corner of Naseby Street was the largest inn in the vicinity, much patronized by travellers to the City and by the horsemen who used the nearby farrier's yard. It was rarely closed. Coaches often arrived in the early hours and the innkeeper was obliged to offer shelter. Even so, though he could see from her manner and her bearing she was a respectable young lady, Daisy's late arrival caused him to view her with suspicion. He called for his wife, a large, uncompromising type of woman, who questioned her thoroughly.

We are required to keep a register of our guests, the wife told her curtly. Daisy nodded and an explanation of her plight came to her in the form of a lie that would normally have caused her to blush, but her face was already flushed. She was an acolyte, she said, on her way to take up holy orders at a convent in St Katharine by the Tower. She had arrived too late in the day and she had no means of crossing the City in safety at this hour. The nuns would not now expect her until the morrow. She had money and she was in need of accommodation for the night. This was a hostelry, was it not? Of course, Sister. The wife was satisfied and Daisy was shown to a room.

The moment the door closed on the innkeeper's wife, Daisy fell back on to the bed. She was still in shock at the events of the evening. First the death of the Duchess, then the fatal though unintentional stabbing of Bates. But she was also exhausted and when she climbed between the sheets she fell into a deep sleep. Next morning she awoke refreshed and ate a hearty breakfast.

The office of Mr Thomas Weston, Merchant, was at Ludgate Hill. Gingerly and a little bewildered, Daisy made her way through the rutted thoroughfares. The narrow streets had no clearly defined footpaths and even on the main roads these were marked not by raised pavements but by wooden posts spaced at intervals of four feet. Walking was a hazard in itself with the swaying bulks of horsedrawn carriages, the trundling menace of wayward handcarts and the incoming tide of people going about their daily business.

At last Ludgate Hill! Daisy peered at the names on the doorways beneath the overhanging upper storeys. Nelson, Graham, Isherwood ... Weston! Thos. Weston, Merchant. A slightly built clerk hunched over open ledgers on a low counter raised his eyebrows as the tinkling doorbell announced her arrival.

'I would like to see Mr Thomas Weston, please,' she told him primly.

'Ah now, miss,' the clerk said, pursing his lips, 'Mr Weston is a very busy man. Is he expecting you?'

'Please tell Mr Weston I am here at the suggestion of the Duke of Buckingham.'

The clerk was visibly impressed. 'What name shall I say, miss?'

'Er....' Daisy coloured slightly. 'Miss Daisy Mason.'

'Miss Daisy Mason,' the clerk repeated carefully. 'Would you take a seat, Miss Mason?'

Daisy remained standing at the low counter, silently repeating to herself. 'Daisy. My name is Daisy Mason.'

4

Thomas Weston was a short, fat, unattractive man with small shifty eyes, too much powder on his double chin, too many unmanly frills and bows on his fussy dress and an air of petulant self-indulgence. Daisy didn't like the look of him at all.

'Come in, Miss ... er...?'

'Miss Daisy Mason,' she said firmly.

'Yes, yes. Miss Mason. Come inside.' The inner office was small and rather shabby with piles of dusty files and ledgers on chairs and side tables. Weston offered her a seat and took his place behind a cluttered desk. 'And what can I do for you, young lady?'

She didn't like his peremptory manner and supercilious tone of voice. It implied that whatever she might want could not be of any great importance. Nor did she like the speculative way he was looking at her. 'I came here with a warrant that entitles me to take part in an undertaking for which, I understand, you are the agent.'

'And what undertaking would that be?'

'The plan to transport a number of settlers to the New World.'

'Ah,' he said condescendingly, but he did not elaborate.

Was he not the man, Daisy wondered, or was he for some reason being deliberately obtuse? 'Are you, sir, or are you not,' she demanded, 'the Mr Weston I have been advised to contact?'

Weston stroked his flabby chin and there was an unpleasant

gleam in his eye. He knew the Duke had paid passage for a former mistress – someone, no doubt, for whom he had no further use. But he had not expected the woman to be quite so young and comely. 'The voyage to the New World is heavily over-subscribed. We have two ships available but both, I am afraid, are already filled to capacity.'

Daisy waited, her face expressionless. She felt he was not telling the whole truth and she didn't trust him.

'There are ways, of course,' he said in a smarmy voice, 'that a single extra passenger might, perhaps, be accommodated. A pretty girl like you might qualify under certain circumstances.'

'I believe I have the necessary *qualifications* now, Mr Weston. I have a warrant and all the required dues have been paid. I also have a copy of the contract between your company and the proposed settlers whom I intend to join. Is this not all I need?'

'You could make certain of your place....' His voice trailed and his stubby fingers drummed on his desk. There was no mistaking his meaning.

'I do believe I am beginning to understand,' Daisy said softly. 'I think you are saying that if I am amenable and, in view of my former profession I should not find that too difficult, then you will ensure I gain my place among the passengers.'

Weston's face was flushed. 'Yes,' he admitted. 'That's it. That is what I'm saying.'

Daisy recalled that the Duchess had referred to the Duke as 'my darling George'. She stood up abruptly. 'I am sure,' she said in a voice that chilled the little merchant, 'that George ... that is, His Grace the Duke, will be most interested to hear of your outrageously improper suggestion, Mr Weston. The Duke has paid my fare in good faith and it is his intention, in due course, to visit me. I am sure he will not look kindly upon the way in which you have attempted to use one of his oldest and dearest friends. I will inform him at once.'

If he had not been so flustered it might have occurred to Weston that Daisy was a little young to be one of the Duke's oldest friends. He hastened to make amends. 'No, no! Please sit down, Miss Mason. I beg of you. I think you misunderstood....'

'I understood perfectly.'

He threw up his arms to cover his confusion. 'I expected a lady somewhat older....'

'I am twenty-five,' she lied.

'Forgive me,' he said. 'The Duke led me to believe you were a lady of a certain profession who wished to begin a new life on the other side of the world. I can see ...'

'My former profession, Mr Weston, is not your concern. I
intend to make this voyage and I will be grateful if you will inform
me of the date of embarkation, the point of departure and any
further details you have available. The Duke, I assure you, will be
most interested to hear of your co-operation or otherwise.'

Weston mopped his brow with a large red handkerchief. 'You
are a remarkable young lady, Miss Mason,' he said, and this time
there was no hint of condescension. 'I will certainly do all in my
power to be of assistance.'

'Then tell me how your plans are progressing.'

Briefly he gave her the background to the proposed voyage.
Already, he explained, there were small settlements in the largely
unexplored territories across the sea, notably in Virginia, financed
and organized by the London Virginia Company. There were
English settlements along the James River in an area known as
Jamestown, so called after His Majesty the King. But this latest
expedition was not going out to join these existing communities,
such as they were. The plan was to establish an entirely new
settlement.

Most of the passengers in the venture were deeply religious
people. They were, in the main, dissenters from the authorized
church in England who had found a temporary sanctuary and
freedom to worship as they wished across the Channel in the
Dutch town of Leyden. But now war between Holland and Spain
was threatened and these English Nonconformists feared the
armies of the Spanish Catholics even more than the prospect of
persecution at home. They had expressed a desire, Weston said, to
emigrate to a place where they could follow their beliefs in peace
and he had agreed to help finance the project.

There were also people of a similar persuasion who wished to
join them from England. The remainder were a mixture of families
and a few individuals who for a variety of reasons wanted to leave
their roots and try their luck in the New World. But these were
very much in the minority. It would be necessary, Weston pointed
out, for any intending traveller to follow a certain code of conduct
and maintain a level of decorum set by the majority. No religion,
thought Daisy, could be any worse than that which she suffered in
her convent days. Weston was watching her, as if awaiting some
comment or reaction, but she merely nodded.

The company behind the project, he explained, was his own.
Or, at least, it had been formed by him: The Company of
Adventurers and Planters. The scheme was that a plantation
should be developed and operated as a joint stock corporation for

a period of seven years. At the end of that time the capital and the accumulated profits were to be distributed among the backers, to be called the Adventurers, and the emigrants, to be called the Planters, in proportion to their shareholding. Every person over the age of sixteen would provide ten pounds and this ten pounds would count as one share.

At the end of the seven years the houses built and the land cultivated would remain the property of the Planter or Planters responsible. Each Planter would have two days per week on which to work on his own property. The rest of the week he would work on the common land and for the common good. The profit made or assets created for the common wealth would, after seven years, be realized and distributed according to shareholdings between the Adventurers in London and the Planters in what was now called New England.

'It must all seem very complex for a young lady to follow,' Weston said, patronizing her again.

Daisy bridled. 'I can follow it perfectly well, Mr Weston.'

'You do understand that as a single young lady you will have no man to do your share of the work?'

'There is always work for a woman,' she said. 'I am sure I'm capable of doing my share.'

'Then you still wish to go?'

'Of course.' Daisy knew she must proceed with caution. She was, after all, a fugitive. She had not killed Bates. It was an accident. Yet she had no way of proving her innocence. There was no point in alienating Weston. She softened her voice. 'As I told the Duke, Mr Weston, I want to start a new life. My prospects here, in London, as I am sure you can understand, are not exactly to my liking. I am willing and eager to become a pioneer in an undeveloped land. The Duke has been good to me and he is interested in my future. It is his intention to follow my progress closely.'

Weston nodded. 'I will make it my personal responsibility, Miss Mason, to ensure that you are properly advised and courteously treated until your departure. Beyond that, of course, as his passenger you will be the responsibility of the ship's master.'

Two ships, it transpired, had been charted to make the voyage. One, the *Speedwell*, had been purchased and fitted out in Holland by the elders of the religious sect from Leyden. The other, the *Mayflower*, was a bigger and better ship bought by the company. The *Mayflower* was to sail, Weston said, within the next few days from London to Southampton. In Southampton, members of the

Southwark Independent Church, who were closely associated with the Leyden congregation, would join up with their English friends from Holland. Along with the people from Southwark, a number of other families and individuals would join the ship here, on the Thames.

'They are all English-speaking?' Daisy asked.

'Oh yes, Miss Mason. They are all English, no Dutch.' He lowered his voice. 'They went to Holland to escape going to gaol.' He consulted a sheet of paper on his desk and his voice returned to normal. 'Now let me see. The *Mayflower* sails from Southwark Dock in two days' time. Early morning, I understand. About seven.'

'I will make my way there,' Daisy said.

'There's a hostelry on the dock front where I'm sure you'll find a decent night's accommodation. The Ship Inn. Right on the dock. It's a good clean place and I can certainly recommend it. I can arrange for a coach to take you there, if you wish.'

'That is most kind of you, Mr Weston,' she said, warming to him at last.

'Tomorrow, perhaps?'

There was a commotion in the street. A crowd had gathered around a crier who was standing on his box and the word that came through loud and clear was 'Murder!'

'I think now, today,' Daisy said, 'if that's possible.'

'Well, certainly,' Weston said. 'If you go down to the dock today you'll have an opportunity to get a good look at the ship. You can probably go aboard, meet the master. Captain Jones is a fine man and a very experienced mariner. I will give you a letter of introduction.'

'You're very kind,' Daisy said.

Weston rang a small handbell on his desk and the clerk from the front office came in.

'Ah, Clifford,' Weston said. 'I want you to take down a letter to Captain Jones of the *Mayflower*. I also want you to stamp this warrant and make certain Miss Mason's name is added to our list of passengers.'

'I thought you said the list was closed,' the clerk reminded him.

'One more name, Clifford, that's all.' He turned to Daisy. 'The stamp of my office attests that your name has been included in the authorized list of passengers.'

The thin, bird-like clerk smiled at Daisy, brought an office chair to the side of Weston's desk and sat down, his pen poised.

'What's all the commotion?' Weston asked, with a nod towards the noise outside.

Given his opening, the clerk's eyes widened and he leaned forward. 'It's the crier, Mr Weston. A grisly murder by all accounts. Somebody bin stabbed to death in an 'ouse in St Giles. They're lookin' for a servant girl.'

Despite the slow-moving traffic and constant hold-ups the coach journey from Weston's office in Ludgate Hill to the docks by Southwark Bridge took less than half an hour. Almost hidden from view, Daisy sat back in the depths of the plush upholstery. She had an inescapable feeling, as she looked out on the offices and coffee houses and small exclusive shops, on the stiff upright merchants tipping their hats to expensively clad ladies out window-shopping, that she had no right to such luxury. It was not that this was the first time she had travelled by coach. The Duchess had sometimes, on a Sunday, taken her by coach to the park. But it was the first time she had ridden in a coach alone and she felt like the impostor she was.

At the huge sprawling Cathedral there was a diversion. Building work was in progress and the driver had to make a left turn. In her uneasy state it seemed to Daisy that Fate was taunting her for this new route took her close to the tall forbidding walls of Newgate Prison. Now, to get out on to Cheapside, they passed through a far less salubrious neighbourhood. Grimy hovels sagged beneath the weight of drooping eaves, ragged slum dwellers stooped in aimless disarray and barefoot urchins gazed with unclosed mouths at the off-course coach. Here was abject poverty, right next door to the flaunted opulence of Ludgate Hill.

With some relief Daisy caught a glimpse of the river as the coach rattled downhill towards Southwark Bridge. Then the broad sweep of the Thames swung into view on her left. She sat forward in the coach, pulled her baggage nearer, ready to alight. The clear blue surface of the water, stained here and there a mottled grey by the bilge from passing barge boats, shone in the afternoon sun.

The coach driver touched his cocked hat, helped her down, told her the fare had been 'taken care of' and bade her good day. She was standing by the door of the dockside hostelry Mr Weston had mentioned, a rather shabby building with a faded sign swinging loose beneath a fixed wooden carving of a schooner, The Ship Inn.

She went inside, hesitated on the uneven floor beneath the low-beamed ceiling, her eyes adjusting to the indoor darkness. To the right a narrow spiralled stairway led upwards. To the left, beyond a low partition, several sailors were huddled around a table. A plumpish girl in a grey sackcloth skirt and a frilly white blouse served them flagons of Old Harry, a popular local drink.

Gathering her apron strings, which one of the younger sailors childishly persisted at every opportunity in pulling loose, the girl greeted Daisy with a bright and cheerful smile, rosy-cheeked from the wind on the river. But from out of the shadows a pale, dark-haired woman with rounded shoulders and a hooked nose waved the girl away. Yes, the woman said, she had a room. She had plenty of rooms. How long did she want to stay?

'Just tonight and tomorrow night,' Daisy said. 'I'm to sail on the ship known as the *Mayflower* early on Thursday morning.'

'Oh, you are, are you?' The woman looked at her warily. 'Not one o' that religious lot, I 'ope. They comes down 'ere, lots of 'em, an' I gets all my rooms ready. But they're too ruddy mean to pay for a decent bed an' board. Rather sleep rough on that old tub.'

Daisy waited, her face without expression.

'Sailin' off to God knows where, by all accounts,' the woman went on. 'Mus' fancy a watery grave, is all I can say. I feel sorry for you, ducks.'

'I am not one of them, I assure you,' Daisy said.

'Then if you're not one o' them,' the woman demanded, suddenly suspicious, 'what are you?'

'I ... I'm a nursing sister. I'm on my way to take up an appointment at the convent hospital in Southampton.'

'Oh.' The woman seemed mollified. 'You're a nun?'

Daisy nodded, blushing slightly. Telling lies was becoming too easy.

'Oh well,' the woman said. 'I suppose you're all right.' Stooping she turned to lead the way. Then she stopped. 'I 'ave to be careful, you know. We gets all sorts in 'ere. Whores an' God knows what else tryin' to book in. After the sailors, if you know what I mean.' She looked up at Daisy. 'No, maybe you don't.'

She led the way up the spiral stairway to a first-floor bedroom. It was barely but adequately furnished with a large comfortable-looking bed, a wardrobe and a wooden table with a basin and a jug for washing. The small, curtained window overlooked the dock.

'This will be very nice, thank you,' Daisy said.

'Two nights, did you say? Payment in advance, if you please.'

Daisy took out her purse and paid what the woman asked.

'An' it's no ladies in the saloon bar.'

· 'I beg your pardon?'

'Women are not allowed to drink at the public bar. Not in my 'ouse, they're not.'

'I'm sure my mother superior would approve.'

'A nun, you say.'

When the woman had gone Daisy threw her dark-blue coat on the bed and flung open the small windows. The air was salty and fresh and there was a strong bracing wind off the river. If she leaned out on the deep sill and looked away to her left she could see the three-cornered flags above the Tower. She took a deep breath, thrust out her chest and unfastened the buttons at her neck.

As she closed her eyes the breeze cooled her hot cheeks and stirred her hair. It was pleasant and refreshing, but when she opened her eyes and looked across the dock wondering which of those tall-masted ships was her *Mayflower* she drew back swiftly, her hand at her throat.

Down below on the dockside a young man was sitting on a capstan. He had been watching admiringly as she took the air. Daisy had caught only a glimpse of him but her impression was of a long, lean individual with a quizzical smile and a wave of fairish hair over one eye.

She moved the curtain an inch and looked out. He was still there, smiling up at her. She tried to put on a haughty look of disdain, but he merely laughed and touched his forelock.

5

The *Mayflower* was a soundly built, solid-looking vessel of some 180 tons. The fore mast and the taller main mast were square-rigged in the conventional manner. On the poop deck at the rear a short mizzen mast, about half the size of the main mast, was rigged to fly a crescent-shaped lateen sail. Raised across the fore deck was a squarish forecastle. On a lower level, between the fore and the poop decks, was a wide middle deck. She was nothing special. Used to trading between the Port of London and the French ports of Bordeaux and La Rochelle, she was a weather-beaten old workhorse, little different to many others anchored on the Thames. But in Daisy Mason's inexperienced eyes she was a big ship waiting to transport her to a world where she could begin her life anew.

On the quayside a queue of men, women and children, surrounded by their belongings, waited patiently. Already Daisy could see, from her bedroom window, people who were obviously passengers and not crew milling about on the middle deck. But the process of embarkation was slow. Whole families shuffled their chattels towards the man at the gangway who scratched his head and lectured them on the disparity between what they had brought with them and what they would be allowed to take on board. Watching like birds of prey, a number of sharp-eyed 'dealers' mingled with the waiting passengers, offering miniscule amounts of cash to 'take off their hands' items they might be obliged to discard.

As darkness fell only a couple of families remained but early next morning the queue had lengthened again. Daisy was standing by her bedroom window when there was a knock and a cheerful voice called out, 'Ready for breakfast, miss.'

She opened the door to the red-cheeked girl who had served in the bar the previous evening. The girl was carrying a tray which held a jug of water, some goat's milk, cheese, bread and a saucer of home made jam. Her name was Polly, she said with a bright smile.

'Daisy,' Daisy said.

The girl looked a little surprised. Evidently she knew her place and was not accustomed to guests introducing themselves by their first names. 'Pleased to meet you, Miss Daisy,' she said. 'I hear tell you're goin' off on a big ship.'

'Yes,' Daisy said. 'This one here.'

The girl came to the tiny window and Daisy pointed out the *Mayflower*.

'How far are you goin' then?'

Daisy remembered what she had told the landlady. 'Only to Southampton.'

'What a shame!' Polly lowered her voice. 'I hear tell that ship is off to sail the seven seas. To unknown lands across the ocean.'

Daisy smiled. 'To a New World, I understand.'

'Ooh! Wouldn't I jus' love to go with it!'

'Would you, Polly? Would you really?'

'Wouldn't I just! Think of all those lovely sailors!'

Daisy laughed, shaking her head as if to say, 'You're incorrigible!' But she couldn't help thinking of the young man she had seen down on the quay the previous evening. She had thought of him several times during the night, once waking with a start and she blushed now at the recollection.

'Mind you,' Polly said more soberly, 'I don't reckon there'll be much fun on that one. I hear tell they're church people, most of 'em. Very strict. No chance of swingin' in a sailor's hammock with them nosin' around.' She laughed and left the room. When she returned she brought a pitcher of water for washing. Daisy was still at the window. 'Don't you want no breakfast, miss?'

Daisy had spotted the young man who had so disturbed her dreams. 'Polly,' she said and something in her voice and manner drew the girl to the window. 'That young man on the steps. At that end.' She pointed to where he was standing on a narrow gangway. 'The one with the light brown hair. Can you see him?'

Polly smiled. 'Oh him! Can't miss him, can you, miss?'

'Do you know him?'

'I seen him in here,' Polly said. 'But only lately. Last few nights he's been in the saloon bar with another man. An older man. Seem to keep themselves to themselves.' She smiled again. 'Too 'andsome for his own good, if you asks me. I think he's called Will.' Her rosy cheeks shining, she inclined her head at Daisy. 'Like the look of him, do you, miss? Fancy him, do you?'

Daisy dismissed the questions with a wave of her hand. 'Of course not, Polly. How can you say such things? It's just that ... he doesn't look like a seaman.'

'Well, he is. I hear tell he's signed up for the trip. Him an' this other man. I think he tol' the men in the bar he's goin' all the way. All the way to this New World.'

The words of the Duchess came back to Daisy: 'If you must get involved with a man make sure he's a top man. If he's a soldier make sure he's a general. If he's a sailor make sure he's an admiral. Always play with the lords and masters, never ever play with the servants.'

'You mean, he's going as an *ordinary* seaman?' she asked.

'Well,' Polly said, 'yes, I think so. But I have to admit he don't seem like no ordinary seaman. Talks very proper, if you know what I mean. Seen better days, if you asks me.'

Daisy attended to her breakfast.

'The ol' witch ...' Polly went on, then corrected herself, 'I mean, the missus here says I ought to try to talk proper when I'm servin' downstairs. An' I do. I try, but when we gets busy I forget. I mean, you can put it on. But then you forget. It's 'cos of the way you were brought up. I mean, if you talk proper all your life it's easy, isn't it? Now you, miss, you talk proper. I mean, you can tell you was well brought up.'

'I was brought up by a duchess,' Daisy said.

'A duchess? A *real* duchess?'

'Oh yes,' Daisy said. 'She was a real duchess. The finest lady I ever knew.'

After breakfast Daisy washed her face in a basin of cold water, tidied her hair and pulled on a shawl. Then she went down the spiral stairway and out on to the sunny quayside. It was a fine, bright morning and a barge was moving silently on the river, gliding in and out of view in the gaps in the line of anchored ships. A large seagull squawked overhead and swooped to claim a crumb from the cobbled apron of the quay and a sparrow hopped stiffly out of its way.

Daisy walked to the corner, passed the dock office, passed the rope and twine merchants and the chandler's shop to where a smoother path led to the ships. She held her head high and her back straight as she had seen the ladies walk in St James's Park. But as she passed the closed doors of the chandlery she felt a tug at her skirts and she looked down. A girl of about fourteen with a dirty face and ragged clothing looked up at her with dark-ringed eyes. Clutching a bundle of rags to her chest she begged, 'Spare a copper, miss. Spare a copper for me an' the babby.' The dirty bundle contained a tiny baby. 'Please, ma'am. I can't feed 'er. I ain't 'ad nuffin' to eat for a week.'

The girl had called her 'miss' and 'ma'am' and was so respectful Daisy decided she must look every inch a lady. Her confidence boosted, she smiled at the less fortunate creature huddled in the shop doorway and loosened her string bag. Then she took out her purse and as she did so a nimble youth appeared as if from nowhere and snatched it from her grasp. The girl with the baby put a hand to her mouth as if the occurrence had shocked her and Daisy was so taken by surprise she was unable to move. But the youth did not get far.

A broad-shouldered, stockily built man with dark intelligent eyes beneath a jaunty-angled seaman's cap, tripped him almost casually and stooped to retrieve the purse. The youth didn't wait. He was up and away down an alley that ran behind the seafront buildings. The girl with the baby backed away with frightened eyes and Daisy cried, 'Wait!' But she, too, ran off and turned a corner out of sight.

The seaman handed Daisy the purse and touched his cap politely. 'Don't you be worryin' about her, miss,' he said in a quietly reassuring voice with an unmistakably Irish lilt. 'Sure it's an old trick. They work together. The two of them and a borrowed baby. The poor little child-mother puts you off your guard and the

galley rat sneaks up and steals your purse. It's as old as the hills
and it only takes a second.'

Daisy had seen the Irishman before. She was certain she'd seen
him with the younger man on the steps of the *Mayflower*'s
narrower gangway and it occurred to her he might be the older
man Polly had mentioned. 'Is that your ship?' she asked. 'The
Mayflower?'

There was a smile in his crinkly eyes. 'In a manner of speakin',
miss. I can't say that I own her. But I can say, in all honesty, I am
employed thereon.'

She laughed. There was something warm and friendly in his
dark seafaring eyes and she liked him instinctively. He seemed like
a man she could trust. 'Actually,' she told him, 'I'm to be a
passenger.'

'Is that a fact?' He looked genuinely surprised. 'You are goin'
on the voyage? All the way?'

'Yes,' she said. 'All the way.'

'With your family, I expect.'

'No. I'm going alone.'

He pushed his cap back. 'You surprise me, miss. I understood it
was families only.'

'I'm on my way to see Captain Jones right now.'

'Have you not been aboard yet?'

Daisy shook her head. 'I believe we are not sailing until
tomorrow.'

'Better get aboard, miss,' he advised, 'and claim your space.
There's whole families of them, markin' out what's theirs. There'll
be little enough room left now and I reckon they'll be wantin' to
hog what they've got all the way across.'

Daisy looked perplexed.

'It's going to be pretty crowded, I can tell you.'

'I stayed here at the Ship Inn last night and I was planning to
stay again tonight.'

'Wouldn't do that,' he said with conviction. 'If I were you, miss,
I'd get my things together and get aboard fast.'

She thanked him and, as another large family, complete with
servants and belongings, arrived by coach, she decided to accept
his advice. Back at the Ship Inn she informed the landlady she was
leaving. The landlady scowled, declared she had no intention of
returning any part of the money Daisy had paid in advance and
scurried off into the dark recesses beyond the spiral stairway.
Daisy sought out the maid, Polly, to say goodbye and left.

At the main gangway the queue had lengthened. Daisy had

nothing cumbersome to carry, only her canvas bag and a small leather case she had bought to carry a few more items she had added to her wardrobe as she passed through the city's markets on her way to Weston's office. She made her way to the head of the queue where the mate, a Mr Clarke, was examining the papers of a man and his family of five.

'Sorry!' Mr Clarke held up a hand to bar her way.

Those in the queue regarded her with hostility.

'I am here to see Captain Jones,' she said primly.

The mate hesitated. 'Cap'n Jones, you say?'

'I am here at the behest of Mr Thomas Weston of the London Company of Adventurers and Planters. Now kindly inform the ship's master of my arrival.'

There was a murmuring in the queue, a disgruntled stir. But Daisy did not flinch before the hostile eyes. The mate was not sure what 'behest' meant but he had certainly heard of Weston. 'Mr Thomas Weston, you say?'

Daisy looked at him wearily. 'Am I to stand here for the rest of the day?'

'What name shall I give?'

'Miss Daisy Mason.'

The mate called a name up the gangway and a small boy who had been sitting astride a coil of rope came running down from the deck in a pair of cut short canvas pants and a flannel shirt that was far too big for him.

'Aye, aye, sir.'

'Tell the captain there's a lady to see him. A Miss Daisy Mason.'

'Yes, Mr Clarke, sir.'

'You'll excuse me, ma'am,' Mr Clarke said, and turned back to the waiting family who had become restless at the interruption.

Within minutes the boy came racing back down the gangway and, out of breath, spoke hurriedly to the mate.

'The cap'n will see you, ma'am,' Mr Clarke told Daisy. To the boy, he said, 'Take Miss Mason aboard.'

The people in the queue, especially the watchful wives, were impressed as, stepping carefully up the slatted planks of the gangway, Daisy followed the boy. There was something about her, something that set her apart from the mainly church ladies who were boarding the ship. Who was she? Why was she alone? Naturally the women watching were curious about her.

Captain Jones was on the poop deck. He was a sturdy, not very tall Welshman. His once dark hair was mostly grey now and he had a deeply lined, weather-beaten face. He was just turned fifty years old. On duty, as now, he wore a royal blue, gold-braided long coat over his canvas work pants and a navy-blue felt hat, flat at the front and cocked at the rear.

In order to save Daisy having to climb even higher or perhaps because he didn't want passengers on the poop, he came down to meet her as she reached the middle or waist deck. 'Ah, Miss Mason,' he greeted her and Daisy was surprised that she seemed to be expected. 'Welcome aboard.'

'You were expecting me?'

'Oh yes. I have a letter from Mr Weston.'

Daisy was impressed. 'But how? I only left him yesterday.'

'The coachman who brought you here also carried the letter.' He looked at her questioningly. 'I believe you stayed at the Ship Inn.'

Daisy nodded. 'Mr Weston recommended it.'

'Ah!' That explained why she had not come aboard sooner. 'I am afraid we are running short of space. I have had to reserve a small corner of the main cabin for you.'

'You are very kind.'

'It was very necessary, miss. There's not much room but I am sure you will be comfortable until we reach Southampton. It's there we might run into trouble. But I'm afraid there's little I can do about it. Families are coming aboard now and laying claim to whole areas between decks. Some have even tried to put up partitions to make their own private quarters.'

'Why do we need to go to Southampton?' Daisy asked. 'Couldn't we go straight off?'

He shook his head. 'We are to meet another ship there,' he explained. 'A ship carrying more church people. They will be travelling alongside us.'

'Across the ocean?'

The captain smiled. He'd had four sons, each of them well able to take care of himself. He was not used to girls and this girl, in some ways, despite her air of self-possession, seemed so young and, despite what that fellow Weston had hinted in his letter, so innocent that he felt a need to protect her.

'Yes,' he said. 'They're coming from Holland and they'll be joining us in Southampton. Then we shall sail together.'

'There may be more room on their ship.'

'I doubt it, miss. I understand it's quite small. Half the size of my ship and mine is not exactly big.'

It was true. The *Mayflower* was not big compared to most of the other ocean-going vessels at anchor on the Thames.

'Their master may be hoping to unload some of his passengers on us,' the captain went on. 'But there's not much chance of that. Some, I am sure, will have to be left behind.' A look of concern crossed Daisy's face and he hastened to reassure her. 'But I wouldn't worry, miss. Mr Weston has instructed me to guarantee your place.'

'And you don't mind that, Captain?'

'I don't know,' he said with mock severity. 'On a voyage such as this we need passengers who can take good care of themselves and not become a burden to the rest.'

'I can take care of myself, Captain,' she said, and he nodded, smiling, as if he had no doubt that she could.

Daisy liked Captain Jones. He had a blunt, forthright manner and he didn't hesitate to say what he meant. But he could also be kind and considerate and he had a brand of quiet authority that instilled confidence.

'I am a trained nurse,' she said. 'I hope that if at any time it becomes necessary you will not hesitate to call on me for assistance.'

'I'll remember that, Miss Mason,' he said, with a nod of approval. 'Thank you.'

He called for the boy to take Daisy down to the main cabin, the large space between decks where many families were already in residence. A small roped-off area had been reserved for her in a corner where two horizontal wooden sleepers, part of a bulkhead support, formed a convenient bench seat.

Daisy sat down thankfully, with her canvas bag and her small case. Here, in her six feet by four feet allotted space, she would have to sleep – at least until they reached Southampton. After that, the captain implied, there might be even less room.

6

The family camped next to Daisy's space were from Gloucestershire and their name was Hopkins. There was a father, a mother and three children, two girls and a boy. Daisy soon made friends with the girls and through them became acquainted with their parents.

The older girl, Constanta, was about fourteen and the little one,

Damaris, announced proudly to anyone who would listen that she was aged three. The boy, Giles, was twelve and seemed to spend his time anywhere but with the family. He and Constanta were the children of Mr Hopkins's first wife now deceased. Mr Hopkins was in his late thirties but the present Mrs Hopkins was in her early twenties, not much older than Daisy.

The parents, Daisy noticed, were civil and pleasant in a reserved way. But they were obviously unsure of her and how to treat her, a young unmarried woman travelling alone. Word had quickly gone round that she was somehow well connected in the City and 'something to do with a Duke'. She wondered what their reaction might be if they knew of her true background and just how tenuous was her link with the gentry.

The Hopkins family were not poor. They had with them, it emerged, a couple of manservants and the younger of these two was constantly being sent ashore to buy extra provisions, mainly because the young Mrs Hopkins kept having afterthoughts. No sooner had he gone down to the quayside store for extra cheese than she realized she needed an extra pat of butter. Upbraided by her husband, who was irritated by her lapses, she became even more forgetful and disorganized. Then, in the mid-afternoon, when the young man was about to be despatched yet again for a single item, Daisy asked if he might be allowed to purchase something for her. Mrs Hopkins was only too pleased to agree and she and Daisy became firm friends.

Most of that day, as they waited in dock on the Thames, there was little for the passengers to do. Daisy spent much of her time talking to Elizabeth Hopkins and inventing games for the children. In the late afternoon a hush fell inside the main cabin as the passengers stood for the communal saying of prayers. Those who were members of the Southwark Independent Church prayed aloud and most of those who were not maintained a respectful silence. But one man, an ill-natured fellow named Billington, had little time for religion and, though he was not and had never been a sailor, he chose these moments to sing shanty songs of a dubious nature.

As the prayer meeting ended Edward, the Hopkins' young manservant, appeared with some freshly baked biscuits from the baker's shop on the quay. Daisy paid him, gave him a coin for himself and was immediately surrounded by the Hopkins children who ignored their young mother's call to order and clamoured for a taste of the biscuits. Laughingly, holding the pastry wrap high, Daisy gave away more than half. Then she went out to the waist deck to take the air and sample some for herself.

Down below on the quayside the queue had grown much shorter but there were still several dealers about, some with small boys waiting to trundle goods away on handcarts. So much had to be left behind, barred earlier by Mr Clarke and now by the second mate Mr Coppin. Goods were hastily disposed of, sold at a quarter or less of their true value. It was a buyer's market. Prospective passengers had little option but to sell. Aboard the ship the space available had diminished steadily throughout the day and those who had been forced to sell off their possessions were resentful to find when they were at last shepherded between decks that many of those who had arrived earlier had more space and had been allowed to retain more of their belongings.

Few voices were raised in protest among the predominantly church members who accepted the situation with resignation. But those who did complain were met with a barrage of abuse from the loud-mouthed Billington. 'Ought to 'ave got 'ere early like the rest of us,' he told the company at large, shocking the ladies in the vicinity and angering their husbands when he added, 'We already spent one night in this bloody hell-hole.'

Daisy raised a hand to the Irishman who was up on the poop deck and he waved back with a smile. The day had been warm with little or no breeze, a bright blue July day, marred only by the occasionally pungent smell of the raw sewage that drifted close in along the dock. Down river the Tower, a recognizable shape in the summer haze, was beginning to blur in the fading light. To Daisy it was a bleak, forbidding place, every bit as frightening as the sinister, high-walled Newgate. Men languished there in cold, airless cells of stone, many of them distinguished gentlemen who had fallen from favour, awaiting their last appointment, an early morning meeting with His Majesty's axeman.

The thought of Bates lying dead on the living-room floor, the knife plunged almost to the hilt in his taut body, the stupefied look of terror and surprise on his face, chilled Daisy's heart and she shuddered. They may not have found him yet. Perhaps the crier had told of another death. There were many murders in the City. With any luck Bates might not be found for several days, at least until she was far away. Who would find him? He had no friends. No tradesmen called at the house. Only the Duchess had friends. A friend or a neighbour might call to enquire about her health. Most of the girls who walked the streets around St Giles were known to the Duchess and she was known to them. Any one of them might call.

The Duchess had done many favours in her time, helping out

with good advice and often with loans of money which invariably turned into gifts. But then, Daisy decided, friends though they were, the fear of catching the dreaded pox would keep most of the girls away. If anyone called it would be a neighbour. She couldn't recall closing the front door. Had she, in her haste, left it open? If she had a neighbour would probably call out down the narrow lobby, get no reply and go inside.

Or perhaps Bates's mongrel dog would raise the alarm. The dog would return, as it usually did, down the long passage alongside the house. At a slow trot, meandering from side to side, nose to the ground, the dog would turn in at the front door and find its master dead on the living-room floor. It would lick his face, stretch out beside him and soon it would start to whimper. Then it would howl and someone would wonder why.

Daisy shivered at the rail and was about to go back to the cabin when she saw something that almost stopped her heart. Across the quay, at the entrance to the Ship Inn, a squad of eight soldiers in their red and black uniforms had lined up. The officer in charge, a sword dangling from his waist in its silver sheath, took the first two men and went inside.

Her heart pounding, Daisy waited. What did they want? Were they looking for her? According to Mr Weston's clerk the crier had mentioned a murder at a house in St Giles and that they were looking for a servant girl. The officer and the two soldiers seemed to be ages inside the inn then when they appeared they were accompanied to the door by the stooping landlady and the barmaid Polly. The landlady was pointing a finger at the *Mayflower*.

Daisy caught her breath as the two soldiers rejoined the ranks and the officer bellowed an order. In the failing light she watched as the squad of eight turned on their heels and in formation made for the ship. People on the quayside stopped what they were doing to watch as the soldiers marched to a halt at the main gangway.

The officer in charge spoke to Mr Coppin, the second mate. Mr Coppin summoned the small boy and sent him off with a message for the captain. At the foot of the gangway the officer posted two of his men and two more at the narrower crew entrance aft of the main bulkhead. Then they were coming aboard, the officer met on deck by Captain Jones.

It was all over. Daisy didn't know what to do, where to turn. She would be arrested, marched off to some foul cell in Newgate, perhaps even the Tower. She went back, trembling now, into the main cabin and sat on the bench in her own space. Absently she began to draw together her few things, ready to pack her canvas bag.

The soldiers in red and black moved slowly among the families in the cabin, peering at faces. They seemed to know who and what they were looking for. Daisy wanted to get it over with. She wanted to stand up and cry, 'All right! I'm here!' But her knees were like jelly and she felt she would be unable to stay on her feet, unable to obey their commands. Then they passed her by, barely gave her a glance and continued on their way.

'What are the soldiers doing?' the Hopkins boy asked his mother.

'I don't know,' Elizabeth Hopkins said. 'What are they doing, Stephen?'

'I hear they're looking for a man,' Mr Hopkins said.

The soldiers went on to search the ship from top to bottom and from stem to stern, though with little help from the crew. And when they left, their search fruitless, they marched smartly back across the quay, like model soldiers in a parade of toys.

As soon as the soldiers had left the main cabin the buzz of voices had resumed. Daisy was bewildered. She had been so convinced they had come for her she had begun to anticipate her fate. In those heart-stopping moments of waiting she had gone through it all. A humiliating arrest in front of all these people; the squad of soldiers marching her off to be charged in the office of the constable; a filthy cell in a terrifying prison; trial for murder and no one to speak in her defence. And then the verdict: the impassive judge, the inevitable sentence of death.

With no grounds for appeal there would be little time to wait. No more than a week, perhaps, before the last day dawned. A baying crowd would gather, eager for the spectacle, the public execution. There would be the scaffold to mount, the masked executioner to face. He was a large man who was recognized wherever he went in the sprawling City. Yet, by tradition, he always wore a mask to his calling. He would climb the steps and stand with his arms folded, the axe at his side, its edge sharpened until it shone like silver in the early morning sunlight. Then the wicker basket would be placed in position, ready to receive the severed head.

All of these images flooded in but that was not all. There were the stories of what happened to the condemned in that week or so of waiting. Daisy had once heard Bates and the Duchess discussing the fate of a French noblewoman arrested in London, accused of plotting against the King and subsequently beheaded in the Tower. The unspeakable things the prison guards did to her, apparently, were commonplace. The guards were said to take advantage of any girl or young woman they knew was soon to be silenced at the block and thrown into an unmarked grave.

She was still trembling. She could barely stand up but she forced herself to her feet and after a moment she left the noisy, crowded cabin and went this time to the lower deck for a breath of fresh air. The Irishman, whose name was Pat Ellis, came and stood beside her at the rail. He was puffing at a crudely wrought pipe, attempting to keep alight a wad of Virginia tobacco. By this time the second mate, Mr Coppin, had brought aboard the last of the would-be emigrant families, the gangways had been raised and the gaps in the bulwarks closed.

'Settled in?' Ellis asked, through a cloud of smoke.

'I have somewhere to lay my head for the night,' she conceded. 'But you were right. There is little room to spare in there.' She looked out across the deserted quayside. 'What were the soldiers looking for?'

'Blowed if I know,' Ellis said. He turned to the second mate who was securing a rope a few feet away. 'What were they after, Mr Coppin? The soldiers.'

The second mate saw Daisy and touched his cap. 'Evenin', miss. I trust you are settled in and comfortable.'

'Comfortable as one can expect,' she said pleasantly.

He smiled and nodded and turned back to Ellis. 'They said they were lookin' for a man. A deserter from one of His Majesty's ships. They say he's been seen aroun' the dock and in the local ale houses. They thought he might have come aboard.'

Ellis laughed and winked at Daisy. 'I can't see him gettin' by you, Mr Coppin. Sure, even the ship's cats are numbered.'

Coppin laughed with him. 'It's the same with Mr Clarke,' he said defensively. 'He's just as keen as I am. We got no room for stowaways.' To Daisy he said, 'Gettin' a bit chilly now, miss. Comes on with nightfall down 'ere on the river, even this time o' year. Be gettin' inside if I were you.'

Daisy accepted the advice graciously. 'Yes, of course,' she said. 'I'll say goodnight to you, gentlemen.'

She was tired and she slept reasonably well that first night on the single mattress the boy brought balanced on his head, 'compliments of the captain'. But the crowded conditions in the main cabin, the coughing and the snoring, the restless children and the fretful babies and the woman who prayed in a low relentless monotone gave a hint of what it would be like in the weeks ahead.

The following day dawned bright and balmy with a pleasant July breeze gently flapping the triangular ensigns at the bowsprit as the *Mayflower* finally left the dock at Southwark and set sail for Southampton. In the light blue morning the clay-coloured Tower, with the King's colours curled idly at the poles and no guards pacing the battlements, looked far less forbidding. Yet as the ship steered a stately course down river Daisy, in the shadow of a longboat, felt like a fugitive stealthily stealing away.

The middle deck soon became crowded as whole families emerged to take the air in the blinding daylight and to watch as the walls of the city and the squat bulk of the Tower were gradually left behind. Now there were fields down to the water's edge, cows grazing, small farms, shacks and outbuildings, cultivated areas of land and acres of open country.

All should have been peace and relaxation on that first leg of the journey but a heated discussion was taking place between a deputation of church elders and the captain. Word had reached the passengers that there might be difficulties in accommodating everyone for the long sea voyage. But for many, who had sold their belongings and abandoned their homes in England, there could be no turning back.

The problem seemed to be that the second ship was much smaller than the *Mayflower*. The people from Holland were hoping to ease their overcrowding by transferring some of their number to the larger vessel. But Captain Jones wouldn't hear of it. His little ship, as he was now calling the *Mayflower*, was already full to capacity.

For the first time, listening to and watching the churchmen and their women, Daisy began to have misgivings about the voyage. Religion ruled their lives. They had shared values and their own strict codes of conduct, but most of all they had their deep-rooted unshakeable faith in God. How this faith differed, if at all, from that of the English or the Roman churches, Daisy had no idea. But this was their voyage, they were in the majority and they would be even more so when the passengers of the two ships joined forces on the other side of the ocean. And she, Daisy Mason, like it or not, was with them. Shanghaied by circumstances, she had become a part of their great adventure.

7

It was again early evening when Daisy saw the Irishman. One foot on the rail on the lower deck he was resting, pipe in hand, after a heavy spell of duty. He smiled at Daisy's approach and she came and stood beside him. She felt drawn to this man and somehow she felt she knew him well and had always known him. Without ever being solemn he was calm and sensible and without, like so many men, being pompous he was confident and sure of himself. He was also old enough to be her father. It was strange, thought Daisy, that after so short an acquaintance they could stand here, side by side, watch the dusk settle on the darkening sea and, without a word being spoken, know that they were together.

'Will you stay on in the New World, Mr Ellis,' she asked, 'or will you return with the ship?'

'I don't know yet,' he said. 'There is talk of a couple of us remainin' behind with the settlement for a year or so with an option to leave at the end of the twelve month. But I don't know. I may be tempted to settle there. I'm gettin' a bit creaky in the bows for sailin' the high seas. An' I have no ties this side of the water. I haven't been back to the old country for many a year.'

'What about your family?'

'Ah, to be sure,' he said, 'there were that many of us that when I did go home now and then to see my old mother she could never remember my name.'

'How sad!'

'Oh, I don't know,' he said cheerfully. 'She had enough trouble rememberin' the names of all those who lived with her. I'm sure it was a relief when one of us got up and left.'

'Were you never married, Mr Ellis?'

'Once,' he said quietly. 'When I was very young. She was called Mary. A lovely girl. Bit like you in some ways an' about your age, too. But I didn't have her for long, less than a year....'

'What happened?'

'She died,' he said, 'and the baby with her.'

Daisy didn't know what to say. She stared in silence at the grey, metallic sea and drew her shawl more tightly about her shoulders.

He turned to her with a smile. 'And what about you? Don't you have a family to return to?'

'I never knew my parents,' Daisy said. 'I was brought up in a convent.' She made a face. 'I hated it. But then I was extremely fortunate. I didn't want to be a nun and so I was sent to work in service for a very gracious lady. She had a fine house in the City and many important friends. She taught me all I know. How to read and write, all the social graces; how to behave at functions and on public occasions. She was determined to make me into a lady like herself.'

'Well, I'd say she's done a pretty good job. You're a fine-lookin' young woman, too, if I may say so. And what I can't understand is why someone like you, with everythin' a girl needs today to find a successful young man in a city like London, would want to go runnin' away to some unknown country.'

Daisy coloured slightly. 'Running away? I'm not running away.'

'Goin' off, I mean,' the Irishman said. 'So far away when there's many a well-off young gent in London just lookin' to make a pampered wife of a young lady like yourself.' He leaned towards her with a grin. 'Why, you could pick an' choose.'

Daisy smiled, pleased with the compliment, though her poise had been ruffled at the suggestion, however innocent, that she might be running away.

There was land to the right, small settlements along the sandy shore and stretches of green almost down to the water's edge. Ahead and away to the left darkness shrouded another shore.

'The Isle of Wight,' Ellis said, anticipating Daisy's question.

'English?'

'Oh yes. Belongs to His Majesty all right, part of the main. I've only ever been there once. Did a couple of days crewin' for a friend. Small boats mostly. They carry provisions across to the penal colony. And sometimes a prisoner in or out.'

Daisy looked at him enquiringly.

'They have a prison on the island. It's a good place to put prisoners serving just a year or two. They work on the land and other jobs.'

'Are they dangerous?'

'No, no,' Ellis assured her. 'They're not hardened criminals. Most of them just serve their time and that's the end of it. Provides a pool of labour for His Majesty. Anyone with any sort of craft is set to work. The rest do farm labourin' and road buildin'. They're not what you'd call dangerous men. They're army deserters, petty thieves, people like that.'

'Like the man the soldiers came looking for?' Daisy asked, steering the conversation round to where she wanted it. 'Was he an army deserter?'

Ellis shook his head. 'No. Worse than that. Y'see, a soldier who deserts his post in time of war is shot if he's caught. But not in peacetime. He just goes to gaol. The man they came lookin' for was not an army deserter. He was a sailor. An' a sailor who deserts his ship ... well, it's a serious matter. Even in peacetime deserting your ship can be treated as a capital offence, 'specially if it's a ship of the King's fleet.'

'Is that what he did? The man they came for?'

'Er ... yes.' Ellis seemed reluctant to discuss the matter further. 'So I understand.'

'Why would they search the *Mayflower*?'

'They made enquiries along the quays at Southwark and somebody told them a man had been asking about a job aboard her.'

'Why would this man want a job aboard a ship if he had just deserted his own?'

Ellis laughed at her persistence. 'I don't know. I think he probably deserted from one of His Majesty's ships and came back to England for some reason of his own. Then when he found they were after him, I expect he had to make a run for it.'

'The girl at the Ship Inn where I stayed said a young man told her he was hoping to find work aboard the *Mayflower*.' Daisy thought of the barmaid, Polly, and her talk of the young man Daisy had seen on the dock at Southwark. The truth was that Daisy had been unable to get the young man out of her mind since the moment he looked up at her window with a smile and a cheeky tug of his forelock. How romantic! she thought. If they were both running away from something perhaps they could run away together. She had dreamed about him several times now and the recollection of those half-awake dreams made her blush. She looked at the Irishman to see if he had read her thoughts. 'She said he was a tall, slim young man with light brown hair and incredibly blue eyes.'

Ellis raised an eyebrow at her. 'Sounds like the girl at the Ship was pretty well smitten with this young fellow.'

'Well, ye-es,' Daisy said. 'Actually I saw him myself once – and he really was quite handsome.'

The Irishman was cautious now, wondering how much she knew.

'What do you suppose happened to him, Mr Ellis?'

'Can't say, miss. He may have taken a job on one of the other ships.'

'Oh, I don't think so. The girl said he was set on sailing with the *Mayflower*. All the way to the New World, she said. I mean, if he was on the run, as they say, that would explain why he wanted to sail to the New World, wouldn't it? Somewhere far away, where they'd never find him, where he could start a new life.'

'I suppose it would, but he'd be out of luck,' Ellis said with a finality that suggested he wanted an end to the discussion. 'He wouldn't get a spot aboard this ship. Captain Jones is not taking on any more crew till we reach Southampton. I know that for certain.'

The passengers were by now well entrenched in their cramped quarters and in a mood to defend their territory. Even those who considered themselves among the most charitable of the church people felt there was simply no room for any more and they were not disposed to make room. At Southampton, for fear of losing the spaces they had claimed, few went ashore and few new passengers were allowed on board without having to face a barrage of questions and hostile stares. Yet a man named John Carver and his entourage were received without rancour and a space large enough for two families was somehow created for them in the main cabin.

Carver, a bald, bearded, upright man in his fifties, was evidently a church elder of some note. Within hours of his arrival passengers were coming to him with their problems and always he received them with courtesy and a natural kindness. By contrast his thin-lipped wife and her dough-faced companion seemed sternly unapproachable. The Carvers had no children of their own and Mrs Carver seemed to disapprove of everyone else's. But they did have a large contingent of servants: two men, two boys and a maidservant.

Daisy watched them as they settled in and her sympathy was drawn at once to the young maid. The girl was small and thin. She had a red rash on her chin, pale sunken cheeks and the largest, saddest eyes Daisy had ever seen. Most of her time was spent running between tasks set by the two women and when spoken to she behaved like a petrified rabbit. She appeared to have absolutely no standing in the Carver household and was even ill-used and ordered to carry out menial jobs by the two servant boys, both of whom were younger than her.

Brushing a strand of lank hair from her large eyes the girl stooped to move a case that was far too heavy for her. Instinctively

Daisy helped her and before hurrying away the girl murmured a
surprised and frightened, 'Thank you, miss.'

She was far from well nourished, Daisy noticed, and her thin
dress, simple and adequate but plain as sackcloth, hung loosely
from the skin and bone of her puny shoulders. Clearly she was
considered of little worth and the stark, uncared-for vulnerability
of her position or perhaps her lack of position touched something
deep and familiar in Daisy. If these people are so religious, she
wondered, where is their charity? The nuns of her childhood were
strict and her life with them had not been easy. But they were
never cruel or consciously unkind.

The arrival of a coach and horses at the quayside caused a stir
and, along with a number of other passengers, Daisy went out on
deck to investigate. It was the *Mayflower*'s second day in dock at
Southampton when the man who was to become their military
leader and adviser joined the settlers. He was a thick-set,
prickly-looking man with red hair, pale-blue eyes and a pointed,
well-trimmed reddish beard.

From the main deck the onlookers watched as the coach driver
and a footman took down a substantial trunk and carried it to the
lowered gangway. Confidently expecting these newcomers to be
turned away the watchers were surprised when the first mate, Mr
Clarke, greeted them with deference and instructed the small boy
to stand by, ready to lead them aboard. At the open door of the
coach the smartly dressed former soldier offered his hand to a
young woman who emerged, shading her eyes in the bright
sunlight, to stand for a moment at the step and look up at the
square-rigged *Mayflower*.

Her clothes, Daisy noted, were of good quality. A blue and
white bonnet, gloves to match and a neat blue and white dress with
a tight bodice, high waist and full skirts swept about her ankles as
she stepped down. Mr Clarke, with the boy in attendance, led
them up the gangway and they were met on deck by the master,
Captain Jones, who shook hands cordially with the man and raised
his hat to the young woman. Obviously they were expected and as
they were led away word went round that they had been allocated
their own cabin.

The red-haired man's name, Daisy discovered later, was
Captain Miles Standish. He and his young wife were from the
north of England. They had travelled down to Southampton from
a town called Chorley in Lancashire to join the expedition to
North America. A soldier by training and inclination Miles
Standish had served in Holland, in the army of Queen Elizabeth,

in support of the Dutch Protestants against the attacks of
marauding Spanish Catholics. At a place called Leyden about
twelve miles from The Hague he had somehow become involved
with the leaders of the exiled English congregation who
worshipped at a church called St Peter's.

Their plan for a new life in a largely undiscovered region of the
world had evidently fired his imagination and his spirit of
adventure and he had volunteered to join them as their military
adviser. Already tales of trouble with the indigenous tribes of
North American Indians had filtered back to England. There was
little doubt that travellers to the New World would need to be in a
position to protect themselves and their families. It was a job Miles
Standish viewed with relish.

The master of the *Mayflower* had been informed that Captain
Standish would be joining his ship at Southampton and should be
afforded the courtesy and consideration to which his rank entitled
him. Though the captain had left the army his role was
semi-official. He was not a member of the previously exiled
congregation from Holland. Nor was he a religious man. But he
was a highly regarded soldier and sources close to the King's court
considered it no bad thing to have a trusted and reliable
representative close to the leadership of the proposed settlement.
Claims to territory and treaties with the natives should and, with
Standish present, would be made in the name of James I.

Miles Standish came from a wealthy and distinguished family.
Three of his forebears had been knighted – one for wounding the
revolutionary Wat Tyler in Smithfield in defence of his king and
two for bravery on the field of battle. Another had been a noted
bishop. Now, though he was no longer in uniform, there was still
something military and distinctive about him. He stepped aboard
wearing a rust-brown doublet with shoulder caps, braid stripes
down the sleeves and white cuffs. Like most of the men he wore
knee breeches with knitted stockings and buckled shoes. But it was
his imperious manner and bearing, not his dress, that set him
apart.

His wife was a small-boned, slightly built woman. But with her
black, almost blue-black hair and her pale porcelain skin, Daisy
could see that many men would find her attractive. There was
something more, too, something fragile and flower-like about her,
a suggestion that she might always be in need of care and
protection. It was a duty, Daisy acknowledged, that many men
might be eager and happy to fulfil.

This dependence on men was not something Daisy admired in a

woman. So many of the street girls she had come to know had been pathetically bound to some worthless male. Daisy had vowed she would never tolerate such a weakness in herself. She had always had to be independent and the Duchess had assured her this was how it should be. It was the only way to survive in the often brutal world of men.

Daisy stood on the fringe of the onlookers and watched as the former army captain and his wife were welcomed on deck. With his pointed beard Standish made a striking figure, but Daisy was more interested in his wife. It was surprising, she reflected, to find someone who appeared so vulnerable joining an expedition such as this. In a fine country house with sufficient domestic staff and a surname held in high regard she would no doubt function well and live the kind of comfortable, unadventurous life to which she was probably born. But here, among strangers and not all of them friendly, Daisy wondered how the delicately wrought Mrs Standish might survive.

Later that evening the talk in the main cabin was that the ship's master had invited Captain and Mrs Standish to dine with him and his senior officers, but only Captain Standish had accepted. Like the lady she was, Mrs Standish had politely declined, announcing that she wished to retire early and leave the evening to her husband and his new-found gentlemen friends.

For some reason she couldn't define, the presence of the young Mrs Standish had unnerved Daisy. She believed she had established a place in the eyes of the ship's master as perhaps the most important and well-connected young woman aboard. Now, for no good reason, she felt her position was threatened.

8

The following morning Daisy sat alone in her confined space in the main cabin. She had brought with her a small cask of water which she used sparingly on a face cloth to wipe the sleep from her eyes and to freshen her cheeks. Fresh water was scarce aboard ship and was for drinking not washing. Sea water, she'd been told, would not lather. The Irishman had warned her and Elizabeth Hopkins had confirmed it: 'Sea water dries and cracks your skin and the wind makes raw meat of it.' Rain water was the only hope of clean fresh water for washing and it hadn't rained for over a week.

The churchwomen, she noticed, scraped back their hair and hid as much of it as they could beneath their tight bonnets. As if it was sinful to do so, they spent little time on their appearance. None wore the paints and powders of the City, but this did not trouble Daisy. Though she'd had access to the Duchess's make-up trays she had only experimented in private and had never shown her face painted in public. It was the virtual impossibility of taking a bath that bothered her most. The journey to the New World, she'd been given to understand, would take several weeks. And nobody would be able to take a bath! Already the atmosphere in the main cabin was oppressive. What would it be like in a few weeks' time? She went out on deck for a breath of fresh air.

It was another bright sunny day, Wednesday, July 26. Nearby, anchored off the West Quay, was the *Speedwell*, the ship that was to accompany the *Mayflower* across the Atlantic. The *Speedwell*, with the Union Flag on her jack-staff and the cross of St George at her stern, had made the short voyage from Holland in just under three days. Anchored for the night of Tuesday out on Southampton Water, she had sailed in and alongside the *Mayflower* at first light.

Already there was a great bustle of activity on the quay. Daisy went to rest her arms on the rail and look down but, as she did so, she was almost bowled over by a tall, slim, muscular young man who came bounding up the gangway and on to the main deck. She felt his hands on her arms to steady her and, as he apologized profusely, she found herself looking up into the eyes she had been dreaming about since she first saw him that day on the dock at Southwark.

'Sorry, ma'am,' he said with genuine concern and then, when he saw that she was not in any way harmed, his tanned, handsome face broke into a smile, 'Clumsy of me.'

In her dreams Daisy had pictured him as a good-looking, roguish, roughneck. A heartbreaker, no doubt. And he still seemed all of these things. But what surprised her was his voice. He had the clear, polished tone of a true member of the gentry.

He released his hold on her. Though she did not appear to object, he was aware that it was not within the bounds of propriety for him to grip her arms in this way. He smiled down at her, but Daisy was unable to speak. She simply gazed up at him, as if he had stepped out of last night's dream.

'I'm sorry, ma'am,' he said again. 'I do hope you are all right.'

The little cabin boy was waiting at the narrow steps to the poop deck. 'Mr Trefor!' he cried. 'This way, Mr Trefor!'

His woollen cap in one hand, the young man backed away, bowing and smiling. Daisy noticed he was barefoot. Only the officers wore shoes on board ship and he was not an officer. He was an ordinary seaman and he was dressed like one, in a leather jerkin and knee breeches.

Daisy blushed in confusion, still unable to find her voice and he turned and followed the boy up to the captain's cabin. Down on the quay with Mr Coppin were two more men. Daisy guessed they, too, were here to see the captain, applicants for the extra crew jobs. She was thrilled to think that the one the cabin boy had called Mr Trefor might be joining them on their long voyage. But with that voice could he really be an ordinary seaman? She hid by a stanchion and waited.

Here, in Southampton, that hectic morning, the ship was finally victualled for the voyage. Supplies stacked on the West Quay were hauled up, swung in over the decks and lowered into the holds. Daisy was surprised there was room for anything more. Already the passengers had brought with them chairs, tables, chests of drawers, cupboards, cradles, trunks, hand looms, spinning wheels, anything they could get past the mates.

According to Daisy's new friend, Elizabeth, there were pots, pans, kettles, lanterns, lamps, buckets, baskets, bottles, crockery, pewter mugs, wooden plates, knives, spoons, salt cellars, hourglasses and steelyards and many other household utensils. Then there were tools. There were spades, hoes, rakes, axes, saws, hammers, chisels, holdfasts, ropes, nails, shovels, seed grain, garden seeds, hooks and twine for fishing and many more.

And according to young Giles Hopkins, stored separately were the weapons and heavier artillery: muskets, powder and shot, swords and daggers, six big guns – two sakers, two minions, two bases – and four small cannon. There were goods for trading, too. Bracelets, chains, rings, strings of beads and ear-rings. 'For the natives,' as Giles put it.

Now they were finding room for the food. Barrels of spiced and salted beef, salted pork, peas and pease pudding, hogsheads of oatmeal and wheat flour, boxes of smoked herring, dried salted cod and dried neats' tongues, sacks of turnips, parsnips, onions, beans and cabbage. There were tubs of pickled eggs and fifty-six pound firkins of butter. And there were many spices: cinnamon, pepper, mace, nutmeg, wormwood and green ginger. There were preserves of roses and clover-gillyflowers, sugar, raisins and prunes. And lots of salt and, for medicinal purposes, bottles of lemon juice. There were also pipes of Dutch gin and French brandy, casks of beer and wine and barrels of spring water.

Daisy watched and waited and when the man called Trefor reappeared he was accompanied by the first mate, Mr Clarke. At the gangway Mr Clarke paused and turned to Trefor and from her vantage point behind the stanchion Daisy could hear clearly what passed between them.

'I want you to know this, Will Trefor,' the first mate said sternly. 'I don't approve of what's been done. I think it's wrong. If it were left to me I'd turn you in. But if Cap'n Jones says you're with us then I must accept his decision. From now on you are a member of this crew. But a very lowly member. You just remember that. What you may have done in the past or what you may have been is no concern of mine. You work for me now. Understand? And you report for duty tomorrow morning at first light.'

The young man smiled and said, 'Aye, aye, sir. Anything you say, Mr Clarke.'

The first mate dismissed him with a curt nod and the man called Trefor went down the gangway and out on to the quay where the Irishman, Pat Ellis, was waiting for him. They spoke briefly, Ellis slapped him on the back and together they went off towards the seamen's tavern.

Will Trefor! So that was his name. And he was now a member of the crew. But what had he done? And what was he before? And how did he get here from Southwark Dock? Mr Ellis would know, Daisy decided, and she resolved to ask him at the first opportunity.

Straining over the rail to look down at the busy scene below, Daisy was so preoccupied with thoughts of Will Trefor that she didn't hear it at first. There was a steady babble of voices and the rumble of horse-drawn carts on the quay but all of that was background noise. There was something else. Daisy listened carefully.

It was there again, the sound of sobbing. Close by someone was sobbing loudly and to Daisy it was the most heart-rending sound she had ever heard, a sound of utter desolation.

She looked around the deck, behind a bulkhead and over a section of dismantled shallop. But there was nothing, no one. Yet the sound was close at hand. She listened again and found it was coming from just below the level of the deck. She went to a narrow doorway, the head of some spiral steps. Two, three, four steps down. It was there again, so close.

To Daisy's right was a tiny landing with a recess. The recess housed a hatch less than eighteen inches square, an opening just wide enough for a slim seaman to squeeze through. The hatch led into the anchor hold where a tarred cable turned a giant cog. In the recess, sitting by the closed trapdoor to the hatch, her head down against her raised knees, and sobbing her heart out was the Carvers' little maidservant Daisy had seen earlier in the main cabin.

'Why?' Daisy asked. 'Whatever is the matter?'

The girl cowered back, her thumb in her mouth. She looked guilty, anxious for some means of escape. But Daisy was blocking her exit.

'What is it?' Daisy asked gently.

The large frightened eyes were dark-rimmed and smudged with tears.

'Nothing is that bad,' Daisy said, coaxing her with a smile.

The girl started to cry again, uncontrollably now, and she sank back against the trap door, reverting to a sitting position, her knees under her chin. Daisy knelt before her, stroked her dark unruly hair and the girl covered her face with her grubby hands.

'What is it?' Daisy prompted. 'Are they working you too hard?'

The small thin body was shaking again.

'Never mind,' Daisy told her. 'You cry as much as you want to. Let it all come out. You'll feel much better.'

Daisy put a comforting arm around the girl's shoulders and the girl rested her head on Daisy's chest. Rocking her gently Daisy murmured soothing words in her ear and gradually the sobbing began to subside. Then, except for one large sob that came every few seconds with a sharp intake of breath, it stopped altogether.

'Sh!' Daisy continued to comfort her until she could feel the girl had relaxed and was breathing calmly and in control. 'All right now?'

The girl nodded and was caught at once by another of the single shuddering sobs. 'Yes,' she said, recovering her breath and almost returning Daisy's involuntary laugh. 'Thank you, miss. Thank you very much.'

'Wait there!' Daisy ordered and she went back up the steps and out to the main cabin for the biscuit bag the Hopkins's manservant had purchased in Southwark on her behalf. The girl accepted the bag readily and, as if amazed that anyone could be so kind, she stared at Daisy in disbelief and munched hungrily at a large piece of pastry. Daisy smiled and sat back against the steps.

'What's the hold, miss?' the girl asked suddenly, her dark round eyes eager for an answer.

Daisy looked puzzled. 'The hold?'

'On the ship, miss. What is it?'

'The hold on the ship?' Daisy said. 'Oh, that's the place where they store the cargo. You know, the things we have to take with us. It's down below. In the bottom, the part that's under the water.'

'Is there rats down there, miss?'

'Rats?' She supposed there would be. She had heard of rats leaving a sinking ship. 'I expect so. If there are rats on board that's where they'll be. Why?'

'They said they'd put me in the hold.'

'Who did?'

'Mrs Carver and Miss Minter.'

'Why did they say that?'

'They gave me some money to go to the shop and I dropped a halfpenny on the deck. It rolled away and over the edge. It fell into the water. It did, miss. Honest, it did. But they didn't believe me. They said I stole it. But I didn't, miss. Honest. I didn't steal it. It just rolled over the side. Now they say if I don't give it back they'll have to punish me. But I haven't got it, miss. They say when we sail they'll get the captain to throw me into the hold.'

'Take no notice of them,' Daisy said in disgust. 'They can't do that. They're just two silly women.'

The girl's mouth fell open at Daisy's lack of respect.

'What's your name?' Daisy asked.

'Prudence, miss.'

'Well, I like you, Prudence,' Daisy said, 'and I shall call you Pru.'

For the first time that morning the girl smiled and her small face was transformed. Daisy thought she looked quite beautiful with her great soulful eyes. 'How old are you?'

'Fifteen, miss.'

'Well, I can tell you this, Pru. The captain of a ship is the person in charge of everything. He makes all the rules. It's his ship and what he decides is the law.'

The girl nodded gravely, taking in every word.

'And he has special powers, too,' Daisy went on. 'He can perform all kinds of duties and ceremonies. Take the service. If someone dies at sea it's the captain's duty to see they are properly buried.'

'Buried?' Pru queried. 'How can you be buried at sea?'

'They have a service and everything. It's just like it is on land, except the coffin is dropped in the water.'

'Dropped in the water?' Pru looked as though she might laugh. 'Wouldn't it float away?'

Daisy laughed and Pru joined in as they pictured a coffin floating away on the high seas.

'It would look funny to another ship,' Daisy said, prolonging the image, encouraging the girl's laughter. 'It would go sailing by, up and down, over the ocean waves. And the people on the other ship would shout, "Ahoy! Is anybody there? Is any *body* there?"'

'Is any *body* there,' Pru repeated and together they rocked with laughter. And for the moment Pru had forgotten her cares.

'Anyhow,' Daisy said, calming down. 'The captain can do all that and he can marry people, too.'

'I'd love to be married,' Pru said, 'and have someone to love. Someone who would love me.'

'Well,' Daisy said with a bright smile, not wanting her to revert to feeling sorry for herself, 'you'll have to find a nice young man and we can ask the captain to perform the ceremony. I don't know though. You're a little young yet, don't you think?'

Pru's normally pale face was flushed. She was excited at the thought that someone might marry her one day and thrilled that someone like Daisy was taking an interest in her. Not wanting the conversation to end she asked quickly, 'What else can he do, miss?'

'The captain? Oh ... he can christen babies.'

Pru was captivated. 'At sea?'

'Of course. He can do all those things. But the point is, our captain, the captain of this ship, Captain Jones, is known to me.'

Pru's eyes widened.

'And it's Captain Jones who decides who goes in the hold. Not your Mrs Fatty Carver or her funny friend.'

Pru was scandalized. It was heresy to speak of her employers in such a way, but she couldn't contain her laughter. Mrs Carver *was* fat. And Miss Minter *was* funny in a peculiar way. Mrs Fatty Carver!

'And I promise you,' Daisy said, 'nothing like that will ever happen to you.'

'Oh, miss!'

'Have a biscuit,' Daisy said.

Pru looked thoughtful. 'Do they really drop the coffin in the water?' she asked, through a mouthful of biscuits.

Daisy laughed. 'Of course they do. And they weight it down so that it sinks, silly.'

Pru nodded slowly and bit into another biscuit. Three biscuits later she stood up, straightened her coarse dress and ran her hands over her wayward hair. She was serious again, sombre even. 'I better go. I'll be in trouble again.'

'Don't forget the bag,' Daisy said. 'You might as well take what's left.' She laughed. 'You've eaten most of them.'

'Oh, miss!' Pru said. 'You're ever so kind.'

'Go on,' Daisy said, 'and keep smiling. You're a pretty girl when you smile. Did you know that?'

Pru smiled brightly in response and ran up the steps to the deck. Daisy waited a few moments to give the girl time to return to the main cabin then she started to follow. But when she emerged into the bright sunlight she paused, her attention drawn to a lone figure on the poop deck. The upper deck aft was out of bounds to the passengers but not, apparently, to the newly arrived army officer. Captain Standish was standing alone up there. He was looking out over the side and he was standing very still.

Daisy wondered why some people had special privileges. The army captain and his wife had been allocated a cabin. There were only four such cabins but, small as they were, they did afford a degree of privacy and were much coveted. Families would readily squeeze into one of these confined spaces rather than share in the communal areas available between decks or in the main cabin.

All four cabins were now taken, one of them by a family named Mullins – father, mother, son and daughter. The girl was about seventeen. Daisy had seen her several times and, in a friendly way, she had returned Daisy's smile. She was probably a nice girl, thought Daisy. But she spent most of her time in or near the family cabin and they had not yet met or been formally introduced. The girl's father, stern-faced and unbending, looked far less friendly.

Up on the poop deck, Captain Standish, eyes narrowed as if he had recognized someone he knew, seemed to be looking with interest at a man on the quay. Daisy followed his gaze and saw that he was watching the man known as Will Trefor.

9

The tavern on the West Quay was a low, ramshackle building where seafaring men sought employment. At a table in the tap room a weather-beaten old sailor would sit most mornings, Sundays included, to give out news of job opportunities. The masters of the various vessels would send details of what crew they required, duration of voyage and what pay could be expected. But the tavern was more than a mere labour exchange for sailors. It was more a club, a precursor of the Seamen's Institute, a place where they could buy a drink, meet old friends and make new ones, a place where they could swap stories, the taller the better.

Pat Ellis and Will Trefor were in there that sunny morning with a young man named John Alden who had signed on as a carpenter with the *Mayflower*. Apprenticed locally, Alden had received a good grounding in his trade and was now out of his indentures. He had lived near boats and the harbour all his life, but he had never wanted to be a sailor and he had never sailed further than Plymouth to the west or Hastings to the east. Yet, when he heard of the twin voyage of the smallish *Mayflower* and the even smaller *Speedwell* to the unknown land across the Atlantic Ocean, he had decided he wanted to be part of it.

John Alden had come with good references from his employer, who had been sorry to lose him, and the first mate, who interviewed him, had liked his frank, open manner from the start. He was a big, strong, broad-shouldered lad, yet he was none too sure of himself. His unworldliness was quick to show in his fresh face and wide innocent eyes but, though he still had a hint of the yokel about him, he was far from stupid. For one thing, he had the makings of a master craftsman. He loved the feel of wood and what he could do with it. But, as he discovered later, it was not this potential that won him his place on board.

According to the law of the land, where more than a certain number of barrels were to be taken out of the country, a cooper had to be employed to cut sufficient staves to ensure the same number of barrels were shipped home again. It was due to this law and for no other reason that John Alden was taken on. Not that he wanted to make a career as a ship's carpenter. Far from it. A handful of coins for a week of a man's life led nowhere. Real and lasting wealth came with the owning of land and property, and there was little chance of that at home in a country where every inch of every acre was already spoken for and staked out by some favourite of the Crown. He wanted to see this New World and try his luck where, it was said, a man could still claim a piece of land and work for something worth having.

'Keep a steady hand, you men!' a voice said.

All three turned to find the second mate, Mr Coppin, standing behind them.

'Glad to have you aboard,' he said, sitting down, 'and to show you I mean it I'll allow you to buy me a drink.'

The young carpenter jumped to his feet. 'What will it be, Mr Coppin?'

'No, lad,' Ellis said, going to the bar. 'We don't let new boys buy the drinks.'

'What do you make of this trip, Mr Coppin?' Will Trefor asked.

The carpenter had noted Will Trefor's accent and manner and was curious to know why he was sailing as an ordinary seaman. But just then he was equally interested in hearing the second mate's reply.

'Well,' Mr Coppin said in his bluff, West Country way, 'I'll tell you. These people are the oddest bunch I ever come across. For a start, they's all religious cranks.' He tapped the side of his head with his forefinger. 'They's supposed to be runnin' away from His Majesty the King. Yet the King knows well enough where they are an' he's watchin' em go. He's lettin' 'em run. An' I reckons as whatever they finds out there, if anythin', then King James will want a pretty big slice on it.'

'You reckon they're being exploited then?' Trefor asked.

'Yes, lad, I do. They must have left comfortable homes, in London or in Holland, with warm beds and cosy firesides and plenty to eat. Even if they survive the voyage an' there's no certainty in that....'

'Why not?' the young carpenter asked.

'Why not? Because the ocean is unpredictable. That's why not. She's like a woman. You never know which way she'll turn. She has strange moods. Sometimes she's calm an' placid an' lovely to look at. Other times she's fiery an' fierce an' howlin' an' screamin' like a wild cat. An' again at other times she's dead. She jus' lies there, not movin' with not a breath of air anywhere an' that's when yer in the doldrums. Yer can't go for'ard and yer can't go back. Yer can't make no progress with her at all.'

Pat Ellis stuck a flagon of ale in the second mate's hand as the young carpenter listened intently.

'Isn't that so, Pat?' Mr Coppin said.

'It's true,' Ellis said. 'The ocean can be pretty treacherous. Short journeys from port to port along the coast or across the Channel, even in the Med, are pretty well charted. But the ocean is different. Once you pull out of sight of land there's little there to guide you. Just the stars, that's all.' He laughed. 'But don't let Mr Coppin put you off, son. He's been there before, so he knows it can be done.'

Young Alden turned back to the mate. 'Is that right, sir?'

'Aye,' Mr Coppin said. 'That's right enough. It can be done. But you needs yer share o' good luck an' good management an' that's for sure.'

'We'll make it, Mr Coppin,' Will Trefor said with a grin. 'You have a damned good crew behind you.'

The others laughed and drank to that but Mr Coppin still added soberly, 'It's not the crew as worries me, lads. It's the passengers. We don't know what their men are made of ... an' so many women an' children.' He shook his head. 'There'll be no warm houses and cosy firesides waitin' on 'em over there. No hot grub or clean beds. There'll be nothin' but what they makes for themselves. An' in the woods there'll be howling wolves an' wild men.' He shrugged. 'But I don't give it no thought now. Nothin' I say can make a difference. We're goin' an' that's that. I just hope their God is goin' with us.'

The young carpenter looked to Ellis and Trefor, eager for some more optimistic view of the venture.

'Sure an' I can't say what it will be like on the other side,' Pat Ellis said, 'but the sooner we go the better.'

Mr Coppin nodded. 'It's the thought of any delays as worries the cap'n. With so many passengers he wants a summer crossin'. A week lost here an' there an' we could be into all kinds of bad weather.'

'I believe the *Mayflower* is in pretty good shape,' Will Trefor said. 'I'm sure she'll see us through. But I'm not so sure about the other little tub. She looks to me as if she's overmasted for her size.'

'An' she leaks like a drunk woman's drawers,' Mr Coppin added.

A young barmaid, barely sixteen, exchanged glances with John Alden as she passed by and the young carpenter looked suitably abashed.

'I'd say there's more here for a young fellow like you,' Pat Ellis said with a laugh.

'There'll be no willing wenches over there, my lad,' Mr Coppin said, joining in the laughter. 'Not unless yer takes a fancy to the wild Indian women.'

Daisy had been down to the shops on the road beyond the quay, keeping an eye open for Will Trefor. She had left the ship hoping to bump into him again, but there was no sign of him. More than likely, she decided, he was sitting the morning out in the Seamen's Tavern. When she returned to the main cabin she found that Prudence was at the centre of a disturbance.

Making her way between the squatting families and their belongings, she paused to watch and listen. At the head of a small group of spectators who had formed a ring round the little maidservant were the two women of the Carver household, Mrs Carver and her companion Miss Minter. Mrs Carver was holding forth, frowning sternly and pursing her lips.

'You swore on the Bible that you did not steal the money you were given to purchase provisions.'

'Yes,' Pru agreed, her voice barely audible, her eyes once again brimful of tears.

'A coin, you said, fell from your clumsy little hand and rolled across the deck and into the sea.'

'Yes, Mrs Carver.'

'And do you still say that?'

'Yes, Miss Minter.'

Mrs Carver thrust her round, fat face at the cowering girl. 'Then we say to you, you little madam, not only are you a thief, you are a liar, too. And you know what happens to liars, don't you? They lose their tongues and they spend the rest of their days wandering about, making funny noises, unable to speak. Struck dumb, by the good Lord Himself who knows them for what they are. Liars! Liars, I say! And you, little thief, are one of them!'

'No, Mrs Carver. It's not true.'

'There is not a grain of repentance in this girl, Miss Minter,' Mrs Carver said. 'She must be punished at once. She must be sent to a place of correction where she can sit in the dark and ponder on her sins. Or, if she so wishes, she can tell more lies. She can tell lies to her heart's content. But only herself will hear them.' Mrs Carver and anyone watching could see the girl was terrified now. 'On board a ship there is such a place and it is down below. Down below in the hold where only the rats live.'

One of the Carvers' young menservants, John Howland, was troubled by the girl's distress. 'I'm sure that Prudence wouldn't tell lies, Mrs Carver,' he began.

Mrs Carver silenced him abruptly. 'Hold your tongue!' she told him. 'If we want your opinion we'll ask for it.'

'But it's not true, Mrs Carver,' Pru said. 'Honestly, I didn't do nothing wrong.'

'Lies, lies and more lies!' the small, fat Mrs Carver boomed, her chest expanding. 'Say no more, child!'

Prudence was on her knees, her narrow shoulders once again racked by sobs.

'We *know* you are telling lies,' Mrs Carver went on, 'because we have the proof!'

With a flourish, from the folds of her full skirt, she produced the crumpled biscuit bag Daisy had given the girl earlier and she held it up for all to see. There was a low murmur from the onlookers.

'This!' Mrs Carver was quivering with rage. 'This is yours, is it not? A bag of biscuits – most of which you have greedily devoured.' Her eyes narrowed and she added venomously, 'If I had wanted you to buy biscuits I would have told you so.'

Pru lowered her hands from her tear-stained cheeks. 'No, ma'am,' she said. 'I didn't buy 'em.'

Mrs Carver looked aghast. 'This is yours, is it not?'

'Yes, ma'am, but ...'

'Yes!' Mrs Carver said triumphantly. 'And how did you come by it? You paid for it with the coin you stole, didn't you? Or do you still deny it?'

Most of the passengers present had gathered as close in as they could to hear the outcome of this one-sided public trial. Twice Elizabeth Hopkins, her three-year-old daughter at her skirts, had murmured, 'Shame!' But, though her sympathy was with Prudence, her utterances were so timid it was not clear whose side she was on.

'Yes, yes, yes,' Prudence sobbed. 'I didn't steal ...'

'Then you are not only a thief and a liar, you are stupid and brazen ...'

Daisy had seen and heard enough.

'No!' she declared in a loud firm voice.

All eyes turned to her in surprise.

'The girl is not stupid, madam. *You* are.'

There was a gasp from the audience, a titter here and there. Mrs Carver's face, already red, was suddenly tinged with purple. Her small eyes blazed at Daisy as she tried to speak but no words would come.

'How dare you!' Miss Minter spluttered.

'I suggest you keep out of this,' Daisy said, with icy calm. 'From what I have seen here, servants have no rights. And you, I understand, are a paid servant like the rest.'

Miss Minter was shocked. She stepped back, her mouth open. And at that moment Mrs Carver's husband, who had witnessed much of the scene from the back of the crowd, decided it was time to come forward.

John Carver was an elder of the congregation from Holland. A dignified man with a quiet and kindly disposition, he had joined the *Mayflower* as the spiritual leader of his people on board. He was a fair-minded man and the heavy-handed action of his wife and her companion had embarrassed him. But even he had been affronted by what appeared to be Daisy's unwarranted intervention.

'You have no cause to speak to these ladies in so offensive a manner, young woman,' he said civilly. 'On behalf of my wife and this other good lady I must ask you to withdraw your remarks, tender your apologies and refrain from entering any further into this discussion.' He threw his wife a mildly reproachful glance. 'This girl is one of my servants. The matter is of no concern to anyone outside of my family.'

'I will comply with your requests, sir,' Daisy said with equal civility, 'on condition these ...' – she weighed her words carefully, – 'these *ladies* will apologize to the girl.'

'Apologize?' Mrs Carver looked as if she might explode. 'Me? Apologize to a servant girl? For what, may I ask?'

Daisy looked down on the diminutive Mrs Carver. 'For making a totally unfounded accusation against her,' she said calmly. 'The girl did not buy the biscuits with stolen money. I gave them to her. Edward, Mr Hopkins's man, bought them at my request when he went to the shop for Mrs Hopkins. He is there, over there.' She pointed a finger at the Hopkins's manservant who shuffled awkwardly at the unexpected attention. 'Is this not so, Edward? Did you not purchase these biscuits for me?'

'I did, miss.' The thin, stooping manservant nodded. 'That I did.'

'I took the bag on deck when I went in search of some fresh air.' With these few words and a twitch of her nose Daisy somehow managed to imply that Mrs Carver was responsible for the stale air in the main cabin. 'I gave some of the biscuits to Mrs Hopkins' children ...'

'That is so.' Elizabeth Hopkins spoke up, pleased that Daisy had come to the rescue of the unfortunate girl.

'I ate some of the biscuits myself,' Daisy went on, 'and only a
few were left when I gave the bag to your girl. If she did "greedily
devour" a few paltry biscuits one can only conclude that you don't
feed her well enough.'

The two women looked chastened but they were unwilling to
recant and accept defeat. Daisy did not hesitate to deliver the *coup
de grâce*.

'And what is more, Mrs Carver,' Daisy said, 'what this girl said
earlier is also true.' She smiled encouragingly at Prudence. 'I saw
her,' she lied, 'drop a coin and chase it to where it rolled out of
reach and into the deep water dock. She was terribly upset.
Fearful of your wrath, no doubt.'

There was a silence in the large cabin. Among the servants
present and also among the older children, the ones who could
understand what had been said, sympathy swung solidly behind
Prudence. But most of the adults felt that Daisy's conduct in
publicly insulting and humiliating the two women could not be
condoned. She ought to have taken Mrs Carver aside and
explained the position. Now everyone, including the two women,
knew there would be much hilarity when the exchanges were
retailed in private.

'I am bound to say,' Mr Carver said in an effort to return the
atmosphere to one of conciliation, 'there appears to have been a
misunderstanding. I do believe, however, my good lady wife is
owed an apology.'

'I agree, Mr Carver,' Daisy said. 'And I will gladly apologize to
your wife if I can have her assurance that no harm or punishment
will come to the girl.'

Carver looked at his wife. What Daisy asked was reasonable and
proper. The maidservant had apparently been entirely blameless.
Mrs Carver looked away, unhappy at the outcome.

'My dear?' Mr Carver insisted.

Mrs Carver gave a peremptory nod.

'Your apology, miss?' he asked quietly.

'By all means,' Daisy said so that all could hear. 'I apologize
wholeheartedly to Mrs Carver for calling her stupid. Some things
are best left unsaid.'

10

At sixty tons, only half the size of the *Mayflower*, the *Speedwell* was a disappointment. The more perceptive of the passengers soon realized there were problems and their disquiet was fuelled further by rumour. It was said the ship's master, a Captain Reynolds, had told Captain Jones of the *Mayflower* that the *Speedwell* was unfit for the proposed Atlantic crossing. Considerable work and adjustments were necessary to make her safe.

It transpired that the church elders from Holland had only themselves to blame. They had bought the *Speedwell* in the Dutch port of Delftshaven without first taking professional advice, without even the benefit of a survey. They had decided that consultation with shipwrights and other experts were a waste of time and money. They had commissioned the rigging and refitting themselves and, in an amateurish fashion, had concentrated more on increasing the passenger accommodation than looking to the ship's essential seaworthiness. They had employed cheap, unskilled and inexperienced labour. Now they were going to have to pay the price.

Captain Reynolds had been engaged in London to command the *Speedwell* and take it across the Atlantic. His first sight of the little ship in Holland had filled him with dismay, but he had not expressed his opinions to his lay employers until after they arrived in England. In Southampton, amongst other able and experienced mariners, he pointed out that the ship was seriously overmasted. There would be severe strain to the seams under even the minimum sail in a moderate wind and in bad weather far too much for the small crew the vessel would carry to contain. He invited the churchmen to seek other advice in the port and they were finally convinced. The vessel had to be made safe and seaworthy and this meant that many of the *Speedwell*'s passengers had to go ashore and wait for the repairs to be carried out. It was not until the end of the first week in August that she was declared fit and ready to sail.

Since the arrival of the *Speedwell* there had been much activity aboard both ships. Daisy had seen little of Pat Ellis and even less of the new man, Will Trefor. Once, when she did see Will Trefor, he was stripped to the waist, his tanned body glistening and his lightish hair shining in the summer sun as he climbed the rigging of the mizzen mast. She was aware she might run into him each time she took to the deck and she was prepared for any such encounter. Then, on the day the *Speedwell* was at last ready to sail, she saw him on the deck below. As he started up the ladder she positioned herself to cross his path. But when he swung his long legs on to the main deck he did not look in Daisy's direction. Instead he hesitated briefly, his attention focused on a figure with a parasol just aft of the main cabin.

Her left hand resting the parasol on her shoulder, her right hand clutching the side, Rose Standish was looking out to the quay, her back to Will Trefor as he approached. Watching from her place in the shade, Daisy sensed that he must have murmured the woman's name or whispered something because Mrs Standish turned sharply under her parasol and put her hand to her mouth in genuine surprise. In his humble seaman's striped jersey Will Trefor stepped forward and took her in his arms.

For a moment Mrs Standish put up no resistance, remaining perfectly still. Locked in his arms she looked small and fragile as if a gentle squeeze might break her. Then she drew back and her dark eyes flashed up at him, but she made no attempt to break away. She listened as he spoke, earnest and imploring, and the longer she listened the more her pale, pretty face registered alarm. But she was not afraid of him. She obviously knew him. She was afraid of what he was saying, what he was doing.

Daisy watched, fascinated. She couldn't hear what Will Trefor was saying or Rose's replies, but it appeared that Rose was trying to deter him gently and with compassion. Again he clasped her to him, holding her prisoner. But at last she broke away, speaking to him sternly now as if to warn him off. He took another step towards her. She shook her head, the palms of her hands against him. He tried to take her in his arms yet again, but this time she turned and hurried to the passage that led to the private cabin she shared with her husband.

Will Trefor stood alone, cap in hand, and suddenly he looked very young, like a lost boy. Daisy felt an urge to rush to his side, to comfort him. But she knew she must not. Even here, in this enclosed, tightly knit community, or perhaps especially here, there were distinctions. Crew were crew. An ordinary seaman had no right to approach a lady passenger, except under orders from a senior officer and probably only then as the bearer of a message. What Will Trefor had done might be expected to bring forth a complaint from Mrs Standish and her soldier husband or even a charge of assault on a respectable married lady. But somehow Daisy didn't think it would.

There was something far deeper in what Daisy had just witnessed than an impertinent sailor accosting a lady. The two obviously knew each other and knew each other well. Daisy's cheeks reddened. Her face burned. She had been prepared to throw herself at this Will Trefor. What a fool she would have seemed when he was so deeply involved with someone else. Daisy felt she had totally misread the situation. She had presumed he was interested in her when he was merely being polite and courteous and nothing more. She felt foolish now, angry at her own stupidity. Yet, on reflection, she decided all was not lost. The 'someone else' was married, was she not?

If you want something badly, the Duchess would say, you should go all out to get it. And, though she had not yet fully faced the fact, Daisy knew she wanted Will Trefor. Better to ignore what she had seen, pretend she had not seen anything. She stayed where she was, watching from the shadows. Will was still there, his broad shoulders sagging in dejection.

It was mealtime on board. Several of the passengers, mainly women, were making their way to the galley where rations were issued daily and cooked over a firebox, an iron tray containing sand on which a fire was built. The main deck was suddenly busy and the passengers skirted round Will Trefor, frowning up at him, seeing him as an inconsiderate and unnecessary obstruction. But Will was oblivious to the crowd, towering above most of them and looking as though he might never move again.

At this point the solid figure of Captain Standish appeared from the deck below. He swung his legs over the side and, head held high in his straight-backed military manner, he strode towards the passage down which his wife had departed. He had missed the little drama by seconds. Apparently preocupied, he seemed unaware of Will Trefor but then he stopped, turned and came back, making his way carefully through the milling throng.

Coolly he asked a question and clearly he didn't like the response. More words were exchanged. Standish became red in the face, his moustache and his short pointed beard twitching angrily. His whole body seemed to bristle as he glared up at Will. Then Will Trefor spun round on his heel and came towards where Daisy was standing. Daisy dodged back out of sight and he swung over the side and down the rope ladder to the deck below.

Daisy was furious. She wanted to know what it was all about and she had no way of finding out. The only person she could ask was Mr Ellis and he was nowhere to be seen. Later that day she was even more furious. As she made her way to the galley to collect her rations she saw Will Trefor, his blanket roll of belongings under one arm, leave the *Mayflower*. What was happening? Had he been dismissed? Had the army captain demanded he must leave?

She had to wait until after midnight, until Pat Ellis was at his post on the master's bridge. She had asked the little cabin boy who, for some reason bashful in her presence, had told her where and when she might find the Irishman. Now, as she left her place in the main cabin in the early hours, stepping over sleeping bodies, she was aware of the potential damage to her reputation.

Already the Carver woman and her companion had begun a murmuring campaign against her. Who was she? A young woman travelling alone, without a family, without a man to protect her. What kind of woman was she? And where did she come from? All of these questions fell slyly from lips pursed in speculation and the implication that she must certainly be a person of dubious character. But none of this prevented Daisy from ascending the narrow ladder to the master's deck in search of Pat Ellis.

She had no business to be on the bridge, the Irishman told her sternly. She must leave at once or he would be compelled to summon assistance and have her removed. She smiled sweetly at him and sat down on a stool, a shawl pulled tightly about her head and shoulders. She had no intention of leaving, she told him, until he had answered her questions.

'And what questions might those be?' he asked.

'What has happened to Will Trefor?'

'The army man objected to his presence.'

'Why?' Daisy demanded. 'Why would he object to his presence?'

'There was something beween them,' the Irishman said. 'Something personal.'

'But surely Captain Jones wouldn't dismiss a member of his crew simply because a passenger wanted him to?'

'It's rather more complicated than that.'

'Tell me.'

Ellis shook his head.

'Please,' she begged. 'I want to know.'

'But you don't know any of the parties involved.'

'I feel as though I know Will Trefor. I feel as though I've known him all my life.'

He frowned. 'Don't say that, Daisy. Don't even think it.'

'Why? Why shouldn't I? He's....'

'I don't want you to get hurt, that's why.'

But it was no use. This only fed her curiosity. 'Why? Why would I get hurt? What is there about this Will Trefor? Does he have the Devil inside him? Would he lead me astray?'

'He's a fine man,' Ellis said firmly.

'Then why would Captain Jones dismiss him?'

The Irishman sighed. 'Well,' he said, 'the captain didn't actually dismiss him. The army man wanted him to, but he refused. And being the true gentleman that he is, Will accepted a position aboard the *Speedwell*. Captain Jones was not too happy about it. He needs all the good men he can get on this voyage. But he was persuaded that some sort of honourable compromise had been reached.'

So Will Trefor had joined the other ship. At least, he would still be travelling to the New World.

'Why did this army man object to him?' Daisy asked.

Ellis threw her a sidelong glance. She looked up at him, pleading with her eyes. He took out his pipe and a pouch of tobacco and she knew he was going to tell her.

'Do you realize, young lady,' he said, 'if Captain Jones or Mr Clarke comes up here and catches you sittin' there, where you have no business to be, then I could be clapped in irons?'

'I'll sit here quietly,' she said. 'I won't even speak. I promise.'

He grinned down at her in disbelief, as if she was promising the impossible. 'One time,' he began, 'a good few years ago now, I had a shore job at the naval college in Dartmouth. I was helping to instruct young midshipmen in the ways of the sea. Will Trefor was a cadet and eventually he came to me to learn about seamanship and navigation. He was a fine lad from a good family and as good a potential officer as any young fellow I'd seen in the King's Navy. He came from a small town somewhere in the North. Cheshire, in fact. His family were country landowners and pretty well off. Their neighbours were mostly landowners, too. It was all country houses up there. Tied cottages, servants, everything. And one of their nearest neighbours had a daughter, name of Rose. Now Will Trefor and this girl Rose were sort of childhood sweethearts. It was taken for granted they would marry when they were old enough. But things didn't turn out that way.

'Will's father was accused of flouting the King's authority and

even being involved in a plot to overthrow him. He was killed
when the King's men came to arrest him. The official verdict was
"Killed whilst attempting to escape". But Will swears they killed
him in cold blood because the King wanted him dead. Will and the
girl Rose eloped, but her family soon found them and brought
them home. Rose was sent to live with relatives in Lancashire and
Will was given the opportunity to enrol at the college. He was
lucky he wasn't sent to some penal colony. But he was very young
and he was obviously not involved in his father's misdeeds. His
tutor, his local minister, several men of substance put in a good
word for him.' Ellis laughed. 'And even so he insisted on adding
his own terms. He agreed to come to Dartmouth, it seems, on
condition that when he'd made his mark in the service of the King
he would be permitted to ask for Rose's hand in marriage.'

Daisy was enthralled. 'And did he?'

'He was well on his way to making his mark an' that's for sure.
He's still only a young man, yet he was third in command aboard a
naval warship. Then when he was in Spain – in the port of Cadiz, I
understand – he heard from a fellow officer that his precious Rose
was to marry a soldier, a captain of the King's Guard. He couldn't
believe it. But, of course, he knew her family didn't want him and
he knew they would be anxious for Rose to forget him. So he
jumped ship.'

'Jumped ship?'

'He deserted. Went absent without leave. He left his post and
made his way back to England across Spain and up through
France. He had very little money so he came to London, found out
where I was staying and came to see me. He knew I'd long since
finished with the Dartmouth job and he knew where I usually
stayed in London between ships. Well, he was in luck. It so
happened I was home an' ready to go to sea again. I was able to let
him have a little money and give him a roof for a few days. And in
that time he found an old school friend of his who is now at work in
the City an' this old friend managed to find out a few things for
him. He found out that Rose had already married a former army
captain named Standish. This Standish was from a very highly
regarded family in Lancashire and was about to set off for New
England and take his young bride with him. Perhaps he thought
he'd better get her as far away from young Will as possible.'

'So you joined the *Mayflower* at Southwark?'

Ellis nodded. 'I did, yes. But Will couldn't join the ship there.
We thought he could at first. We thought there'd be no problem.
Then we heard the King's men were searching all the merchant

ships in dock in the City of London. If they'd caught him they'd have locked him up an' thrown away the key. So we had to think again. I signed up myself an' got to work on Captain Jones. I've known him a long time an' I suppose he trusts my judgement. I told him all about Will's Dartmouth background, his skill as a navigator, what a fine all-round seaman he is – I wanted him to make Will one of his officers an' I was pretty sure that when the going got rough he would have. The captain said he couldn't take on any more crew until we reached Southampton. Company orders. So Will came aboard when we docked here – officially, anyway – and signed on for the voyage. Then he fell foul of this army fellow.'

'What does he see in her, Mr Ellis?'

Ellis hesitated. 'Well,' he said, 'I don't know really. She's a bit too frail-looking for my liking.' He smiled down at Daisy. 'An' not nearly as pretty as some.'

Daisy was pleased with the implied compliment. 'But what would make a man do all that? I mean, desert his ship and follow here here. If she's already married....'

'Love, I suppose. Men do some very odd things when a woman is involved.'

'You think he was in love with her?'

'I suppose he must have been.'

'You think he still is?'

'Oh, I expect so. But he'll get over it.'

'Do you think so? Do you really think so?'

Ellis suddenly felt sorry for her. She was so eager, so anxious to hear his reply. He nodded. 'Oh, yes,' he said with a conviction he didn't feel. 'I'm sure he will.'

Wisps of cloud drifted, like tobacco smoke, across the high moon. And there was a movement close by. Ellis put a finger to his lips. It might only have been a gust of wind stirring the rigging or one of the ship's cats chasing a shadow, but he couldn't be sure. He pocketed his pipe and went to secure a spar that was working loose. Daisy watched as he tied his knots.

'It can be pretty dangerous up here for someone who doesn't know her way around,' Ellis said softly. 'A spar swinging loose has been known to knock a man overboard.'

'Was Will on board when the soldiers came?' she asked.

'Oh yes. He was here. But they would never have found him. Not in a million years. There are places on a ship they'd never dream of looking.'

'And he was on board all the way down from London?'

'In the hold.' He tested the ropes holding the spar, then turned to face her. 'Better go now, eh?' He kissed her lightly on the forehead. 'An' stop worrying about Will Trefor. In fact, I think you'd do well to forget all about him now, don't you?'

11

Now, at last, for the passengers of the two ships, the great day dawned – or so they thought. August the fifth in the year 1620. Some small rearrangement of accommodation between the two vessels had been achieved though not entirely without acrimony. The storage of equipment and provisions had been checked and re-checked, the longboats had been hoisted in and everyone who should be was aboard.

The orders that morning came thick and fast and in the sudden clamour Daisy, jostled by the crowd on the main deck of the *Mayflower*, strained to identify the different commands. First the anchor was raised, trailing green weed and dripping sea water as it swung inwards to be secured in its resting place. Then the first mate gave the order to cut the ribbons on the foresail and let it fall. Next the crew, to the rhythm of a shanty, hoisted the main yard and sheeted the main sail. Officers at their posts rasped out the orders and, like the children watching, Daisy was caught up in the mounting excitement. Close by, Giles Hopkins, aged twelve, decided he wanted to be a sailor.

Make fast the halyards! Set your topsail! Haul taut the bowline! The orders carried on the early morning breeze. Hoist the mizzen! Hold the tiller! And finally: Boy to the top! Shake out the flag! Mariners, stand by!

Cirrus clouds, like locks of pale grey hair, flecked the blue sky as the two ships nosed out, a wind from the north billowing their sails. Firm and steady they set off down Southampton Water and the passengers dashed to look back at the town they were leaving behind. Then, as the line of the shore grew thinner and the excitement of leaving port died away, the crew became quietly absorbed in their duties. Subdued now, the passengers spoke in low tones as if casting off had given them a foretaste and a sudden realization of the weeks of isolation that lay ahead.

At mid-morning Daisy saw Rose Standish. She was staring across at the *Speedwell* until, at the approach of her husband, she hurriedly withdrew. Daisy looked for some sign of Will Trefor on the smaller ship but could make out only figures here and there and none that resembled Will. In fact Will was down below where the ship was taking on too much water and with the first mate of the *Speedwell* he was attempting to improve the performance of the pumps.

For those first few days the sea was calm and there was only a light wind, yet Captain Reynolds of the *Speedwell*, early on the evening of the tenth, was forced to fly a distress signal. Both ships hove to and Mr Coppin from the *Mayflower* went aboard. The *Speedwell* was leaking badly, Captain Reynolds said. He dared not allow her to face the open sea.

The church leaders aboard the *Speedwell* were taken below to examine the hull where they could see for themselves that the ship was taking on more water than the pumps could control. The master of the *Mayflower* was consulted but Captain Jones could offer no more help or solution to the problem than Captain Reynolds. He could only suggest they should put back to the nearest harbour where a closer examination could be made and whatever repairs might be necessary could be undertaken. The nearest port was Dartmouth.

In Dartmouth a thorough examination was carried out. This time qualified shipwrights were called in and the hull of the *Speedwell* was checked from stem to stern. The verdict was that until the leaks had been completely and expertly plugged there was no hope of the *Speedwell* setting sail. This meant more delay and more expense and for many of the would-be settlers it was the end of the road. There were too many obstacles. An omen, they said, that the project was doomed.

There was suspicion, too, about how the communal money was being spent and a growing distrust of the organizers. Almost penniless some of the passengers took their families ashore and abandoned the venture. But gradually the work was done and on 23rd August, with 120 passengers crowded aboard the two ships, the *Mayflower* and the *Speedwell* set sail in a second attempt to cross the Atlantic.

Their troubles were far from over. They were barely out of sight of the green and pleasant Dartmouth coastline with only a few miles of the 3,000 mile voyage behind them when Captain Reynolds was again forced to raise the alarm. Once more his ship was leaking badly and in grave danger of sinking. Even with the pumps working full out they could not contain the powerful swell of the ocean. Again the *Mayflower* was hailed alongside and Captain Jones agreed there was no alternative. The *Speedwell* must go back.

Dismay turned to despair and though many aboard the *Mayflower* wanted to carry on without the smaller ship, Captain Jones was concerned for her passengers and crew. As Captain Reynolds set a course for home, the master of the *Mayflower* felt he was honour bound to escort the leaking vessel to a safe harbour.

To prevent the masts from opening up the vessel's splitting seams still further it proved necessary to hoist as little of the *Speedwell*'s sail as was practicable. This made for a slow and anxious return as the captain, forced to ride the waves as lightly as he and his pilots knew how, kept all hands at the gruelling task of baling out. With an exhausted and demoralized crew the *Speedwell* at last limped into the haven of Plymouth Hoe where yet another examination of the ship's hull was commissioned. The passengers, with little means of paying for food or accommodation, were taken ashore. But the people of Plymouth showed them great kindness and many of the local people took them in.

The *Mayflower* anchored by the Barbican. Festooned with little flags the harbour, with its newly painted houses, the upper storeys overhanging the walkways along the quay, seemed a bright and pleasant place, a cheerful contrast to the sombre atmosphere of anger and frustration on board. Among the passengers of both ships were those who muttered darkly about abandoning the 'whole idiotic business', selling what there was to sell and returning to London. But none of this exasperation touched the church people who consoled themselves with the confident belief that when the time was right God would allow them to go.

It was in the midst of this discontent that John Alden, the cooper taken on in Southampton, fell foul of the head of one of the more influential families. The family by the name of Mullins – father, mother, eighteen-year-old daughter and six-year-old son – had apparently warranted special attention. Like Captain Standish and his wife, they had been allocated one of the private cabins aft. The daughter, Priscilla Mullins, was a tall slim girl with brown hair, greenish eyes and a fair complexion. She was not beautiful – or even conventionally pretty – but she was so decorous in her manner that to a working lad like John she seemed to personify all that was best in a woman.

The girl's father, a prosperous merchant in the City of London, had left a comfortable home in Dorking and sold everything he owned to avail himself of the even greater prosperity to be found in the New World where, it was said, opportunity was boundless. At once he had allied himself with the congregations from London and Holland. In them he recognized the proprieties he sought for his wife and family and he respected the standards and values of their leaders. When it came to his notice that a young seaman had taken more than a passing fancy to his daughter he was less than pleased. The young seaman was John Alden.

Mr Mullins complained to the captain. The captain, with far more on his mind than such trivia, instructed his second mate to deal with the seaman concerned. Mr Coppin was highly amused and the next time he came across the young carpenter he gripped him by the scruff of the neck, no easy task as John Alden was well over six feet, a good six inches taller than the squat but sturdily built mate.

'What's this I 'ear? Ogling young ladies now, are we? Frightening the skirts off 'em with your lewd looks and murky longings?'

'What?' John was bewildered. 'I don't know what....'

Mr Coppin, who clearly did not take the matter seriously, laughed in his face. 'Complaints from me lady's chamber. Dirty young devil bin eyeing 'em up!'

With surprising strength in his wrist John easily wrested the mate's hand away and asked calmly but without a trace of insolence what he was supposed to have done.

'A cat may look at a queen,' Mr Coppin said, still highly amused, 'but not on this ship. You can be flogged at the wheel. You can be made to walk the plank, blindfold with yer 'ands tied behind yer back!'

'For goodness' sake, Mr Coppin,' John said, 'may I know the nature of my offence?'

Apparently he had been looking at a girl. The girl's father had complained to the captain. She was not for the eyes of common seamen, the father had said. But I'm not a common seaman, John protested. Mr Coppin raised his bushy eyebrows. O-oh! Is that so? Do I tell the lads down below that? Young John is not as common as you lot, is that it? Did the girl herself complain? John demanded. No, it was her father. And Mr Mullins would be much obliged if you would save your staring eyes for tap-room trollops in seafront taverns. Pray keep yer common orbs off his precious daughter Priscilla!

'Priscilla!' John Alden's frank, open face was alight. 'Is that her name then? Priscilla! Priscilla Mullins! What a beautiful name. What a beautiful girl. Have you seen her, Mr Coppin? Priscilla.' He held his strong, bare arms up to the sun. 'Priscilla!'

Mr Coppin shook his head in mock resignation. 'Sorry, Cap'n ... Mr Mullins,' he said to himself. 'I tried....'

The new examination of the *Speedwell* determined that the movement of the ship through the water and the strain of the top-heavy masts, even in a light breeze, opened up the seams, let in water and closed again when the pressure was eased. The shipwright's report concluded that if the *Speedwell* was to be made fit and safe for a transatlantic voyage it would need to be completely re-rigged. The settlers simply could not afford it. There was no alternative. They must leave the vessel behind so that it might be sold to defray costs. The shipwright, the repairs assessors, harbour dues – all had to be paid. But what was to be done with the *Speedwell*'s passengers? There was little or no room for any more aboard the *Mayflower*.

The problem was eased slightly when, after all the facts had been made known, a number of the *Speedwell* passengers decided they had endured enough disappointment and frustration and voted to abandon the project. They took their belongings, and such equipment and provisions as were left were somehow accommodated aboard the *Mayflower*. The master of the *Speedwell*, Captain Reynolds, and most of his crew seemed well pleased with the opportunity to get out of their contracts, happy to ship out of Plymouth on less perilous ventures. Only Will Trefor wanted to stay and promptly put in a request to be transferred back to the larger ship.

Deciding on the final 100 passengers, Captain Jones's absolute maximum, was no easy task. Those who had travelled down from Southwark Dock in the *Mayflower* were unwilling to give up an inch of the space they had made their own. Coaxing from them any sort of compromise was proving impossible and in the end it was suggested that a number of domestic staff should be left behind.

Several of the families had two or more servants but were reluctant to dispense with their services. They argued that they were going to need as much cheap labour as they could get when they reached their destination. It was also deemed unchristian to abandon faithful staff in Plymouth where they were strangers with little hope of finding employment. But three of the menservants and a lady's maid elected to leave, were paid off and given the price of a single coach ticket back to London. Still there were too many bodies for too little space.

The decisions as to who should go and who should be allowed to stay were taken on the main deck of the *Mayflower* with Captain Jones insisting on a reduction in numbers and the church elders asking for volunteers. Almost every one of the servants had spent his or her life in service and was alarmed and bewildered at the prospect of being put ashore. Daisy watched the scene with growing pity for those facing dismissal. Then she noticed a small group had gathered around the Carver family.

Church elder John Carver, his wife and his wife's companion had a staff of five: two menservants, two boys and the fifteen-year-old maid Prudence. Mrs Carver, apparently, had decided she had no further use for Prudence. With her companion, Miss Minter, she appeared to be taking great satisfaction in singling the girl out.

Captain Jones was clearly not happy with the selection of the little servant girl. Looking somewhat abashed John Carver was also at odds with his wife over her choice. The other Carver servants, whether consciously or not, had edged away from Prudence and the girl was standing alone now, with her tiny cloth bag of possessions, outside the family circle. But Mrs Carver was adamant. She would not give up any of her male servants. They would all be required in the new country and they were all required now.

For Prudence dismissal meant she must go ashore and seek whatever shelter she could find. Her severance pay as a lowly maid was even less than the pittance an adult servant would receive and obviously insufficient for her immediate needs. The girl could not be left, Captain Jones insisted. If put ashore she might fall into all kinds of bad company. It was up to the church to protect her, he told Carver, not abandon her. She was little more than a child.

Prudence gripped her bag. Her large dark eyes, smudged even darker now, darted from one to another of her impersonal elders as they debated her fate. The hard, unflinching countenance of Mrs Carver looked down on her with fat cheeks and pouting lips and there was thinly disguised venom in Miss Minter's long-nosed, supercilious gaze. Even the worried frown of Mr Carver, who knew that what his wife was proposing was unacceptable to any caring Christian, was of little help. Hadn't he too much else on his mind to become embroiled in a minor domestic issue? Only the captain seemed to care.

'She is not coming,' Mrs Carver said. 'We do not need her and that's an end to it.'

The girl's lips quivered as she saw the look of resignation in Captain Jones's eyes.

'Go along now,' Mrs Carver said brusquely.

'There is a convent here,' Mr Carver offered weakly.

Prudence turned away, her eyes cast down, her chin on her narrow chest. If she was to be a waif, in her threadbare frock and scuffed canvas shoes she already looked the part.

'I don't know what's going on here,' Daisy Mason said, edging her way into the group around the Carver family, 'but I offered Prudence a position with me this morning and Prudence accepted it. Obviously you have not given her an opportunity to explain.'

For once Mrs Carver was at a loss for words.

To the captain, Daisy said, 'I need a maid, Captain Jones. I have taken this girl into my employ.'

'We are attempting to reduce the numbers,' Mrs Carver muttered crossly.

Daisy rounded on her. 'Then I suggest you reduce your domestic staff still further. You have four male servants.' She cast an eye over the two men, who shuffled uneasily, and the two boys, who looked down at their boots. Then she raised her eyebrows at the two women. 'I really can't think what you ladies want with *four* men.'

The two women looked as if they were about to explode but Mr Carver and the captain, who threw a remonstrative glance at Daisy, did their best to calm them.

Mr Carver said, 'We have a meeting shortly, Captain Jones. Several more of our people have expressed a wish not to take part in the voyage – in view of our experiences so far. Perhaps we could wait a little longer. There may yet be a satisfactory solution.'

Captain Jones nodded. 'Very well. But the matter must be resolved by this evening.'

'Whatever the outcome,' Daisy said decisively, 'this girl works for me now and she will stay with me.' Then, mocking Mrs Carver's grand manner, she added, 'I have no intention of crossing the Atlantic without a maid.'

The captain touched his hat and there was the hint of a smile behind his eyes as he withdrew. Prudence was hopping on one foot in delight.

'Come, Prudence,' Daisy said, leading the way. 'I will explain your duties.'

As the crowd dispersed the two women were left to scowl and, giving vent to her anger, Mrs Carver proclaimed, 'A woman who leaves her bed in the middle of the night to visit common seamen is not a fit person to employ an impressionable girl.'

But, fortunately for Mrs Carver, Daisy Mason had gone out of earshot.

The *Mayflower* was no more than 90 feet in length and her weight was a little less than 120 tons. The captain, anxious to set sail, had agreed to take 100 passengers – though not without misgiving. He was not entirely confident his ship was big enough to carry so many across the notoriously difficult and hazardous ocean and already he was well behind schedule. In accepting the command he had anticipated a summer crossing. He had fully expected to sail from Southampton in mid-July at the latest and in mild balmy weather. With all the delays and false starts six valuable weeks had been lost and he could now expect to meet and have to contend with strong seas and buffeting crosswinds. There was certain to be a good deal of discomfort for his passengers and still more bickering and disharmony – not to mention the very real dangers that lay ahead for so heavily laden a vessel.

It was the first week in September before they were ready to sail. Even then, after numerous meetings and much discussion in private between the families involved and though many had opted to remain in England with the vague assurance that there would be other, follow-up voyages, there were still 102 passengers to accommodate.

Captain Jones now called a final pre-embarkation meeting with the church elders, representatives of the other passengers and his first and second mates. Mr Clarke, the first mate, reported that the stores of provisions and equipment had been rearranged to make room for what could be taken from the *Speedwell* and had been secured to ensure there would be no shifting of cargo in heavy seas. The shallop, a large open boat they would use to go ashore at the end of their voyage, a boat that could carry between twenty and thirty men, had now been dismantled to make more room. Parts of the shallop, Mr Clarke told the meeting, had been distributed to serve as partitions or tables in the main cabin and below to construct temporary quarters for passengers. When the new land was sighted it would be reassembled.

The 102 had now taken up every available space. Small play areas had been set aside for the children, toilet and washing arrangements had been established, dining areas had been designated and a routine drawn up for mealtimes. Hatches had been battened down, the crew were all present and correct and the

Mayflower was again ready to sail. Satisfied that everything was in order Captain Jones, from the poop deck, gave the command to cast off.

As the ship drew clear of the Barbican steps many of the passengers strained for a last look at the port of Plymouth in the sad knowledge that this might well be their last ever look at the land of their birth. Here, in the neat little streets from the town to the waterfront, people sat by their own firesides and slept in adequate beds. There was work to come in from and go out to. There were bright new houses and a bakery and a dairy and an inn at the end of the quay. Where the settlers were going there was nothing. If they wanted all this they would have to build it for themselves.

The Irishman, Pat Ellis, looked up from his post on the lower deck and waved a hand at Will Trefor who was clinging to the mizzen mast. Captain Jones had not liked the way in which he had lost Will Trefor to the *Speedwell* and if only to reassert his authority he had taken him back. Will acknowledged Pat's wave and from the main deck Captain Miles Standish saw the exchange, frowning when he realized the former naval officer was on board after all. With the girl Prudence at her side, Daisy Mason saw Will Trefor, too, and decided there and then that he was for her and she would have him one day – no matter what.

12

Just before noon that September morning the crowds along the quays and down Southside Street beneath the Hoe began to disperse. Men went about their business, women gripped children by the hand and began to drift away, and many who had joined in the cheers of farewell fell silent now, shaking their heads at the folly of such an undertaking. Several local seamen had sailed or claimed to have sailed out of Plymouth to Virginia and all were agreed on the hazards that lay ahead for the band of hopefuls aboard the overcrowded vessel.

From the *Mayflower* the dark contours of the town – the sprawl of streets and houses along the quays, the blackened warehouse walls to the west, the mud flats to the east – were now indistinguishable in the midday sun. Only the majestic new fort built by Drake was a clear silhouette on the skyline. Up on the poop deck Captain Jones knew he was flouting an established transatlantic convention: out in spring, back in autumn. Already it was early autumn. The summer was over and they were only just setting out.

Used to running consignments of cognac and wine from Gascony or taking rolls of cloth to France or Belgium, the *Mayflower* creaked under the weight of her 102 passeners and her heavily stocked holds. But the weather was fine and only the most pessimistic questioned her ability to see the job through. As they headed out into the Channel they were met by a light, east-north-east wind and sufficient sail was hoisted to take full advantage. Careful to avoid the treacherous Eddystone Rocks the captain set a steady course to the south-west.

Normally a mild-mannered man Captain Jones was in an irritable mood for most of that first day. He'd had enough of the frustrations of the *Speedwell*, the delays, the changes of plan, the bickering and the posturing of the so-called religious leaders who seemed to disagree over even the most mundane of matters. Nor had his crew much time for the constantly complaining landlubbers.

The journey down from the port of London had been reasonably quiet and harmonious, but from the moment the exiles from Holland arrived in the *Speedwell* there had been nothing but ill-feeling and an undercurrent of discontent. Of the wives, many seemed petty and spiteful and only concerned with the needs of their own little circles. To make matters worse many had an infuriatingly self-righteous attitude to others as if only their way was the right way and everyone else was a poor misguided sinner. At least, this was how they appeared to members of the crew.

There was little sympathy then when some hours out they sighted the Manacles, turned a few points west, met the long rolling swell of the Atlantic and most of the passengers were seasick. Few, if any, had experienced the sudden switch-back motion with which they were now faced. Yet, curiously, for one who had never been to sea, Daisy Mason was not among those unfortunates who became pale and retched at every roll and sway of the lurching ship. Even more curiously, nor was the wife of the soldier, Captain Standish.

On only the second day out the delicate, flower-like Rose surprised Daisy when she appeared at the entrance to Daisy's tiny makeshift quarters in the main cabin. The area which Daisy now occupied with the girl Prudence was partitioned off on one side by a small section of the shallop and on the other by a blanket slung on a rope. Daisy recognized Rose Standish at once and didn't know whether to smile and welcome her in or wait to hear the purpose of her visit.

'Yes?' she enquired.

Rose Standish was dressed in dark green: a good quality ankle-length skirt and a tight-fitting bodice. Thrown back about her shoulders and loosely tied was a short cloak, crimson in colour. Her head was covered by a dark green coif, a close-fitting cap that came down over her ears and became a muffler. Her oval face looked pink, her lips slightly blue, and the wind had whipped some colour into her usually pale cheeks. She had black shiny hair that formed a widow's peak and made her face seem heart-shaped, but she was only conventionally pretty, no great beauty. It was not easy to see, thought Daisy, why two such men as her husband and Will Trefor should find her so compelling. But then, hadn't the Duchess always said that men are totally unpredictable in their choice of women?

Noting Daisy's hesitant surprise, Rose Standish smiled and said, 'I hope I am not intruding. Perhaps I have called at an inconvenient time.'

Daisy responded quickly. 'No, please come in. Sit down.'

There was a stool Pat Ellis had found for her. Rose Standish sat down, looking around for where Daisy might sit. Daisy perched on the edge of the low mattress.

'I ...' Rose began awkwardly. 'I saw what you did....'

Daisy looked blank.

'About the servant girl. I was on the deck the day you rescued the servant girl from the Carvers. They were quite prepared to put her ashore, poor girl. I saw what was happening and had it occurred to me I do believe I would have done the same. I am in need of a maidservant.'

Daisy shook her head. 'I don't think Prudence would want to leave me, Mrs Standish. Not now. No matter what you were prepared to pay her.'

'Oh no!' Rose seemed genuinely surprised. 'I'm so sorry. You misunderstand me. I have no intention of trying to steal away your girl. I'm sure she will be devoted to you forever now.' She took a deep breath and smiled, and Daisy could see that many men would indeed find her attractive.

'I'm making an awful mess of this,' Rose continued with an

infectious laugh. 'Please allow me to begin again. I came to see you because I admired what you did. May I say you showed a very real compassion for that poor girl. You showed these church people what true charity is.' She came to a halt, wondering if yet again she had said the wrong thing. 'You are not one of these church people, are you?'

Daisy shook her head. 'No,' she said positively. 'I am not. Thank God!'

The added oath struck them both as funny and they laughed like schoolgirls.

"Well,' Daisy said, as their mirth subsided. 'I'm sure you know what I mean.'

Daisy had matched Rose's slightly flat North Country tones with her own carefully modulated, Sunday afternoon, St James's Park accent. She waited now, curious to know the true purpose of her visit, and Rose seemed to sense the unasked question.

'As I said, to take that girl in was an act of true charity. I came to see you because I felt I would like to have a friend with such a generous nature. I know few of the passengers and I have no friends among the ladies. As we are to be shipbound for several weeks, I was hoping you might accept my offer of unconditional friendship.'

Daisy was charmed. 'Of course,' she said warmly. 'Of course I will. I'm very pleased to make your acquaintance, Mrs Standish.'

Rose held out her hand. 'I hope you will call me Rose and allow me to call you by your christian name, your truly christian name.'

'Daisy,' Daisy said, with a smile. 'Daisy Mason.'

Rose stood up. 'Good,' she said. 'I must go now. I would like you to take some refreshment with me. When my husband goes off to one of those interminable meetings I will ask you into my sumptuous temporary home. It's at least three inches larger than yours.'

They laughed and Daisy said, 'I'll look forward to it.'

'You can tell me all about yourself and how you came to win the dubious honour of sharing in this highly disorganized journey into the unknown.'

Daisy was not sure about that but Rose went on to say, 'And I will tell you how I came to be so unfortunate.'

They laughed again and Rose turned to leave. Daisy liked her. It was difficult not to, and she really was quite a beauty in her bone-china way, especially when she laughed and her eyes brimmed with her own brand of merriment. She was also far from the weak and spoiled young woman Daisy had imagined her to be.

'Let's meet again soon,' Daisy said with enthusiasm.

Rose agreed. 'And I must say again how much I admire the way you defied the Carvers. The girl must have thought you were her fairy godmother. Especially the way she is.'

Daisy's smile was checked. 'The way she is?'

'Why yes,' Rose said innocently. Then she put her hand to her mouth. 'You didn't know?'

'Didn't know what?'

'Well....' Rose was embarrassed. 'I'm sorry. I'm probably entirely wrong. I mean ...'

'What is it?'

'Nothing. Please forget I said anything.'

'You said you wanted us to be friends,' Daisy reminded her. 'If there is something I should know I'd be grateful if you would tell me.'

Rose shrugged helplessly. 'I'm sorry. I may be wrong, Daisy, but I don't think so. When I was coming here across the main deck I saw your girl carrying a washing basket. It's very windy out there and she had to hold on to the ropes. In the wind and from a side view I must say, with her skirts windswept, she looked very pregnant.'

'Pregnant?'

'Well on the way, I would say,' Rose told her gently. 'Several months.'

Daisy frowned. 'What a fool I am! How could I not have noticed?'

Prudence always stood a little round-shouldered. Her skirts were a size too big, cut down to fit in length but still full around the waist. It might not be readily noticeable. Daisy felt certain Mrs Carver didn't know or Prudence would have been abandoned earlier. But it would explain the tears on the stairway. The heart-breaking 'what's to become of me?' look.

'The poor girl,' Daisy said, after a moment. 'I must talk to her at once. She must rest.' Then she laughed. 'A baby! We'll have a baby to take care of! Oh, Rose! I do hope you are right about this.'

'You do?'

'Why yes, of course. We are going to need children in our New World. Lots of them. This little one can be a beginning.'

'Miles and I want children ...' Rose smiled wistfully, as though her imagination was racing ahead. Then she added softly, 'I would love to help.'

Daisy nodded confidently. 'Prudence will be all right. I'll see to that. She is only a baby herself. Barely fifteen. I'll help her all I can.'

'And so will I,' Rose promised, 'if you will allow me.'

When Prudence returned Daisy did not mention the visit of Rose Standish. Nor did she refer to her newly acquired knowledge. But looking at Prudence in a new light she was soon convinced that Rose was not mistaken.

That evening Daisy and Prudence took a late meal of salted cod, rye bread and barley wine with the Hopkins family at the communal table on the waist deck. Like most of the servants aboard, the Hopkins' two men waited on their employer and his family, only taking their own meal when their employer and all the other employers had left the table. This practice resulted in a full table of servants after every meal, but Prudence was no longer among them. Daisy had told her she was a companion not a maid and instructed her to sit beside her. Shyly Prudence had done as she was told. Eyebrows had been raised but nothing was said. At least, not openly.

Later, when they returned to their section of the main cabin, Daisy sat on the stool and Prudence sat on the bed as they sorted through the day's wash. Daisy had been planning to alter a dress to fit Prudence, who was pitifully short of clothing. Now, in view of the girl's expanding waist-line, she would have to alter her plans.

'Pru,' Daisy said gently, 'you never told me how you came to be working for the Carvers.'

'Mrs Carver took me on in Southampton, miss,' Prudence said.

'You hadn't been with her long then?'

'No, miss.'

The Carvers had fled from Yorkshire to Leyden in Holland to escape the persecution and religious intolerance at home. In Holland they could worship without fear though this latitude, they felt, would provide only a temporary and precarious freedom. Mr Carver had been a leading figure in the negotiations to make a permanent move to New England. Subsequently, before transferring to the *Mayflower*, he and his family had sailed to Southampton in the ill-fated *Speedwell* – though Prudence knew nothing of all this.

'You didn't come with them in the other ship then?'

'No, miss,' Prudence said, blushing a deep red as if she was being interrogated, accused of some crime.

Daisy laughed. 'Come on, Pru,' she said. 'Tell me about yourself. What did you do before you were taken on by the Carvers? Where did you live? And what about your family?'

She had rarely been asked anything about herself and the

questions worried her. 'I ain't done nothin' wrong, miss. Honest.'

'Pru, for goodness sake! I'm your friend. I'm sure you haven't done anything wrong. I just want to know about you, that's all. Where you came from. Who you worked for before the Carvers. Where you lived.'

'I lived in an 'ome, miss, when I was small.'

'What kind of a home? A poor house?'

'Yes, miss.'

'Were you born there?'

'I don't think so, miss.'

'What about your mother?'

'I don't know much about my mother.' She glanced at Daisy as if she was about to reveal a long kept secret. 'I asked about her once. I asked the master's wife an' she said I didn't need to know about things like that. But there was another lady, a seamstress. She used to show us how to mend our clothes. She told me my mother was just a young girl. She said she died 'cos of me.'

'She died in childbirth?'

'Yes, miss. That's what this lady said. An' then my mother died an' an old widder woman took me in. Her name was Miss Tucker an' she didn't have no children of 'er own. I can on'y jus' remember 'er. She was very old an' she wore a black shawl on 'er 'ead all the time an' she stooped right over as if she'd lost somethin' on the floor. I think I was on'y about five when *she* died. It was 'er what called me Prudence. They called me Prudence Tucker at the 'ome.'

'Did you like it there?'

Prudence shrugged her narrow shoulders. 'I don't know really. Sometimes it was all right.'

'Then Mrs Carver brought you from the poor house?'

'No, no, miss. I was there till I was twelve. Then I got sent to a big 'ouse in the country at Fareham where there was a lot of servants. I was a scullery maid. Then one day we was told we were all being taken to Southampton for the trade.'

'The *trade*?' Daisy queried.

'Yes, miss. They said the 'ouse was bein' closed down an' we would be found work at Southampton. That's when Mrs Carver and Miss Minter took me, but I didn't like them very much.'

'And they didn't know about the baby?'

Prudence shot Daisy a look of alarm, her mouth open.

'Don't worry,' Daisy said. 'I'm not angry with you.'

'Oh, miss, you know!'

'We would all get to know sooner or later, Pru. Can't hide a baby forever, can we?'

Unable to look at Daisy, Pru hung her head.

'How far on are you?' Daisy asked in a quiet, comforting tone.

'I'm not sure, miss.

'You must know when it happened.'

The big round eyes brimmed with tears.

'Now look, Pru, I am not angry with you. I am not going to throw you out or ... or drop you in the sea in a sack or ... or hang you upside down from the highest mast.'

Prudence almost smiled.

'So don't worry. Just tell me all about it and we can decide what we have to do. All right?'

She nodded and sniffed away the threat of tears.

'When did it happen?' Daisy asked again.

'It was at Fareham, miss. There were these two 'ouseboys an' they stole this wine an' stuff from the cellars when 'is lordship an' milady were away. It was around last Candlemas. They took me to the barn to see a new calf what 'ad jus' bin born. But I didn't see no calf. They 'ad this cider an' some wine. They said we was 'avin' a party. Well, I 'adn't tasted nothin' like that afore. I suppose I must 'ave 'ad too much 'cos I don't remember what 'appened next. There was two of 'em, miss. But I reckon to know which one it was as done it.'

'You didn't tell anyone?'

'No, miss. The boys were in a lot of trouble stealing from the 'ouse. I didn't want no one to know I bin with 'em. When 'is lordship came back he sent 'em to gaol in Winchester an' I thought I might be sent there, too. So I said nothin' to no one.'

Daisy smiled. 'Well,' she said, 'now I know why I found you crying on the stairway. But it's nothing to worry about. If you want this little baby and you want to keep it then you shall. We'll take good care of it. Together. You and me.'

What Daisy was saying dawned only slowly on Prudence. She had never dreamed that she might be allowed to keep the baby and she hadn't dared to think what might become of it. All she had felt certain of was that it would be taken from her. No one would believe she was a fit and proper person to keep it and care for it.

'You do want it, don't you?' Daisy asked.

'Oh, miss. I'd love it an' protect it always....'

'Good,' Daisy said. 'Then we must make plans. Babies need things. Clothes for a start. They don't pop out fully dressed, you know.'

Prudence laughed with joy. 'But what will people say?'

'What people?' Daisy asked dismissively. 'The only people who matter are you and me and the baby. The baby is ours, part of our family. I never had a family of my own, Pru. Not a real family. And neither did you. But we can make sure this little one has.'

'Oh, Miss Daisy. I'm ever so grateful to you.'

Daisy brushed her gratitude aside. 'We must begin at once. I will have to inform the captain. We have a young lady on board who is expecting her first baby and as far as we can tell it's only a few weeks away. You will need extra rations. We must build up your strength.'

Prudence felt that a great weight had been lifted from her shoulders. She looked at Daisy now with love in her eyes. She had never loved anyone so much as she loved Miss Daisy.

'I do love you, Miss Daisy,' she said spontaneously.

'Save it for the baby,' Daisy said with a smile. 'A baby needs all the love you can give it.'

13

Daisy resolved to see the captain at once. He was on the poop deck with Mr Clarke and as the first mate came down to enquire the nature of her business she told him firmly it was the captain she wished to see. Courteous as always to a lady, Captain Jones came down the narrow rope ladder and touched his hat at his determined visitor. Daisy told him about the baby, how she intended to take care of her maidservant personally and how the girl would require extra rations.

Not surprisingly Captain Jones was less than enthusiastic about the extra rations. The provisions set aside for his crew, he told her, were sparse enough. It was essential that his men received their full quota. Extra provisions for individual passengers could only be authorized by the passengers themselves. He suggested she should put her request to Mr Carver.

'The baby won't be any trouble, Captain,' Daisy said. 'I promise. There are more than enough ladies willing and able to care for the little thing. I'm sure it will cause no problems for you or your crew.'

'I wish your maidservant well, Miss Mason,' the captain said, 'and I am sure, as you say, there are plenty of capable ladies on hand. But I fear we may not go quite so smoothly as I had hoped.' He nodded towards the north where heavy storm clouds had gathered on the horizon. 'We could be in for a rough passage.'

Daisy held on to the rope ladder as she followed his gaze. The clouds looked black and dark blue.

'Is the girl in good health?' he asked.

'She is small, not very strong – but then, I don't know. A woman finds a strength from within when it comes to producing a child.'

'Has she been sick?'

'A little seasick, I believe. But no more than most.'

'See Mr Carver,' the captain said again. 'Tell him I suggested you ask him.' Then his eyes crinkled in a smile. 'Call upon him as a true Christian gentleman, Miss Mason.'

The early days of the voyage out had passed with a fair wind and a gently rolling sea under warm skies. Most of the passengers had quickly recovered from their initial bouts of seasickness and, though many were still pale-faced and unable to take the roll of the deck in their stride, they had settled into a patient routine. But all was not well.

This latest development, a maidservant's baby, was only one in a series of possible complications that troubled Captain Jones in those early, outwardly smooth-running days. The most serious problem was a growing disaffection between passengers and crew. From the outset the passengers had proved poor sailors and less than resilient in face of the elements. They had complained constantly about wet decks, water seeping into the cabins and the increasingly stale air indoors. None of which he could do very much about.

Captain Jones was more than tired of the self-righteous elders who came to see him on a variety of pretexts and always to complain. In the growing number of disputes beween passengers and crew, because of his conviction that the churchmen were, in the main, a discontented ill-natured lot, he would invariably side with his crew. In many ways this was understandable but in the case of one seaman it seemed to the passengers that the captain's instinctive loyalty was being carried a little too far.

The seaman was a large uncouth fellow, foul-mouthed and with little respect for anyone on board, including his captain. During their early bouts of seasickness he had mercilessly taunted and tormented the passengers whom he delighted in calling 'land-lubbers'. Most of them were new to the perils of the ocean and in their misery and lack of a will to retaliate he had assumed they were frightened of him. Threatening anyone who crossed him, he promised to throw them overboard at dead of night after robbing them of all their possessions. Few took him seriously but there were many complaints about his language and behaviour. Yet Captain Jones, tired of what he put down to the petty whining of his passengers, had taken no action.

On one occasion, as she entered the narrow passage from the deck to the galleys, Daisy Mason found the seaman, whose name was Dyke, barring her way. He was the worse for gin but, seeing an attractive young woman, he stood his ground, swaying arrogantly from side to side and looking her over in a lewd and suggestive manner. Daisy ordered him to stand aside. He was no more than a great slab of dirty grease, she told him, not fit to walk the boards with real gentlemen. Dyke laughed this off and with a flourish and a mocking bow stepped aside. But, though the contempt in Daisy's voice had rankled, there was little improvement in his manners and he continued to terrorize the passengers, constantly challenging and threatening the men and frightening the ladies with obscenities and crude vulgarity.

John Carver, after a deputation of senior churchmen had confronted him, was at last prevailed upon to approach the captain with a complaint on behalf of all the passengers. Dyke had committed an outrage by relieving himself in full view of the main deck at a time when several ladies were taking the air. The man had gone far enough, they declared. He must be disciplined. Captain Jones, anxious to maintain his authority over his crew and keen not to be seen to yield too readily to pressure from the churchmen, tried to generalize the complaint. His crew, he pointed out, were labouring under considerable difficulties aboard such a crowded ship and living in quarters even more cramped than those of the passengers. Naturally there were tensions, he said. John Carver made it clear that most of the complaints concerned one man, the seaman named Dyke. But even so nothing was done and Dyke went unchecked.

From her meeting with the captain Daisy had gone at once to the Carvers' quarters in the main cabin. Mrs Carver and Miss Minter did not hide their hostility. Daisy said she had a request to make of Mrs Carver's husband, but Mr Carver was busy with so many other matters she had decided to approach his good lady wife. Mrs Carver was mollified and more than a little curious. Daisy told her the maidservant Prudence was pregnant. Many months pregnant, in fact, with a baby due in only three to four weeks. An expression of smug satisfaction slowly suffused the squat Mrs Carver's puffy features and the taller, thinner Miss Minter could barely suppress a lip-twisting smirk. But Daisy was not deterred.

The girl, Daisy explained, had been cruelly taken advantage of at the home of the family from whom Mrs Carver had acquired her. The Duke, the girl's previous employer, was as yet unaware of her condition. But when the *Mayflower* returned to England, she said, he would be notified at once. With this, though not actually saying so, Daisy implied that the baby might be of noble blood. There was no need, she assured herself, to mention that a lowly houseboy was responsible. Mrs Carver was a snob and Daisy was prepared to use any such weakness to achieve her goal.

If the baby was to survive the girl would need extra nourishment and the captain had advised Daisy that only the passengers' acknowledged leader, Mr Carver, could authorize that. Mrs Carver basked for a moment in the reflected glory. Choosing her moment, Daisy assured Mrs Carver that the girl Prudence harboured no ill-feeling towards her or Miss Minter and nor did she. Mrs Carver frowned. She felt that gestures of conciliation should be her prerogative. But Daisy hurried on to say she was sure both ladies were of a truly charitable disposition and would not allow any personal difference to influence their response to the will of God.

'The will of God?' Mrs Carver echoed and she and Miss Minter exchanged glances.

'It is surely the will of God that this young woman is soon to bear a child. I feel it is our duty, as women, to help our younger sister in whatever way we can.'

Both Mrs Carver and Miss Minter sensed that they were somehow being manipulated and they didn't like it. Their first response to the news that Prudence was pregnant had been this air of smug satisfaction. But Daisy's approach made their only possible reaction, as Christian ladies, one of charity and understanding. Mrs Carver maintained a coolly formal front towards Daisy, but agreed to speak to her husband on the girl's behalf.

'A truly Christian act,' Daisy responded, 'from a truly Christian lady. Thank you, ma'am. Thank you so much.'

And though Mrs Carver searched Daisy's bland expression for a hint of irony she found none.

News of the expected birth travelled fast and from her obscurity as a ladies' maid Prudence became known and recognized throughout the ship. Still extremely shy and embarrassed by all the attention she stayed close to Daisy. But among the women passengers there was considerable interest and even rejoicing in her condition and several came to see her and wish her well. It was as if the impending arrival of a new baby confirmed the validity of their undertaking, a sign of approval and encouragement from the Almighty.

Among those who came was the previously aloof Priscilla Mullins whose family had warranted the allocation of a private cabin. If she could be of assistance, she told Daisy, she would be only too willing to help. Pleasantly surprised by the unexpected figure at her makeshift door, Daisy had invited her in and the tall slim Priscilla had stayed for much of the afternoon. She loved babies, she said, and she hoped one day to have ten, possibly more. Ten babies! Prudence stared at her wide-eyed and open-mouthed and Daisy laughed. We'd better find you a husband first, Miss Mullins, she said. And as Prudence blushed and lowered her eyes, she added kindly, 'Any girl can have *one* baby without benefit of clergy, but *ten*!'

Prudence found her voice at last and looking directly at Priscilla she said, 'There is a boy, miss.'

Priscilla raised her eyebrows. 'A boy?'

'For you, miss. I 'eard tell at the servants' table once ... an' I seen the way 'e looks at you.'

Priscilla laughed, unsure of how she should respond.

'Pru,' Daisy said lightly, 'you're embarrassing our guest. Who is this fellow and why don't I know of him?'

'I think I know who Pru means,' Priscilla said. 'I'm afraid my father has warned him off.'

Daisy was puzzled. 'Not one of the servants?'

'Oh no, miss,' Prudence said quickly. 'He's a carpenter. 'is name's John an' 'e's very 'andsome.'

'Sounds like you have a rival, Miss Mullins.'

'Oh, Miss Daisy,' Prudence said, hiding her face again.

Priscilla laughed and said, 'You must call me Priscilla.'

Daisy held out a hand. 'Daisy,' she said, 'and as you know, this is Pru.'

'I would like us to be friends,' Priscilla said, and so they were.

Elizabeth Hopkins was another who was delighted with the news of Pru's baby. Though it was early days for her, she was pregnant again. Prudence wanted to know what it was like, the actual process of having a baby. Was it painful? There was nothing to fear, Elizabeth assured her. It's painful at the time but it's the kind of pain that goes away completely and is soon forgotten, like toothache – she laughed – when the cause of the trouble is extracted.

But one unfortunate outcome of Pru's condition was its effect on her relationship with a young passenger named Maurice Tinker. Maurice was a thin, slightly stooping young man with a sallow complexion and an air of being sadly out of place in the robust company of the crew and the younger male passengers. He'd be happier sewing a sampler, Daisy had remarked with a laugh. But then she realized that Prudence was genuinely fond of him.

'I quite like 'im really, miss,' she admitted. But now, now there was a baby on the way, the hope of even a mild flirtation with the sad-eyed young man was gone. 'He wouldn't be interested in me though,' she said. 'I mean, would 'e? With the baby an' that.'

Daisy was about to make another joke about Maurice Tinker but she didn't. It occurred to her that there was still a long voyage ahead and in the New World there would not be all that many eligible young ladies around. Maurice was from a good family and financially, in the long run, he could prove quite a good catch. It was possible that in time he would again consider Prudence, baby or no baby. But none of this was uppermost in Daisy's mind. She had not caught more than a glimpse of Will Trefor since they left port and she decided it was time they were properly introduced. She went in search of Pat Ellis to find out what she could.

Ellis was down on the lower deck, checking the water levels. He looked worried. 'Hello there,' he said with a frown. 'Not seen much of you lately.'

'No,' Daisy agreed. 'I've been settling in.'

He was busy with the rigging and though he smiled affably enough she could see that something was giving him cause for concern. She turned and looked out to sea. The light was poor and there was a tension in the air, a foreboding. Then suddenly a fierce squall whipped up and took her breath away.

'Better off inside,' Ellis said. 'I reckon we're in for some rough weather.'

Dark clouds hung low on the horizon.

'How soon?' Daisy asked.

'Hard to say. But it won't be long. If I were you I'd try to keep things off the deck. Even in the main cabin. Try to hang things up off the floor. We're goin to be shippin' water.'

'Did you hear about the baby?'

He smiled and held on to his hat as another squall lashed at the decks. 'Better keep that little girl of yours well fed and well wrapped up. Keepin' dry is goin' to be the big problem.'

'You make it sound serious.'

'It *is* serious. I been through a few Atlantic storms in my time an', believe me, they can be pretty bad.'

'Does the captain know?'

Ellis laughed. 'Oh, yes. The captain knows all right. But he isn't goin' to go around frightenin' his passengers, is he now? Don't you worry. Cap'n Jones knows what's on the way an' he knows how best to handle it. He's a good skipper. One of the best. But there's not a lot he can do about the water. We're all goin' to get pretty wet in the next few days.'

'They say we're carrying too much weight for a ship of this size.'

Ellis nodded. 'Too much cargo, too many people.'

'Are we in danger, Mr Ellis?'

'There's always some danger at sea,' Ellis answered.

'I heard tell of a ship that got lost on this route only two years ago,' she said.

Ellis fixed his eyes on the darkening horizon.

'Mr Ellis?'

'I wouldn't want to worry you....'

'Is it true? I won't say anything to anyone else.'

'The truth is that two years ago this month a party of church people set out from Gravesend in a bigger ship than this. She was overcrowded, one hundred and eighty passengers and crew, and they were advised not to attempt a crossing at this time of year. But our ship is in much better shape.'

'What happened?'

'It was the ship. She wasn't up to it. She was already limpin' an' low in the water before she left the Thames. They ran into a gale an' they were driven off course. The clouds were solid. No stars to guide 'em. They were days, then weeks off course. An' as the winter came in things got worse. The crew was overworked an' weak. They ran short of food an' water. Six of 'em died. Then the master, a Cap'n Maggner, died.

'The ship was out of control by now, blown an' tossed about the ocean like a cork in a whirlpool. What remained of the crew an' some of the passengers did what they could to bring her to rights. But there was nothin' left, no food, no water an' no dry clothin'. They were cold an' wet all the time an' as the days went by more an' more of 'em died of the flux. It was September when they set out an' they didn't see land until March of last year. Only fifty of 'em survived out of one eighty.'

'Terrible tales of the high seas,' a voice behind them came with a laugh. 'Is he trying to scare you, miss?'

They turned to see Will Trefor, who was swaying back and forth as he held on to a guy rope, his hair blowing wild in the wind.

Ellis introduced him to Daisy. 'I don't know if you two have met....'

'We have now,' Trefor said and he touched his forelock as he had on the quay at Southwark.

Daisy felt her pulse quicken. 'Mr Ellis tells me we are running into some bad weather.'

'We certainly are,' he agreed and she noticed again his well-bred accent. It seemed so incongruous coming from a man in a seaman's torn and dirty jersey.

'He was telling me,' she said, 'about a ship that set out two years ago. It was overcrowded like ours ...'

'Maggner's ship,' Trefor cut in. 'We are not like that, miss. This is a far better tub. We have a better crew and there is no better master than Captain Jones. I should take no heed of crazy Irishmen.'

'Crazy am I?' Ellis said mildly.

The second mate, Mr Coppin, leaned over the side of the deck above and called down instructions to the two men.

'Aye, aye, sir!' Ellis called back. To Daisy he said, 'Better be off now. We have work to do.'

'Aye, aye, sir,' Daisy said and she went to the steps where, momentarily, Will Trefor barred her way.

'There is something I wish to ask of you, Miss Mason,' he said quietly. 'I would like to call on you, if I may.'

Daisy was outwardly composed but her heart was racing. 'I will be in my quarters this evening, Mr Trefor,' she told him. 'Between seven and eight.'

14

Will Trefor took Daisy at her word. That evening, as the threatened storm failed to materialize, he appeared in the main cabin and, stepping carefully between the temporary homes of several families, found his way to Daisy's partitioned space. He had made an effort to dress for the occasion in a deep crimson shirt, a pair of grey breeches buttoned just below the knee and black, high-buckled shoes. He had even taken a comb to his wayward locks. Prudence saw him coming, sensed her mistress would want to be alone with him and quietly slipped away.

He stood in the entrance, his head almost touching the ceiling of the wide cabin. 'You are the young lady I first saw at Southwark Dock, are you not? At a window of the Ship Inn.'

Daisy was sitting on the stool, a sewing box in her lap. 'I stayed there for just one night before I came aboard. You waved to me from the quay.' She looked up at him. 'Very forward of you, I must say.'

He smiled, ignoring the mild reprimand. 'And I didn't see you again until Southampton. Now I wonder why that was. Such a lovely lady.'

'You didn't see me, Mr Trefor, because you were stowed away in the hold. You stayed out of sight until Southampton. Then you went off and joined the *Speedwell.*'

'And damned near drowned,' he added, looking at her curiously, not sure how much she knew about him. 'How do you know I stowed away?'

'Mr Ellis told me.'

He looked up at the ceiling. 'That crazy Irishman.'

'Mr Ellis is one of the nicest men I have ever met,' Daisy said and she obviously meant it. 'He is also one of the most sane.'

Will Trefor was touched by her loyalty to his old friend and intrigued by her forthright manner. 'I am sure that is so, miss.'

Pat Ellis had commended her to him with the words, 'Sure an' if I was young enough I'd be after her myself.' Will had then been curious to meet her. He had a vague recollection of bumping into her once on the foredeck but now he had met her formally and conversed with her, albeit only briefly, he understood what Pat had meant. There was 'something about her'. Something *different*.

Daisy didn't want Will to leave. She wanted to talk to him, to detain him for as long as possible. 'I would offer you something to eat, a glass of wine....'

He dismissed this with a wave of his hand. 'When a gentleman calls upon a lady it is not the prospect of food or drink that lures him. He comes to bask in the radiance of her presence.'

Daisy laughed aloud. 'Do you always talk such rubbish?'

He laughed with her. 'In some quarters such rubbish is expected.'

'You said you wished to call on me,' she reminded him, 'as there is something you wish to ask of me. I agreed firstly because I was curious to know what you wish to ask and secondly because I thought you might prove – how shall I say? – *interesting*.'

'Interesting?'

'A man who is pursued across London by a company of the King's men and escapes by stowing away in the hold of a merchant ship, at least, a man who is so obviously not a common criminal, sounds interesting – wouldn't you say?'

Will smiled and leaned closer to her. 'Just how much did our Irish friend tell you about me?'

'He told me you were once an officer of His Majesty's Navy. He also told me that, for reasons of your own, you left your ship. "Deserted" is, I understand the word. You left your ship in some port in Spain and made your way back to England. You are a fugitive, Mr Trefor, are you not?'

'We are all fugitives,' he said, 'one way or another.'

Daisy looked at him sharply.

'We are all running away from something, Miss Mason,' he continued. 'What are *you* running away from?'

She blushed. 'I am not running away from anything.'

'The manner of your reply would suggest that you are.'

He was teasing her and fortunately she realized it.

'That may be so,' she replied coolly. 'But I don't have half the King's men after me.'

'Ah! But you would have,' he told her gallantly, 'if they had witnessed your beauty and your grace.'

She laughed again. 'You are incorrigible, Mr Trefor. And you are the one who is crazy – not Mr Ellis.'

It was light-hearted banter, but Daisy was pleased with the compliment.

'Are we to be friends?' he asked hopefully.

'I don't see why not,' she responded.

'Then may I call you Daisy?'

'Why, ye-es,' she said, a little surprised. 'That *is* my name.'

'I hope you will regard me as a friend,' he said, 'and call me Will.'

She nodded. A friend? Is that all? 'You said,' she reminded him again, 'there was something you wanted to ask me.'

'Yes,' he said, 'there is. A favour. I wanted to ask a favour of you.'

'A favour?'

'A young lady called to see you. Her name is Rose.'

Daisy came back to reality. 'Mrs Standish.'

A frown creased his tanned features. 'Her name is Rose Chelford.'

'Oh, but surely, she is married to a Captain Standish, is she not?'

Still frowning, he shook his head.

'I don't understand.'

'Miss Mason,' he said. 'Daisy.' His voice was suddenly earnest, all the gaiety gone. 'Rose Chelford and I have known each other all our lives. We were together as children, in Cheshire. She loves me, Daisy. She always has.'

Daisy didn't want to hear this, yet she found herself asking, 'If she loves you why did she marry this Captain Standish?'

Will seemed eager to tell her. 'My father,' he said, 'was a Privy Councillor but he fell out of favour with the King. He was accused of being anti-Royalist. It was said he had once been a supporter of Robert Devereux, the Earl of Essex, and his enemies brought this to the attention of His Majesty. My family was systematically discredited. We were robbed of our home and our land was confiscated. I was too young to do much about it, I'm afraid, and I was packed off to naval college. I lost my birthright and I lost Rose. My family was in disgrace and Rose's father was not happy about her relationship with me. He did everything he could to end it. He even sent her away to live with relatives in Lancashire.

'At college I had a good friend whose home was in Lancaster and through him Rose and I were able, from time to time, whenever he went home in fact, to exchange letters. From what I could gather Rose was discovered reading one of my letters and she was forbidden to correspond with me or to contact me in any way. I was told by my commanding officer I would be dealt with severely if I persisted in "pestering" the young lady and my friend was charged with a breach of discipline for acting as a go-between. Though how delivering a few love letters constitutes a breach of discipline....' His voice trailed. 'I testified that he had absolutely no knowledge of what was in the letters or that Rose's family disapproved and he got away with a reprimand. Even so I was responsible for getting him into trouble and I felt badly about it.

'I heard nothing of Rose for some months and it was during that time she was introduced to this army fellow – Standish. I'm sure she was coerced into marrying him. The engagement was announced almost as soon as they met and eventually Rose was persuaded to go through a form of marriage with him. The wedding was arranged very quickly, probably because they wanted it to take place whilst I was at sea. Her father knew I was not a man to give up without a fight and I suppose he didn't want any spectre turning up at the feast. When I heard about it I was in port in Spain. I left at once for England.' He smiled wryly. 'I had some wild idea I would ride up on a white charger, scoop Rose up and carry her off before anyone could stop me. When I heard Standish planned to take her away to North America I vowed I would follow them and win her back.'

Daisy was still seated on the low stool. Will Trefor was still standing, high above her, by the narrow entrance. He stepped forward and went down on one knee like a man proposing marriage. Daisy felt drawn to him, fixed and held in the blueness of his eyes.

'I wanted to ask you ...' he began.

She waited, her mouth slightly open in anticipation. Beyond the partition the noise in the main cabin was a continuous low buzz, a monotony of voices, of children's shrieks, of people moving and things being moved. She wanted to cup his noble head in her hands, to draw him closer and kiss him lightly on the lips.

'... if you would pass on a message I have for her.'

It was just the two of them, Daisy leaning forward, Will on one knee, everything else obliterated. Then his request broke the spell.

'Oh,' she said in a voice that sounded distant, alien even to herself. 'I don't know. I don't think that would be quite proper. I mean, Captain Standish ...'

'Forget Captain Standish,' he interrupted rudely. 'If we are friends, Daisy, surely you could do me this one small favour.'

Daisy hesitated in dismay.

'I have been asked,' he said quietly. 'No, I have been *ordered* by the ship's master to stay away from Standish and his quarters. But you could go there for me, give Rose a message.'

The following morning, like hostile hordes preparing to attack, the black menacing clouds still hung low on the horizon to the west. Their presence seemed to give an added chill to the air as greyer clouds hid the sun and the lone ship ploughed on through choppy waters.

Daisy's maid and companion, Prudence, came running into the main cabin with a fistful of nails. Mr Ellis had told her he had scrounged them from the carpenter, John Alden. Miss Daisy was to use them to hang up everything she could off the deck, ready for when the storm came.

But Pru's eyes were alight with bigger news than this. Mr Ellis, she said, had asked John Alden to make a crib for the baby and John had said he would. Oh yes, and she had called upon Mrs Standish as instructed. Mrs Standish would be pleased to see Miss Daisy at any time after two and before five o'clock this afternoon.

By no means clear in her own mind what she wanted to say to

Rose Standish, Daisy had reluctantly agreed to deliver a message from Will Trefor. She was confused and unsure of her motives. It was wrong, she told herself, to take part in such deception. To deliver a message of love from a young man to another man's wife was indefensible. But would she have such qualms if the young man involved was someone other than Will Trefor?

Rose Standish welcomed Daisy at the door of her cabin soon after two o'clock. The cabin was small but larger than many of the spaces occupied by parents with children. There was a bed, a table and two chairs, even a small clothes cupboard – and Daisy was impressed. The captain must be an important man, she concluded.

She was to learn later that Captain Standish was a military adviser and strategist of some note and the church leaders had been quick to encourage his interest in joining them. Stories of marauding Indians had persuaded them that a man such as Standish would indeed be an asset when they at last set foot in what might well prove less than friendly territory.

'I am so glad to see you,' Rose said. 'Do come in.'

In her fragile way Rose looked as pretty as ever and there was a youthfulness about her, that of the young wife who has never had to toil or drudge in dull domesticity. It was reflected, too, in minor matters of dress. Where most married women tied their caps beneath their chins, young girls pinned their caps to their hair and so did Rose.

'My husband will be here shortly,' she said, 'but he will not stay long. He is to attend a meeting of the elders. There is some problem, I understand, with an objectionable member of the crew.'

Almost as she spoke Miles Standish filled the doorway behind Daisy. He was not as tall as Will Trefor but he was broad-shouldered and solidly built. His military bearing made him seem taller than he was and even out of uniform, as he was now, it was somehow obvious that he was or had been a soldier. His reddish hair fell in curls on his forehead just above his bushy eyebrows and his ginger moustache and beard were in need of a trim. His pale eyes were steady and uncompromising and with a glint that suggested here was a man who was used to power and the exercise of authority.

Rose introduced him to Daisy and he took Daisy's hand and bowed to touch it with his lips. 'I am indeed pleased to make your acquaintance, Miss Mason,' he said. 'Rose has told me about you and your quite charming indifference to pompous religious ladies.'

'Miles!' Rose laughed with mock reproval.

Daisy was not sure how she should respond. 'I don't know what I ought to say to that.'

'Don't say anything,' he told her, holding up his hands. 'I am sorry if I embarrass you.' He smiled. 'But if it's of any interest I can't stand those silly women either.'

Daisy laughed. 'But you wouldn't dream of saying so.'

He winked an eye conspiratorially and Daisy noticed the powerful bulk of his shoulders as he turned to kiss Rose lightly on the cheek.

'Enjoy your *tête-à-tête*,' he said and he withdrew.

Daisy looked at Rose, again marvelled that such fragile beauty could attract two such men.

Rose held a chair for her. 'Tell me about the baby and Prudence – how is Prudence?'

'Oh, she's very well,' Daisy said, sitting down, 'now that she knows we all support her and want her to have the baby.' She laughed. 'I actually saw it move yesterday. Pru was sitting quietly on the floor and I saw this little kick. There was no mistake. A really strong kick.'

Rose was thrilled. 'Oh, I do wish I could see that.'

'Well, you probably can,' Daisy told her. 'It happens often. usually in the evening when we are sitting down and everything is quiet. Or, at least, as quiet as it can be in that awful cabin. I think the baby kicks out to see if anyone is there, because it makes Pru jump and we laugh and make a noise. It goes still then as if it's satisfied we haven't gone away.'

'I have begun to make some little garments,' Rose said.

'I'm afraid that's something I'm not very good at,' Daisy admitted. 'But I must try. The ship's carpenter has promised to make a crib.'

'It's all so exciting,' Rose said. 'I do wish that Miles and I....' She shrugged her narrow shoulders. 'He insists we must have our own roof over our heads and our feet firmly on dry land before we even think of having children. Miles is a soldier, as you know. Very well organized. Everything in its proper place.'

She was not criticizing her husband. She clearly accepted that this was the way he was.

'He's quite handsome,' Daisy said.

Rose smiled. 'Yes,' she agreed. 'All the ladies seem to like him. He can be quite charming, too, when he wants to be. But sometimes he appears very strict and hard. And he doesn't suffer fools. Right now the church people have asked him to lead a deputation to see the captain about that awful seaman Dyke.'

'But they have already asked the captain to do something about him and he has refused. He said the passengers are always complaining and the crew has enough to put up with without being disciplined over trivial matters.'

'I know,' Rose said. 'But this time, I understand, Dyke has attempted to molest one of the servant girls.'

'I have come across him twice now and I have told him what I thought of him. You have to be firm with men like him, Rose. They are usually bullies and cowards.'

'I'm afraid not everyone is that strong. I must say I was glad to get away from him. He barred my way on the stairs and I threatened to tell my husband. Fortunately for him he allowed me to pass. But now, I understand, he is almost permanently the worse for drink. I fear the consequences for anyone who falls foul of him.'

'Did you tell your husband?'

'Good heavens, no! Miles would be terribly angry.'

'You really are very fond of him, aren't you?'

'Miles? Well, of course. He's my husband.'

Daisy had not exactly been eager to pass on the message from Will. But now, in view of Rose's obvious devotion to her husband, it didn't seem so important. 'It's just that I had a visit from a member of the crew. A young man who claims to know you.'

Rose looked at her sharply.

'His name is Will Trefor. He said he saw you come to visit me and as I knew you he asked if I would deliver a message. A very personal message.'

'A message?'

'I told him I couldn't possibly to that. You are a married lady.'

Rose's expression gave nothing away and Daisy was caught up in the momentum of what she had started.

'He said you are not married. Not in the eyes of God.'

Rose's cheeks were suddenly hot and red.

'He said that you and he ...'

Rose turned away.

'... that you and he have been friends since childhood.'

'Did he say that we were lovers, too? Or did he merely imply that?'

'He just said that in the eyes of God you and Captain Standish are not married.'

'Oh, Daisy.' Rose turned to confront her. 'What am I going to do with him?'

'He is a very determined young man,' Daisy told her. 'He

deserted his ship and took a job as an ordinary seaman – just to be near you.'

'We were parted by our family circumstances. After what happened with his father my family didn't want me to see Will ever again.'

'And you? Did you want to see him again?'

'I was just a child. I hadn't met anyone else. Will was the only young man I knew. And I had always known him. But then, when I moved to Lancashire, I met Miles.'

'Did you never love Will?'

'Oh yes, of course I did. As a dear, dear friend. But not in the way a woman loves a man. Not in the way he claims to love me. I love Miles in that way, Daisy. No one else.'

Before she met Miles Standish, Daisy would have welcomed such a declaration. It would have left the way open for her to pursue Will. But now she was confused. She should have felt elated. But she didn't.

Rose was waiting, watching her. 'You said Will asked you to deliver a message.'

'Yes,' Daisy said. 'He asked me to tell you he will follow you to the ends of the earth. He will never give up and one day you will be his again and his alone.'

15

Accompanied by Captain Standish three of the most senior elders – William Brewster, the acknowledged head of the church congregation, his deputy William Bradford and the man whom the passengers as a whole had elected as their governor, John Carver – made up the deputation that called upon the ship's master that grey September afternoon. Captain Jones had agreed to meet them in his cramped quarters just below the poop deck, but there was little room to invite them in and he could only stand at his door to hear what the four men had to say.

Once again their complaint was about the foul-mouthed seaman called Dyke who persistently threatened to rob passengers of whatever valuables they possessed before throwing the men overboard and violating the women. Dyke had now committed a gross and totally unacceptable offence. He had cornered the maidservant of a Mrs Winslow and subjected the girl, Ellen, to a disgusting ordeal. The four demanded action.

Captain Jones was surprisingly reluctant to give them any assurance. Perhaps, he suggested, they should keep a closer watch on their womenfolk. The ship, he pointed out, was seriously overcrowded. Against his judgement he had been persuaded to allow far too many passengers on board. Ideally he should have half as many passengers and twice as many crew. His men were labouring under considerable difficulties. Every man had at least three jobs to do and he did not propose to risk alienating them by disciplining one of their number.

'In the main,' William Brewster conceded, 'the crew are good men. They have shown our people much kindness and in many ways. Most of them, I assure you, are well thought of and give little cause for concern. The main problem rests with this one man. He was an unfortunate choice, if I may say so.'

'No, sir,' the captain told him tartly, 'you may not say so. This one man is at this moment down below manning the central pump. It is a strenuous task. It requires a strong man. This man was chosen for his size and strength. He is a big man, strong and powerful. He knows his job and he does it well. We *need* him. What would you have me do? Clap him in irons?'

'I would have you warn him, Captain,' Miles Standish broke in, unhappy with Brewster's meek approach, 'that if he should frighten or harm any of our people again he will have me to deal with.'

The captain looked Standish up and down. 'He is a very large man.'

Standish drew his cape aside to reveal a slim-barrelled pistol at his waistband. 'And I have a very efficient flintlock.'

'Gentlemen!' The elderly Brewster raised his hands in alarm. 'There must be no violence. Please!' To Standish he said, 'I am afraid we could not condone the use of arms. Not in our name.'

'Nobody will use arms against a member of my crew,' the captain warned. 'I will not allow it.'

'You will not *allow* it?' Standish appeared to question his authority.

'I am the master of this ship,' Captain Jones reminded him. 'If any person threatens to take arms against me or any member of my crew I will have that person restrained, returned with me to England and handed over to His Majesty's Constable. Such a person would be a danger to everyone aboard.' And quietly he added, 'I might remind you also, sir, that as master of this ship I have it in my power to try and if found guilty to execute said person.'

'Gentlemen, please!' Brewster and the other two churchmen were agitated now, concerned that the point of their deputation appeared to have been lost. 'We came here to ask for your advice and assistance, Captain. We request that you have a restraining word with the man who is at the root of our present differences. The man named Dyke.'

'I make no promises,' the captain said. 'But I will tell you this.' He looked to the horizon. 'Those clouds you see, gentlemen, mean that we are in for a very rough few days. Believe me, when the going gets difficult, you and I will be grateful for a man like Dyke.'

The four men left the half-deck below the poop feeling they had achieved precisely nothing. Miles Standish was furious. 'I swear,' he said, 'if that animal Dyke comes anywhere near *my* wife I shall kill him.'

The church elders were shocked.

'We must pray,' William Brewster said.

'The Lord will deliver us,' said John Carver.

Down in the pump room the seaman Dyke was working alongside Will Trefor. Both men were up to their elbows in grease and though a cold east wind was blowing above decks the sweat was rolling from them, coursing their grimy faces, salting their lips, pooling at their throats and glistening on their naked arms and chests. One of the pumps had jammed and Dyke was attempting to free it manually, his biceps bulging and straining as if they would surely burst.

Dyke was well over six feet tall and he looked almost half as wide. He had huge shoulders and hands to match and a contempt for heavy work that many a ship's master had turned to good use. He was first to lift an outsize bale or coil a sail-dragged rope, displaying his physical prowess with pride. And less proud men made no attempt to deter him, artfully praising his efforts and pretending to marvel at his strength.

'One of these days, Dyke,' Will Trefor told him, 'you are going to bust your gut.'

But Dyke merely laughed and complained that he was hungry. He could eat a horse, he said. He was always hungry and he had been known to steal the rations of other seamen – a court martial offence in the King's Navy and an equally serious crime aboard a merchant ship. Stealing another man's food was one of the worst crimes a serving man, soldier or sailor, could commit. But where Dyke was concerned nobody dared to complain.

Dyke was also a compulsive scavenger. There was rarely anything edible left on the communal table in the crew's quarters and the servants made certain that little remained of the passengers' leftovers. But what there was he would invariably consume. From stale bread to rotting vegetables to suspect beef, he would devour almost anything. And when told such an indiscriminate habit could lead to food poisoning and an early grave he would merely snort and mouth the standard retort: 'Better than dying of hunger.' But he was not just hungry for food, he confided to Will Trefor. He was hungry for a woman, too.

'From what I hear,' Will admonished him mildly, 'you are always hungry for a woman. They say that when you go ashore all the whores in Christendom go into hiding.'

'Nah! That is not so. They can't get enough of me.' He laughed coarsely. 'They stand in line. Wait their turn. An' they keep on coming back for more.'

'And they don't charge you anything, I suppose?'

'Nah! They don't charge me. They would willingly *pay* me!' He laughed uproariously and the jammed pump moved for him. 'I reckon we should turn this old tub into a whore ship. What do you say, Trefor? Throw all those bible-punching preachers an' God-gobblers overboard an' jus' keep the women!'

'You really are an uncouth animal, aren't you, Dyke?'

Dyke released the pump. He was never quite sure how he should deal with Will Trefor. Though mentally slow, even he recognized that Will was no ordinary seaman. Dyke was not sure what he was. He had heard it said that Trefor was a spy for the officer classes. Yet the man could tackle most of the jobs on board ship and he was not afraid to get his hands dirty. He was also the only member of the crew – apart from that upstart of a carpenter who was not a real seaman anyway – who was clearly not afraid of him.

'Who are you calling an animal?' he demanded.

Will Trefor faced him across the pump, suddenly tired of the man's bluster. 'You, Dyke. I'm calling you a great lumbering, uncouth oaf with the brain of a flea, the instincts of a rabbit and the proclivities of a pig.'

'The what?'

'You are not fit to look at the ladies aboard this ship.'

Dyke was slow-thinking but quick to react when he believed he had thought something through. He looked warily at the tanned, handsome face, expecting a smile, an assurance that it was all a joke, that Trefor didn't mean it. But Will didn't smile.

'I'm warning you, Dyke,' he said sternly. 'I am telling you to stay away from the ladies aboard this ship or else.'

'Or else what? What can *you* do? I'll beat you to a pulp.'

'You have the brawn,' Will said, 'I grant you that. You could probably thrash me to within an inch of my life, as they say. But the brawn is *all* you have. I have the brains. I would recover and when I did you would never be able to live in peace again.'

'What are you talking about?'

'Think about it. You would never be able to sleep or fall ill or even take a nap. Because I would be there – waiting for an opportunity.'

Dyke put his hands to the sides of his head as if the thinking hurt. 'You're mad!'

'That's right. I'm mad. Completely mad.' Will smiled now, injecting a gleam of madness in his eye. 'Scared now, are we? Scared of what I might do?'

'Me? Scared of you?' Dyke let out a loud, yet not totally convincing roar of laughter. But it made him feel better and he recovered his bravado. 'I could eat you for breakfast.'

'A cannibal, too, eh?'

Dyke frowned. 'Who are you, anyway? Where do yer come from? An' where yer bin?'

'I've been at sea.'

'Where? Where yer bin?'

Will told him.

'Wait! Wait a minute!' Dyke's brain was working overtime. 'Those are not merchant routes. Those are King's Navy routes. Yer bin in the King's Navy, ain't yer? An' yer talk like an officer. Yer bin an officer in the King's Navy, ain't yer? An' now yer just a ratin' on a merchant ship.' A dim light had appeared in Dyke's eyes. 'I know,' he said. 'I know about you. Yer bin kicked out, ain't yer? Yer bin court-martialled an' kicked out.'

Will smiled and shook his head.

'Then what?' Dyke was watching him closely, but Will merely smiled again and turned back to greasing the pump.

It was some time later, when Dyke was taking his break on a double pallet in the first hold, that the answer occurred to him. He sat up in excitement. That was it! Will Trefor was a Navy deserter! Hadn't a search party boarded the ship back at Southwark? And even Dyke could see the possibilities. Blackmail for a start! A bounty, maybe! A King's ransom! Him an' that fancy voice. Mr Midshipman Trefor, at least. More likely a lieutenant. Dyke wondered if the master or Mr Clarke knew.

Two decks higher, Daisy Mason was looking for Will Trefor. There was no sign of him but she found Pat Ellis.

'A good thing, too,' Ellis said in response to what she told him. Then the Irishman smiled as if something had just occurred to him. 'If Mrs Standish is not interested in Will, I'd say that leaves the door open for someone else, wouldn't you?'

Daisy avoided his eye. 'I don't know what you mean.'

'Come on, Daisy,' Ellis laughed. 'We both know you like Will. An' so you should. He's a fine young fellow.'

'I'm sure he'll be very upset,' she said, refusing to be drawn.

'It's a matter of time, that's all. He's young. His pride's been hurt. But he'll get over it.'

The ship plunged downwards and Daisy gripped his arm.

'A young man needs a young woman,' Ellis said. 'An' you're the best-looking young woman aboard this old wreck – including Mrs Rose what's-her-name?'

Daisy smiled up at him and the ship lurched again, throwing them together. To the north the dark clouds merged and hid from view the gas-green daylight. A howling gust of wind whipped the slackened sails and sent a shudder through the plunging decks. Waves hit the sides, smashing upwards and outwards like shots from a cannon.

'Better get inside,' Ellis warned, his eyes scanning the low-hung clouds. 'This could be the big one.'

Daisy didn't want to go inside. So many bodies, living and sleeping in such close proximity and in so cramped and enclosed a space had rendered the air in the main cabin foul and almost unbearable. But then the rain came, a windswept drizzle at first then a chilling downpour, and she turned and ran for cover.

The sky darkened. Black clouds, veined by long fingers of lightning and backed by a dull rolling thunder, were the signal for seamen to scamper unbidden up rope ladders and over wet rolling boards to lower the sails. Down and up plunged the *Mayflower*, down and up as tall spumes of grey water crashed over the bowsprit, flooded the decks and swirled away with a dark-green froth-topped flourish. Great climbing waves opened up ahead like the jaws of some enormous whale and closed on the nose of the storm-tossed ship. Up and over walls of water the lurching vessel ploughed on as all hands fought to bring in the sails, to batten the hatches and to wedge and secure the shifting cargo in the lower holds.

In the main cabin families huddled together silenced, save for the whimpers of small children, by a fear and dread of the raging storm, a phenomenon none there had experienced and some believed to be a sure sign of the wrath of God. Determined to keep her balance, Daisy stepped gingerly in the narrow divisions that edged the territory of each family group. With heartfelt sympathy she acknowledged the pale faces, the tinges of green under young chins and the anxious stillness of worried mothers. It would only take one child to be seasick now and they would all start.

Pru's friend Maurice Tinker was huddled in a corner where his parents had settled. Mrs Tinker was slumped on the floor of the cabin with her head in her husband's lap. She had been ill for days with a sickness which the doctor had put down more to melancholia than anything physical. Mr Tinker, sitting precariously on a low stool, stared into space as if his heart and mind were elsewhere and he was present in body only.

'Have you seen Prudence?' Daisy asked Maurice.

He shook his head and looked as if he was about to vomit. 'Can't we open one of the scuttles, miss?' he asked as if Daisy was a person in authority. 'Get some fresh air in here. It's foul. My mother can't breathe.'

Holding her breath against the stench, Daisy nodded in agreement. It was certainly foul but she was not sure they should tamper with the hatches. 'The water's very high out there,' she said. 'We'd get drenched.'

The young man looked at the faces turned towards him. Tense, non-committal expressions. All hated the stench, were sickened by the fetid air. All were gagging for a fresh clean wind. But none would take the lead.

The ship lurched yet again. Belongings slid to starboard. A child cried and another joined in. The ship rose and then dipped, as if on a giant roller coaster, and several women and children screamed.

'Better wait until we're back on an even keel,' someone warned.

But Maurice found he had raised their hopes. Unwashed bodies, unchanged babies, the imminence of seasickness, the raw sewage and waste the failed pump had allowed to seep into the ballast – all gave rise to a ghastly combination of smells. The jammed pump, one of two designed to draw off the bilge, was working again thanks to Dyke, but the temporary stoppage had made matters worse.

'In God's name,' a voice cried out, 'will someone please open a hatch?'

It was all the encouragement Maurice needed. He reached up and, not without difficulty, succeeded in releasing the grips on a two foot square hatch. The trap flew back on its hinges and a rising wave swept in. All those near scrambled away, falling over the bodies of others in an effort to escape a drenching.

As the prow of the ship rose water ran down the outside deck and into the big cabin. As the prow dipped sheets of heavy rain slanted in. Out in the dark someone was shouting orders, the voice carried on the howling wind, and after several attempts the trap was heaved to and closed. Then it flew back with a resounding slap and more rain poured in. A head appeared now at the opening to bellow obscenities into the cabin. Apparently it was much easier to open the trap than to close it and for it to stay down someone on the inside had to secure the grips.

Maurice Tinker slithered as best he could to beneath the opening, ready to slot the grips into place. A seaman out on the deck saw him below, yelled an instruction through the hatch and with the help of two others forced the trap door up and over and slammed it down. Maurice tried to press home the grips but he hadn't the strength and the rain and the waves were only partly cut off.

By now most of the floor in the main cabin was under half an inch of water that swirled and eddied back and forth with every lurch of the ship until everywhere was wet underfoot. Many of the passengers rushed to lift boxes and cases and sundry belongings but as they huddled together, arms full, they found there was nowhere dry to put anything down. Parents were tired and angry, children were crying and in a crowded corner a boy of four was violently sick.

The storm showed no sign of abating as the ship ploughed on, down and up, down and up, and sometimes it seemed to stay down for a frightening few seconds longer. Then it would shudder from stem to stern and the anger and frustration of the passengers would turn again to fear. Daisy made her way to her own small compartment where most of her belongings with Pru's little bag of possessions had been hung on nails. But there was no sign of Pru.

One of the Hopkins girls, Constanta, who was fourteen, was sitting on an upturned basket, her head between her knees. Damaris, the three year old, was sitting on her mother's knee, all of her thumb rammed in her mouth, her head back against her mother's breast as she watched wide-eyed. Elizabeth Hopkins gave Daisy a look of helpless resignation and Daisy could only nod and smile in sympathy. Children, and some of the adults now, were vomiting all around. But there was no sign of Prudence and no one had seen her since the storm began.

16

With the grips on the hatch not fully closed water from the deck above channelled through the gap with every tilt of the ship. Maurice Tinker, who had made the mistake of opening the hatch, could still not close it tight. A strong forward thrust of the two grips was required and Maurice needed all the strength he could muster and probably more. But he could only just reach the grips and he had nothing to stand on.

One of the churchmen went up the two steps at the door of the cabin to ask for assistance but was told bluntly to get back inside. Then the second mate, Mr Coppin, came in out of the driving rain. Mr Coppin, who had the necessary strength and knew exactly what was required, was too short to reach the grips and this seemed to annoy him. He stamped out of the cabin, went back to the waist deck and sent in the seaman Dyke.

Dyke's reputation was by now well known and several of the women cowered back out of his way. He laughed aloud, strode across to the partly closed scuttle, knocked it upwards with the palms of his hands and as it fell back slammed both grips into position. Water ran off the inside edge and dripped to a halt.

Hands on hips, he turned and surveyed the scene around him. He laughed again, his large feet planted firmly on the wet floor of the cabin, and began to taunt the unfortunate occupants. Before the night was through, he forecast, they would all be dead, food for the fishes. 'Abandon all hope!' he boomed, recalling the words of preachers he had heard on the streets of London. 'Repent ye sinners.'

At the far end of the long cabin, Miles Standish and John Carver were deep in discussion, their heads together. They were out of earshot but Standish recognized Dyke and saw that by his aggressive stance and manner he was intimidating those passengers nearest to him.

'What is that seaman doing in here?' he demanded.

'Wait!' Carver counselled quietly. 'The Almighty will deal with him, Captain Standish. We have prayed for deliverance....'

But Standish had little faith in the power of prayer. 'Then allow me to be your deliverer.'

He strode through the cabin with Carver close behind, urging him to refrain from hasty action. Daisy Mason saw them coming. She glanced across at Dyke. Brave as he was, Standish was clearly no match physically for the belligerent giant.

'You!' Standish bellowed in his deep, authoritative voice. 'You have no business in here. Report to your superior officer at once. I order you!'

'An' who might you be?' Dyke asked with contempt.

'Captain Standish of His Majesty's Military Reserve. And I am ordering you to report to your superior officer.'

Dyke's tone lost a little of its assurance. 'You can't order me about.'

'I ordered you to leave this cabin at once.' Standish took a step nearer. 'Did I not make myself clear?'

From behind Standish, John Carver attempted to calm the situation. 'I am sure there is no need …'

'This is my affair, Mr Carver,' Standish told him, 'and mine alone.'

A silence had fallen on the long cabin. Even the children, aware that something was afoot, were less restive.

Standish spoke clearly and a little louder than before, conscious of playing to an audience. 'I will deal with this individual and in my own way.'

'An' what way might that be?' Dyke enquired.

'My patience is running out,' Standish warned him.

'Why, I could sling you o'erboard with one 'and,' Dyke said. 'Why should I tek 'eed o' you?'

'Because, you impudent dolt,' Standish told him, 'I am an officer of His Majesty the King. And also, at this moment, perhaps more impressively than that, I have a rather powerful ally.' He drew his waistcoat aside to reveal his flintlock pistol. 'I will count to three. At the end of that time my ally here will ensure you are never able to fulfil your disgusting threats.'

Daisy put a hand to her mouth to conceal her smile. There was no doubt what Standish meant and some of the ladies present were almost as shocked by this as they had been by Dyke.

'We'll see about that,' Dyke muttered.

Standish drew the pistol from his waistband, cocked the catch and, with the barest hint of a smile, aimed at Dyke's crotch. 'We most certainly will.'

As if the slight twitch of Standish's moustache had in some way lessened the tension and offered him an opportunity to save his face, Dyke laughed scornfully and moved away. 'Got to 'ave a gun, eh?'

'As effective, I'd say, as any of your bullying.'

Dyke started to swagger slowly towards the exit.

'Move!' Standish ordered, his mood suddenly changed and his pistol raised.

Dyke hurried out into the driving wind and the high drenching waves that continued to lash the decks. Then Standish adjusted the pistol and replaced it, out of sight, behind his waistcoat. There was a murmur throughout the cabin and though most of the churchmen present deplored the aggression and threatened violence of the scene they had just witnessed, several of the ladies smiled and nodded their approval at Standish.

Daisy clapped her hands and exclaimed in a voice that carried: 'Bravo, Captain! And thank you.'

Standish looked across at her and held her gaze for a disconcertingly long moment. It was a look unbecoming of a married gentleman and those ladies who missed little were quick to notice.

Though others, too, had expressed appreciation, John Carver was less enthusiastic. 'We cannot condone violence of any kind, Captain Standish. I am sure you are aware of that.'

'Where we are going, Mr Carver,' Standish said, without giving Carver his full attention, 'we may well have to meet violence with violence. If only in self-defence.'

Carver frowned.

'Defence is my responsibility in this enterprise, is it not?' Standish said, turning to him. 'I came along as a soldier. None can foretell that our negotiations with the natives will be peaceful. We may not be welcome.'

These were facts that Carver was not yet willing to face. 'For now, sir,' he said, 'I am sure the Lord will deal with this unfortunate individual and in His own good time. Our people will pray for him.'

But Standish was only half-listening. His attention had strayed again and at that moment he had eyes only for Daisy Mason who was anxiously questioning Maurice Tinker. Maurice was mopping water into a bucket and feeling foolish and embarrassed. By opening the scuttle he had added to the general discomfort and indirectly caused the confrontation beween Dyke and the army man. Daisy wanted to know when he last saw Prudence.

It was some time ago, Maurice told her; long before he opened the scuttle. Everyone was complaining about the foul air and Pru looked as if she was about to pass out. She was *green*, he said. She wanted fresh air. Couldn't breathe, she said. And she was worried about the baby. But he told her she mustn't even think of going out on deck. The wind was howling and screaming and the waves were ten, fifteen feet high. Strong enough to sweep her away. But she wouldn't listen. She said she would die if she had to stay indoors.

Daisy was worried. It was wild and dark out on deck. Pru could have been swept overboard and no one would know. 'Haven't you *any* idea where she went?'

'I think she must have gone out by the forward door,' Maurice said. 'There was a seaman at this door. Sending people back in, he was. Said it was too dangerous outside. She could only have gone out through that end.'

Squelching water underfoot, Daisy ran to the forward door and out into a narrow passage. Perhaps Mr Ellis had seen Pru and taken care of her, she thought. But then it occurred to her that Mr Ellis would be at his post and far too busy to concern himself with individual passengers. Perhaps she was with Rose Standish.

There was a huddle of men and women ahead where the passage opened out and rain slanted in from the deck. Three of the men were attempting to lift a sagging body that seemed bereft of life. Daisy ran, anxiety gripping her throat. 'What is it?' she asked. 'What's happened?'

But the wind screamed through the timbers, a black cloud hid the moon and she became just another shadowy figure, her questions unheard. She struggled through the tight knot of onlookers to where she could see for herself what was happening.

'Woman fainted,' someone told her. 'Passed right out.'

The men lifted the woman and called out for people to 'Stand back!' and 'Make way!', their voices muffled by the wind. But the woman they supported was not Prudence and Daisy rushed out to the heaving deck where a seaman, cursing her stupidity, gripped her by the arms. Waves were still lashing the decks and within seconds she was drenched from head to toe.

The seaman wanted her to go back inside but Daisy refused, screaming through the gale that she was going forward. He tried hard to restrain her but, fearing more of the passengers might follow her example, he was anxious to return to his post. He gripped her hand and guided it to a rope, a lifeline that ran from one end of the deck to the other.

Grasping the rope with both hands Daisy broke away from the seaman and holding fast made her way forward. Again a giant wave slapped her full in the face but, gasping for breath, she steadied herself, disregarded the warning cry of another seaman and hauled herself along the rope, hand over hand, until she was level with the passage that led to the cabin of Rose and Miles Standish.

The moon seemed to race across the sky as wispy scuds of cloud sped by and there was only intermittent light. The surrounding sea was a black void and though the force of the waves had lessened the wind still howled and screamed through the beleaguered ship.

Choosing her moment Daisy dashed across the deck to the shelter of the passage. The up and down movement of the bows seemed more pronounced in the narrow gangway and she suddenly felt queasy. She closed her eyes, shook off the feeling and made her way to Rose's door. She knocked lightly, called Rose's name. But there was no reply.

Despite the wind and the twisting and creaking of the ship it was quieter here. There was not the chatter of the main cabin, the interminable buzz of people. Daisy tried the door and it opened outwards. Rose Standish was lying on the low bed, her face to the wall.

Daisy went to her, touched her shoulder. 'Rose,' she said softly.

Rose turned her head. Dried tears marked dark rivulets down her white cheeks and her face had a ghastly pallor. Her eyes were sunken slightly and her lips were pale and dry. For an awful moment Daisy thought of the Duchess and the way the Duchess had looked on her death bed. But then Rose raised a smile and the impression was dispelled.

'Oh, Daisy!' she said hoarsely. 'I've been sick. It was awful. I think I must have lost half of my insides.'

Daisy sat on the edge of the bed.

Rose looked frail, her face pale against the white coverlet. 'It's so good of you to come.'

'To be truthful,' Daisy said, 'I came in search of Prudence. There's no sign of her in the big cabin. No one seems to have seen her since early in the storm. I hoped I might find her here with you.'

Behind them Rose's husband Miles filled the doorway. 'I'm afraid my wife has been violently seasick. She is not used to such turbulence.'

Daisy rose to her feet. 'The storm has affected many in this way.'

'But not everyone,' Standish said, looking at her frankly.

His disconcerting eyes disturbed Daisy and she averted her gaze. The ship took another downward lurch and seemed to hang suspended before righting itself. Rose let out a little scream and Daisy fell forward. She had carefully avoided falling towards Standish and she found herself again sitting on Rose's bed.

'This can't go on much longer,' she said, referring to the storm. 'There must be an end to it soon.'

'It can,' Standish said firmly, 'and it will.'

Daisy looked up at him, surprised at his blunt contradiction. She was merely attempting to reassure his wife.

'I must ask of what assistance I can be to the ship's master,' he told Rose importantly. Then he paused and looked at Daisy again. 'I would like you to stay here, Miss Mason, and take care of my wife. She needs to have someone with her. At least, until the storm is over.'

'I'm sorry,' Daisy said. 'I came here in search of my maid.'

'Your maidservant?' he said, his eyebrows raised.

'She is missing from our quarters in the main cabin. I can't think where she can be.'

'I hardly think the whereabouts of your maidservant is of greater importance than the welfare of ...'

Rose tried to raise herself. 'I'm all right, Miles, really I am. Daisy must find the girl.'

'Why? Why must she find the girl?' her husband demanded scornfully. 'She's probably holed up somewhere with one of the servant boys.'

It was not the sort of remark a gentleman should make in the presence of ladies but Miles Standish, apparently, was not always a gentleman.

Daisy regarded him with an undisguised contempt. 'My maidservant is my responsibility, Captain Standish. Your wife is not. What's more, my maidservant is barely fifteen years old and she is pregnant.'

Standish laughed shortly. 'Then she can't come to much harm, can she?'

'Miles!' Rose was embarrassed by her husband's cavalier attitude.

'My presence is, I am sure, required on the upper deck,' he said curtly. 'I shall expect you to comply with my ... er ... *request*, Miss Mason, and stay with my wife until I return.'

With that he turned on his heel and left them alone. Rose made an effort and sat up straight. 'Please don't think ill of him, Daisy. I think he must be very tired.'

'The gentry always treat ordinary folk as unimportant,' Daisy said. 'It's as if Prudence doesn't matter. She could have been swept overboard for all he cares.'

'That isn't true,' Rose said in defence of her husband.

'I'm afraid it is, Rose. These people are all the same. People like your husband are brought up to believe in privilege....' Daisy stopped short, remembering that she was supposed to be one of 'these people'.

Rose looked at her curiously, then a wan smile eased her pale face. 'Don't you worry about me,' she said. 'Go and find Prudence. She can't be far away. And we must think of the baby.'

Daisy appeared to hesitate as if she was torn two ways. But she was not thinking of Rose. She was wondering how much of herself she had given away.

'I'll be all right, Daisy. Truly I will.'

Daisy looked at Rose vacantly for a moment then she nodded, smiled encouragingly and left to resume her search. Prudence was not likely to be 'holed up' with some servant boy as Standish had suggested, but her absence was worrying. Braving the storm, Daisy clung once again to the lifeline and made her way back.

Near the entrance to the main cabin a small terrier was tethered to a post. Each time a large wave exploded on the deck the bedraggled little dog was swept over the edge through a gap in the bulwark. Shivering and wet it clung on, eyes wild, and each time succeeded in scrambling back.

As Daisy watched, waiting for a lull in the storm, a young man she recognized as the ship's carpenter, John Alden, staggered out on to the sloping, windswept deck, untied the knot and picked up the whimpering pet. Again choosing her moment, Daisy dashed from her lifeline and the young carpenter held open the door.

'You shouldn't be out there, miss,' he said, following her inside. 'And nor should this little fellow.'

Daisy smiled up at him and took the wet, frightened dog. 'I'll find his owner,' she promised. She liked John Alden. He was a simple man, good at his work, a carpenter not a seaman, and he was patently honest and trustworthy. As Pru said, 'A nice person.' He was usually cheerful, too, but now he seemed downcast. 'What is it, John?' she asked. 'What's wrong?'

He looked embarrassed. 'I was worried,' he said. 'About Priscilla. I been up to her cabin to see if she was safe an' ol' Mr Mullins gave me a rare tickin' off.'

'Did you see Priscilla?'

'Oh no, miss. He wouldn't let me see her. I said I'd come to see if she was safe an' he said yes, she was safe from the storm an' safe from ruffians like me. I mean, I don't know what he thinks I am.'

Daisy laid a hand on his arm. 'It's what Priscilla thinks that matters, John. Not what her father thinks.'

'Her father doesn't like me an' I don't know why. Probably thinks I'm not good enough for her.'

'You're as good as any man, John Alden,' Daisy told him. 'And better than most.'

'Thank you, miss,' he said simply. Then he held the little dog's chin and looked into its still frightened eyes. 'You're in good hands now, my friend.'

Daisy found the owner who, with a sick wife and two small children to care for, had forgotten about his dog. One of the children, a small girl, took the terrier gratefully and, wet as it was, held it tightly in her arms. Maurice Tinker was still mopping up water.

'Prudence,' Daisy said. 'Has she been back?'

Maurice looked as worried now as Daisy. 'I haven't seen her. I just tried to go out on deck to look for her but I was told to get back inside.'

'Didn't she say where she was going or ... or anything?'

'She was scared and sort of sick-looking. Like I said, it was awful in here and she said she just had to get out. She said something about a place of her own....'

Towards the forward end Mrs Carver and Miss Minter, together with other members of their church, were kneeling on the wet floor. Their pale faces almost hidden in swathes of dark clothing, they looked like bundles of rags. They were praying and the low rumbling sound of prayer filled the cabin. It was just like a church service, thought Daisy. Then she realized it *was* a service. It was conducted by John Carver, those in prayer responding to his invocations. Daisy turned to leave and was confronted by Miles Standish.

'Excuse me,' she said and she walked to the door.

A place of her own! Of course! Daisy knew now where to look. Why hadn't she thought of it before?

'Miss Mason.' Standish had followed her. 'My wife....'

'Your wife is well able to take care of herself,' Daisy told him and she went out again into the night.

Sliding on the watery deck she grabbed the lifeline and hauled herself level with the narrow entrance to the spiral stairway. Two, three, four wet steps down. The tiny landing, the raised recess, away from the crashing waves and out of harm's way. This was where Prudence spent her most private moments. This was her own secret place. And sure enough this was where she was.

She was sitting quite still, her head against the trap door of the hatch, her eyes half-closed, and she was startled to see Daisy. 'Oh, miss! Did you want me? I was scared with the storm....'

'It's all right,' Daisy said. 'Can I come in?'

Prudence made room and Daisy squeezed in beside her. 'I know it's your own secret place,' Daisy said with a smile, 'but perhaps you'll allow me to stay for a while. At least, until the storm is over.'

17

The poop was deserted, exposed as it was to the full force of the gale. Captain Jones, his first mate Mr Clarke and Pat Ellis were in a huddle just below on the partly sheltered waist deck. The Irishman had been down in the first hold with Will Trefor securing the shifting freight when just before midnight the ship had gone into one of its more prolonged downward curves. As it hung suspended there had been a moment when, side on to a massive swell, it seemed certain to keel over. Women and children screamed and even experienced seamen gripped any fixture close to hand and held on grimly, fearing the worst. Families clung together, lips moved in silent prayer and many believed the end was nigh. It was then that throughout the vessel there was an ominously long drawn-out creaking of timber and a resounding snap was heard above the storm.

The captain was aware that the gale-force winds were straining the top hamper and putting the seams of the vessel under excessive pressure. This was causing leaks between decks and a steaming dampness that only added to the discomfort of his passengers. Now one of the ship's main beams had bowed almost to breaking point and a substantial crack had appeared. Ellis had reported to the captain at once. Captain Jones had then sent his first mate to investigate and Mr Clarke had confirmed the extent of the damage. As the three conferred they were joined now by the second mate Mr Coppin. In a trough of mounting waves the ship lay hove to, water flooding the decks and seeping in through every open seam. Some members of the crew, Mr Coppin told them, were not behaving as well as they should. They had been quick to grasp the seriousness of the situation and their anxiety had soon conveyed itself to the passengers.

Captain Jones was anxious not to alarm his passengers, especially the women and children. He felt they had suffered enough. Racked with aches and pains, gagging on foul air, they were wet, cold, hungry and thoroughly miserable, and he knew it would take very little to set off a dangerous panic. He also knew he could not hope to keep the extent of the damage from them for long.

The rolling ship had somehow come out of that heart-stopping lurch and riding high on the black, moon-streaked ocean with cascades of water streaming from all sides was back on an even keel. In the main cabin and below decks passengers were murmuring darkly. They wanted to know exactly what was happening.

Several of the men converged on John Carver and his closest associates demanding that yet another deputation of elders should confront the captain. There were questions that must be answered. What terrible damage had befallen the ship? Could it be repaired? Were the captain and his crew still in control? Had the ship been blown off course? Were they lost and how much longer would the storm continue? How much longer could the ship hold out?

Carver appeared alone and uninvited on the waist deck to inform Captain Jones of the serious drop in morale and the deteriorating situation among the passengers. The captain decided he could allay their fears no longer and invited Carver and a small committee of elders to assemble, along with senior members of his crew, by his quarters under the poop. There he told them the true position.

The ship, as they knew, had laboured with great difficulty, taking a great deal of water on board and suffering a sustained battering from the elements. Unfortunately one of the main beams which held the ship's hull in position had cracked under the strain and could at any moment break in two. If this happened, Captain Jones told them, the ship would slowly begin to disintegrate. There was little he could do, he explained, but steer the ship into the wind and hope to ride out the storm.

The leading churchmen – Carver, Brewster, Bradford – had been joined by a younger, serious-looking man named Edward

Winslow. Together with Mr Mullins, Priscilla's father, and Stephen Hopkins, Elizabeth's husband, representing the non-church passengers, they all agreed with the captain that they should do their utmost to foster an atmosphere of calm. Carver, for the churchmen, announced that they would continue with prayers in the main cabin and a service would be held in which the Lord would be asked to watch over the little ship and all aboard her. The service would be open to everyone, including the crew. Having little faith in the Almighty some of the sailors present turned away to scoff at this but Captain Jones rebuked them. He wanted his passengers to be kept calm and he didn't care how it was done.

The *Mayflower* had sailed, the ship's officers agreed, as near as they could say, about half-way across the Atlantic. Captain Jones admitted to these leading passengers he was now by no means sure of his position. The first and second mates pointed out that the prevailing winds and the main currents were running strong in an easterly direction. Some of the more experienced members of the crew, they said, felt it would be wiser, therefore, to give up and try to make it back to England. The storm showed little sign of abating and there were no safe havens within striking distance. Staying on course or even trying to hold the position they had they would face very heavy odds.

If they headed for home, Mr Clarke said, the closer they got to England the more likely they were to run into a friendly ship. They might even find one of the main trading lanes with the chance of meeting several ships. They might then be relieved of some of their passengers and escorted safely home. Going forward they faced only the unknown. There would be no friendly welcome even if they succeeded and the possibility, if not the probability, of starvation in a hostile land caught in the grip of a bleak winter.

But there was also a strong feeling that they should carry on – not least among the crew. Most of the ordinary seamen were not cushioned by guarantees. If they failed to fulfil their contracts there would be nothing for them and their earnings, in some cases, were urgently awaited by the wives and families they had left behind. Debts had been incurred. There were loans to be repaid. For some of the passengers, too, the prospect of a return to England was grim. Having sold everything they owned to finance their emigration they would be faced with destitution.

The arguments ranged back and forth. Some, having come this far, were prepared to risk their lives. There was no saying they would make it back to England, they argued. If they headed for home and were swept too far off course they might be picked up by Spaniards, their goods confiscated, their fate unknown. Worse still, they might run into one of a number of pirate ships said to be operating east of the Azores. Yet there were those, mainly among the crew, who believed the dangers which lay ahead were far too great. The decision, finally, after he had heard all sides rested with Captain Jones.

The captain brought the little conference to an end with the promise of prompt and decisive action. A great deal, he said, would depend on the extent of the damage. True to his word, as soon as the meeting broke up, he summoned the young carpenter, John Alden, and together with his senior officers they went down to the hold.

John had been engaged as a cooper but his training as a carpenter had endowed him with skills so obviously superior to those of the ship's joiner, who was really a sailor with a little knowledge of woodwork, that he had been called upon to carry out all of the more intricate tasks. The breaking up of the shallop had been largely supervised by John and it was done in such a manner that it would not be too difficult to put together again. It was John the captain looked to now.

By lantern light they saw that a main cross beam that buttressed the centre mast as it passed through the waist deck had cracked where it was bolted to the mast and was sagging at the break. Anticipating a call from the captain John had already studied the damage and planned a method of repair.

It so happened – the churchmen believed miraculously and by the grace of God – that a giant jack had been shipped along with the rest of the settlers' cargo. An accessory to the printing press William Brewster and others had installed and operated in exile, it had come from Holland on the *Speedwell*. It was a new piece of equipment, something Brewster couldn't bear to leave behind. One day, he hoped, he would have another printing press and the jack would have its uses. Others saw it as a practical aid to jacking up and careening the boats they planned to build so no objections had been raised and he had been allowed to bring it along. It was to prove their saviour.

The beam on one side of the mast was firm and undamaged. John proposed to set the jack beneath the break, cut a strong prop long enough to reach from the jack to the beam and try to force the beam back into position by working the jack. Then he would bind a strong splint across the break and put a permanent prop in place, lashed to the mast. With the upper deck reinforced where the mast came through and secured to the beam below the new structure should be sound enough to take the pressure of the mast.

Almost before John had finished outlining his plans Captain Jones had authorized the bringing up of the jack. John went to work at once and there was no shortage of willing helpers. All night long they toiled until, as the first light broke on the horizon, the beam was bound and secured and the damage repaired.

This done, attention was turned to the various leaks in the hull. Fortunately none turned out to be serious, although they had caused a good deal of discomfort below decks. For the next couple of days, John said, if the ship was held steady and the water was baled he would plug the leaks temporarily. Then, when the weather eased he would make them good on a more permanent basis.

As the young man returned to his bunk to sleep what the captain called 'the sleep of the just', passengers and several crew members crowded into the first hold to marvel at the feat of engineering he had accomplished. Among them Pat Ellis found himself standing close to Mr Mullins who had watched the young carpenter retire modestly to the acclaim of all present.

'Remarkable!' Mr Mullins murmured. 'Quite remarkable!'

Aware of Mr Mullins' attitude to John and aware, too, that Mr Mullins considered himself on a higher intellectual plane than most ordinary mortals, a serous thinker who more often than not had his head in a book, Ellis said with a smile, 'There are times when the skill and knowledge of a practical man are worth centuries of poets and philosophers.'

Encouraged by the repair and as the wind had dropped slightly, Captain Jones brought the *Mayflower* round towards the west with the declared intention of 'going on'. But scarcely had the ship resumed its voyage than it was tossed and buffeted again in a suddenly raging sea. The wind shrieked and whined in the rigging and large greyish white waves lashed the bulkhead and soaked through the already wet decks to the cabins and holds below.

Day after day the galley fires were washed out and there were no hot meals to relieve the misery. Again and again, after a relatively calm morning, a storm blew up and the sea raged so violently against the stricken vessel that the captain was compelled to take in every stitch of canvas. Once more the ship was allowed to drift, helpless and barely under control. Buffetted and beaten by towering waves, rolled over as far as the gunwales and thrown high in the water only to pitch forward in a frightening, roller-coaster dive the little ship shook and rattled her passengers like pebbles in a tin.

In the main cabin and in all the enclosed spaces the need to keep out the seeping water blocked out the fresh air, too, and in all the congested areas the atmosphere was foul. Unwashed bodies, stale clothing, the stench of urine, the soiled garments of babies and small children and the reek of dried vomit made breathing almost unbearable. For the sake of their lungs many were forced to risk the hazards of the open deck.

It was at the height of this second onslaught from the storm that the young manservant, John Howland, with the permission of his employer Mr Carver, offered his services to the captain. With several members of the crew laid low by sickness or injury all extra hands, provided they were young and agile, were welcome. Young Howland was at once despatched to check some fittings that appeared to be working loose. But no sooner had he begun to climb a grating to take a closer look than a huge swell lifted the nose of the ship well clear of the water and he was caught off balance. With nothing to cling to he was thrown overboard and he fell with a scream, his arms flailing.

At that moment the halyards from the topsail were blown outwards in the following wind and by the greatest good fortune young Howland's hand was brushed by a passing strand. In an incredibly opportune reflex action he grasped it tight and held fast and as the halyards ran out he was carried deep under the surface of the waves. But he held on, faced wth certain death by drowning should he let go.

Young Howland's luck was certainly in. His plight had been spotted from an upper deck and the cry went up at once, 'Man overboard!' Those near at hand rushed to halt the rapidly uncoiling rope and bravely, sliding and falling in the slush of the heaving lower deck, they hung on until the young man was hauled to the surface. Gasping for breath and half-drowned he was drawn alongside with a boat-hook by a man called Thomas English, the master of sails and rigging, and as the roll of the ship brought him near and to within their grasp several pairs of hands reached out.

The cries of 'Man overboard!' had brought Daisy Mason and Prudence from their refuge and to the head of the rain-lashed spiral steps. It looked to them that a seaman had been thrown into the sea and was clinging for his life to a slim line of rope. They watched in alarm as members of the crew battled to bring him close to where their outstretched hands could haul him back.

Daisy recognized the bobbing head in the water, the

straw-coloured hair darkened now by the grey Atlantic. He was one of the Carvers' servants, one of Pru's former colleagues. The ship lurched and Daisy held Pru tight.

'Isn't he one of the Carvers' men?' she yelled above the whistling and howling of the wind.

'It's John. John Howland,' Prudence yelled back.

A man with a second boat-hook had a grip on the young servant's clothing and was hauling him in. He was unconscious. Perhaps he had already drowned. Certainly the question foremost on the lips of his rescuers and those watching from the decks was: is he still alive?

Daisy relaxed her grip on Prudence as the saturated bundle was hauled aboard the lower deck. Howland was Pru's friend, the only one of the Carvers' servants who had cared for her and she was concerned now for his safety. Foolishly she started down a rope ladder and Daisy grabbed at her clothing to restrain her. But the ship lurched yet again and Pru slid downwards, lost her footing and fell the rest of the way. As she hit the deck below she was hurled against a stanchion. Then the ship rode a huge wave and on the slanting boards Pru's inert body began to slide in the fast-flowing foam towards an open rail.

Daisy saw the danger and screamed and from the quarter deck above a long body dropped down, fell in the slush of water and scrambled crab-fashion after the sliding girl. It was Will Trefor and with one arm around a post he gripped and held on to the unconscious maid. Someone threw him a line. He dragged the girl towards him by her clothing and tied the rope loosely under her arms to avoid putting pressure on her bulging stomach. Then he called out to his helpers and they hauled Pru's body towards them up the deck, the water swirling and eddying around her. Daisy watched open-mouthed. Pru was not moving. Was she just unconscious? And the baby? What about the baby?

Will Trefor was carefully hauling himself up the still sloping deck by way of the lifeline as Daisy clung to the foot of the rope ladder.

'Is she...?' Daisy began.

'Get back up there!' he ordered. 'Get back up and inside!'

'Is she all right?'

'Knocked out, that's all. She knocked her head.'

Three seamen were attending to John Howland. He was lying face down and one of the men was pressing heavily upon him to expel the sea water from his lungs. Others were carrying Prudence to the shelter of the first hold.

Will drew himself up beside Daisy, towering over her. 'What was she doing, for God's sake? A pregnant girl!'

'You saved her life,' Daisy told him.

'And damned near lost my own,' he said. 'Now get back to the cabin and stay there. And that's an order.'

Daisy faced him defiantly.

"Go on!' he said. 'Move! Out here you are a danger to the crew. We have enough to worry about without silly women getting in the way.'

She pushed him aside. 'I'm going to Prudence. With all you clever men around she might need a "silly" woman.'

18

The ship's doctor was a man called Giles Heale who did what he could for the wet and miserable passengers though he had few medical supplies. What was shipped at the outset had proved totally inadequate for his needs. He had nothing for upset stomachs, the most common complaint. His supply of settling powders had been used up in the first major outbreak of seasickness. And he was not and never had been a physician. He was a surgeon, a man who had once, after a shark attack in the Caribbean, successfully amputated a seaman's leg above the knee, without anaesthetic, and thus halted the onset of gangrene.

Unlike many ship's doctors who during the long hours at sea sought solace in mind-numbing insobriety, Dr Heale was no maudlin alcoholic. He had been chosen in the early days – when Captain Jones and the Company of Merchant Adventurers cared about not offending the church people and their elders – because he was a non-drinker. But now, his only antidote for all ills, including his own, came in small kegs of which there was still a good supply. Brandy was all he had to offer his patients.

On Dr Heale's instructions the seaman took Prudence from the hold to his own cramped quarters. Pru had recovered consciousness but she lay on the doctor's bunk, holding her stomach with both hands, her large eyes dark-ringed and sunken in their sockets, her small face deathly pale.

'John?' she asked weakly as Daisy appeared at the door.

'John is all right,' Daisy told her. 'Dr Heale has seen to him. It's you we are concerned with now.'

The doctor put a tin mug to Pru's lips. She tasted the brandy and shuddered but he made her gulp it down and she coughed as the fiery liquid hit the back of her throat. Dr Heale smiled and nodded as if his patient was now cured of whatever ailed her.

'She'll be all right,' he said. 'If you keep her warm.'

Prudence was wet from head to toe but there was no change of clothing to hand. Daisy looked at Dr Heale.

'There is little we can do,' he said defensively, 'until the storm subsides.'

Daisy turned him aside, away from Pru. 'What about the baby, Doctor? Will the baby be all right?'

Dr Heale frowned. He looked back at Prudence as if he hadn't realized she was pregnant. 'Oh, the baby! Oh, the baby should be all right. It's nice and warm in there, you know. The baby is better off than any of us.'

'But she took a nasty knock when she fell.'

'Unborn babies are very resilient,' he assured her. 'She'll be all right and so will the baby. You'll see. I'll take a look at her again when things calm down. See if we can spot the little mite kicking out.'

Daisy nodded. It was obvious he didn't know any more than she did.

'She can stay here,' he said. 'Have a little rest – and when she's feeling better you can take her back to her own bed.'

The long dark afternoon lengthened into evening and although the wind still whistled and howled through the rigging the swell of the ocean levelled off and waves no longer lashed the decks. There was no moon and with little light from the stars and no break on the surrounding horizon the sky hung low, an enormous black canopy over a sable sea. From the master's quarters below the poop came the yellow light of a swaying lantern where Captain Jones sat alone, guessing the position of his little ship and attempting to plot a course.

In the main cabin, now that the ship had regained a certain equilibrium it was possible to mop the floor of water. Territories were re-established. Families returned to their own spaces and Daisy returned to hers. The items she had hung from the bulwark were relatively dry. Daisy made a bed for Prudence and as she turned to go back to the doctor's quarters Will Trefor filled the makeshift doorway. Daisy's hand went instinctively to her hair.

He smiled down at her. 'Some ladies look even nicer when they're all windswept and wet.'

'I'm afraid I'm not one of them,' she said primly. 'The truth is, I'm a city girl at heart. I would like nothing better than to sit in a steaming hot bathtub then spend an hour with my hairdresser.' A city girl! Daisy checked herself. She had given a different account of herself to others and she wondered now how much Will Trefor knew or had guessed about her. 'At least, what I mean is, I would certainly like to be in the City right now. Preferably dining at The Queen's.'

Will listened with the slightly amused look he seemed to reserve for conversations with Daisy. 'If you and I ever get back to the old country I'll take you there. I promise! Dinner at The Queen's. A banquet!'

'And what will we have at this banquet?'

'We'll have whatever takes your fancy. Fish, fowl, the finest venison – anything you want. And if they haven't got it I shall insist they send out at once and get it.'

'Anything I want?'

'Anything at all.' He put the tips of his fingers to his lips and kissed them as if savouring some delectable dish. 'And the desserts....'

Daisy smiled wryly. 'Our just desserts, perhaps.'

But Will dismissed the interruption. 'And we will wash it all down with the finest wines the Queen's cellars can serve up.'

'Wine indeed!'

'We'll drink all night!'

Daisy shook her head. 'I don't think so. You seem to have forgotten I'm a lady. I am not one of your seamen's tavern drinking companions.' She threw him a look of disapproval. 'You show a distinct lack of respect. I will have respect, Mr Trefor. Especially from a lowly member of the ship's crew.'

'Daisy!' he protested, pretending to be hurt. Then more seriously, he added, 'I came to apologize for speaking to you in the way I did. But you and Prudence were foolish to venture out on deck....'

'Respect, Mr Trefor. I demand respect.'

As on that previous occasion he went down on one knee. 'I respect you more than any other woman on this ship, Daisy Mason. You have more ... more spirit, more courage, more character than all of these church people ...'

'I agree,' she said, cutting him short. 'But I am still a lady.'

He took her hand and held it to his lips. 'A fine lady. Believe me, Daisy, you have my total respect.'

'Good,' she said.

He let her hand drop and came to his feet. 'I only hope I can win back yours.'

'You saved my girl's life today,' she said. 'I will not forget that.'

'What about the baby?'

'Dr Heale thinks the baby will be all right. As he says, babies in the womb are well protected.'

'I hear he once cut a baby from a dead woman,' Will said. 'She'd fallen from a window and died instantly, but the baby was still alive.'

Daisy nodded. Dr Heale may be good with the knife, she thought, but he knew little more than she did when it came to careful nursing. The problem now was to keep Prudence warm. 'I must go,' she said. 'I want to bring Prudence back here, get her out of her wet clothing.'

Will stepped aside to allow her to pass. 'Perhaps I can help. I could carry her....'

'Thank you,' Daisy said and he followed her across the main cabin. 'Thanks to your friend Mr Ellis,' she told him, 'not all our things are wet. Mr Ellis gave me some nails....'

'What is there between you and Pat Ellis?' Will asked suddenly, in her wake.

Daisy stopped and looked back at him.

'Why is he so concerned about you? He treats you as if you were his own daughter. In fact, he told me he wished you were his daughter. He told me if ever I cause you any problems I'll have him to deal with.' He laughed. 'I've known Pat Ellis for a long time now yet there he was threatening me.'

'What kind of problem might you cause me, Mr Trefor?'

'That's what I asked him,' Will said. 'You know all about me. You even know all about me and Rose.'

Daisy nodded. 'And so does Captain Standish.'

Will merely smiled. 'Let us get one thing clear, Daisy. I knew Rose before Miles Standish ever set eyes on her. A fancy ceremony in a church can't cancel out what we meant to each other. Rose is mine – not his.'

'I must hurry,' Daisy said and he followed. 'I must see Prudence. I must find a way to keep her warm.'

'There are many ways of keeping a girl warm.'

Again Daisy looked back at him, a warning in her look.

'I mean, body warmth is what's required,' he said, 'and another person's body warmth is best.'

She stopped and eyed him suspiciously, ready to pounce on the merest hint of a smile. But he seemed serious. 'Body warmth?'

'Take off her wet clothing,' he said. 'Dry her out, put her to bed naked and find someone to get in beside her. They must be naked, too, and they must hold her tight. Hug her until she's warm. It's the best way there is. It could be the *only* way, under the circumstances.'

Daisy looked sceptical.

'She's a pretty little thing,' he said. 'Shouldn't be any shortage of volunteers.'

'Prudence is eight months pregnant,' Daisy reminded him. 'She is in danger of losing her baby.'

Will faced her seriously. 'If you want to keep that girl warm then put her to bed, take off your own clothes, climb in beside her and hold her in your arms.'

'I couldn't do that.'

'Why not? A sailor would do it for another sailor.'

'I've heard about sailors,' Daisy said flatly.

Will laughed, then serious again he said, 'It's true. Believe me. It's something we were taught at Dartmouth.'

Daisy could see the sense in what he was saying. But she didn't know if she could do it. As they left the main cabin they were met by Maurice Tinker.

'Pru, Miss Mason,' he said anxiously. 'Is she all right? I heard she....'

'I think so, Maurice,' Daisy told him. 'The doctor has seen her.'

He nodded and went on his way.

'If you don't think you can do it yourself,' Will said, 'why not ask him? She'd be safe enough with him.'

Mr Coppin came down the ladder into the crew's mess. One of the booms required re-roping and now the swell had calmed a little he wanted the job done. Dyke was hunched in a corner, squatting down on his huge haunches. Will Trefor was bending over him.

'I want two men,' Mr Coppin said.

'Aye, aye, sir,' Will responded. 'But I'm afraid Seaman Dyke is not well. I'll go up and find someone else.'

'I'm all right I tell you.' Dyke was clearly irritated at the suggestion that he might not be fit. But his face was grey and pallid with a hint of green about his hairy gills. 'I'm as well as the next man.'

'You don't look well.' Mr Coppin agreed with Will. 'We can get someone else.'

Dyke stood up, swaying slightly. He was fit and he would prove it. Admitting to weakness was for lesser men. 'I'm all right, sir. Nothin' wrong with me.'

Mr Coppin looked at Will and Will shrugged. 'Well, if you're sure,' the mate said. 'Maybe a bit of fresh air will do you good.'

Dyke glared at him. 'Fresh air? I don't need no fresh air. I ain't seasick. I ain't never bin seasick in me life. No, sir.'

'All right,' Mr Coppin said. 'I believe you. If you say you're well enough, then all right. But somebody has to go up and rope that boom – and go now.'

'Aye, aye, sir,' Dyke said. 'We're on our way.'

Will Trefor climbed the ladder and Dyke lumbered up after him. Will knew that Dyke was not well but he also knew there was no arguing with the big man. Probably it was something he'd eaten. For the last few days there had been no hot meals and a number of uncooked and suspect dishes on offer. Yet Dyke had continued to devour anything that came his way.

The rain was still heavy, sweeping in long sheets across the empty decks with only the yellow glow from the swinging lantern below the poop and a pale, cloud-crossed moon. But it was easy to spot the loose spar with its flapping halyards. Will Trefor and Dyke climbed to the upper deck and edged out to grasp the wayward ropes. Several were loose and the two men set about securing them as correctly as they could in the poor light and the driving rain.

In charge of the store of firearms, Miles Standish had sought Captain Jones's permission to check on the gunpowder which was stored apart from the rest of the cargo. It might well have been damaged, he suggested, or washed away in the storm. With a seaman accompanying him he had checked the barrels and was pleased to return the padlock keys to the captain in the knowledge that the precious powder had come to no harm.

As he left the master's quarters Captain Standish was spotted by Dyke whose temper in concert with his stomach was in turmoil. Dyke had not forgotten the confrontation with Standish. In the presence of passengers in the main cabin Standish had humiliated him. There was a score to be settled here and Dyke saw his opportunity. Instead of tightening the ropes on a lower, secondary spar Dyke released it and with a malicious heave sent it swinging out across the upper deck. There was every chance it would knock Standish from the deck to serious injury below or even overboard. From behind Dyke in the darkness Will Trefor tried to warn him. 'Get down, man!'

Standish looked up, saw the danger and dropped to the deck. Will pushed ahead of Dyke, gripped the ropes and tried to haul the wayward spar back into place.

'Give me a hand!' he demanded of Dyke who, though still holding his bulging stomach, was laughing aloud.

Dyke hauled the spar in with him and together they secured it in position. Will looked at Dyke but Dyke merely moaned and gripped his stomach. Clearly he was in pain. It could have been an accident, of course. But Will didn't think so. Nor did Miles Standish.

Standish was still down on the deck, crouching warily. 'You men up there!' he yelled. 'What in God's name is going on?'

But there was no reply and as soon as he felt it was safe to do so Standish stormed back to the master's quarters. He would see about this. Someone had made a deliberate attempt to injure him.

Captain Jones had enough problems. He had turned his ship around and was now, he hoped, back on course. He couldn't wait to spot land, put these people ashore and head for home. They had caused him nothing but trouble. Yet he knew in his heart his ship was dangerously overloaded and his passengers were not entirely to blame. There were arguments on both sides. But, fair-minded though he was, with this little respite from the damaging storm, he was in no mood for further aggravation. It took all the patience he could muster to listen to Miles Standish.

'I am sure it was an accident,' was his first reaction.

'Damned dangerous accident.' Standish was still angry. 'I might have been killed.'

'I am sure it was an accident, Captain Standish,' he repeated, for once giving him his title. But Standish would not be placated and Captain Jones felt obliged to pull on a topcoat and go out on deck to investigate.

The rain was still lashing the storm-tossed ship and the respite was only relative. It was still black and wet and dangerous out on deck. Will Trefor had summoned help and Dyke, doubled up and in great pain, had been guided down. Nobody liked the man but, for all his great size and former strength, he seemed weak and vulnerable and he was undoubtedly sick. Will had stayed on the upper deck to finish coiling the overlap of halyard.

When Standish saw Will he stopped in his tracks and pointed an accusing finger. 'You!'

Captain Jones intervened. 'Were you up there when this spar swung free, Trefor?'

'Yes, Cap'n,' Will admitted.

The captain liked Will Trefor. He was no trouble, a good and conscientious worker and a fine seaman. He obviously came from good stock, probably from a more elevated background than himself, and he was also something of a mystery man. But it was not Captain Jones's way to probe into the private affairs of the men he employed. If they could do the work they said they could do and if they were not habitual criminals then they were acceptable. Even Dyke, who had a foul mouth and too often upset his passengers, was a good man to have in a crisis.

'What happened?' he asked.

'You can see what happened,' Standish cut in. 'He tried to kill me.'

Will remained silent.

Captain Jones looked from one to the other, sensing the animosity beween them. Of Standish he asked, 'You know this man?'

'Unfortunately,' Standish answered, 'yes.'

The captain waited but neither man was prepared to elaborate. It appeared to be something personal to them and he had no wish to become involved. Nor did he wish to prejudge a member of his crew. This, too, was not his way. 'Is your work done?' he asked Will. 'Ropes secured?'

'Yes, sir.'

'Then go below now. I will deal with this matter in the morning.' To Standish he indicated that they should return to his cabin. 'Please....'

Standish glared at Will who simply swung a leg over the side and made his way down the ladder to the lower deck.

19

Down below in the crew's cramped quarters Dyke's condition had worsened. Too heavy for a hammock he normally rolled his bed out on the boards. That night he lay slumped in a corner, half-sitting, his huge legs splayed outwards, his gnarled head in his big hands. He was moaning so pitifully that even those members of the crew who feared and disliked him most felt sorry for him.

Pat Ellis was kneeling beside him, trying to soothe him with words but without success. Then when Will Trefor appeared Ellis went to him at once and took him aside. 'This is serious,' the Irishman said. 'The man's in agony. We better fetch Doc Heale. Dyke doesn't want him but I say we better get him anyway or it's a priest he'll be ...'

'There's not much Heale can do,' Will said. 'He's out of stomach pills and potions. All he has is brandy.'

'Better fetch him though. I reckon it's some kind of food poisoning.'

Will went over to Dyke and stooped to speak to him. 'Could you take a drink, Dyke old fellow? Might ease the pain a little.'

'Couldn't take a thing, Will. Me guts are fit to bust.'

'Has anything like this happened before?'

'Never as bad.' He rolled away from Will and turned his head to the wall, moaning low and so forlornly that others gathered round.

'It must be something he's eaten,' Will decided. 'What has he had? Does anyone know? It's the first thing the doctor will ask.'

'He ate that stew,' one of the men said, making a face. 'That 'orrible filthy stuff they sent down yesterday. No one wanted it. It was cold and mushy, never bin 'otted up 'cos all the fires were out. It was standing over on that locker all day. Bet there were cockroaches an' all sorts in it this mornin'. Didn't stop ol' Dyke though. He scoffed the lot.'

'Nah!' Dyke turned his head briefly, surprising them with the vehemence of his denial.

But others had seen him, too. He had grabbed the bowl of unappetizing hash and spooned it down, great mouthfuls of barely cooked meat, as he always did with whatever came his way. Perhaps he needed it, thought Will. Perhaps such a big man needed to be constantly stoked up. He certainly worked hard and he used up a lot of energy in the process. He also loved to demonstrate his considerable strength.

Dr Heale arrived with Pat Ellis and the group around Dyke broke up to allow the professional man room to work.

Ellis spoke quietly to Will. 'What have you bin up to?'

'You mean up there? The business with the boom?'

Ellis nodded, suppressing a smile. 'Tried to kill someone is what I hear.'

'It was Standish.' Will regarded him levelly. 'And it was not me.'

'What happened?'

'I'm not absolutely sure,' Will said. 'Dyke and I were up there securing some ropes on one of the middle spars. Dyke released a lower boom, it swung out and nearly took Standish with it. It might have been an accident. And it might not. I can't say for sure. But Standish went mad. Called in the captain.'

'Well, the word is it was you who tried to finish off Standish. And it doesn't look good, Will. Naturally, our military man will believe it was you.'

'I didn't do anything,' Will said. 'He can believe what the hell he likes.'

Dyke had stopped moaning. The doctor had insisted he swallowed some brandy but when he refused a second draught the doubters were at last convinced he was seriously ill.

'Try to keep him warm,' Dr Heale told those who were standing near. 'I know it's difficult with everything so wet, but I don't want him catching a fever.'

Several pairs of hands removed his clothing and the big man offered no resistance. He never wore anything under his jersey or pants and to strip him was a quick and simple operation. They dried him as best they could then wrapped him naked in a blanket – naked, that is, except for his woollen hat. Again he stretched out on the boards, wanting only to be left alone.

'How bad is it, Dr Heale?' Pat Ellis asked respectfully and the doctor drew him and Will Trefor aside.

'It's very bad,' the doctor said. 'But to be honest, I don't know what it is. Most likely it's some form of food poisoning. But it could be....' He hesitated then lowered his voice. 'Well, you've seen enough, I'm sure. You know as well as I do what it could be.'

'We've been at sea for weeks,' Ellis said. 'If Dyke had the plague it would have shown itself by now.'

The plague was common to London and the bigger cities at home, the result of overcrowded hovels, bad hygiene and the disease-carrying black rat. Once started it was impossible to combat, capable of engulfing and exterminating entire populations. The merest hint of its presence could create havoc and strike terror in the heart.

'Please,' Dr Heale begged, 'keep your voice down.'

'We have the conditions,' Will Trefor said quietly, 'for starting our own plague.'

'For all our sakes you must not say such things,' the doctor told him. 'I am speaking to you two in confidence. The plague could sweep through this little ship like a house fire. I can't say it is the plague, only that it could be. And I don't want to spread any rumours. You understand? People are frightened enough as it is. It could cause a panic.'

Dyke was mumbling incoherently. Again he held his stomach with both hands, writhing in agony. Then he let out a long, low, harrowing moan.

'I'm afraid I've done all I can here,' Dr Heale said. 'Perhaps it would be appropriate to summon a priest.'

'Why not?' Will agreed. 'If I know Dyke it'll make him sit up and fight.'

'Or lie down and die,' Ellis said.

There was no love for Dyke among the crew, only a compassion at the severity of his suffering. Among the passengers there was not even this. When the request went up to the main cabin for one of the church elders to administer the last rites there was a grim satisfaction among those he had tormented. The oldest of the churchmen, Mr Brewster, embarrassed by what he called their unworthy response, rebuked those who smirked, told them they should feel ashamed and promptly offered his services. No matter what his previous way of life had been, if the man was seriously ill and close to death he was entitled to make his peace with his Maker. Few of the passengers were so charitable. Some even laughed aloud when they heard the bully Dyke was rolling on the boards in agony. It served him right, they said. It was no more than he deserved.

Despite the doctor's assurance that Dyke's condition was not contagious those members of the crew who normally bunked down closest to Dyke moved a little further away. Inevitably someone had murmured the dreaded word 'plague', thus conjuring up the images of cartloads of emaciated corpses and the accompanying cries of 'Bring out your dead!' that so terrified the masses. There was little doubt that such an outbreak would bring a rapid and sorry end to the voyage. Inevitably, too, the tale of the plague ship sprang to the minds of many.

It was the old story of the merchant ship bringing passengers and cargo from the Far East, a ship upon which the plague had run riot. Most of the passengers and many of the crew had died and been consigned to the deep. A messenger, rowing ashore with a request for help, had been reviled, stoned to death, his body and his boat burned. The ship had been forced to seek harbour elsewhere, sailing from port to port in growing desperation. But the fearful news had travelled ahead of her and entry everywhere was denied. In one port a shot had been delivered across her bows and she had been forced to withdraw. Eventually all of those on board were dead, the ship was set alight and, after drifting aimlessly for several days, she sank off the coast of Brittany.

There were many variations of this story and countless embellishments. One was the oft-told tale that on calm nights, a few leagues out of Dinard, a ghost ship is sometimes seen, full-masted and ablaze from stem to stern. On deck, huddled close together, are the doomed passengers and crew, their faces white with eyeless sockets, their mouths opened wide in soundless screams, their hands outstretched in supplication as the blazing vessel glides silently from sight as eerily as she came.

The story of the plague ship may or may not have been true but such tales sent tremors of apprehension throughout the seafaring community. Already the more credulous members of the *Mayflower* crew were forecasting the worst. Yet, conscious of their fears, William Brewster approached Dyke's bedside with the offer of prayer and the heartfelt advice that he should ask the Almighty for the forgiveness of his sins. Dyke's reply was an incoherent mumble. The following morning, after a night of restless moaning, Dyke was dead.

He had suffered ominous symptoms: fever, abdominal pain, severe vomiting and diarrhoea. And in the end, as he tried to raise himself from his makeshift bed, he had collapsed shaking in a cold sweat and with ice-cold hands and feet. Dr Heale, in consultation with the captain and a passenger named Samuel Fuller, who was also a doctor, went to great lengths to make it known that Dyke had died simply of food poisoning and nothing else. There was no question of anything infectious and there was no cause for concern.

For all that the burial was hastily arranged. That same morning the huge body was rolled into a shroud made from six large flour sacks and, after a short service conducted by the captain with Mr Brewster reading the lesson, sent sliding to the bottom of the sea. Only a few members of the crew, those who had worked with Dyke, were present, Will Trefor and Pat Ellis among them.

As William Brewster murmured a prayer, his eyes raised to the clouded heavens, his psalter clutched to his breast, Pat Ellis said quietly, 'Somebody must have loved him once. Even if it was only his mother.'

'You think he had a mother?' Will said in mock surprise.

But there was nothing malicious in their gentle banter. Others, unable to contain their glee, openly celebrated Dyke's death. And others, especially among the churchmen, swore it was a visitation, divine retribution from the sure hand of God.

For the first time in three days the fires were alight and the aroma of steaming broth drifted out from the galleys. Passengers queued for their share and their family's share. Daisy fed Prudence the first hot meal to pass her lips since some time before the storm and Pru responded. Daisy had slept or tried to sleep with Pru in her arms, her naked body enfolding the girl's. Some warmth had passed between them but Daisy was not by nature a warm-blooded girl herself and her efforts had not met with great success. Prudence was still a deathly pale colour and the tinge of blue around her lips worried Daisy.

Dr Heale's answer was more brandy but Daisy feared this was a little too strong for Prudence to take. It made her drowsy and, after the initial boost, even more in need of warmth. The broth, too, made little difference. Pru was still cold, shivering intermittently. Again Daisy undressed and climbed in under the blanket to hold her tightly in her arms. And it was only a few minutes later that there was a slight flurry at the curtain as if someone had entered their space.

Daisy was tired, dozing with her eyes closed and the sound in her semi-somnolent state was like the rustle of a bird, a hedge sparrow perhaps, taking flight. She opened her eyes and turned to look over her shoulder. Rose Standish was standing this side of the curtain.

Rose looked surprised, startled even, to see them in bed at midday, and a little embarrassed. She was holding a folded blanket. 'I brought this,' she began apologetically. 'For Prudence. For extra warmth.'

Daisy started to get up and remembered she was naked. Her bare leg was out from the bedclothes, her bare shoulder exposed. Her flaxen hair, lank and lifeless now from lack of care, had fallen across her face.

'I ... I thought it might help,' Rose said. 'It's dry.'

Daisy nodded and smiled but before she could stand up Rose had gone. She stepped out from under the blanket, tucked Prudence in and put the extra blanket over her. Then she dressed herself quickly in her still damp clothing. What on earth, she wondered, had gone through Rose's mind. She had looked quite shocked. Daisy pulled her dress straight, laughed quietly and spontaneously and thought poor Rose! What did she think they were doing? She would have to go along at once and explain. Prudence was asleep, breathing normally. She looked quiet enough, Daisy decided, and safe for now.

Out on the deck Daisy stood for a moment, holding on to a stanchion as the prow of the ship rose and fell. She wanted to compose herself and think of an opening, something perfectly natural and without apology, something that would explain to Rose what she had seen.

The sky was dark, a grey October sky, heavy with low cloud. She shivered as the raw wind whistled again through the rigging and pinned her damp clothing to her body. Why was it so dark in the early afternoon? Where was the sun?

She raised her pale face skyward and to her surprise there was a break in the clouds and a splash of sunlight splayed long, thin fingers that touched the white crests of the dark water, turning them red and orange and gold. She closed her eyes, welcoming the unexpected warmth with a smile – and watching her from a higher deck Will Trefor was caught, open-mouthed, and held entranced by her simple unadorned beauty.

Will's feelings towards Daisy Mason had been ambiguous from the start. As a young man on the dock at Southwark he had been drawn naturally to the unusually attractive girl at the upstairs window of the Ship Inn. Pat Ellis had confirmed his conviction that Daisy was no ordinary young woman and she had occupied his thoughts more frequently than he cared to admit. At the same time he had been constrained by his devotion to the pursuit of Rose Standish. Rose had become the focus of all the fire in his heart, his resolve to right the wrongs inflicted upon him and his family. She had been taken from him along with much else and he was determined to take her back. Through Rose he would settle a number of scores – though he had not given a thought to how Rose might feel.

And now, here was this girl. Daisy Mason. Strong, self-possessed, dignified, yet utterly feminine. After weeks at sea, cramped in confined quarters without adequate food and with little water to spare for the washing of bodies or clothing, enduring storms and sickness and despair, many of the passengers resembled corpses risen from the grave in a painting of the Day of Resurrection. Yet, amongst all this, the girl known as Daisy Mason looked like an alabaster saint.

He swung down a rope ladder to drop before her. With only the barest hint of a smile, Daisy eyed him warily.

'How is Prudence?' he asked politely.

'A little better,' she told him.

'Did you do as I suggested?'

'Yes, Will Trefor,' she said coolly. 'I did as you suggested. I took off all of my clothing and I tried to warm the poor girl. But I'm afraid it made little difference.'

'Strange,' he said. 'Your body warmth should have made a lot of difference.'

'I don't think my body warmth, as you call it, can be all that warm.' She looked up at him coyly. 'And I don't think it's a subject I should be discussing with someone I barely know.'

'It works, Daisy. Believe me, it works.' There was a light in his eyes now, a compulsion to cross the bounds of propriety – a defence, perhaps, against the danger of taking her too seriously. He smiled and added, 'I'll show you if you like.'

Primly Daisy averted her eyes. 'What on earth are you suggesting, Mr Trefor?'

'I suggest we make a bed somewhere,' he said with a grin. 'We take off all of our clothing and you allow me to ... er ... warm you up a little.'

'Out of my way, you insolent man!' She pushed him aside, but she was not entirely displeased. Even if he was not treating her as a lady should be treated he obviously found her attractive. Then as she went on her way the thought occurred to her that he would not dare to say such a thing to some women. She frowned as his laugh followed her along the deck and her cheeks were burning as she approached Rose's cabin.

Daisy wanted to explain to Rose Standish about body warmth. She stood for several seconds at the cabin door, unsure of what to say, where to begin. Priscilla Mullins's parents entered the passage and she stepped aside to allow them to pass. Mr Mullins acknowledged her presence with a curt nod and his wife smiled weakly at her. Then, as they entered their own cabin, Mrs Mullins glanced back as if in response to some remark her husband had made.

There was a movement inside Rose's cabin and Daisy summoned up the courage to knock lightly. She wanted to have a quiet chat with Rose, nothing more. It had not occurred to her that Miles Standish might be in and she was surprised when he opened the door.

'Ah!' he said and over his shoulder he informed his wife, 'It appears we have a visitor, dear.'

Rose was sitting on the narrow bed she shared with her husband. She looked ill, her skin taut and pale, her dark eyes sunken, her hair like a judge's black cap. With a wan smile she came unsteadily to her feet and invited Daisy in.

20

'Rose,' Daisy began, concerned at Rose's appearance.

'A little late to be calling now, is it not?' Miles Standish hovered behind her. 'My wife needed you at the height of the storm, Miss Mason. Not now, when a measure of tranquillity has been restored.'

'My duty lay elsewhere,' Daisy told him curtly.

'Oh yes?' His chin rose as he confronted her. 'You find the needs of a servant girl more pressing than the sickness of a lady? People like us must maintain our position and there are certain things we will do well to remember. A lady is a lady: a servant is a servant.'

'The girl needed me,' Daisy said, angry now. 'Mrs Standish did not.'

Rose was embarrassed. 'Miles, darling, please.'

'My wife was sick....'

'Rose was simply seasick, like most of the other passengers. The girl is pregnant. She had a fall and we were extremely concerned – not just for her but for her baby.'

'How is she?' Rose asked. 'And the baby?'

'She's resting right now,' Daisy said. 'She must be kept warm ...'

'Pregnant,' Miles Standish said with distaste. 'Who in his right mind would bring a pregnant servant girl on a jaunt like this? I would have thought you would have known better.'

'Daisy didn't bring the girl,' Rose told him. 'She took her over from the Carvers. I told you about it, Miles. Daisy didn't know the girl was pregnant.'

'I see.' Standish nodded thoughtfully. To Daisy he said, 'In that case, if I were you I'd give her back. If you took her on in good faith and only discovered her condition later I'd say you were entitled to give her back. No question about it. She is not your responsibility.'

'Give her back?' Daisy looked at him askance. 'The poor girl doesn't belong to me. I can't *give her back*. I'm afraid I was not brought up to treat people as possessions.'

'Really?' Miles Standish was offended. 'And how *were* you brought up, Miss Mason?'

'Miles!' Rose admonished him.

'I think I should leave, Rose,' Daisy said, 'before I say something we might all regret.'

But Standish was not deterred. 'My wife,' he went on, 'has told me of your friendship with the Duke.'

Daisy didn't like the stress he put on the word friendship. She looked him squarely in the eye, challenging him to say more.

'You know him well, I understand.'

'Well enough,' she said.

Fortunately Daisy's Duchess, over a long period, had told her a good deal about her friend the Duke and his family. She had actually seen the Duke's wife and his two small daughters in the park.

'You will know his two younger brothers, Tom and Harry.'

'My acquaintance is with the Duke's lady wife.'

'And his sister Melanie?'

'I know his two small daughters.'

'Ah yes!' Standish said. 'Beautiful children. So like their mother, don't you think? The lovely Isabella.'

Again Rose was embarrassed. 'Miles! Daisy is my friend. She did not come here to be interrogated. She came to see *me*.'

'After seeing to her servant, no doubt.'

'What Daisy does with her servant is her own affair.'

Daisy glanced sharply at Rose, but the remark was plainly innocent.

Miles Standish bowed slightly and smiled. 'Of course,' he said. 'I'm sorry. I had no right to speak to you in that way. I was, perhaps, over-anxious for the welfare of my wife.'

He held Daisy's gaze just a little longer than was necessary and Daisy felt there was something more than a mere apology in his expression. Despite his often abrasive manner, he was a handsome and attractive man. Even his impulsive and fiery approach was not without charm. Daisy felt drawn to him and later, on reflection, she wondered if, as with Will Trefor, she would find all well-bred, arrogant gentlemen attractive. And yet again she wondered why a pale slip of a girl like Rose Standish should have such a hold on the affections of two such men.

Standish decided he would take a walk on deck and Rose was left to restore the friendly relatonship she felt her husband had damaged. Her seasickness and subsequent debility had left her

pale and wan, even more fragile-looking than before, a poor
specimen beside Daisy in her apparently robust health.

'Don't you ever get seasick, Daisy?' she asked when they were
alone.

Daisy laughed and shook her head. 'I think I must have an iron
constitution or something. When I was quite young I worked in a
hospital. I must have developed an immunity to most common
ailments. Certainly the sight of someone vomiting doesn't affect
me as much as it seems to affect some people.' She gripped her
lower lip in her teeth. Had she again given too much of herself
away? 'I ... I've just been lucky, I suppose.'

'You worked in a hospital?'

'My mother thought I ought to see the inside of such places,' she
lied. 'I didn't really work there. It was a convent hospital and I
sometimes helped the nurses on the wards.'

'How interesting!' Rose said with obvious sincerity. 'I wish my
mother had allowed me to do something like that.'

Daisy guessed that Rose had led a very sheltered and restricted
life. It was surprising that Will Trefor had ever been allowed to
spend time alone with her.

'I would have loved to have done something like that,' Rose
went on. 'But I was never allowed to mix with ordinary people. I
think it's a great mistake, don't you, to shelter young ladies too
much? Although, I suppose, in a way it was because I had never
been allowed to do anything or go anywhere outside my own
family circle or away from people of my own kind that I was so
willing to come with Miles on this voyage. It was the sense of
adventure, the promise of pastures new.

'I could have waited for Miles to establish himself in the New
World and then send for me. That's what my parents wanted,
especially my father. But it was my chance to escape. I'd been
protected and cossetted all my life and I was eager to get away.
But I'm afraid I'm not too well equipped for what lies ahead.'
Rose looked at Daisy with frank and open admiration. 'You seem
– I don't know – so much more capable than I am.'

'In many ways,' Daisy said, 'I, too, have led a sheltered life.'
But she didn't want to discuss her own background. She turned the
conversation back to Rose. 'I'm surprised you were able to spend
so much time with Will Trefor.'

Rose laughed nervously. 'We were children. Our family estates
adjoined each other. and there were other children. We were
rarely alone together. My younger sister was with us most of the
time and Will's two cousins. It was just that one day when I was

sixteen and Will was nearly eighteen and we knew he would be going away to college he told me he loved me. He said I must say I loved him and promise I would never love anyone else.'

'And you promised?'

'I was sixteen,' she protested. 'I didn't *know* anyone else. I hadn't even met Miles.' Her voice softened as she thought back to those distant summers. 'It was Cheshire – the trees and the meadows and the lake, the whole lovely flat countryside. You could see for miles, away into the distance. One way there was nothing but sunlit fields and little shady woods. The other way lay the village and all the tiny dwellings huddled around the church. You could tell the time of day by the cows blocking the lane outside our gates every morning and every evening. It was our own enchanted land. Anything we wanted to happen could happen there.

'Will had a tutor, a tall thin man who came to the hall every afternoon and when we saw him going back down the path to the village we would run across the fields and Will and his cousins would run to meet us. We had a den, our own special place by the lake where our land met theirs. We were children, Daisy. We'd always known each other. It was as if we were related.'

'Will told me you and he were inseparable.'

Rose threw her a sidelong glance. 'Inseparable?' She laughed. 'Well, I don't know. I was certainly not with him when he got into trouble with the gypsies. Will and one of his cousins were caught in the woods with two of the gypsy girls and there was a terrible row. A great band of gypsy men marched on the Hall where Will and his family lived. There was nearly a riot.'

'What happened?'

'Will's father met them at the gate and it was all smoothed over somehow. He was such a lovely, charming man. I suppose he talked to them nicely and gave them a few pieces of silver – something like that. Will was under a cloud for weeks but I suspect his father was secretly amused by it all.'

'Young men do these things,' Daisy agreed, 'and they get into trouble. It's nothing new. But what Will did for you, Rose, that was different. He deserted his ship and he was not just an immature young man. He was an officer of His Majesty's Navy. If the naval authorities ever catch up with him he'll be in serious trouble and it isn't something that can be smoothed over. It won't be a matter of giving some gypsy a few pieces of silver. He'll be court-martialled. And he did it for you.'

'Oh, Daisy!' Rose was tired now. 'You don't understand. We

were just children. We lived in a world of our own. In those days Will wanted to be a poet wandering the country, living close to nature and writing love poems. It was all so different then. It was our childhood. We believed in fairy tales and dreams that came true and people who lived happily ever after. But, of course, life is not like that. Dreams very rarely come true and if they do it's not always in the way you hoped they would. People like us, people like Will – we have no excuse. We must do what we know is right, what is best.'

'Best for who?' Daisy asked.

'In families like ours,' Rose insisted, 'one must make sacrifices. We must go where our duty lies, not where our hearts want to take us.'

Daisy had a glimpse of Rose's world, a world to which she could never belong. Membership was registered at birth and from then on, through all the impressionable years, the little members were sedulously honed by circumstance and design. It was not difficult to break out in later life and join the real world, but it was virtually impossible to break in. Even by marriage. No matter how rich or famous, a husband or wife from outside the system would always remain an outsider. Yet Daisy didn't envy Rose and she couldn't dislike her. Rose was the kind of person who would be liked and accepted at any level of society.

'I'm married now,' Rose said, 'and I love my husband.'

'And you don't love Will?' Daisy asked.

Rose smiled sadly and, though her smile momentarily lit her face, she looked even more frail. 'I can't say that, Daisy. Will is a part of me, a part of my past.'

'Yet you love your husband?'

'I believe it's perfectly possible to love two men at the same time, don't you?'

'I believe,' Daisy said carefully, 'that it's possible to choose any one of many men and live your life quite happily, faithful only to him, to bear his children, to stay with him until death, yet never really love him at all. I see that all around me. But it's not for me. I intend to wait until I find the one man, the *only* one.'

'And if you find him, how will you know?'

'I'll know,' she said. 'He may not even exist. We may never even meet. But if he does and we do, I'll know.'

'And I thought you were so ... so self-sufficient.' Rose laughed. 'You're just a romantic ...'

'Fool?' Daisy supplied the word. 'Yes,' she admitted. 'I probably am.'

'Well,' Rose said warmly, 'I hope you find him. You deserve to.'

'Enough of this foolishness!' It was Daisy's turn to laugh. Then seriously she said, 'I came here to explain. About Prudence.'

Rose looked concerned.

'You know it was Will who saved her? She would surely have been swept overboard and lost.'

Rose nodded. 'Do you think it has done any damage to the baby?'

'It's too early to say. Dr Heale says we can only wait and see. Poor man. I don't think he knows any more than we do. He has few medicines, as you know, and little else, apart from his brandy.'

'It would be awful if she lost the baby.'

'We must ask the church people to pray for her. They seemed to succeed in ridding us of that dreadful sailor.'

'Wasn't that strange?' Rose said. 'What do you think he died of?'

'Food poisoning,' Daisy said decisively. She had no wish to subscribe to the scaremongering rumours of a plague. 'He would eat anything he could lay his hands on. He was disgusting.'

'How sad,' Rose said. 'But I suppose it could be a blessing in one way. If he had lived I fear he would have caused trouble with Miles.'

'Well,' Daisy said, 'from what I hear he tried to kill your husband. What happened, I understand, was that he swung a heavy bar out across the top deck knowing your husband was up there. It nearly knocked your husband into the sea.'

Rose looked aghast. 'Miles didn't tell me.'

'No,' Daisy said. 'Your husband prefers to believe it was Will Trefor. Both Will and this man Dyke were up there at the time.'

'Oh no. Will would never do a thing like that. Whatever else he may be, Will Trefor is a gentleman.'

Daisy smiled. 'Don't they say that all's fair in love and war?'

There was a light knock at the door. Daisy opened it to Maurice Tinker, the young man who was a friend of Prudence. He seemed agitated. 'Miss Mason,' he said anxiously. 'I'm sorry to intrude. But can you come? Pru is asking for you.'

'Oh,' Daisy said. 'Yes. Yes, I'll come at once.'

Rose stretched out a hand. 'You'll keep me informed?'

'Yes, of course,' Daisy assured her.

Only later did it occur to Daisy that she had failed to mention the reason for her visit. She had not explained why she was lying naked next to Prudence, but it no longer seemed important.

On the way back she was waylaid by John Alden, the carpenter.

He had moulded and shaved the crib he was making for Pru's baby to near perfection. All it required was a final smoothing of any rough edges and a good polish.

'Miss Mason,' he said eagerly, 'can you spare me a moment? I have something to show you.'

Daisy shook her head. 'I'm sorry, John. Not now,' she said and she hurried on.

'Pru wants her,' Maurice explained to the disappointed carpenter. 'I think she's taken a turn for the worse.'

'I want this man charged with this offence,' Miles Standish demanded. 'If you think I am going to allow someone to try to kill me and get away with it then you don't know me very well.'

'That is true,' Captain Jones agreed. 'I don't know you very well. But I have learned, I believe, as much as I need to know.'

'And what, sir, does that mean?'

The captain stood up behind his desk. 'It can mean whatever you want it to mean,' he said. 'And hear this, *Captain* Standish. This is not the army. This is a merchant ship. *My* ship. And I do things my way. I need every experienced seaman I can lay my hands on. And I have just lost one. A damned good worker.'

'A bully and a brute,' Standish said.

'That may be so,' the captain conceded. 'But he was also a strong, seasoned and conscientious seaman. The kind of hand I need on this God-forsaken voyage. And Will Trefor is another. I have no intention of wasting time charging him with an offence he may or may not have committed.'

'Captain Jones,' Standish persisted, 'you know as well as I do, I am entitled to a hearing on this matter. If I don't get it I shall not forget. We may be cut adrift from civilized ways just now but if we are to survive and establish any kind of order we must bring with us the recognized and accepted codes of conduct honoured in our own country.'

'What exactly do you expect of me?'

'I accept, the way things are at the present time, that you cannot punish this man in an appropriate manner. To clap him in irons would, I agree, be a waste of labour. I would, however, like the charge to be made and laid against his name in order that he may be punished when circumstances permit.'

'You are assuming he is guilty.'

'I know he is guilty.'

'I will ask one of my officers to look into the matter and make a report.'

'I look forward to reading it.'

'I did not say I would make the report available to you or to anyone else. I will have the matter investigated. If I feel there is anything contained therein which you ought to know then you will be informed.'

'I suggest Mr Clarke would be the right man ...'

'Mr Clarke, as you well know, is my first mate and my senior pilot. He is far too busy to be taken away from his post on ... on ...' – Captain Jones hesitated. There was nothing to be gained by antagonizing the arrogant Standish further – 'on non-naval matters.'

'Then who?'

'I don't know,' the captain said wearily. 'I will give it some thought.' But he could see he was not going to get rid of Standish that easily. 'Possibly my ship's doctor is the man. The work Dr Heale can do is limited at present due to lack of supplies. I think he might find the time. I will ask him this evening. But I shall not insist. He will do the job only if he is willing.'

Standish nodded. The captain clearly considered the whole business a waste of time. But he had got his way. 'And if he is not you will appoint someone else.'

Captain Jones ignored this. 'I would ask that you do not approach Dr Heale or attempt to discuss the matter with him prior to his inquiry and until I have his findings to hand.'

'Of course not,' Standish answered, as if offended that the captain should think he might.

'Then, please, leave it with me.'

Standish bowed. 'Thank you, Captain,' he said. 'I look forward to hearing the outcome.'

21

'Daisy Mason!'

Daisy looked up to find Will Trefor sliding down a narrow rope ladder to join her on the waist deck in the early evening shadows.

'I'm on watch, Daisy,' he said. 'I only have a minute. But there is something I want to ask you.'

Wisps of cloud raced across the moon in the fading light. Daisy offered her face up to him, willing him to take her in his arms. Living as she did in such close proximity to so many family groups she had never felt so lonely, so solitary. She wanted someone who was close to her and to her alone. True, she had Prudence and the baby. But Pru had the baby and the baby had Pru. Mother and child. They were as close as two people could ever get to each other. Daisy had no illusions. She was merely a caretaker, someone to watch over them. She wanted someone of her own: a man. She wanted Will Trefor.

He looked at her uncertainly, as if reluctant to ask. 'There is something I would like you to do for me.'

'Anything,' Daisy said brightly. Then, embarrassed at her own eagerness, she added, 'If I can, of course.'

Will had not noticed her embarrassment. He was too busy hiding his own. 'No,' he said, turning back to the ladder. 'It's unfair. I have no right to involve you.'

'What is it?' Daisy's curiosity was aroused. 'You can trust me. I thought we were friends.'

Will turned again to face her and gripped her squarely by the shoulders. The ship rolled and needing little encouragement she fell against him. He held her away from him and looked into her eyes. 'I ... I have to see Rose,' he said earnestly. 'I must see her soon.'

Daisy held her breath and tried to ignore the sudden void in her stomach, the feeling of emptiness, the sheer desolation.

'Her husband is telling lies about me. I want Rose to hear the truth and hear it from me. Then she can decide for herself what she wants to believe.'

'Captain Standish is telling lies about you?'

'There was an accident. You must have heard about it. It's all around the ship. Standish is saying I tried to kill him. He was almost hit by a loose spar. It swung out of control and just missed him. I was there at the time and for that reason he believes I was responsible.'

'I did hear something....'

'He claims I did it intentionally.'

'And did you?'

'No, no, Daisy. I swear it.

'Then it was an accident.'

'Not exactly,' Will admitted. 'It was Dyke. You know how Dyke was. Dyke evidently had some grudge against Standish. He tried to hit him with the loose beam. It might have worked, too. Could have knocked Standish out and hurled him overboard. We would never have found him in that foul weather. He'd have been swept away at once. Of course he believes I have a motive and, therefore, it was me. I don't think he even knew that Dyke was there. It was very dark. But Dyke admitted to me he'd done it deliberately. And now Dyke is dead and I can't prove it.'

Daisy was torn by mixed emotions. She wanted to help him but she resented his concern for Rose.

'If I can tell Rose to her face that what Standish says is not true....' His eyes glinted in the moonlight. 'I must go back to my post. I'll be off watch in an hour or so then I can go and see her. But I can't visit her alone. That's what I want to ask of you, Daisy. Will you come with me?'

Daisy nodded. She found she was unable to speak and she was angry with herself, angry that her eyes had watered.

'One hour,' he said and he hugged her affectionately, like a close friend, before swinging back up the ladder.

Daisy put her head inside the main cabin. The odour and the chaos of so many men, women and children, of damp clothing and bedding made a daunting prospect. She caught the eye of Maurice Tinker and beckoned him to her side.

'Would you look in on Pru for me, Maurice? See if she's all right?'

'I just did, Miss Mason,' Maurice said. 'She's sleeping like a baby.'

Reassured Daisy returned to the open deck. The ship was still rising and dipping and occasionally pitching dangerously but the air, at least, was fresh. Daisy clung to a stanchion and gazed out into the darkness where no lights shone and only an intermittent glint of silver from the clouded moon streaked the black water.

There was a movement in the shadows and Daisy turned away, not wanting to pry. John Alden was embracing Priscilla Mullins. Despite John's obvious good character, his skill as a craftsman and the high regard in which he was now held by captain and crew alike, Mr Mullins still did not see him as an acceptable suitor for his daughter's hand. These were stolen moments.

The two figures in the dark had merged into one and in her heart Daisy wished them well. Then suddenly she felt that she was trespassing. The dark was not for her. The dark was for lovers. Not wishing to disturb them she went back inside.

Among the passengers there was an eerie stillness as if the storm had taken so much from them they could only wait, with a kind of numb resignation, for the next onslaught. Prudence was still asleep. Daisy sat by her bed and watched over her, realizing yet again that Pru, so heavy with child, was little more than a child herself.

The ship's boy had turned the sandglass and called the half-hour. Now he swung the bell that tolled the hour and Will Trefor was relieved of his post. As Daisy dozed on her stool, Maurice Tinker shook her gently and told her that Will was waiting for her out on deck. She went to meet him and his smile of greeting filled her with doubt. She wanted to pull away, resenting the role in which she had been cast. She wanted to say no, I can't do this! But his eagerness swept her along, his arm about her shoulder as together they went to Rose's cabin.

A young manservant who, for reasons of his own, was keen to cultivate the goodwill of Captain Standish witnessed their approach. Aware of the strained relations between the two men he ran off at once to inform the army captain that his wife had visitors.

Daisy knocked lightly and looked inside. Rose was alone at a small hand-loom. Her black hair was pinned up, exposing her delicate white neck. She was hunched over her work, a piece of thread at her lips, and her face looked pale and drawn. Without malice, Daisy could not help but notice how thin and frail she was and wonder again at her undeniable power to attract men.

'Where is Miles, Rose?' she asked.

'I don't know,' Rose said pleasantly. 'He went off in rather a temper, I fear. But do come in, Daisy. Is it Miles you came to see?'

'Well, no,' Daisy told her. 'We wanted to make certain you were alone. And if so I could act as chaperon.'

'We?'

'You have a visitor.' Daisy looked over her shoulder at the man waiting in the narrow companion-way. 'Will Trefor is here to see you.'

'Oh, but he shouldn't!' Rose looked alarmed. 'He knows he shouldn't.'

Will emerged from behind Daisy. He looked adoringly at Rose and, helplessly, Rose gazed back at him. It didn't seem to matter to him that Rose was a mere shadow of the girl he had known in those Cheshire fields. It didn't seem to matter that she was another man's wife. He had known her in his youth and she had made a deep and lasting impression upon him. She was still his Rose and this stinking hell of a ship was no place for a girl like her. She was in poor health and this tiny airless cabin was a death trap. He wanted to lift her in his arms and carry her back through time to those leafy days where the dew glistened on a blade of grass in the morning sun and everything was new.

'You should not come here, Will,' she scolded him. 'You know how Miles is.'

'It's about Miles,' Will said.

Rose looked at him sharply and then at Daisy. 'Miles? Has something happened to Miles?'

'No, no,' Daisy assured her. 'Nothing like that.'

'Miles has told the captain I tried to kill him,' Will said coldly. 'There is absolutely no truth in it, Rose, and I am sure you would never believe such a libel. But I wanted you to hear it from me, face to face. There was an accident on the upper deck. A loose beam. Enough to knock a man overboard. Your husband chooses to believe it was not an accident. I was working on the upper deck at the time and he claims I was responsible, that I tried to kill him. I came here to tell you this is not so. I would never do such a thing, as I'm sure you know. Even though your husband is a conceited, arrogant, trouble-making fellow, I would not stoop so low. If I wanted to harm him I would do it openly and certainly not without warning him first.'

'Oh, Will,' Rose said. 'Please ...'

'Your husband is aware that I held a commission with His Majesty's Fleet. I have my honour to uphold. But, though he has slandered me with false accusations, it's not your husband who concerns me. It's you, Rose. My only concern is that you should know the truth.'

'We will all know the truth shortly.' Miles Standish had appeared in the doorway. 'When the result of the inquiry is made known.' He stepped inside the tiny cabin to put himself between his wife and Will. 'But for now, sir, I must ask you to explain your impertinence in visiting my wife in my absence.'

'I brought Mr Trefor here, Captain Standish,' Daisy volunteered. 'I have been present the whole time.'

Standish ignored her. 'Your explanation, sir?'

'I came to tell your wife that your accusations are groundless,' Will told him. 'You know my background, Standish.'

'Yes; as I understand it, you deserted your ship.'

'You know my background,' Will repeated, 'but the people whose minds you are attempting to poison against me do not. And I am not in a position to explain myself.'

'You claim to be a gentleman, but nothing in your behaviour verifies your claim.'

'And you are behaving like a gentleman?' Will taunted him. 'Why not tell the truth? You have no proof I was responsible. You just want to *believe* I was.'

'I cannot discuss this matter whilst it is under investigation. I have given my word to Captain Jones. And, of course, as a gentleman I am honour bound to keep it.'

Daisy was uneasy now. None of this concerned her and she felt like an intruder. She turned to leave.

'Wait!' Will Trefor held up a hand. 'Since we are here, the three of us, and we have Miss Mason as our witness, there is something more I wish to say to you.'

'I have *nothing* more to say to you,' Standish told him. 'Nothing at all.'

'Then hear this,' Will said. 'You may be married to Rose, you may be her husband and she may be your wife in the eyes of the Church ...'

'In the eyes of God, man!'

Will shrugged. 'If you wish. But in my eyes and in Rose's eyes that is *all* you are. Your marriage was a marriage of convenience, arranged by two self-seeking families without regard to Rose's feelings.'

'Rose's feelings? What do you know of Rose's feelings?'

Will turned to Rose and her eyes didn't flinch as she held his gaze. In his presence her cheeks had regained some of the colour they had lost, her eyes were brighter.

'Tell him, Rose,' Will urged her gently. 'Tell him of the day we went to Derbyshire. Tell him how we climbed our peak ... how we looked down from that great height and saw the valley and the white splash of water where the fall met the stream ... tell him, Rose. Tell him how you loved me then, when you were seventeen. Tell him what we told each other.'

Daisy was heartsick. She wanted to leave, to be anywhere but here. She gripped her lower lip between her teeth, wanted to pass but Will and Standish were in her way. Will, the lock of light-brown hair low on his brow, the blue eyes pleading with Rose. Standish, thick-set and solid, his body taut beneath his rust-brown doublet.

'We were just children ...' Rose said lamely, her voice trailing.

Standish could contain his anger no longer. 'How dare you! How dare you speak to my wife in ...'

'Wife? Wife?' Will mocked him. 'What is a wife? A wife is a possession to you. Like a house or a carriage. Rose is not one of your possessions. Rose is the girl I met when I was young. We were meant to meet and we met and our fate was sealed. You are simply someone who came along later. You don't love Rose the way I do. You don't *know* her the way I do. You never could.'

'Rose,' Standish said in a low, measured tone. His face was flushed as he fought to control his temper. Disconcerted at the look in his wife's eyes, he felt he was losing her. 'Tell this … this man he is wrong. Tell him he has made a dreadful mistake.'

'There is no mistake,' Will said.

Rose was trapped, torn between the two. 'Oh, Will,' she said despairingly. 'Why did you come? Why did you follow me? You knew I was married to Miles. You know my place must be with my husband.'

'None of that matters now,' Will insisted. 'You cannot be bound by such a marriage. It was just an arrangement. You didn't want to marry him. Your father wanted you to marry him. You had no option. And I'm afraid it was my fault. When you needed me I was not there. But I'm here now.' His voice dropped as if his words were for her ears only. 'Tell me you don't feel the way I do. Look me in the eyes and tell me those days meant nothing to you. Tell me – if you can.'

'Tell him, Rose,' her husband said, 'and let's be rid of him.'

But Will Trefor's eyes were burning into hers and her usually pale face was hot and flushed.

'Will,' Rose said at last, her lips trembling. 'It was a long time ago. It seems as though it all took place in another life. I …'

'*And this, too, is a rose,*' Will quoted softly. '*A rose of yet another hue.*'

'Don't,' Rose said. 'Please don't.'

'Rose?' Standish put an arm about his wife's shoulder.

'*A rose of yet another hue,*' Will murmured, '*but none so fair as the Rose I knew.*'

Rose averted her eyes, turned away from him and hid her face against her husband's chest.

'Are you satisfied now?' Standish demanded. 'Your foolishness has at last succeeded in upsetting my wife.'

The exchange between Will and Rose had apparently been lost on Standish but Daisy had witnessed the scene and sensed the pull of the past that held them.

Will smiled as if he had found the answer he wanted. 'Not satisfied, no. Not yet. Not until I have her back where she belongs. But I am pleased to have the answer to what I came here to find out.'

'And what might that be?'

'I would have thought that was obvious. Even to an insensitive wretch like you.'

'Get out!' Standish was angry now. 'Get out and stay away from my wife. Get back to below decks where you belong. I will deal with you when I'm ready.'

'I shall look forward to that,' Will said and he turned on his heel and left.

Rose sat down, her hands covering her face. Standish stared, as if awaiting some declaration, some affirmation of her loyalty. But she was not yet ready to face him. Daisy hesitated. Should she go to Rose, comfort her? Or should she leave her alone with her husband?

'I would be grateful if you would leave us now, Miss Mason,' Standish resolved her dilemma. 'Thank you for your assistance.'

Daisy wondered what, if any, assistance she had been. She turned to leave, then looked back. But Rose remained seated, her face hidden.

Outside in the passage the ship's boy hovered as if he had been awaiting his opportunity. 'Miss Myson!' he cried anxiously in his high-pitched Cockney accent. 'Miss Myson, miss! I bin sent t' git yer. It's yer moid. They fink she's 'avin' 'er boiby.'

22

Rose Standish heard the boy and hurried after Daisy. 'I must come with you!'

'Where are you going?' her husband asked in surprise.

Perhaps she saw an opportunity to evade his more probing questions but Rose didn't wait to reply. She rushed after Daisy who by now was hurrying back along the open deck to the main cabin.

'Surely it's too early?' she asked at Daisy's heels.

The terrors of the storm, the cramped cabin, the lack of suitable food had all contributed, but Pru's fall from the ladder was the prime cause of this latest emergency. And Rose was right. It *was* too early for Pru to give birth.

Will Trefor was waiting at the threshold of the cabin. Rose followed Daisy, aware of Will but rushing past him, and was in turn followed by her husband who threw Will a warning glance and hurried inside.

Towards the corner where Daisy had set up her limited, partitioned space a small crowd had gathered. A buzz of animated conversation filled the long, wide cabin. Daisy and Rose picked a way through the tight knot of onlookers who grudgingly made a path for them. But when Miles Standish appeared the crush eased and the watchers drew back with rather more alacrity. Standish was known as a man of some authority and a man whose temper had a notoriously short fuse.

The little crowd of mainly women and girls had for once an air of happy anticipation. The prospect of a birth had cheered them considerably. It would be the first major happening they'd had cause to celebrate since leaving Plymouth. Everyone aboard the storm-tossed vessel was worn out and tired and eager for relief, something to brighten their day.

Behind the curtain Pru was attended by Dr Heale. Mrs Carver knelt solicitously at Pru's bedside, mopping the girl's feverish brow and murmuring words of quiet encouragement. When Daisy appeared the older woman looked up and smiled weakly. Daisy accepted her presence without comment. Perhaps, she thought, this is part of some self-imposed penance for her previously callous behaviour.

Pru's eyes were closed. Her head moved restlessly from side to side. Dr Heale turned to Daisy and Rose and answered their unasked question. 'I'd say the baby is well on its way.'

'But surely it isn't due yet,' Daisy said.

'The baby will come,' Dr Heale said, 'when he or she is ready. They always do. And I believe this little one is ready now.'

Daisy and Rose Standish looked at each other in surprise. But Mrs Carver nodded in agreement with the doctor.

Beyond the partition the little crowd of well-wishers were quieter now. Waiting for the news that might, perhaps, be heralded by a baby's cry, they were ready and eager to send up a cheer at the first hint from within.

Miles Standish came unannounced and, as if by right, brushed aside the curtain.

'Captain Standish!' The doctor was affronted. 'There is call for privacy here.'

But Standish took in the uncertainty and bewilderment of those present and promptly took over. 'My God!' His nose twitched at the foul air. 'The atmosphere in here is dreadful. What a welcome for a new born! I wouldn't be surprised if the poor little mite refused to come out.'

'Miles!' Rose was shocked by her husband's indelicacy.

'How in Heaven's name,' he demanded, 'can the poor girl breathe?'

'There is so little space anywhere,' Dr Heale told him.

Standish looked at his wife. 'It is quieter and more private in our cabin.'

Rose was thrilled. 'Oh, Miles! Could we?'

He nodded. 'I can move out for a while. This is no place for the birth of a baby.' He looked questioningly at Dr Heale. 'Doctor?'

Dr Heale agreed at once. 'It would certainly be better for both mother and child. If you are sure....'

Standish wasted no time, eager to appear gallant in his wife's eyes and put the intrusion of Will Trefor out of her mind. 'Wrap the girl up well.'

Daisy covered Prudence with a blanket and Mrs Carver stood aside as he lifted the girl in his arms.

'Go, Rose,' he said. 'Lead the way.'

Rose hurried back to her own cabin to prepare the bed. Daisy's eyes were on Miles Standish, this fiery, unpredictable man who held Prudence tightly in the blanket and ordered, 'After you, Miss Mason. And tell those idiots out there to make way.'

Daisy threw back the curtain and those outside fell away to make a clear passage as the solid, stocky figure of Captain Standish emerged cradling the frail, semi-conscious girl in his arms. He strode out, head high, there was a surge and the path closed behind him.

Many of those nearest, especially among the older women, were shocked by what they saw. With sharp intakes of breath they witnessed the deep dark shadows under Pru's eyes and her pale wan little face. They had not expected her to look so ill. She was only having a baby, after all.

It was raining again and sudden gusts of wind swept the rain into the faces of those who dared to peer or venture out. Standish shouldered his way into the tiny cabin and with great care set the girl down on the bed Rose had prepared for her.

Watching him, Daisy was surprised at his patently genuine concern. He was a strong man physically with a quick temper and a quirky impatience. But there was clearly a more gentle side to his nature. For the first time Daisy could understand how a girl like Rose could come to love him.

Nodding his approval Dr Heale, a small slight man, hovered behind Standish. He was in a state of agitation and his lack of composure caused Standish to revert to his more usual boorish manner.

'You have delivered babies before, I hope?'

'Of course,' the little doctor told him and offended by the implied questioning of his credentials he was stung into taking control. 'I would be obliged if you would leave us now, Captain Standish. You have done what you can and we are grateful.'

Standish, who had gone down on one knee at the low bedside to rub Pru's cold hands in his own, stood up abruptly. 'Yes,' he said. 'Of course.' He kissed his wife on the cheek. 'I will ask Captain Jones to find some place where I can lay my head for the night.'

Rose looked adoringly at her husband, as if the episode with Will Trefor was totally forgotten. 'Yes, my love,' she said. 'Take care.'

As Standish left the companion-way he saw Will who was watching from afar. He hesitated, then decided he had nothing more to say to him and went off in search of Captain Jones.

In the cabin Prudence had begun to stir, rolling from side to side as her contractions became more frequent and more prolonged. Dr Heale had a foreboding that this would be no easy labour. For one thing the girl was uncommonly small and by no means ideally built for child-bearing. He had known women in the slums of the city to deliver their own babies and with little difficulty. 'Like shelling peas', as the colloquialism went. But this was different. His concern, he assured himself, was more than justified.

Pru's gamin-like face was waxen now, and green at the gills, and her huge eyes in their dark sockets dilated as her head rolled back. Rose took out a tiny frill of a handkerchief she had previously sprinkled with rose water and waved it ineffectually under Pru's nose. Daisy held the little maid's hand and spoke to her softly with words of comfort and encouragement. Dr Heale knelt at the foot of the bed. Prudence, with her knees bent and her legs as wide apart as they would go, bore down on herself and pushed as instructed to expel her baby.

'Good!' Dr Heale exclaimed and Rose and Daisy exchanged a bright, eager smile.

Among the passengers many of the mothers had given or offered baby wraps, swaddling-clothes, knitted shawls or blankets. John the carpenter had finished the crib. The ship's captain, realizing the uplifting effect the arrival of a new and healthy baby could have on his demoralized passengers and crew, had ordered rations of goat's milk and whatever food the baby might need to be made available if its girl-mother was too weak to feed it. Everything was ready.

To many, both men and women, aboard the floundering ship as

they made their tentative way towards a new world and a new way of life, the impending birth of this baby marked a resurgence of hope and optimism. Throughout the *Mayflower*, even amongst the crew who were heartily tired of the long haul in cramped and overcrowded quarters and the uncomfortable and often hazardous working conditions in mid-Atlantic storms and high seas, there was a build up of joy awaiting release. Everyone wanted something to celebrate – and what better than a new-born babe?

Most of the crew had promised themselves they would wet the baby's head with several tots of Dutch gin or French brandy and jugs of beer and it was generally expected that Captain Jones would release enough extra provisions to afford a celebration. If they could run into calmer waters there could be a gathering on deck, a baptism followed by a great party with everyone invited.

The ship's carpenter was feeling rightfully proud that his lovingly crafted crib, ready and waiting for its intended occupant, had been so well received. Many had been to his workshop to admire his workmanship and to praise its neat lines. Also, John Alden's secret trysts with his Priscilla had been discovered and forbidden by an outraged and indignant Mr Mullins, but risking her father's wrath further Priscilla had persuaded her mother to accompany her to view her young suitor's creation. Mrs Mullins had been highly impressed with both the crib and her daughter's gentle giant of a boyfriend and had promised to speak to Mr Mullins.

According to John Carver and other spiritual leaders the new baby would be a source of joy to them all, a release from the tensions and privations of the previous weeks. Heralded by a perceptible easing of the stormy weather the new life about to begin in their midst was perhaps, they felt, a sign from the Almighty that the worst was over.

Dr Heale had shared none of this joy. He had been quiet and subdued since Pru entered the later stages of labour and Daisy had noted his apprehensive manner. It was not that she doubted his competence; it was his demeanour. There was a pessimism in his actions, as if he foresaw that all would not go well. Then, when the contractions ceased and Pru's writhing body fell back to lie still in sheer exhaustion, he looked up from the tiny bundle cradled in his arms, his face a picture of total desolation.

There was an eerie moment of complete silence and both Daisy and Rose knew that something was wrong. Something was dreadfully wrong.

Dr Heale closed up the cloth that enfolded the bundle and set it down on a cushion away from the bed. Daisy moved towards it but his arm barred the way. 'No,' he said. 'No, Miss Mason. I'm sorry.'

Rose stared open-mouthed from one to the other, realizing yet not wanting to accept the truth.

'The baby is dead,' Daisy said, and the doctor nodded. 'But why?' she asked. 'Why?'

'Please.' Dr Heale ushered them towards the door, as far from Pru as they could go inside the tiny cabin. 'I'm afraid the poor little mite was premature,' he told them. 'Arrived far too soon.'

'Oh, no!' Rose stifled a cry, her hands to her mouth. 'I was so looking forward to this baby.'

'We all were,' Daisy said. 'The whole ship. Passengers, crew, everyone.'

Dr Heale turned away. Daisy put a hand on his thin, rounded shoulder, and he looked back at her. 'There was nothing I could do,' he began, but his voice broke and he turned away again, stooping slightly.

Daisy knelt beside the bed. 'What about Pru?' she asked. 'Is she all right?'

The doctor took control of himself. 'I'm sure she is,' he said. 'But there are things I must do.' With his eyes he indicated Rose who was sobbing quietly into her handkerchief. 'I would be grateful if....'

Daisy understood. She put a shawl around Rose's shoulders and led her outside. Miles Standish was waiting at the end of the short passage, just out of the slanting rain. He came to meet them, aware at once that all was not well.

As much as anyone Captain Jones was dismayed and disappointed at the sad news. His passengers and to some extent his crew had been diverted by the anticipation of the baby's birth. Now, with nothing to celebrate, he feared they might sink into a collective melancholy that could do nothing but harm to their already shaken morale.

It was still unwise to venture out on deck. The roll of the ship was such that an unwary passenger could at any time be pitched into the sea. Yet the air in the main cabin and in the first hold, which also housed many passengers, was still foul. It was stale and motionless, and the presence of too many bodies in too little space was barely endurable. Added to this the prolonged lack of hot meals and dry clothing had rendered most of the passengers, adults as well as children, seriously weakened.

With the lack of fresh vegetables and too much reliance on salted meat, the captain feared an outbreak of scurvy or, with the true cause of the death of Seaman Dyke unresolved, something worse. Without delay he consulted Dr Heale and several of the church elders and, despite the need to conserve provisions, ordered extra rations for everyone. To the task of supervising the rekindling of the fires in the galleys and the production of hot food he appointed his second mate, Mr Coppin.

By now it was early November, almost sixty days since the *Mayflower* sailed out of Plymouth Sound, and it was time they were in sight of land. But there was as yet no cry of excitement from the look-out man in the crow's nest, no swarm of shrieking gulls to greet the bow, no driftwood riding the swell or any other sign that land was close at hand. And the captain and his pilots, though certain they were on course for the coast of North America, knew they were being driven further and further to the north, away from their planned destination.

There was also the troublesome business of the army man, Standish. Captain Jones wanted the matter cleared up as soon as possible and with no ill-feeling carrying through to the difficult days ahead. He asked Dr Heale if, in view of the stress of the baby's death, he wished to be relieved of the onerous task of conducting the inquiry. But the doctor said no. He had been impressed with Standish, a man he had previously considered rather quick-tempered and arrogant. In giving up his own bed to the pregnant servant girl, Standish had shown unexpected compassion. The doctor promised Captain Jones he would carry out his investigation within the next few days.

It was now the Irishman Ellis sought a meeting with Captain Jones. He had heard of the doctor's proposed inquiry, but he was also aware of the need for skilled officers of the watch. Mr Clarke, the first mate, had gone down with a stomach disorder and the list of qualified officers was already small. Sensing an opportunity to make his friend and shipmate indispensable, Pat Ellis reminded the captain that Will Trefor was no ordinary seaman.

Will Trefor, Ellis again pointed out, had been an officer of the King's Fleet. Ellis had known him since Dartmouth days, had taught him all he knew and could confidently recommend him as a reliable and resourceful pilot. Captain Jones was impressed but, again, not surprisingly wanted to know why such a man had undertaken to ship out as an ordinary seaman. Ellis liked and trusted the captain and asked if he might speak in the strictest confidence.

'If there is something I find I cannot condone, Mr Ellis,' the captain told him, 'then I will have to say so. I may also feel duty bound to record it in my log.'

'Then I must not put my friend at risk, Captain.'

'I cannot be expected to sanction rogues or criminals.'

'No, sir,' Ellis agreed. 'Of course not. But suppose I was to tell you nothin' of Will Trefor? Suppose I was to tell you the tale of another? So that I might judge your reaction to these other circumstances?'

The captain smiled. He liked Ellis and respected his skills. Good as his own pilots were, Mr Clarke and Mr Coppin were not in the Irishman's class. And like them, Pat Ellis was an honourable man, a man he could trust. He said, 'I'm listening, Mr Ellis.'

'You're a romantic sort of fellow, Captain,' Ellis began in his soft Irish brogue.

'I am?' the captain asked with a smile of surprise.

'You must be, sir. Or you would not love the sea as you do. Some men love the sea. Some men love women. Some men love both. Now this man, this man I will tell you about, loved the sea and just one woman.'

The captain waited with a tolerant but knowing look in his eyes, happy to take a few minutes' break from the pressures of his command.

'This man,' Ellis went on, 'when he was young fell for a girl from a well-placed rich family. Now don't misunderstand me, Cap'n. His own family were rich an' pretty well off, too. Landowners they were, in the north of England. An' everything was fine. Then this young man's father fell foul of the King. The land was confiscated, the father was executed an' the boy was despatched to Naval College.'

Captain Jones, despite his air of polite scepticism, was interested.

'The boy became a fine sailor, a seaman in the best tradition. Sure, hadn't his grandfather sailed with Drake? An' he was soon commissioned in the King's Fleet. He served well an' with distinction, didn't he now? An' he always intended to return an' marry his childhood sweetheart. But by this time the girl had moved with her family an' a marriage had been arranged for her. A marriage to a soldier at that! A soldier of good rank an' from a noble family. Now when our sailor-boy hears of this he does an unfortunate thing.'

The captain leaned forward, his eyes narrowed.

'But then he was young an' foolish,' Ellis said, 'an' he was eager to win back his lost lady love.'

'What did he do?'

'I'm afraid he jumped ship. He went absent in the port of Cadiz an' made his way back to England – only to find the young lady was already a bride. She was about to sail on a voyage into the unknown with her new husband. So he signed on for that self-same voyage as an ordinary seaman in an effort to win the girl back.'

'And?'

'Well, that's all, sir. For now. But the story is far from over.'

23

'As you are no doubt aware,' Captain Jones said, 'Mr Clarke is temporarily indisposed and my cover is stretched to the limit. I cannot afford to have any of my officers fall sick. I need a replacement.' He looked up at the tall young man who stood before his narrow desk. 'I am prepared to offer you a commission for the remainder of our voyage, an opportunity I hope you will accept.'

'Thank you, Captain,' Will Trefor said. 'I'm honoured.'

He could do the job well enough. That was no problem. But he didn't want to discuss his qualifications. That would only lead to questions and more questions, questions he had no wish to answer.

'I expect you are wondering why I chose you.'

Will was silent, his expression giving nothing away.

'I chose you because I am reliably informed you have the right background and training, Mr Trefor.'

Will noted the prefix. He was 'Mister' now.'

'Let's say a little bird told me all about you.'

'A little Irish bird, sir?'

Captain Jones smiled. 'Don't be hard on him, son. He has only the best of motives. He knows I need an extra man. He knows, too, that if you do a good job for me I will report this to the authorities back home. My word is highly regarded, I assure you, even in the King's Fleet. I am sure I am in a position to help you with whatever difficulties you may have in that quarter.'

Will nodded politely. 'When do I commence my...?'

'Mr Coppin will show you the new roster. Oh and Mr Trefor, Mr

Ellis tells me he has a spare doublet. I would like you to wear it when you are on duty.' He stood up. 'I am pleased to welcome you as one of my officers. A contract will be drawn up accordingly.'

'Thank you, sir.' Will turned ot leave.

'And Mr Trefor....'

'Sir?'

'There is just one other thing. I have to say this and I trust you won't see it as an unwarranted intrusion in your personal affairs. I would be obliged if you would stay well away from Captain Standish. He appears to hold some sort of grudge against you and I cannot afford ill-feeling between important passengers and my officers.'

'I understand, sir.'

'He has asked me to hold an inquiry into the incident which occurred on the upper deck. I suppose you know he claims you were responsible.'

'Yes.'

'And were you?'

'Of course not, sir.'

'I have asked Dr Heale to carry out the inquiry. You will have ample opportunity to tell him what part, if any, you played in this rather odd affair. In the meantime, it would help if you would steer clear of Standish ... and Mrs Standish.'

Will raised his eyebrows.

'She is a married lady, Mr Trefor.'

'Not in my eyes, Captain.'

'Well, she is in *my* eyes. She is Mrs Standish, the wife of one of my passengers. No matter who she was when you knew her, she is Mrs Standish now. Please remember that.'

Wihout another word, Will bowed and left. Pat Ellis was on watch. Will crossed the poop deck and went straight up the narrow ladder to the bridge.

'What's the idea?' he demanded. 'What have you been telling the captain?'

The Irishman, nearing the end of his watch, was removing the pegs from the compass rose, marking a slate as he did so and clearing the board for the next man. Deliberately taking his time over the task he turned slowly and smiled. 'Now calm down, Mr Trefor,' he said, peg in hand. 'From this day forward you are an officer of the watch an' you must behave like one.'

'Captain Jones knows all about me and he got it all from you. Do you realize what this means? It means I can't go home. I will have to stay in this God-forsaken New World – if there is such a place and if we ever find it!'

'Acquit yourself well an' the captain will see you right. He's a good man, Will, an' he promised me that much. He needs a reliable officer an' that's what you are. I had to tell him that. I owed it to the passengers, the crew, the ship. You're wasted on sloppin' out an' ropin' in. You're an officer, for God's sake! That's what you were trained to be an' that's what the captain needs right now.'

'What did you tell him about Rose Standish and me?'

'I told him everythin'; the whole story. So you better stay away from her, son. Standish reckons you tried to kill him an' if you don't stay away from his wife you'll be supplyin' yourself with a motive. Stay away from them, Will, an' deny everythin'. I told the captain it was Dyke not you. That's why I told him the rest, how it all began. Will Trefor is a gentleman, I said. A man like Will Trefor would never stoop so low. If he wanted to kill Standish, I said, he would do it openly, give him a chance to defend himself. Oh, the captain believes me right enough. But he says we need proof. Standish insists it was you. So don't go makin' it easy for him.'

The sea was calmer now, though there were still sudden and unexpected swells. Stomachs lurched and heaved but had little left to expel and the sound of retching rent the air. With the news of the baby's death a melancholy pallor had settled on many faces and throughout the ship there was an air of despondency and gloom.

The passengers were visibly weaker and many members of the church were frequently on their knees in prayer. One of the oldest of the elders, an already gaunt and emaciated man, knelt for so long on the hard boards of the main cabin he was unable to stand without assistance. Others lay in self-induced stupors, dreaming of an eventual deliverance. But most were pessimistic. The ship, they believed, was only temporarily becalmed in a lull before yet another storm.

John Carver, who had officiated at the burial of the seaman Dyke, now arranged for a short service to be held on deck for the committal of Pru's dead baby to the deep. Naturally, though the baby had never lived outside its mother's womb, it was to the settlers a much sadder and more affecting occurrence than the death of the man whom none had mourned. With the loss of the baby it was as if much of the hope invested in the voyage had evaporated.

With the mate, Mr Coppin, Mr Carver paid a visit to the carpenter. A small wooden box was required. The beautifully carved crib stood abandoned on John Alden's bench. Mr Coppin suggested the carpenter should make a lid for it and it could then be used as a coffin. Though practical, to Mr Carver it seemed an insensitive suggestion. It would be a great shame, he pointed out, to lose such a lovely ornate piece of workmanship. There would be other babies once the colony was established. Such a beautiful crib could be passed on from household to household in memory of the little one they had lost.

This was a nice idea, Mr Coppin agreed, but other families might not want it. They might consider the crib to be unlucky. Reluctantly Mr Carver and John Alden admitted this might well be the case and Mr Coppin pressed home his argument. People are funny about these things, he said. They're very superstitious. But his motive was not entirely altruistic. He had a backlog of urgent work for the carpenter – for one thing, there was a constant need for caulking below decks – and he didn't want him spending time making a coffin which, after all, would only be thrown overboard.

However simple and straightforward he was instructed to make something, John Alden would take his time and create a minor work of art. He was that kind of carpenter. Mr Coppin was firm and persuasive and both Mr Carver and John had little option but to accept what he said. With a heavy heart John began to make a lid for his beloved crib.

Prudence was not well enough to attend the ceremony on deck. Daisy had broken the news about the baby and she had sunk almost immediately into a deep sleep. She was too tired to cry or even to respond and Daisy wondered if she had fully understood. Out on the deck with a fair wind blowing up astern, many of the passengers and several off-duty members of the crew gathered for the short service. Hands raised to heaven, Mr Carver began with a prayer.

Captain Jones, in his cocked hat and best blue and gold long coat, read a passage from his King James' Bible, the gospel according to Mark: *And they brought young children to him, that he should teach them: and his disciples rebuked those that brought them. But when Jesus saw it, he was much displeased, and said unto them, Suffer the little children to come unto me, and forbid them not: for of such is the Kingdom of God. Verily I say unto you, Whosoever shall not receive the Kingdom of God as a little child, he shall not enter therein.*

More prayers, and the carved crib with its makeshift lid was placed on a plank of timber balanced on a hastily constructed stand. At Carver's bidding the plank was allowed to tilt and slowly the crib slid forward, gathered momentum and plunged into the swirling waters. A hymn, sung with gusto for so physically weakened a congregation, followed and the sad little ceremony was over, a final tear wrung from many who had few tears left to shed.

It was two days before Prudence regained the strength to leave the cabin of Rose Standish, two days before she fully realized what had happened. She returned to the quarters she shared with Daisy and was in such a sad and despairing state that Daisy feared for her sanity. Daisy had heard how women were often depressed, sometimes suicidal, for a period after giving birth, even women who had borne babies that were alive and well. The effect on a simple girl like Pru, who had *lost* a baby, could be devastating. She might do something silly. She might try to harm herself in some way. Daisy consulted the less than adequate Dr Heale.

The doctor agreed there was the possibility of Prudence, melancholy as she was, doing something foolish. But his own morale was at a low ebb and he could only point out that most of the passengers were now in a state of abject despair. There was little anyone could do. What was needed was a new diversion. The sight of land, for instance! But he did suggest that a close watch should be kept on the girl, day and night if possible. Daisy enlisted the help of Pru's friend, Maurice Tinker, and together they contrived to keep her under constant surveillance.

Later that day Dr Heale paid a second visit to Pru's bedside but he had really come to see Daisy. He took her aside. 'There is a matter I wish to discuss with you, Miss Mason, with your permission. About Captain Standish.'

'Oh´ yes,' Daisy said. 'I have thanked the captain and Mrs Standish for taking Prudence in. It was so kind of them and they were so good to her. To be honest, I was a little surprised that Captain Standish could be so ... so considerate.'

The doctor smiled. 'He can be a difficult man.'

'But I believe,' Daisy said, 'his heart is in the right place.'

'Yes,' the doctor agreed. 'It was about Captain Standish.' He hesitated. 'As you may know, I have been asked by the ship's master to carry out an investigation into an accident which occurred on the upper deck. It seems some kind of bar came loose one night and as it swung out it came perilously close to knocking Captain Standish overboard. Captain Standish is of the opinion it was done deliberately.'

Daisy laughed. 'Who would do such a thing?'

The doctor shared her incredulity. 'Exactly – but there were two men working on that deck at the time. One a man called Trefor, who I understand has since been appointed an officer of the watch.'

'As a reward?'

The little doctor smiled. 'Now, my dear. You must not say such things. And the other was the man who died, the huge fellow Dyke.'

'Will Trefor would never do a thing like that.'

'Er ... no,' Dr Heale said tentatively and a little surprised. Her conviction implied that she knew the man and knew him well. 'I am inclined to agree. But Captain Standish believes he would and did.'

Daisy shook her head.

'I know, I know,' the doctor said. 'But Captain Standish is not easy to convince – though I have it on excellent authority that Dyke was the man responsible. It was not an accident. It was done deliberately and it was done by this man Dyke.'

'On excellent authority.'

'Another officer of the watch – Mr Ellis – told me Dyke had confessed this to him and had expressed regret that he had not succeeded.'

'I know Mr Ellis,' Daisy told him. 'If Mr Ellis told you that then you can be sure it is the truth.'

'I agree,' the doctor said. 'The problem is, we have no absolute proof. All we have is Mr Ellis's word. We don't even have a denial from Mr Trefor. He absolutely refuses to confirm or deny he was responsible. A matter of honour, he says. He is insulted that we should pose the question. Refuses to discuss it.'

Daisy could well imagine Will Trefor's response to the doctor's timid probing.

'Now, as far as we know, Dyke had no motive,' the doctor continued. 'People have told us he had some sort of confrontation with Captain Standish, but nobody will admit to being present and seeing what actually happened.'

'I was there,' Daisy said spontaneously.

'You were? Why, that's excellent, my dear. Can you tell me exactly what took place?'

It occurred to Daisy that her evidence would oppose Captain Standish, a man she had only recently come to respect. The way he had helped Pru had surprised and impressed her. Yet she was convinced he was wrong about Will. Will Trefor would never do such a thing. She was sure of that and she felt it was only right to say so.

'Miss Mason?'

'This man Dyke was in the main cabin,' she said. 'He was terrorizing passengers, as he had on many previous occasions, threatening to steal their belongings, taunting them for being seasick and making objectionable remarks to the ladies present. He was a crude and offensive oaf of a fellow.'

'Was he reported to the captain?'

'Mr Carver was present and I believe there had already been considerable friction between the passengers and Captain Jones about this man. The captain, I suppose, felt that a lot of the complaints were unjustified and of little foundation. I suspect Mr Carver didn't really want to involve him.'

'I see.'

'But Captain Standish was there.' She smiled. 'And quite effective he was, too.'

'Captain Standish is not a big man,' Dr Heale said. 'At least, not compared to a man like Dyke.'

'True,' Daisy agreed. 'But Captain Standish ordered Dyke out of the cabin, made a few threats then produced a pistol.' She laughed aloud at the recollection. 'He frightened the life out of Seaman Dyke.'

'Captain Standish drew a pistol on Dyke?' The doctor was intrigued. 'Nobody has told me of this.'

'Several people were present. Mr Carver, for one.'

'And who else?'

'Oh, quite a number of passengers. I can name most of them.'

'Good, good! Excellent!' the doctor said. 'And what happened?'

'Well,' Daisy told him, 'Dyke departed in a hurry, swearing to take his revenge. I suppose you could say he was humiliated by Captain Standish, made to look foolish. In Dyke's eyes that might well have seemed sufficient motive for murder.'

'Yes! Yes, thank you. Thank you, my dear. Most helpful!'

Almost at once Daisy had misgivings about what she had told the doctor. She felt it was only fair to defend Will, yet she had no wish to alienate Miles Standish. And alienated he would be. He was not a man to take an impartial view. He would be convinced that for some reason she had done this to spite him. Yet the doctor needed to know what happened that day in the main cabin. She just wished he had heard it from someone else.

But for Daisy there were other more pressing matters. Prudence had at last realized she had lost her baby. The infant had been committed to the deep and she was left feeling drained and empty. Most nights she cried herself to sleep, sobbing into her pillow in the early hours of the morning.

Daisy sat beside her, stroking her hair and attempting to console her with quiet words of comfort. There was time yet. She was only young. She had her whole life ahead of her in a new country, a new world. In time she would find someone, someone she could love and who would love her. She would marry him and they would have children. And her children would have a father in a way the lost little one would never have had a father. But Daisy's efforts were of little avail. For now, Prudence was inconsolable.

Towards the end of this long and tortuous voyage there would be another birth and another death. Elizabeth Hopkins would add a baby boy to her family of three children – two daughters and a son – and the new arrival would be named, appropriately it seemed, Oceanus. Early in November one of the servants, a young man by the name of William, who had been ill for several days with severe stomach pains, would die in his sleep and on Tuesday the seventh be buried at sea. But by then everyone aboard was even more dispirited and neither of these events had quite the impact of Pru's unexpected loss.

24

Maurice Tinker, the slightly built and almost girlish youth, son of Mr and Mrs Thomas Tinker, did what he could to cheer up Pru. So often was he at her side that many of the passengers berthed in the main cabin assumed he had been the father of her child. But he was more like a nurse than a lover and Daisy was charmed by the solicitous way in which he helped to take care of his young friend.

Still the tears and the mood of desolation persisted until one evening Daisy noticed a change in Prudence. It was no gradual change this. Nor had Pru grown weary of mourning. It was such a sudden change that Daisy could only conclude it was the result of something specific. Something had happened. Something quite dramatic. And Daisy couldn't think what it might be. Prudence was transformed. She was calmer now and more composed, blessed with a new serenity. The pain, apparently, had eased. The trauma, it seemed, was over. Daisy decided it was best not to ask what had happened. She would wait until Pru volunteered the information.

Though she guessed it was in some way connected to a visit Pru had made to her hideaway on the spiral stairway, Daisy knew nothing more. Pru had taken to retiring there whenever she wanted to be alone and she was often missing for long periods. But so long as she knew where Pru was, Daisy didn't mind. Since Pru's confinement their roles had been somewhat reversed. Daisy had, in many ways, become Pru's maid. Yet she was happy with this. She wanted Pru to recover in her own time and she explained to Maurice Tinker the importance of Pru's hiding place on the stairs. Maurice had left her alone there, as if he understood instinctively her need for solitude, and though he was rarely far away he never attempted to intrude.

So something had happened. A visitation, perhaps? A sign from above? The church people, less sceptical than Daisy, would certainly attribute any change for the better to divine intervention or what they called 'the will of God'. Still Daisy didn't ask and when the time was right, as Daisy guessed she would, Prudence wanted to tell her all about it.

'I feel better now, Miss Daisy,' she said, without any prompting.

'Do you, Pru?'

'I just 'ave to face up to what 'appened.'

Daisy waited for the dam to burst, for it all to come flooding out.

'Everyone 'as bin ever so kind. Maurice ... an' Mrs Standish ... an' Captain Standish ... an', most of all, you.' Her eyes were shining as they had not shone for weeks. 'I feel stronger now an' I want to get back to doin' me work. I can do things for you again an' ... an' for Mrs Standish, too, if you tell me.'

'I'm glad you feel better,' Daisy told her with a smile. 'But we must take things slowly. We don't want you falling ill again.'

'I've bin goin' to the stairs,' Pru said.

Daisy nodded. 'You have thought everything over now, is that it?'

'Well yes, miss,' Pru said. 'But more than that. I 'ad a little talk.'

'Oh?' Daisy was curious. 'And with whom did you have a little talk?'

'With Mr Ellis. You know Mr Ellis, miss.'

'I see,' Daisy said.

'He was lovely.' Pru's eyes misted over. 'He told me things.'

'Oh?' Daisy said. 'What kind of things?'

'About my baby. About what 'appens when a baby dies. He found me on the stairs an' 'e said 'e could see I was sad – an' was it about the baby? I told 'im it was. I told 'im I wished I 'adn't bin saved from goin' overboard 'cos then I could 'ave died with me baby. He said that was a wicked thing to say an' 'is friend, Mr Trefor, would be most upset to 'ear me talkin' like that. Mr Trefor, 'e said, 'ad risked 'is life to save me an' 'e couldn't believe 'ow ungrateful I was. I said I was sorry an' it was just that I'd lost me baby. I wasn't really ungrateful. If I'd 'ad a little boy, I told 'im, I would 'ave called 'im Will after Mr Trefor. Just as I was goin' to call me little girl Daisy after you, miss.'

Daisy was touched. 'Don't mind Mr Ellis....'

'Oh no, miss,' Pru said, springing to his defence. 'He was lovely. He told me all about babies that are born dead an' what 'appens to 'em. You see, miss, I don't know if you know this but when a new baby is born its soul is pure white. "White as the driven snow", Mr Ellis said. There's not a mark on it. Nothin' but the most pure brilliant white.'

'Of course,' Daisy said in agreement, as if humouring a small child.

Pru's large round eyes widened even further. 'A soul is white in the beginnin' but it gets stained by sin. When we commit a sin it leaves a mark, a sort of stain, on our souls. Doesn't matter 'ow small the sin is, it always leaves a mark.'

'Mr Ellis told you this?'

'Yes, miss. He said the angels in 'eaven get the babies ready to be born. They give 'em pure white souls, but sometimes the angels get tired of sendin' babies into the world only to find their souls get stained with sin. So they sort of rebel an' stop givin' out souls. Well, you can't live without a soul so the new babies die. An' those babies are so clean an' pure they go straight up to 'eaven. Mr Ellis says they're very lucky. They don't 'ave to go through all the dangers an' temptations of this world before they get there. They go straight up to 'eaven, straight into the next world an' a life of everlastin' 'appinesss where nothin' bad can ever 'appen to 'em. That's what Mr Ellis says. An' that's why we should always be pleased an' 'appy when a new baby dies before it's born. We should be glad, 'e says, not sad.'

'Glad?'

'Glad,' Pru said with absolute conviction. 'We should be glad because that baby 'as gone straight to 'eaven.'

'I see,' Daisy said, hearing the Irishman's voice in this fanciful notion and marvelling again at his power to persuade. 'That's a lovely idea, Pru.'

Pru smiled and Daisy felt that in her heart Pru was as innocent as the baby she had lost.

'I'm sure your baby will be happy now,' she said, 'wherever she is.'

Pru took on an air of serenity and went about her work with a new vigour. She even seemed to enjoy her chores, and several of the women in the main cabin commented on her rapid and robust recovery. Daisy, to the delight of the members of the church, replied that Pru had received a sign from God that all was well with her lost child and she should now get on with her life. Daisy couldn't wait to confront and congratulate the sagacious Irishman.

Recently though, except to wave to him as he came down from the poop, Daisy had seen little of Mr Ellis. The first mate was still indisposed and along with the other ship's officers Pat Ellis had been helping to cover by putting in extra hours. The watch was a long and tiring duty for a man alone on the bridge without the burden of overtime elsewhere, but the situation was set to ease with the addition of Will Trefor to the duty roster. Daisy was pleased when she saw the Irishman leaning on the side and looking out to sea on the waist deck and she hurried out to join him.

'And where have you been hiding, Mister Patrick Ellis?' she asked, quietly mocking his soft Irish brogue and wearing her brightest smile.

It was a blustery day with the wind still whipping the sails but, after the weather they had endured, the sea seemed almost calm.

'On watch most of the time,' Ellis told her, matching her smile, 'an' I'm dog-tired.'

'You look cheerful enough, for all that.'

'An' so I am.' He looked around to ensure there was no one within earshot. 'Listen, Daisy,' he said, 'keep this to yourself, you understand? We don't want to go raisin' any false hopes, do we now?'

'What is it?'

'Well, they say we are off course. Headin' due north instead of west. Now I'm not so sure about that. We may be off course an' we may be further north than we ought to be, but I reckon we're headin' west all right.' He lowered his voice still further and Daisy had to lean closer to him in the swirling wind. 'I reckon we're within striking distance of a landfall.'

'A landfall?'

'We are not far from land.'

'Really?' Daisy peered into the distance but there was nothing on the grey, encircling horizon. Nothing. Just the swell of the ocean all around. Her sudden rush of excitement subsided. 'How can you tell?'

'Well,' Ellis said, 'we're not there yet, but I can smell it.'

'You can smell it?' Daisy laughed. 'Is it that bad?'

'No, darlin'. A seafarin' man can smell the land. There's a sort of subtle change in the air. It smells different. The ocean begins to look different.'

'How different?'

'You can see where the water changes. Gets a little greener here an' there. An' you see things. Bits o' driftwood, more foam. An' watch out for the gulls. The birds'll come sweepin' in all of a sudden an' start to circle the bows. You'll see.'

'But that's marvellous news.'

'Well, don't you go spreadin' it around. Not yet. They don't agree wit' me on the watch. Calculations differ. Their newfangled gadgets tell them they're some way off yet. But I *know*.' He tapped his nose. 'I can smell it, I tell you.'

'What about Captain Jones?'

'Captain Jones is sayin' nothin'. Too smart for that is the captain. He knows there are ways of tellin' when land is near without all this fussin' with the compass an' the traverse table an' the quadrant – all essential aids to navigation, I grant you. But there are times when you might just as well follow your nose.'

'What will it be like? This land?'

'Ah, it'll be fine. Just fine. Hard at first, but things'll get better. An' if anyone can make a success of it these people will. This has been one hell of a voyage an' they're still here. They've come through it all. They're survivors, Daisy. Not all of them, of course. But quite a few of them will settle down an' make a go of it. If they can get through this first winter they'll be all right. You'll see. An' they'll build somethin' wonderful.'

'You have such faith in them?'

'I have faith in them because they have faith in God. That's what they have that most other settlers don't have. Their belief in God. It'll see them through, one way or another. Believe me.'

Daisy smiled. 'That's what I wanted to see you about,' she told him. 'God.'

'God?'

'Yes,' Daisy said. 'I want to thank you for bringing my little maidservant out of her depression. It was so kind....'

'Oh!' He laughed. 'The poor girl was sittin' on the steps to the cable hold. Breakin' her heart, she was.'

'And you helped her to put it all back together again.'

He raised his eyebrows at her.

'She told me what you said. About babies that die and go straight to heaven.'

'Did she now?'

'It was a lovely thing to tell her,' Daisy said warmly. 'But where on earth did you get it all from?'

'About the babies with no souls? At home in Ireland, of course. Where else?' He laughed. 'I was a child once, you know. Strange as it may seem. An' I was sent to church school – Roman Cat'lic – as a little lad. We had nuns for teachers an' they taught us all about heaven an' hell an' the wrath of God. An', to be sure, that's about *all* they taught us. Every mornin' we'd sit in a little circle wit' our mouths wide open an' this weird old woman would invoke the Almighty. She was all in black with her head covered an' her spooky white face pokin' out an' she would raise her hands to the roof an' beseech the Lord to have mercy on the souls of us poor wretched sinners. We were about seven years old at the time.

'We'd sit there scared stiff o' this Almighty God, this great presence loomin' over us, the one you can't see but you *know* is there, an' there'd be the threat of eternal fire lickin' at our toes.' Ellis laughed again and looked down at Daisy. 'An' there was the parish priest. You know, I can't remember a single word of what he said but he could put the fear of God in us with just one lift of his great bushy eyebrows. He was a big fellow or, at least, he seemed big to us little ones an' he had this wispy reddish hair that stuck out all over the place an' these pale eyes that followed you everywhere. He wore scarlet robes, too, that billowed out behind him when he strode from the chapel to the schoolhouse. An' he was always gruntin' an' snortin', and he had great tufts of red hair comin' from his nose. I had nightmares about him when I was a small boy. I suppose he must have been mixed up in my mind with my idea of the Devil. In my dreams he'd be chasin' me with his robes on fire an' flames flowin' from his nostrils an' his pale eyes ablaze....'

He stopped in mid-sentence and grinned at Daisy whose mouth had fallen open as she listened like the children he described. Then she thumped him on the chest and laughed at her own attitude of wide-eyed innocence.

'As I said,' he continued more soberly, 'I can't remember a single word of what the priest said but I've never forgotten some of the things those nuns told us. We were about as pure as could be then – round about the time of our First Communion – an' they told us all about the sins of the world an' the terrible temptations that lay ahead.' He laughed. 'We couldn't wait to get out into the wicked world an' be tempted.'

Daisy leaned against him, her face turned away from the biting wind, and listened to the lilt of his strong, soothing Irish voice.

'The notion that babies born dead go straight to heaven – now that's one of the things that stuck in my mind. We'd all sit up straight an' listen as Sister Mary or Monica or whatever her name was went on an' on. Straight in, she'd say, straight in those babies go to a special place on the right hand of God. Sure an' she'd have us all wishin' we'd been born dead.'

'Prudence is like a child,' Daisy said. 'She may be almost sixteen years old and she may have given birth, but in her head and in her heart she's still only a child.'

'She's a good girl, Daisy,' Ellis said. 'An' if she's your maidservant you're responsible for her. You see that you take good care of her now.'

'I will,' she told him. 'And I'm grateful to you. I didn't realize you were a religious man.'

He looked surprised. 'Religious? Me?'

'You're a Roman Catholic.'

'Ah!' he said. 'I was once. When I had no choice an' no mind of my own.'

'But what you said to Prudence....'

'You don't have to believe a story to tell it, Daisy. Myself, I don't believe a word of it.'

A seaman went by, touching his forelock at Daisy and smiling at the Irishman. 'Beginnin' to think you might be right, Mr Ellis,' he called out, against the wind. 'It's in the air!'

'He means about a landfall,' Ellis told Daisy.

But that was Thursday, the ninth of November, and though the wind dropped and the battered *Mayflower* eased more smoothly through the undulating surface of a calmer sea there was, as yet, no sign of land.

There was now an air of stillness about the ship. Most of the passengers remained by their personal belongings, taking scant interest in anything, even what little food was on offer. They were weak not only in body but in spirit, haunted by the dread of another body-racking storm. Darkness came early and to most the night was welcome. They fell asleep where they lay, cold and exhausted. They'd had no information of how near or far they were from their destination – even their leaders were silent, their questions for once unasked. It was as if they were so battered and bruised by their experience they no longer feared what lay ahead. They were just too tired to care.

Next morning at first light the look-out man in the crow's nest struggled to his feet. Barefoot and stiff with cold on the low-sided, eight-foot-wide platform he peered out at the grey, misty dawn, rubbed his eyes and peered again. There was a thin dark line on the horizon. The young seaman held his breath. It was there all right, no mistake. He scrambled a few feet up the halyards, looked again. It was land. Land! His arms through the ropes he hung in the rigging as he cupped his hands and yelled down to the silent decks where the only sound was the swish and splash of the water against the rise and fall of the bow. 'Land ho!'

The second mate, Mr Coppin, was on watch and the captain, roused from his bunk by the look-out's cry, was quick to join him. Down below, passengers stirred, dimly aware that most of the crew were already out on deck, and the growing commotion became a rumble of excitement which swept through the cabins. No, they were not dreaming. There it was again. The cry that many had come to believe they would never hear. 'Land ho!' And again. 'Land ho!'

At last! At long last the end of their ordeal was in sight. Out on deck they gathered to stand and stare through the swirling mist at the distant shoreline, barely able to contain their excitement. John Carver and William Brewster dropped to their knees in prayer of thanksgiving and other men, their wives, children and servants followed their example. But there were those, too, who viewed the prospect with mixed feelings.

Miles Standish stood against the side, a protective arm around his wife Rose, aware that his responsibility as military adviser to the settlers was only now about to begin. Daisy Mason, standing outside the main cabin, her hands resting on the shoulders of her maid Prudence, wondered how without a man they would fare in this harsh new world. Up on the poop deck the *Mayflower*'s newest officer pondered his future. Had he been wrong to pursue his youthful dream? Could one ever relive the past? And, more to the point, did Rose not want him? Did he not want *her*? Was it only the dream he wanted, not the reality? Will Trefor was as confused now as he was at the outset of his strange personal odyssey. But one thing he *did* know. Sooner or later the *Mayflower* would be returning home and back in England he was a wanted man. Dare he return? Dare he ever return?

25

The original agreement had been for the settlers to land somewhere close to the mouth of the Hudson River. Captain Jones calculated they had arrived too far north. What they actually saw in the grey dawn of that November morning was part of the shoreline of Cape Cod.

The captain at once called a meeting with John Carver and other leading churchmen. It was the start of a fine day, he said, and the wind was light, blowing in from the north-east. He felt they ought to do an about turn, attempt a landing not here but some distance down the coast where they had authority to land. They all agreed; the *Mayflower* was turned around and they headed south.

All morning they sailed down the outside of the narrow neck of land that enclosed the Bay of Cape Cod until they ran into dangerous waters. Towering breakers began to buffet the ship and they were suddenly swept into the turbulent shoal waters off the southern extremity of the neck, the area which would later become known as Pollock Rip. Then, before they could retreat, they were caught in the cross currents and enormous waves reared all around them.

The captain held on and his expert seamanship guided them through towards the safer waters of Nantucket Sound, but suddenly the wind dropped and the ship began to drift out of control. Captain Jones's only option now was to sail clear of the shoals and taking advantage of the first gust of wind he swung his ship round and headed for the open sea. Once clear of the treacherous currents the *Mayflower* sailed in a wide arc for the northern tip of the cape, eventually finding shelter within the bay.

Tacking in close to the shore Captain Jones found a wide harbour and dropped anchor as near to land as he safely could. His passengers were tired and weary of the sea and many were obviously in poor health. Their first enthusiasm at the sight of the New World had waned in the wake of the subsequent delays and they were eager now to go ashore.

From the ship giant oak trees, junipers and pines and even flocks of fowl could be seen, but the aspect was bleak. The trees were bare and there was no sign of human habitation. Several of the women wailed in disappointment. Though they'd had no idea of what to expect they simply did not like what they saw. If they had sailed on time, in the summer as planned, the captain pointed out, things would have been very different. As it was they were faced with a cold and desolate winter.

At once arguments broke out amongst the passengers. Most were heartily sick of life aboard the overcrowded, reeking ship and were eager to feel solid earth beneath their feet. But some argued that they should wait for the weather to improve and then attempt to sail south again where they might at least find settlements or some sign of human life.

Most members of the crew were also tired of the cramped conditions aboard ship and were anxious to get under way for the voyage home. Some were even in favour of dumping the cargo of disgruntled passengers and their baggage with them. Sensing trouble the captain sought to cool tempers and conduct a reasonable discussion. It was at this point that the oldest of the church leaders, William Brewster, whose long beard had turned white, recalled the advice they had been given before leaving England and this was brought to the captain's attention.

As the arguments raged back and forth between the various groups, each with its own ideas of what course ought to be taken, Captain Jones called a further meeting, this time of heads of households. They had been advised, he reminded them and as Mr Brewster had pointed out, to elect from amongst themselves a governor and a governing body who would run the colony they planned to found and run it in a civilized and equitable manner.

At this a degree of calm was restored and an agreement stating the settlers' avowed aims was drafted. They would found a colony, they would draw up a table of laws to preserve good order and they would evolve a code by which they might live in harmony. But first they would pledge themselves to work together to achieve these aims. It was Saturday, November the eleventh, 1620, and the agreement was signed by the heads of households on behalf of themselves, their wives, sons, daughters and servants. Forty-one men signed, but no women. Women were considered incapable of entering into any such agreement.

Daisy Mason declared that as she was not to be a signatory to the document she saw no reason why she should be bound by its terms. Neither John Carver nor Captain Jones were surprised at her outspoken reaction. Pat Ellis and Will Trefor were highly amused when they heard of it. And Miles Standish was even more intrigued than he already was by this self-possessed young woman who did not hesitate to defy any man with whom she disagreed and his interest in her was stimulated still further. But none of the women offered their support.

In addition, Mrs Carver and her companion, who had recently come to regard her more favourably, revised their judgment yet again. She was a brazen upstart, they decided, who refused to accept her proper place. Elizabeth Hopkins was too engrossed in her new baby and the needs of her other children to take much notice and another of Daisy's friends, Dorothy Bradford, had become remote and withdrawn as if the torment of the voyage had robbed her of her confidence. Most of the other women were apathetic, schooled all their lives into leaving matters of business and politics to their husbands. Even Rose Standish could only muster a wan smile, as if Daisy was attempting to change the nature of the universe.

When the forty-one signatures were appended a vote was taken and John Carver was elected first governor of the new colony. He was to hold the office for one year and most of the passengers were happy to leave the administration in his hands. At fifty-four Mr Carver was among the oldest of the settlers and he was known and respected by almost all of them.

The first move under the new agreement, a decision taken immediately after the meeting, was to send fifteen men ashore to collect wood, take a good look around and search for any sign of human life. Miles Standish was appointed leader.

Setting out with great enthusiasm, aware that one of them would be the first of the settlers to set foot in the New World, the fifteen-strong party pulled away in the longboat and headed for the shore. Yet when the question was asked later, having been distracted by the need to negotiate swirling currents and then slippery rocks underfoot, no one could remember exactly who had reached the shore first. Just as sometimes, someone commented, no one can remember exactly whose foot stepped in the house first at New Year.

The explorers were heartened to find good black soil, hardening though it was with the onset of winter. Among the trees they recognized birch and ash and walnut, and again they saw wild fowl. But finding no sign of human life they filled their casks with fresh spring water and returned to the ship. For the stoves in the galleys they brought trimmed branches of juniper and the sweet odour given off by the crackling boughs permeated the whole ship for days and replaced much of the fetid air in the poorly ventilated cabins.

Though the weather was bad – heavy, driving rain and a bitterly cold wind – the fifteen returned again later in the day to bring back more wood and more of the precious spring water. In their absence others had not been idle. The shallop, the long sail boat, which they had dismantled and used to make partitions, bunks, tables, benches in various parts of the ship, now had to be put together again. The parts were assembled on board and the next day taken ashore to where John Alden set to work. It was a slow process and even with many helpers the job took almost two weeks to finish.

Despite the weather every passenger and every member of crew who was fit to walk managed to wade through the ice-cold water to set foot ashore. The opportunity to bathe and wash clothing in fresh water was too great to resist. Nor was the chance to cook on an even keel wasted. Huge bonfires were built and attempts were made to dry out the clothing. But the rain rarely let up and the bitter wind lashing the rain in their faces as they waded back to the small boats that would return them to the ship brought coughs and colds and aching joints.

Captain Jones had decided now that the harbour he had chosen was not going to provide a safe haven for his ship. The wintry conditions were worsening rapidly and he informed the new governor, John Carver, that those passengers who wished to stay must make up their minds where they wished to be put ashore. The rest must abandon their quest and go home with him to England – unless within the next few days a safe harbour could be found.

None of the passengers wanted to go through an ordeal similar to the voyage out. Yet ashore they faced a whole winter without decent shelter and with no chance of making a start on the hardening ground. John Alden was urged to hurry with the rebuilding of the shallop but he was a man who could only work at his own meticulous pace and though tempers frayed around him it made little difference. It was decided that suitable quarters ashore should be set up as soon as possible and in a more favourable location.

An expedition was despatched to find the site, again with Miles Standish in charge. Most of the men he had taken previously went with him but this time he insisted that Will Trefor went, too. Standish had returned from the afternoon trip to find Will standing close to Rose on deck. Though there was no evidence they had so much as exchanged glances Standish, a quickly suspicious man, had bridled at the sight. He had decided he would not leave the ship in future unless Will Trefor was also going ashore.

Diplomatically Captain Jones suggested the small party would be wise to take a member of crew with them, a man used to ship-to-shore signals and vice versa, and he asked Will if he would mind going along. Though he could guess the captain's true motive, as the newest and most junior of the ship's officers, Will had little choice.

The party set out on the morning of Wednesday, November the fifteenth. Each man carried a sword and a musket, and provisions for a week were landed with them. Stepping out in single file the fifteen headed north along the beach, grassy dunes to their left, the dull grey sea to their right. The wind had dropped, the tide made little sound on the smooth sand and only the occasional squawk of a bird rising from a thicket broke the silence.

As before the prospect seemed bleak. But then, within a mile, to stay with the shore, they were forced to breast a hillock of sand and as they dragged their feet to the top, energy drained in the sliding climb, they were startled to see a party of six Indians and a mongrel dog coming towards them. Both parties halted in their tracks. Then a friendly cry of greeting went up from Miles Standish and the others joined in. The Indians turned at once and fled inland.

Standish and his men followed but the Indians were not burdened by packs and equipment and, far fitter than their pursuers, they soon disappeared. The sand along the shore ran some way into the woods and further hampered the settlers' progress. But it did show footprints. Fanning out they expected to come across some kind of settlement and at one point they found what appeared to be an old graveyard. Probing and digging they unearthed a skull and a few bones and the remains of some bows and arrows. Standish ordered his men to return everything to the ground and, as near as possible, to leave the place as they had found it.

Moving on they came to an abandoned shack and inside, to their surprise, they found a large rusty kettle which was certainly of European origin. Had it belonged, perhaps, to some shipwrecked sailor? Again they found small mounds of earth but these did not look like graves. They dug down and uncovered a basket of maize. Digging further they found another. Corn of recent growth filled three or four baskets. About thirty ears, some red, some yellow, some tinged with blue. Even this small amount would help to replenish their diminished stock. They decided they would take what they could carry, promising themselves that if the owners could be found they would replace what they had taken as soon as they had reaped their own first harvest.

The big kettle was filled with maize, hooked on to the long, trimmed branch of a tree and carried between two of the men. Most of the men filled their pockets, too, but along with their swords and their muskets and their own supplies they were unable to carry more. With the intention of returning when the shallop was ready they covered the remainder of the maize and restored the mounds of earth. A little later, on the opposite bank of a river, they saw two canoes drawn up at the water's edge. But they had no time to investigate before darkness fell and they returned to their camp for the night.

Tell-tale signs of the Indians were all around: footprints in the sand, man-made formations of pebbles on the beach, strange markings on the trees. And, whether with justification or not, they felt their every move was being closely watched. Standish ordered that sentries be posted throughout the night in case of attack. Swords were to hand and muskets were primed, a slow-burning match kept alight. Then, as they finished their meal and bedded down, it began to rain and there was a steady downpour. Every man was soaked to the skin and as dawn crept up on the horizon they emptied their pockets of the sticky mess of maize ruined by the rain.

With the aim of reaching and following the shoreline they set off to make their way back to where the longboat which brought them would pick them up. They had planned to follow their own tracks through the trees but the rain-soaked ground offered few clues and they were soon forced to halt and take their bearings. In twos and threes they spread out, heading in the same general direction, and it was now that coming to some higher ground Will Trefor paused on top of a small hill to assess the terrain that lay ahead. Not far away across what looked like a narrow track through the woods he saw where a sapling had been drawn down and secured. On the path lay a coil of rough twine. It was a man-made trap.

Coming along the track through the trees, closely followed by Dorothy Bradford's husband William, was Miles Standish. They were heading directly for the obstacle in their path and though they would certainly encounter the young tree Will realized they might not see the rope. Without hesitation he cupped his hands and called a warning. 'Look out! Look out, man! There's a trap!'

Miles Standish turned his head in the direction of the cry and came to an abrupt halt. Will cried out again but Bradford passed his leader and carried on, leaving Standish to take the message. At once, as Bradford disturbed the foliage, a loop caught around his foot and the bent sapling was released. As it swung back into its rightful, upright position, the loop tightened about his ankle and Bradford was hauled upside down in the air.

Bradford was more shocked than hurt and had suffered only minor bruising, mainly to his dignity. Quickly he was cut free and the explorers fell to examining the trap. Earlier they had come across the severed heads of deer, deer's feet and harts' horns, and they concluded the trap was not intended for them but for the red deer they occasionally glimpsed through the thorny thickets that tore at their clothing and scraped their hands. They were intrigued at the ingenuity of the trap, so simple yet so effective that they decided to take the rope back with them to show their comrades aboard the *Mayflower*.

On they went until they glimpsed the steel-grey sea glinting in a rare ray of sunlight. Clear of the woods they marched along the shore until they came up and over a scrub-covered sandy mound and were delighted by what they saw. Three healthy-looking bucks and several partridges hovered at the water's edge and settled like a blanket on the ground was a large flock of wild geese. But their gunpowder was wet and useless, and at their approach the deer raced for the cover of the bushes and the birds lifted off and away *en masse* in a great cloud of flapping wings.

Even so they were happy they could report back to their families and friends that there was food in abundance, sufficient game to discount any fear of starvation. Pleased and excited by their findings so far they continued the tiring trudge back along the sandy shore in talkative mood. But it was heavy going and their ebullience was short-lived. Before long the sky darkened and the rain fell yet again. Head down, each man was left alone with his thoughts.

Leading the column Miles Standish found himself perplexed, forced to reconsider his allegation against Will Trefor. Was it the result of some kind of paranoia? As so often in the past, had he allowed his ridiculously fiery temper to get the better of him? It was Trefor who had warned him and saved him from the trap. For all Will Trefor knew or any of them knew the trap could have been a killing device with a fixed arrow that shot through the heart of its prey on impact. Will Trefor had not hesitated to warn him of the danger.

26

When the expedition returned to the ship there was much to discuss. Obviously Captain Jones had to retain sufficient food and drink to see him and his crew through the long voyage home and he was keeping a careful watch on what was left, rationing everyone aboard, including himself. The men were eager to go ashore again and, with dry powder, replenish the dwindling stocks.

But despite the good news they brought the explorers found the mood, especially among the women, surprisingly unresponsive and subdued. Most had pinned their hopes so much on reaching this New World that the bleak, forbidding landscape had proved a sadly disappointing anticlimax. Anything, they had persuaded themselves, would be an improvement on conditions aboard the cramped and overburdened ship. Now, with a suggestion of snow in the driving rain, the icy wind and the manifestly uninviting shore there was little to cheer them. Even the birth of a boy child to Susannah, the wife of one William White, had done little to raise their spirits.

Along with several other young women Daisy Mason and Prudence had again ventured ashore, partly for the sensation of feeling solid earth beneath their feet but also to seize the opportunity to wash more clothing in fresh water. With much ribaldry the heftier sailors had carried the girls from the small boats through the shallower water to the shore, watched and frowned upon by the churchmen and women aboard ship.

Daisy and Prudence washed themselves and a complete change of clothing in the pool of fresh water. They also laundered garments for Rose Standish and Elizabeth Hopkins, drying the clothes before a small bonfire on the beach until the rain returned to send them back to the boats. Refreshed and in a more cheerful mood, Daisy soon realized that the feeling of despair amongst the women passengers was far more serious than she had thought. William Bradord's wife, Dorothy, seemed to be affected more than most.

'She's taken funny, Miss Daisy,' Prudence reported.

Daisy liked Dorothy Bradford. During the voyage they had become good friends. She hurried now to Dorothy's bedside. 'The men are searching for a suitable place to settle,' she told her. 'It shouldn't take long. They've found corn and maize and land that's already been tilled for sowing. And there's fish and fowl, and deer running in the woods. Plenty to sustain us. Mr Carver says come the spring we should be well established.'

'But it's so cold,' Dorothy murmured. 'My bones are frozen through. I'll never be the same.'

'They say the summers here are much, much better than at home. It won't be long, Dorothy. We'll be into the spring before we know it.'

Dorothy couldn't raise a smile. She turned her head aside, into her pillow. Rose Standish had arrived to collect her washing. She stood beside Daisy and they exchanged frowns, recognizing that this previously strong and resilient young woman was seriously depressed.

Daisy knelt on one knee and said softly, 'We have fires now in the galleys. Rose will stay with you and I'll bring some hot soup.'

But there was no response.

Mrs Carver came from her end of the main cabin to see what was happening. 'Mrs Bradford,' she said sternly. 'We must be strong at this time and support our menfolk. We must be of good heart and pray for the improvement in the weather which will surely come. You are aware that despair is a sin, are you not?'

Daisy indicated that Mrs Carver's voice and manner were too harsh and of little comfort. Mrs Carver, who as the wife of the new governor clearly believed she had a duty and a right to censure the wives of lesser men, turned away impatiently. Rose Standish also turned away.

'Rose?' Daisy followed her. 'We mustn't give up now. It's the weather, that's all. It can only get better. If we had arrived here in the summer we would be delighted with the beauty of the place.'

'How do you know?'

'Mr Clarke told Mr Ellis. Mr Clarke has been along this coast before. He says it's beautiful and there are lots of safe harbours with good fishing and good hunting. He says we'll be thrilled with the place by spring.'

Rose smiled wanly. 'Those of us who survive 'til then.'

'Don't you dare talk like that, Rose Standish,' Daisy scolded her with mock severity. 'You are going to survive. We all are.'

Unexpectedly Rose put both of her arms around Daisy and hugged her tightly. 'Take good care of yourself, Daisy,' she said, 'and find yourself a husband. You are strong and determined and with a good man at your side ....'

'And where would I find a good man amongst this lot?'

'There's Will. Will Trefor. You'd make a fine couple. In fact, I'd say you were made for each other.'

Daisy looked genuinely surprised. 'Will is only here because of you, Rose.'

'Will is here for his own reasons,' Rose said. 'It's true we were close once. But we were young and there was nothing to it really. Then everything went wrong for Will. His home was taken. His family was destroyed. He was lost and he was hurt and he wanted to hit back. And somehow, in his imagination, I became mixed up in all that. But for me, whatever there was between us was over a long time ago. I love my husband.' She looked Daisy in the eye. 'Really I do. Miles is a difficult man. I don't deny that. And I know few people can understand him. But I can and I do. I know him and all his faults and I still love him.' She put a hand on Daisy's arm. 'In a different way, I love Will – and I love you. And I think you and Will could be very happy together.'

A woman nearby, crouched on a stool, was sobbing bitterly into her hands.

'What is it?' Daisy asked.

Rose touched the woman's shoulder. 'What is it, Mrs Mullins? What on earth is the matter?'

'I want to go home,' Mrs Mullins sobbed. 'We came here to find a new life for ourselves and our children and there's nothing here. Nothing. I have relatives and friends at home.'

'You have friends here, Mrs Mullins,' Daisy told her.

Mrs Mullins' daughter, Priscilla, returned from the galley with a tin mug of steaming broth. Whenever she could now Priscilla spent time with John Alden, but the young carpenter was busy on the beach rebuilding the shallop. In the absence of her father, who was in a seemingly endless series of meetings with other men of his standing in the shipboard community, she had brought her mother from the lonely confines of their private quarters to be among others in the main cabin. But the general mood of despondency and gloom had upset rather than cheered her. 'Come on, Mother,' Priscilla urged. 'Don't let Joseph hear you.'

Priscilla's little brother chose that moment to come running in from the deck. 'They found some Injun tents! Full o' bows an' arrows an' things! They saw Injuns, too, an' they was wearing war paint!'

'Shut up, Joseph,' Priscilla said as her mother howled. 'For goodness sake!'

Two of the sailors who were standing by to float the reconstructed shallop had wandered a little way along the beach and inland when by chance they came across two abandoned wigwams. The Indian dwellings, they discovered, were made from long saplings bent into an arc and stuck into the ground at each end to make a shelter. The structure was then covered with a thick matting.

Inside the first wigwam there was room to stand. Mats lay strewn about the floor and the interior walls were covered with a finer, more decorative and more delicately woven matting. The thickest mats were spread beside a fireplace for use as beds. The chimney for the fire was a wide open hole in the top with a mat to cover it as required. A stack of bullrushes and some twine for the weaving of the mats lay in a heap.

There were wooden bowls and basins and dishes. There were baskets made from crab shells and there were many ornaments, harts' horns, eagles' claws, the feet of deer. And at the side of the recently extinguished fire was a cooked herring on a wooden platter, evidence that the Indians who lived there had fled at the approach of the seamen. Unarmed and conscious that they were trespassing the two seamen had raced back to the shallop on the beach.

A small party, carrying muskets and swords, had returned with them to examine their find. But though they waited in the hope of meeting and making friendly contact with the owners the Indians did not appear. There was much of interest in the two dwellings but nothing to suggest the Indians were in any way hostile. Certainly there was no sign of slings or arrows. If they had weapons, the party concluded, they would be hunting weapons and no doubt they had taken those with them.

The shallop was ready at last and though the weather had deteriorated still further and snow storms blurred their vision the settlers knew they had little time to waste. Captain Jones was anxious to set sail and he wanted an early decision. Did they want to stay or did they want to go home?

To those racked with coughs and colds and aching joints, the alternative seemed equally bleak. Either go ashore and possibly perish from starvation or at the hands of the natives, or stay aboard and endure the nightmare of a return voyage. To the rescue came the second mate, Mr Coppin, the only man with first-hand knowledge of the bay. He had been here once with a fishing vessel and he told now of a really fine harbour to the north.

On Tuesday, the fifth of December, a new expedition was organized and this time the party was headed by the settlers' new governor, John Carver. Of the passengers he was to be accompanied by William Bradford, Edward Winslow, Miles Standish, Richard Warren, John Howland, Edward Tilley, Stephen Hopkins, John Allerton and Edward Dotey. Of the crew, Mr Clarke and Mr Coppin, the first and second mates, Will Trefor and two ordinary seamen.

The following morning Governor Carver led his party aboard the shallop in the face of a piercingly cold north-east wind. With their prime object the finding of a suitable haven the explorers this time were acutely aware of the presence of Indians. The settlers were, after all, the intruders, the governor pointed out. They would be seen by the Indians as a potential threat. It was essential then to seek them out and establish good relations before any hostility could grow between them.

The inherent dangers of such a trip had not been lost on the wives left aboard the *Mayflower* and many of them, already sick and dispirited, were demoralized still further. Miles Standish embraced Rose in the privacy of their small cabin and promised to return unscathed. Will Trefor, as he joined the men descending into the shallop moored alongside, looked back and realized he was looking not for Rose but for Daisy Mason. Daisy was standing with Prudence on the main deck. He held her gaze briefly and her eyes communicated her concern. Pat Ellis, who was the only ship's officer to remain as cover with Captain Jones, noted the exchange with approval.

As always the weather dictated their course and the shallop followed the shoreline in a wide arc instead of attempting to cross the windswept bay. They had intended to make an early start but for various reasons the party had been slow to embark and that first morning they had lost precious daylight hours. Now, after sailing some twenty miles down the coast of the deep bay, they found an inlet and headed for the beach. The plan was to spend the night in a sheltered spot and carry on exploring in a wide semi-circle from first light.

As they approached the flat, sandy shore they were surprised to see as many as a dozen Indians who promptly scattered. The men from the shallop rapidly built for themselves a small stockade as shelter from the wind and any missiles that might come their way. With difficulty in the wintry conditions they also built a bonfire and set up sentries for the night.

Some distance along the coast another bonfire was blazing

merrily, confirming that the Indians were still in the vicinity. Early next morning, after John Carver had insisted on saying prayers, the party was divided into two groups. One group was to stay with the shallop. The other was to remain ashore to explore and investigate the area as a potential place to settle.

The party aboard the shallop reported that the inlet was really a small bay and the water was deep enough to sustain a vessel the size of the *Mayflower*, but the party on shore were less enthusiastic. The soil, they said, was poor and there was no reliable source of fresh water.

The shore party had found a dead grampus on the beach close to where they had seen the Indians the previous day. It was about fifteen feet long, fat and fleshy and promised a good yield of oil. But they had little time to spend on their find. They followed the tracks of the Indians and came to a stretch of water that later came to be known as Great Pond. Deeper into the woods they found what appeared to be an abandoned Indian burial ground. The place was dark and damp and had an eerie quality. But again Carver insisted on offering up prayers, this time kneeling to pray aloud that the dead might rest in peace. The explorers were eager to leave and even some of his closest colleagues were a little embarrassed at Carver's piety.

'Bloomin' spooky, if you ask me,' one of the seamen muttered, having learned to moderate his language in the presence of the churchmen.

The weather did not improve as the day wore on and the shore party returned to the beach early, built two huge bonfires and prepared to settle down for the night. The place was not really suitable, they had decided, for a permanent settlement. Tomorrow they would press on around the bay.

As before, sentries were posted for the night. It proved a wise precaution. Two of the guards out on patrol came racing back with a call to arms. The men were roused, a few musket shots were fired into the darkness and there was the unmistakable sound of someone or some*thing* beating a retreat.

At first light they were on their feet again, stamping about in the icy cold, stacking their equipment ready for a return to the shallop at high tide. Undeterred by a murmuring impatience John Carver led them in a short prayer, then they settled down to eat breakfast. Within minutes there was a blood-curdling cry from the woods and one of the guards came running with the news that the cry had come from a party of Indians. As he broke though the bracken, gasping for breath, arrows rained through the air all around him and the explorers dived for their weapons.

Miles Standish, whose automatic musket of flint and steel was more sophisticated than any of the other weapons, fired in the direction of where he judged the arrows had come from. Then he fired a second volley, giving the others time to prime their pieces. As a military man he took command now and ordered them to hold their fire.

Some of the men, foolishly as it turned out, had left their weapons along with other items of equipment on the beach ready for boarding the shallop. They ran there now to retrieve them. The Indians shrieked and danced in the woods then came forward to cut off those on the beach.

There were about thirty Indians in all and their leader moved to the fore and fired three arrows. From the makeshift stockade three musket shots were fired in reply and at the third shot there was a strangled cry as if someone had been hit. The Indians turned and fled.

When the shallop came in a small party of men, armed with muskets and led by Miles Standish, were left to shadow its progress along the shore. The purpose was to make it plain to the Indians that they were not in any way afraid of them. But there was now no sign of the Indians and after about half a mile the shore party was picked up.

Continuing the tour of the bay the shallop covered well over forty miles without finding Mr Coppin's harbour. And again, as the day wore on, the weather worsened. Even deep into Cape Cod Bay, a good twenty miles from the Atlantic Ocean, the sea was so rough that the hinges on the rudder of the shallop sheared through and were snapped off. Without any means of steering, the boat was now at the mercy of the oncoming storm.

Guided by the squat, hunched figure of Mr Coppin, the men aboard the shallop fought hard to get their oars into the water and row clear of the beach. But it was not without a tense and strenuous struggle that the sailors on board succeeded in bringing the shallop under a degree of control. With skilled seamanship the small vessel was gradually pulled away from the treacherous waves that thundered in to crash and break on the rocky shore.

Mr Coppins now believed they were close to the safe harbour for which they were searching. Running under a minimum of sail he had his small crew use their oars to hold a steady course and as the shallop sped between two promontories he was convinced he had found his haven. With only the early evening stars to guide him in the raging gale he turned the shallop from heading north to due west but as they made the turn the mast snapped, breaking in three places and bringing its sail down on top of them.

At one of the oars Will Trefor urged the others on. 'If you are men,' he cried, 'row like fury!' And they responded as Mr Coppin kept them to a course which in the snow-filled darkness he could only guess at.

Their luck was in. Suddenly they found they had run aground on a white sandy beach. Only later did they realize they had been hurled through a minefield of jagged rocks to the only safe landing place in several miles of coast.

Some, wary of Indians, decided to spend the night aboard the shallop. Others, anxious to stretch their weary limbs, gathered up brushwood, built bonfires and attempted to steam the chill from their tired bodies. Next morning the day dawned fine and sunny and the sea was calm.

They had landed, they discovered, on a tiny island in a wide, natural harbour. It was uninhabited and as Mr Clarke, the first mate, had been the first man to step ashore they named it Clarke's Island. It was only about a mile wide but it was well wooded with oak, pine, beech, walnut, sassafras, vine and dense stretches of tanglewood. They baled out the shallop, attempted to dry out their clothing and their wet bed-rolls and were thankful that the following day, the tenth of December, was a Sunday. At least, John Carver would insist they observed the day of rest.

On the Monday, somewhat refreshed, they boarded the shallop and explored the harbour. They were pleased to find it was quite large, not only large enough to contain the *Mayflower* but capable of holding several ships of comparable size and providing good shelter in all weathers. The water was sufficiently deep and there were many good places to land.

Four or five years earlier, Mr Coppin told them, he had seen a map in which the harbour here had been called Plimoth. Great good fortune, he said, had steered them clear of perilous rocks and a remarkable coincidence had brought them to this most appropriately named sanctuary. But the men of the church would countenance neither good fortune nor coincidence. It was entirely, they insisted, the work of God.

Miles Standish had been more than impressed with the skill of the seamen and the tenacity of Will Trefor in particular. As one of the youngest and fittest of the oarsmen Will had played a decisive role in bringing the boat to safety. Standish offered him his neckcloth with which to bind his sorely blistered right hand and a gulp at his personal brandy flask. Will accepted both with good grace but said little.

When the explorers finally went ashore they were delighted to find a number of abandoned cornfields and freshwater streams. There was timber within easy reach and several sites looked suitable for the building of their settlement. It was not perfect. Much of the soil had been overworked and no wide river cut a highway into the interior as did the Hudson River further south. But there was no argument. It was the best they could find and with the depth of winter fast approaching they decided it would have to do.

Back at the *Mayflower* tragedy awaited them.

27

Mrs Bradford's depression had deepened. The spectacle of so many passengers suffering from debilitating colds and an unsightly scurvy, a common complaint on long voyages, suggested to her distracted mind that the ship's company had fallen prey to the dreaded plague and she was convinced that all aboard the *Mayflower*, including herself, were doomed. This deep pessimism also led her to accept the more lurid tales of marauding Indians and running packs of voracious wolves. She was certain the shore party, decapitated by savages, their headless bodies torn apart by wild animals, would never return.

Early on the morning of the eighth of December, four days before the shore party returned, she was seen on the main deck, white-faced and dressed in a floor-length nightdress, declaiming to the skies. In a totally uncharacteristic manner she appeared to be railing against the unfair and arbitrary nature of fate and the lack of intervention from a remote and unfeeling God.

Twelve-year-old Joseph Mullins, who had been at his post below the poop as self-appointed 'extra look-out', rushed back to the private cabin he shared with his parents and his sister and awoke the seventeen-year-old Priscilla. 'You should see Mrs Bradford,' he told her. 'Talking to herself, she is. An' shouting her head off!'

In the main cabin Daisy Mason's handmaid, Prudence, lay awake. She was thinking of her baby 'basking in a heavenly glow', as Mr Ellis had put it, when she heard Mrs Bradford's raised voice. Others stirred in their separate sections and went back to their fitful sleeps and restless dreams, but Prudence got up, pulled on her long dress and went out on deck to see what was happening. With Priscilla and Joseph she saw Mrs Bradford in her flowing nightgown, flitting to and fro like an anxious ghost, her face almost white. Joseph said she was 'scary' and 'off her head'.

Mrs Bradford ran to the rail and hurled defiance at the wind but her words were thrown back in her face. She made strange noises, her voice starting low down and rising slowly through a long rumbling scale to a high-pitched shriek. The two girls and the small boy huddled together and watched open-mouthed.

'She's gone mad,' Joseph said, his eyes wide with excitement, and the girls could only agree.

'I must tell my mistress,' Prudence said.

But the Irishman, Mr Ellis, whom Prudence loved and trusted, had spotted Mrs Bradford's odd behaviour and was coming down a ladder from the upper deck to investigate. All three ran to meet him.

'What's this?' he asked, catching the boy Joseph. 'What's going on here?'

'It's Mrs Bradford,' Priscilla told him. 'We think she's gone mad.'

Ellis followed them a short distance along the deck until they came to a halt. Mrs Bradford had climbed up on to the side of the ship with only a slim guy rope to steady her. With her free hand outstretched she was again raging at the wind and the rain and the relatively calm sea, heaping abuse on the elements.

Should she fall there was no support, nothing below her but the cold grey water. A sudden gust of wind or a lurch of the prow could cause her to lose her grip on the rope and hurl her overboard. Ellis cautioned the excited youngsters to be quiet and remain where they were. Then he crept up silently on Mrs Bradford from behind. It appeared to him that at any moment, in her demented state, the lady might throw herself into the sea and he wanted to position himself where he could grab and hold her.

By that strange telepathy that assembles onlookers others had appeared to watch in silence.

'She goin' t' jump in?' a small friend of Joseph asked.

'Hush!' whispered his mother.

Pat Ellis was almost there, close behind Mrs Bradford and, as she raised both arms to the heavens and her flowing nightgown flapped in the wind, he grabbed her around the waist and pulled her back from the brink. With the unpredictability of the unhinged she didn't struggle. She simply turned and smiled in an oddly coquettish manner at her saviour as he helped her down.

Two of the watching women came forward to take her into their care and one put a cloak about her shoulders. As they led her away she paused, brushed young Joseph Mullins' cheek lovingly with her knuckles and called him John, the name of the small son she and her husband had left in Holland.

Prudence ran to tell Daisy what had happened but Priscilla warned her little brother not to mention any of this to their mother. Priscilla knew that her mother was in a similarly depressed state of mind and an account of Mrs Bradford's moments of madness, especially as Joseph would no doubt describe them, would do nothing to aid her recovery.

Disappointed in the outcome, Joseph and his friend went off to resume their look-out. They had hoped Mrs Bradford would jump and there would be cries of 'Man overboard!' and great activity on deck. But they had to be content with a fierce argument on the subject of alarms. When a lady goes overboard do you call 'Woman overboard!'? Of course not, Joseph's friend insisted. It's always '*Man* overboard!' How do you know? Joseph demanded. And why would anyone shout *man* if it was a woman?

The women in Mrs Bradford's section of the main cabin rallied round and brought her hot soup and words of comfort. Some spoke of feeling much refreshed after going ashore to wash clothing and bathe themselves and their children in fresh water. Perhaps, it was suggested, such an excursion would help raise Mrs Bradford's spirits and morale.

A trip ashore was planned for ten o'clock the following morning but Captain Jones did not welcome the proposal. The party, he said, would not have adequate protection. He could only spare two seamen and the male passengers who had been left behind by the main shore party were not those in the best of health.

A deputation of the more robust of the ladies led by Eleanor Billington, a large noisy Cockney woman who, though not so ill-natured as her husband, was scornful of physical weakness, convinced the captain they could take care of themselves. It was agreed that four of the remaining men armed with muskets and two seamen to manage the boat would take eight of the ladies, including Mrs Bradford, ashore. They were to stay close to the beach and venture no further than the first freshwater pool.

At ten the next day the shore party assembled, the two seamen steadied the longboat and the ladies began to descend the rope ladder from the waist deck. The sea was far from calm that morning, swirling green and bumping the boat against the ship in the swell from a daunting cross current. The first two ladies were helped down and guided to the narrow bench seats. Then came Mrs Bradford.

Tallish, slim, still white-faced, her long dark locks swept by the wind, Mrs Bradford began her descent. She seemed calm and composed, fully recovered from her odd behaviour of the previous day. But the casual way she held the ladder set her apart from the previous two and as her foot touched the bobbing longboat she raised her head. One hand holding on to a rope rung she drew a long strand of her black hair from across her eyes and, looking up at the ladies who were waiting to follow, she smiled sweetly.

In that suspended moment, a moment that many of those present would long remember, there was no mistaking the look in her eyes. She was happy now, content in her madness, totally relaxed in her new found release from sanity.

One of those watching from the deck was Daisy Mason. She opened her mouth, sensing what was about to happen, but no sound came out. Others were similarly dumbstruck as Mrs Bradford, toying with one foot on the longboat, suddenly turned away and flung herself at the turbulent sea.

Somebody shrieked. The seaman holding fast to a ship's rope let it go and his end of the longboat swung outwards in the current. His mate clambered over the seats but the boat rose with the water and the two women already on the boat screamed, terrified of being thrown overboard.

The whirling swell levelled briefly, the boat steadied and anxious faces peered out in search of Mrs Bradford. But she was gone. It had happened in an instant and she had been swept away on a rising wave. If she had planned to thwart those concerned for her safety she could not have chosen a more opportune moment.

The two seamen in the boat were fully occupied attempting to calm their hysterical passengers and restore order. Neither thought to follow Mrs Bradford into the icy water. But any such rescue attempt would almost certainly have failed. She had gone and her body was never to be found.

The women in the boat were helped back aboard the *Mayflower* and into the arms of comforting friends. Mrs Carver, on the main deck, was scathing.

'Suicide!' she cried. 'That's what it was! That young woman deliberately drowned herself. And that's a sinful way to die. A downright sinful act – the punishment for which is to burn forever in everlasting fire!'

'Shut up, woman!' Daisy ordered. 'If you have nothing good to say then shut up!'

'How dare you speak to me in that way!'

'If you call yourself a Christian then, for God's sake, shut up!'

'That young woman killed herself. She has a husband out there, risking his life to find a place where he can make a home for her. She has a small child waiting for news in Leyden. Yet she killed herself! She has committed a crime, a sin against Almighty God.'

'Mrs Bradford was under great strain,' Daisy said, calmly now. 'The woman who fell into the sea was not the Dorothy Bradford we knew and respected.'

'Fell into the sea,' Mrs Carver scoffed. 'That woman did not fall into the sea. She deliberately killed herself.'

Daisy looked at the other women who were gathered at the top of the rope ladder. 'Of those of us who saw what happened,' she said challengingly, 'only you, Mrs Carver, believe Mrs Bradford did what she did deliberately. The rest of us are quite certain she was struck by a wave and carried away in the current.' She looked for support from the watching women. 'I am sure that is what Mr Bradford would prefer to hear on his return.'

There was a nodding of heads, a murmur of agreement.

'As you say, Mrs Carver,' Daisy continued, 'Mrs Bradford's husband has been away from the ship, searching for a place where we might settle. Who knows what terrors he and the others have had to face? Are we to greet him with the news that his wife grew tired of waiting and threw her life away? Surely not.'

The agreement was more vocal now and one of the seamen said, 'She was just about to step into the boat when that big wave 'it us. There was nothin' any of us could do.'

Daisy nodded her encouragement. 'And there was nothing Mrs Bradford could do to save herself. It was an accident, Mrs Carver. A dreadful accident.'

Mrs Carver remained silent. She couldn't stand this Daisy Mason, this woman who always seemed to get the better of her, this ... this upstart. Who is she anyway? she asked herself. Where did she come from? She was not a member of the church. She had no family with her, no travelling companion. Who is she? And who does she think she is?

'Is it true Mrs Bradford chucked herself overboard?' young Joseph Mullins asked later.

'No, Joseph,' his sister told him scoldingly. 'It is not true. Mrs Bradford was swept away by a huge wave as she was getting into the longboat.'

*

When the shallop returned, early on the morning of Tuesday, December the twelfth, the members of the main shore party, though cold and wet in the driving rain, were in good spirits. They had at last agreed on the place where they would settle. They would build their new homes, they had decided, on high ground overlooking the bay. Nearby a wide area of land had in recent years been cleared and corn had been planted. A fast-flowing stream ran down the hillside to a safe harbour for the smaller boats, drained the site and provided a constant supply of fresh water. There was also a fair-sized hillock which offered a commanding view of all approaches and was later to be given the sombre name of Burial Hill. Miles Standish had noted it was a good spot to put the small cannon the settlers had brought with them.

It was not an ideal place to settle. It was not close to some large inland waterway like the Charles River further north and there was no really deep water harbour like the one found later in Massachusetts Bay. The area cleared earlier by Indians had already been over-cultivated and the soil was no longer at its best. But the settlers did not realize any of this or, perhaps, they did not want to. They needed shelter and they were determined to find what they could all agree was an acceptable place to settle. Here, they believed, they had found it.

As they climbed wearily aboard the *Mayflower* they were greeted by their families and those who had stayed behind. But as they brought their good news they were quick to sense the air of foreboding, the fact that all was not well on board the parent vessel. Captain Jones was among the first to greet them and at once he took aside the governor, John Carver, explained that Mrs Bradford had drowned in an unfortunate accident and asked for his assistance in informing her husband. William Bradford was led away from the milling crowd on the main deck and up to the captain's private quarters where between them Carver and the captain told him he had lost his wife.

Bradford had returned to the *Mayflower* elated at having found a place to settle. They could make plans, he would tell Dorothy, plans for a new permanent home and through Captain Jones they could send instructions back to Holland for their son John to join them. The news, he hoped, would serve to ease his wife's depression. Now all his hopes and plans for the future meant nothing.

In the captain's cabin he sat down unsteadily and held his head in his hands. After all the trials of the weeks at sea, the disappointment in the dismal landscape, the prospect of a bleak winter ahead, his world was suddenly empty and without purpose. Quietly Captain Jones stepped out of the tiny cabin and closed the door, leaving the two men inside to kneel in silent prayer.

Among those on the main deck to greet the returning men, Daisy strained on tiptoe for a glimpse of Will Trefor. As he came aboard she squeezed through the press of bodies and called his name. 'Will! Over here!'

He looked up and smiled and made his way towards her.

Daisy was jumping up and down, hoping he would take her in his arms and kiss her on the lips as other men greeted their wives. But she was not his wife. And when he reached her he simply took her hand and held it gently.

He was wearing a woollen hat and his unruly light brown hair stuck out at angles in wet darkened strands like the straw of a scarecrow. He grinned down at her and she laughed as the rain fell on her upturned face and in that moment Daisy felt he might do it.

But the moment passed and he didn't kiss her. They simply stood close together, slightly embarrassed, knowing they had started something but not knowing how to proceed.

It could only have been seconds but the longer they waited the less certain Daisy became. Perhaps it was just her imagination. Perhaps Will didn't feel quite the way she did. Again she looked up at him and this time she saw what previously, in her excitement, she had missed. He was weary, desperately tired. He needed sleep, a good long rest.

She walked him towards his quarters, to the steps that led below where the crew bunked, and Pat Ellis stepped forward to help her. But suddenly she stopped. She would take him to the main cabin, she announced, to her bed space, as her guest, where she could take care of him herself. Prudence would bring hot soup from the galleys. The fires were burning now and there was hot soup for everyone. And then, when he was warm and dry, he could lie down and sleep.

Will hesitated, blinking down at her, too tired to think clearly, and Pat slapped him on the back and told him conditions were chaotic down below. He should take advantage of the young lady's kind offer. Will merely shrugged and put up no resistance as Daisy steered him without further discussion to her own private corner of the main cabin.

All of the men from the shallop, it transpired, were deperately tired and in need of a rest. Will seemed dazed as if in a trance and he was cold and shivering. As with Prudence earlier, Daisy knew he must somehow be kept warm. In her small partitioned space she removed his wet jerkin and sat him down on her low bed. She plucked off his 'Monmouth', the seaman's woollen hat, and with her fingers brushed back his hair before covering his face with a towel. Then, as Will held the towel to his face, she turned from her tender ministrations and drew the thin curtain across the narrow entrance and across the prying eyes of Mrs John Carver and her companion, Miss Minter, who had chosen to hover close by.

With difficulty she eased off Will's sand-caked buckled shoes, and his knee-high stockings made wet marks on the wooden floor. Slowly and carefully she peeled them off and his bare feet were revealed, red and raw like slabs of frozen meat.

Will stared down at them, trying to focus. There was no feeling in them and they looked as though they belonged to someone else. Daisy towelled them dry and tried to warm them between her hands as Will closed his eyes and sat back in weary compliance. All he wanted was to shed his wet clothing and fall asleep.

Prudence arrived now with a bowl of steaming soup, the savour of which revived Will long enough for him to devour it gratefully and within seconds. Daisy took Prudence aside and told her she was going to put Mr Trefor to bed. She didn't want any visitors or intruders and she wanted Prudence to stand guard at the curtain and refuse entry to absolutely everyone.

Happy to comply, Prudence nodded and smiled brightly. She liked Mr Trefor and she loved Miss Daisy. She loved Miss Daisy more than anyone else aboard the whole ship. In the whole world, in fact. And though she was not very clever and didn't know very much, she knew enough to know that Miss Daisy was in love with Mr Trefor.

Nobody would get past that curtain. Nobody, Prudence told herself, and with her arms folded high across her chest and her small face set in a frown of fierce determination she took up her position at the entrance, seated on Daisy's wooden stool.

28

Behind the curtain Daisy removed Will's shirt and towelled his shoulders and chest. All of his clothing was wet, she realized, and would have to be removed. Without hesitation she released the buttons and pegs and peeled his mud-stained breeches down and off. Acting swiftly now and dispassionately, like a nurse, she stripped him naked. Will was too tired to resist or to attempt to cover himself.

Daisy dried him carefully, the whole length of his body down to his long legs and his half-frozen feet. Treating him like an invalid, she helped him to lie down and, freed of his clothing, Will stretched out on the narrow bed. He sighed and shivered slightly as she drew the blankets up and over him and it crossed her mind that she might herself undress and lie with him, allow the warmth of her body to seep into his. At Will's suggestion she had done this for Prudence, but she blushed at so wanton a thought for she knew in her heart that with Will it was not strictly necessary.

For a moment she sat beside him on the edge of the bed and with her fingers brushed the hair back from his forehead. Then suddenly, as she stood up to leave, he gripped her hand. She stopped and smiled down at him. He looked up at her in gratitude, put her fingers to his lips, released her hand and closed his eyes.

She wanted him. She wanted to climb in beside him and hold him. But she didn't want to take advantage of him like this, in his sleep. When the time came, *if* the time came, she wanted him to know exactly who he was with and exactly what he was doing. She gathered up the wet clothing and went in search of Pat Ellis.

Out in the main cabin Mrs Carver and her companion watched open-mouthed as Daisy, the small bundle under her arm, passed nearby. They stared at each other in disbelief. She, an unmarried woman, had a man in her quarters, a man who from the evidence before their eyes must be stark naked!

Pat Ellis took the clothing, asked Daisy to wait for him on deck and returned from down below with a dry shirt and some fresh breeches. He handed her his hip flask, too, and asked her to give Will a good warming shot of what he called 'the old fire water' when he awoke.

Will Trefor slept all that day until early evening and when he did at last wake up he was surprised to find where he was, alone in the curtained quarters of Miss Daisy Mason. He closed his eyes to collect his thoughts and the events and images of the past few days came flooding back, a jumble of faces and places and fleeting impressions. The desperate rowing between treacherous rocks, the shallop hurtling out of control, the trek along the wind-whipped shore and inland through the muddied woods, the black nights and the cold, the icy, mind-numbing cold.

Beneath the blankets, he realized, he was naked. But at least he was dry. For the first time in days he was warm and dry and waking up was not such a stiff and painful process. He took in his surroundings. Hanging on a peg were a pair of breeches and a shirt – *his* clothing, but not what he had been wearing. He thought of Daisy, remembering her soft hands as she undressed him, and his first instinct was to jump up and get dressed. But then, perversely, he changed his mind. It was not *his* fault he was naked. Perhaps, he thought with a smile, when she returned he might persuade the lovely Miss Daisy to join him.

He stretched himself luxuriously in the bed. This was so much better than a sandy dug-out in a howling wind with only the sour faces of the settlers, especially the sanctimonious ones, and the even more sour faces of the duty seamen to welcome the dawn. He couldn't fully recall what had been agreed back there. All he knew was that they had found a site and the settlers would soon be leaving the ship. And once Captain Jones was rid of them, as he had said so often, he would set sail for England.

Will was not sure what he wanted to do. He could stay, of course, in the so-called New World, attempt to carve out some sort of future for himself and, in truth, that might not be such a bad prospect. Those who had been here before – Stephen Hopkins had been to Virginia, Captain Jones and his first mate, John Clarke, had transported cattle across the Atlantic and Mr Coppin had actually fished in Cape Cod Bay – all said there were good, rich seasons, especially summer and autumn. It was an option, perhaps his only option. For what awaited him at home?

There was his inheritance from the estate of his mother. But there was also a possible death sentence. He had deserted his ship. True, he had deserted not in wartime but in a time of peace. In wartime, as in the battles against Spain, desertion was considered an insult to the Crown and met with summary execution. In Will's case, though he had deserted his ship in peacetime, his desertion, in view of his family history, might also be considered an insult to the Crown, equally punishable by death.

He had made a fool of himself, chasing across Europe and across England in search of a love he'd known for only a short time as a very young man. A boy, really. He didn't love Rose. He knew that now. He merely loved what she represented for him, that special time in his youth, those few enchanted years before his family was torn apart at the whim of a capricious monarch. He didn't believe his father had been party to treason or any other crime, apart from evading taxes wherever he could just like all the gentry. But whatever the reason those days were gone, lost forever. And Rose, as she was then, was lost with them. Will was fond of her still and he wished her well, but he knew she no longer meant anything special to him.

Rose's husband, Miles Standish, was in Will's opinion a hot-head and at times insufferably pompous. He was also, Will conceded, a resourceful leader and a man of impeccable military background and it was a tribute to his spirit of adventure that he had chosen to come on such a perilous mission. But Will was not sure that Standish had been wise to bring Rose along. Rose was not a strong girl. She had always seemed to Will to be of a fine delicate nature and, like her namesake, she flowered best in an English country garden. Preferably, thought Will, a garden in Cheshire.

Will wanted to return, to re-establish his position as a man of substance. He didn't relish the prospect of spending the rest of his days in some colonial outpost. But the more he thought about it the more he wanted to be part of what was going on here, too. Far more than he had realized this unknown landscape had caught his imagination and the fortitude of the churchmen, though he found their religious fervour at times a little difficult to take, had deeply impressed him. Men like Carver, Bradford, Brewster, Winslow were exceptional men. And they were *good* men. They knew right from wrong and they were determined to live by what was right. They were willing to make rules and abide by those rules for the common good. They were *civilized* men.

Prudence came in with a bag of washing. She stopped short, her large eyes wide in her small face. 'Ooh, Mr Trefor! I thought you were asleep.'

Will grinned as she attempted to avert her gaze from the hair on his chest. 'I was just about to get up, Pru,' he announced and made as if to throw back the blankets.

'Ooh!' Prudence cried again and she dropped the bag and ran outside.

Swiftly Will pulled on the dry breeches and the shirt from the peg on the wall. Then he took the cork from Pat Ellis's brandy flask, held the flask to his lips and threw back his head. For a moment he closed his eyes, relishing the taste of the warming liquid. Good old Pat, he thought. He certainly knew how to revive a man.

Barefoot he went outside, thanked the wide-eyed Prudence and asked her to thank her mistress for him. On his way out of the main cabin, aware of their interest in his presence, he bowed politely at Mrs Carver and her companion and when they looked shocked gave them a cheerful smile.

Down below in the crew's quarters he handed Pat Ellis the flask. 'Looks as though the old ship will soon be on her way,' he said. 'Once the decks are cleared of passengers the captain will up anchor and away home.'

'I don't think so,' Pat told him. 'If this harbour you found is good enough to see us through the winter it's my guess he'll wait for spring. I would. But I'll tell you this for sure, when we do go you should come wit' us.'

The ship's boy knocked lightly and Standish opened the door of his cabin.

'Cap'n would like to see you, Cap'n Standish, sir,' the boy announced in his high-pitched, unbroken voice. 'In 'is quarters, if you please, sir.'

Standish nodded and turned back to where Rose lay sick and pale. He sat beside her on the bed, took her hand, his ruddy face stiff and anxious. 'You must rest, Rose. Keep up your strength and your spirits. There's so much for us to look forward to now. They say the springs and summers are lovely here, more English than in England. Long, hot, summer days. Beautiful rivers and streams and trees and ....'

Her eyes were closed.

'Rose,' he whispered. 'Rose, love. Things can only get better for us. I promise you.'

She opened her eyes, squeezed his hand, smiled weakly. 'I know,' she said. 'I have a chill, that's all. I just need to rest.'

'We had a meeting,' he told her with enthusiasm, 'and it was all decided. As soon as we agree on the best site we are going to build a fort and a common house where we can all live if we have to, then we are going to build cottages, one for every family. We are going to map out the site into plots and then lots will be drawn. Each family will have its own plot. Except for the governor. John Carver will have a corner site where we can build the Governor's House. And us, my dear. Our name will not be in the draw for plots. We will have our own place by the fort where I will have my command.'

Instead of pleasing Rose the prospect appeared to alarm her. 'Why? Why must you be the one ...?'

'Because I'm a soldier,' he told her. 'The defence of the colony will be my responsibility. There are many Indian tribes along this coast and in the interior. We must be ready to fight them.'

'But they might not want to fight.'

'That's true. They may even want to make friends with us and I sincerely hope they do. But in the beginning we must make it clear we have weapons superior to theirs and that we are not afraid of them. We would prefer to be their friends but if they make any attempt to take what is ours then we will fight and defeat them.'

'Oh, Miles, this is their country. They were here before us. We are the intruders.'

'We will set up our colony, my dear, and if they wish to live alongside us in peace they will have to behave themselves. We have much to teach them.'

Rose frowned and the light from their single lamp flickered on her fragile features. 'They may have much to teach *us*,' she murmured softly.

Standish smiled. 'This is not for you to worry about, Rose. Not now. You must conserve your strength.'

Rose returned his smile, too tired to argue.

'I am informed the ship's captain wishes to see me,' he said quietly.

'The captain?'

'I'll not be long,' he assured her, gently withdrawing his hand from hers. 'I have some brandy in the locker. It would warm you, help you to sleep.'

Rose made a face. 'I know, but I can't drink it, Miles. It burns my throat.'

'I'll not be long,' he promised.

Captain Jones was in his cabin. With him was Giles Heale, the ship's doctor. 'Ah!' the captain said. 'Step inside.'

There was little room in the captain's quarters but Standish squeezed in to sit on a low stool and face him across the small desk.

'We will soon be moving into this safe harbour, as you know,'

Captain Jones began, 'and then, if we are berthed safely, we will unload our cargo. There will be little time for talk.'

Standish waited for him to come to the point.

'You will recall you asked – nay, *demanded* that I hold an inquiry into the conduct of one of my officers.'

Standish shifted uneasily on the stool. He had demanded an inquiry in the heat of the moment. His feelings towards Will Trefor had become rather more ambiguous since then.

'You alleged that one of my officers made an attempt on your life – an extremely serious allegation.'

Standish opened his mouth but the captain held up a hand and continued, 'As you know, in compliance with your request, I asked the doctor here to conduct an investigation.' He looked at Dr Heale, inviting him to speak. 'Doctor?'

In making his request Standish had indicated that he would prefer one of the church elders, Carver or Brewster perhaps, to carry out the investigation. But Captain Jones had insisted it was for him, as ship's captain, to decide and he had no intention of involving any of the passengers. Later, on reflection, Standish had been glad the captain had taken that line. If his accusation was proved groundless he had no wish to appear wrong – and not a little hot-headed – in the eyes of the people who held him in high regard and had appointed him their military leader.

Dr Heale coughed. 'I ... er, interviewed several members of crew, Captain Standish,' he began nervously, 'but I am pleased to say I was unable to bring my enquiries to a satisfactory conclusion.'

Standish raised his eyebrows. 'Pleased?'

'Yes,' the doctor went on, gaining confidence. 'I, of course, interviewed Mr Trefor, the officer you accused. He told me that on the night in question he was attending to the ropes, here on the top deck, with a shipmate, a man called Dyke. Mr Trefor was busy to starboard, Dyke to port, when the bowsprit suddenly swung inwards from the port side. It happened just as you came from the captain's cabin. Mr Trefor agreed that it would certainly appear, and would seem so to you, that an attempt had been made to knock you overboard.' He paused. 'From the position of the two men, only Dyke could have done what you suggest.'

'Is that what Trefor says?'

The little doctor had no intention of allowing Standish to bully him. 'No, sir. That is what I say.'

'And what does Trefor say?'

'Mr Trefor says it was quite possibly an accident.'

'It was not an accident,' Standish said stubbornly. 'Someone tried to kill me. Captain Jones admitted at the time it was a most unlikely accident.' He looked at the captain. 'You practically told me that the bow, sir, even if unroped, would not swing inwards in such a way of its own accord. It would have to be pushed.'

'Captain Jones did say that,' the doctor intervened, 'and after a demonstration for my benefit by the first officer, Mr Clarke, I concluded that he was right. It would have to be pushed. I believe, sir, there *was* an attempt by someone to cause you bodily harm, even to cause your death. It is unlikely that you would have been recovered from such a turbulent sea, especially at night.'

'Thank you,' Standish said with a note of triumph and vindication in his voice. 'Thank you, very much.'

'However,' Dr Heale continued, 'there is nothing to suggest that Mr Trefor was involved. If anyone tried to kill you, sir, it was Dyke.'

'Ah, and Dyke is dead,' Standish scoffed. 'How convenient. How very convenient.'

'I have to tell you,' the doctor said, 'that though the evidence was not conclusive I am certain it was Dyke and not, as you alleged, Mr Trefor.'

'You seafarers,' Standish said. 'You always band together.'

Captain Jones, who had listened patiently to all this, had other matters to which he must attend. But he could not allow the slur to go unchallenged. 'I deeply resent that remark, Captain Standish, and I must ask you to withdraw it.'

Standish waved a hand at him and shook his head in submission. 'I'm sorry,' he said. 'Consider it withdrawn. But you must agree the dead man cannot defend himself.'

'There is more,' Dr Heale said. 'It emerged in the course of my enquiries that Dyke had reason to hold a grudge against you. By all accounts he was a difficult and in many ways an unpleasant man and I can vouch for that from my own experience of him. I understand that on one occasion when he was being particularly insulting to passengers in the main cabin you cautioned him and ordered him to leave.'

'That is correct.'

'At the point of a pistol, I believe.'

'Yes.'

'Well, of course, there is no question in the circumstances your action was justified. But a man such as Dyke would most certainly harbour a grudge. Would you not agree?'

'I suppose so,' Standish conceded.

'So we have established a motive.'

'Surely not sufficient motive to kill someone.'

'I disagree,' the doctor said. 'Dyke was a violent man. His violence, I understand, required little provocation.'

Captain Jones was eager to speed up the proceedings. 'You are not convinced?'

Standish shrugged. 'Not entirely.'

The captain picked up a leaf of paper from his desk. 'Then perhaps this will entirely convince you. It's a statement from one of my officers – Mr Ellis – whom you may or may not know.'

'I think I know the man,' Standish said, with a hint of disdain. 'An Irish fellow.'

Captain Jones eyed him for a moment. 'I am as aware, sir, as you are that in some quarters an Irishman is regarded and portrayed as a figure of fun. I can assure you, however, that my Mr Ellis is one of the most sound and capable men I have ever known.'

Standish held up both hands in mock humility. 'I stand rebuked.'

'In his statement,' the captain continued, picking up the paper again, 'Mr Ellis has the following to say: *I was present at the death of Seaman Dyke who had been laid low by a mystery illness. He was incoherent towards the end but before lapsing into this unfortunate condition he told me clearly and in a straightforward, unemotional manner how he had tried to kill one of the passengers, a Mr Standish, with a bowsprit. He swung the bowsprit at this gentleman with the intention of knocking him overboard at night in a heavy sea whereby he might be rid of,* in his own words, *this jumped-up little fart of a man.*

Standish's face turned an even deeper red and his indignation boiled up. But looking directly at him now, Captain Jones went on, 'Somewhere in his distant past Dyke had been a Roman Catholic. At death's door he decided he would make his peace with God. He wanted to make a last confession. In the absence of a priest he asked Mr Ellis to stand in as one and it was then he confessed to attempted murder.'

'I understood the Roman Catholic confessional was inviolable. No priest must reveal what he hears there.'

'Mr Ellis is not a priest.'

Standish stood up. 'Is that all?'

'Er ... no.' Captain Jones turned to Dr Heale. 'Thank you for your work on this, Doctor. I am grateful to you. I believe, as far as you and I are concerned, the matter is now closed.'

Dr Heale edged his way past Standish. 'Thank you, Captain.'
He bowed slightly. 'Gentlemen.'

As the doctor left Captain Jones indicated he had not yet
finished with Miles Standish and the military man resumed his
seat.

29

Captain Jones faced Miles Standish across the narrow desk. 'I
want to talk to you about Will Trefor,' he said gruffly. 'But first I
must correct any mistaken impression you may have gained.'

Standish listened, barely masking his impatience.

'I want you to know I have not dealt with your complaint lightly.
I believed your request for an inquiry was, in your eyes, fully
justified. And I believe that inquiry has been properly and
conscientiously carried out. As regards Will Trefor I am confident
our conclusions – mine and Dr Heale's – are soundly based.

'This young man was an officer in the King's Navy. Naturally
when he applied to me to be taken on as an ordinary seaman I was
more than a little surprised. And *wary*, too. His bearing and his
obviously superior knowledge and training set him apart from the
average crewman. I needed to know more and to his credit he was
open and frank. He answered all my questions and I engaged him.
And I'm damned glad I did!

'He was trained, I understand, as a midshipman at Dartmouth.
He received his commission and became a junior officer in the
King's Fleet. For personal reasons he chose at the outset to
damage a highly promising career by deserting his ship. He left his
ship in Spain, arrived in the Port of London and, as I am now
aware, hid in the hold of my ship until we docked in
Southampton.' The hint of a smile crossed the captain's rugged
features. 'Then he had the cheek to ask me for a job.'

'Deserting one's ship is a very serious offence, Captain,'
Standish said solemnly. 'Not one which I would have thought a
man like you would knowingly condone.'

'We must look at the circumstances,' the captain countered.
'Trefor was a supernumerary, a young officer still undergoing

training. He was not essential to his ship's complement. We were not at war. He did not put his ship or his shipmates in any danger. He did not desert in the face of the enemy.' He paused, then added quietly, 'He deserted, I understand, because of a lady.'

Standish's face darkened. 'You refer to my wife.'

'A young man's pride bruises easily,' the captain said. 'Trefor's pride was hurt by the humiliation and injustice his family suffered.'

'Injustice? You accuse His Majesty of injustice?'

'I am impressed with your loyalty to the Crown, sir,' Captain Jones told him, 'but I will thank you not to attempt to misinterpret my words. I refer to the injustice as it appeared to Will Trefor. He was the innocent victim of his father's folly. He lost his home, everything, and tied in with all of that was his adolescent love for your wife. What he did was wrong. He should not have pursued Mrs Standish. She was now a respectable married woman. He ought to have accepted that. But he didn't. He made a fool of himself and he probably knows it. But he is not the first man to make a fool of himself over a woman. I would have thought you could find it in your heart to forgive him. After all, there is no harm done.'

Standish remained silent.

'You have my word that Dr Heale's report was complete and true, and that Will Trefor was not in any way involved in Dyke's attempt to harm you. Trefor was a naval officer, an honourable young man. Hardly likely to stoop to murder.' Captain Jones smiled. 'I realize relations between the King's Navy and His Majesty's Army are not always as they should be, but *murder*?'

Standish refused to return his smile. 'I wonder,' he said, 'why you are so concerned for this man Trefor.'

'Several reasons,' the captain replied coolly. 'First of all, when my chief officer went sick at the height of the storm I was a man short. Will Trefor turned out to be everything he said he was. A first-class pilot. A strong, resourceful man at the helm. Just what I needed. I also heard, from my second mate Mr Coppin, that when the rudder broke on the shallop and the mast snapped it was Trefor who shouldered the bulk of the rowing. He probably saved the lives of those men – you among them. Not to mention saving the shallop.'

Standish thought of the deer trap in the woods along the coast, how William Bradford had been caught by the leg and hoisted aloft upside down. Apart from the indignity it was damned painful and Bradford's leg had troubled him since. It was Will Trefor who had saved Standish then, too.

'All right.' Standish stood up to leave, unable to shake off his belligerence. 'I agree he is a useful man to have on hand. But I don't have to *like* the fellow.'

Captain Jones looked disappointed. 'I'm sorry you said that. Because there is something more.'

Standish turned back to face him.

'As you can imagine,' the captain said, 'Will Trefor is in considerable trouble at home. If he sets foot on Southampton Dock or in any other English port he is likely to be clapped in irons.'

'So?'

'On my return to London I hope to speak on his behalf. I intend to approach the Admiral of the King's Fleet. In my opinion, it would be a great pity if a young officer of Will Trefor's calibre is lost over a private matter such as this. When the facts are made known he may be pardoned and reinstated. I would like your permission to say why it was he deserted.'

'My wife's name must not be brought into this.'

'It would be no reflection on your good lady. On the contrary, it would be a tribute to her integrity ...'

'No.'

'Well, of course, I would not mention her name without your approval ....'

'Good,' Standish said with an air of finality. Then suddenly he added, 'People believe what they want to believe. They would say there must have been something. She must have encouraged him in some way.'

'Some people, perhaps. But such people are of little consequence. The whole business would soon be forgotten. Especially if you are to settle permanently over here.'

Standish shook his head. 'If we do decide to settle here we will still want to go home from time to time.'

Captain Jones could not hide his disappointment.

'So what exactly do you hope to achieve?' Standish felt obliged to ask.

'I will ask that Mr Trefor be severely reprimanded and barred from holding a commission with His Majesty's Fleet for a period of five years. I will suggest that he would then be in a position to add to his already considerable experience as a naval officer by serving with a merchant ship. I would gladly take him on as first officer on any ship of mine.'

'He may not want that. He may decide to stay on this side of the Atlantic.'

'Then he would have that option.'

There was a pause, a moment of hesitation.

'A letter from you,' the captain prompted gently, 'in praise of the contribution he has made to the cause of the new settlement which is, after all, to be established in the name of our sovereign ....'

But Standish turned away. 'I must leave you, Captain,' he said brusquely. 'I have work to do.'

Excitement was running high aboard the *Mayflower*. Eager to see the proposed site the settlers were anxious to set sail. Everything they had taken ashore was now brought back by shallop or longboat and restowed in the ship. Then, on Friday, December the fifteenth, Captain Jones weighed anchor and eased his vessel from its temporary shallow resting place into the rolling expanse of Cape Cod Bay. With the shallop leading the way the *Mayflower* sailed out across the twenty-four mile stretch of water to within five miles of the chosen harbour only to find in the strong north-easterly wind it was impossible to make a safe entrance.

There was great disappointment on board, a feeling of anticlimax at the end of so promising a day. But with professional patience Captain Jones tacked steadily all night. Next morning, with the wind in his favour, he tried again. This time there was no problem but no sooner had they passed between the narrow strips of land that formed the entrance than the wind changed direction and again raged from the north-east.

They had made it just in time, Captain Jones announced. A stroke of sheer good fortune! The churchmen, of course, did not see it that way. Once again, they decided, it was the hand of God. He had halted the gale to allow them time to enter in safely. It was a good omen, they said, a sign that this was indeed the place where they should stay and make their homes.

All that morning Captain Jones edged the *Mayflower* slowly round the new, smaller bay, anxious to satisfy himself the harbour was as good as he had been told. Reassured at last he took still more time to find the most suitable place to anchor and in the late afternoon he found what he was looking for, but by then it was too late to go ashore. That Saturday, December the sixteenth, he secured his vessel with three anchors in the sheltered spot where it could safely remain until the following spring.

The next day prayers were said on deck and as always the Sabbath was strictly observed. Passengers stared with hope and wonderment at the pleasant if wintry-looking landscape and spent their day of rest conversing in hushed tones and quiet speculation. Inside the main cabin there was the usual subdued feeling of Sunday with people quietly mingling or calling on friends and acquaintances.

Daisy Mason sat for a long time with Elizabeth Hopkins' baby sleeping peacefully in her lap and a clear view of the door. When someone entered she would look up with apparent unconcern but always she was hoping it would be Will. Only later did she learn he had been on duty all day.

Prudence was missing for most of the afternoon and Daisy guessed she was with Maurice Tinker. Prudence and Maurice had been spending more and more time together in recent days. Quiet and gentle and given to reading poetry, Maurice was teaching Pru to read and they seemed content to spend all of their free time in her hiding place. John Alden and Priscilla Mullins were not so fortunate.

Despite all the evidence in John's favour, Mr Mullins still did not fully approve of his daughter's friendship with the young carpenter and Priscilla's troublesome little brother had been briefed to keep a watchful eye on their whereabouts. The boy Joseph saw it as an opportunity to get his own back on his big sister for the many times she had censured him in the past.

At dawn on the Monday two parties set out, one in the shallop, the other in the longboat, to explore the inner coast, report back on the most suitable sites and ensure there was no immediate danger from marauding Indians. The men were mustered on the sandy' shore, guards were left to protect the boats and Miles Standish led the combined party several miles to the north. Within a short distance they came across more abandoned cornfields and it soon became obvious the whole area had once been occupied.

Though the ground was frozen hard they found the soil was good, black and fertile-looking underneath. The woods were dense with a variety of trees and the settlers were delighted to find plum and cherry trees in abundance. Satisfied with this initial reconnaissance they returned the following day to search for the source of the main river and determined to fix on a site. Some favoured the island, Clarke's Island as they had christened it. It would be easier to defend, they argued, than a site on the mainland. But they finally accepted it was far too small. Others favoured the banks of the river upstream but the woods there were far too dense, would need a lot of clearance work, and the river ran far too shallow.

The debate continued despite the need for urgency and it was mid-week before the decision was made. The chosen place was the high ground overlooking the bay in the area known to the local Indians as Patuxet, but named Plimoth some six or seven years earlier by the English explorer John Smith, who had also given the whole coastline the name of New England.

The settlers were eager to make a start. They wanted to build some communal shelter as soon as possible. Christmas was almost upon them and, tired of the cramped conditions aboard ship, they had a vague, unspoken hope of celebrating the festive season on land. But towards that weekend a violent storm blew up, they were unable to go from ship to shore and their plans for unloading goods and equipment were maddeningly delayed.

On Saturday the weather improved and every man who was fit enough was taken ashore. The felling of trees and the stripping and cutting of timber began. Sunday was Christmas Eve and, though there was a need to get on with their work, they did not abandon their faith and the day was spent in rest and prayer.

John Carver as governor and other church elders took the opportunity to circulate among the families to offer reassurance and to visit the many who had fallen sick. But during the night the families huddled aboard the *Mayflower* suffered a new setback when a series of shrieks and strange noises from the mainland kept them awake. Among the women there was an outbreak of panic and hysteria and many of the men were equally scared, but at daybreak the only sign of life along the frost-bound shore was a flock of squawking gulls swarming an inlet.

Christmas Day, it was decided, would not be a holiday and every available man returned to the task of felling trees and trimming the logs for cutting. As a precaution, Miles Standish and a small, specially selected squad of men with muskets patrolled the area around where the party of tree fellers worked. They found nothing untoward, no sign of Indians lurking in the vicinity. Yet, as darkness fell and they prepared to end their labours for the day, they were startled by more wild shrieks and strange noises. Muskets at the ready, Standish and his squad went to investigate the fringe of the forest but again they found nothing.

Most of the men returned that evening to their families aboard the *Mayflower*, but twenty or so remained to guard the logs and to sharpen the cutting tools for the morning. Aboard the ship some effort was made to celebrate Christmas but most of the men were too tired to take part. Two things happened to lighten the occasion.

Although the supply of beer carried for the passengers had long since been consumed Captain Jones decided to release some of the ship's private stock. It meant there would be less to sustain himself and his crew on the return journey, but he was a kindly man at heart. He recognized the fortitude of his long-suffering passengers and judged it was the least he could do.

The other event to gladden the hearts of the settlers had occurred that morning when John Alden appeared with a large sack of small toys he had fashioned out of bits of surplus wood during the long hours at sea. Every child received a doll or a toy soldier or the model of a small boat. This was their first Christmas on this side of the Atlantic and for many the little wooden toys became more precious than anything they received in the years to come.

The carpenter, John, was still pained by the recollection of the lovingly crafted crib he had converted into a tiny coffin sliding into a cold grey sea. For the girl Prudence who had lost her baby he had made a special carving as a memento. It was a replica of the crib, small enough to hold in the palm of the hand, with the infant Jesus, a halo about his head, sleeping like a newborn babe, the whole in a smooth whitewood. It was a gesture that further endeared him to Priscilla Mullins and a gift that Pru was to cherish for the rest of her life.

By the end of that week a site had been chosen for a cannon platform. It was to be built on top of a small hill with a good view of the surrounding country. Here they would build their fort, a fort it would be difficult to take by surprise. The settlement, they decided, would be built inside a stockade. Houses would form a main street which they would call Leyden Street in honour of the town in Holland where many of them had lived in self-imposed exile, out of reach of religious persecution. But first they resolved to construct a large common house where they could store the items they wanted to bring ashore and provide shelter for a good number of the settlers until individual houses were erected.

At this point the single men among the settlers were asked to join with families and in this way the number of houses immediately required was reduced to nineteen. Priscilla Mullins, naturally, wanted John Alden to join with her family and this was quietly indicated to Governor Carver who tactfully refrained from mentioning the arrangement to Priscilla's father. As it happened William Mullins was one of those most affected by the cold and the feelings of mental and physical exhaustion many were suffering and he had lost much of his fire. Recognizing that, besides being a fine upstanding young man, John was one of the ablest of the journeymen and more likely to provide them with a good roof and sound furniture than most, Mrs Mullins tacitly went along with the suggestion.

The work went slowly yet considering the voyage the men had survived, the privations they had endured and how weak they were from the lack of adequate food in the often bitterly cold weather they did remarkably well. But there was a price to pay in hacking coughs, sore throats, streaming colds and sudden sneezes, germs passed from one to another, attacks they were too weak to shake off and some were so seriously affected it gradually became clear they might not have the strength or, more importantly, the will to survive the winter.

Still more ominous, since the death of Dorothy Bradford, a new and darker possibility had occurred to more than one of the less devout, men as well as women. Though it was considered a sin even to contemplate such an act, suicide as a quick way out of all their misery sometimes seemed an increasingly inviting option. Aware of the dangerously low spirits, John Carver and the church elders released more of the settlers' dwindling food stocks, increased each family's rations and worked hard to maintain morale. But the spectre of death cast a long shadow over their efforts.

Already, on the fourth of December aboard the *Mayflower*, one of the menservants, a man called Thompson, had died of cold and exhaustion. On the sixth a boy servant, Jasper More, employed by the Carver family, had died as the ship waited in the bay of Cape Cod. Next and the first to die in the small harbour at Plimoth was a single man named Britteridge. A servant named Prower died on Christmas Eve and another, a man named Langemore, died in the last week of 1620.

30

The New Year came in with the threat of an epidemic. First to go was a much respected man named Degory Priest who had left his wife and two young daughters in Holland that they might join him in the New World only when he had made a home for them there. He died on January the first.

The keeper of the settlers' accounts, one Christopher Martin, an abrasive and unpopular man of forty, who had recently lost his two menservants, now fell ill himself. The passenger named Fuller, who was also a doctor, saw that Martin was so weak he was unlikely to survive more than a few days and sent at once for Governor Carver.

Carver took over Martin's accounts and spent the night in prayer at the sick man's bedside. Then Martin fell into a deep sleep and never regained consciousness. His body, like the others, was taken out in the longboat, weighted with stones from the shore and committed to the wider expanse of Cape Cod Bay.

On the ninth day of the New Year there was at last some encouraging news. The common house was almost ready for occupation. Lots were drawn for sites along both sides of the main street and the men who had worked on the common house were free to begin building their own homes. But again there were delays when torrential rain brought work to a standstill.

By Sunday the fourteenth most of the men were either camping ashore in a series of dug-outs covered by turf resting on wooden posts or sheltered in the common house which was almost overflowing with beds and bed rolls. The declared aim of the church elders was to bring all the settlers from the *Mayflower* for their first full service on dry land, but that morning before daybreak those aboard the ship were shocked to see the common house ablaze.

Many of the women watching from afar were convinced the settlement had been surrounded by savages, burned to the ground and all of their menfolk murdered. The truth was the fire was confined to the newly thatched roof. A spark had set the dry underside alight and though the blaze had sprung up rapidly it had died down just as fast in the heavy rain and no great damage had been done. But the women, convinced that vicious savages were responsible, were reluctant to accept this simple explanation.

By the twentieth, using both the shallop and the longboat, the settlers had ferried most of the food and equipment from the ship to be stored in the common house. All the *Mayflower* holds were cleared of the passengers' goods and chattels and only a few of the men, women and children remained on board. Daisy Mason was one of them.

As if she was in some way immune to minor ailments Daisy was strangely untouched by the proliferation of colds and fevers all around her. Prudence had been feverish and Rose Standish had been far from well and perhaps in ministering to them Daisy had little time to brood and allow herself, as many did, to fall sick. But there was no escaping the saddening results of the epidemic.

Over the months at sea Daisy had come to know most of the 102 passengers who had sailed out of Plymouth, England, at least by sight if not by name. Mr Priest she had known and liked and his loss had seemed especially sad. He was a good man, anxious to see again the family he had left behind and full of plans for the future. His two small daughters were the children of his first marriage. As a young widower he had married the sister of one of the senior churchmen, Isaac Allerton. And though he had never actually said so, Daisy had the impression he was worried that his second wife, Sarah, might not have as strong a commitment to his girls as did their natural mother. Now the poor man was dead and his new wife and his young daughters would have to fend for themselves.

Prudence had been especially concerned at the death of the Carvers' servant boy, Jasper More. It was not that she was fond of Jasper in any way. It was simply that he had a little sister, Ellen, who was no more than eight years old. Ellen was in service to the Winslow family and, though there were two older brothers, it was Jasper she seemed to cling to, Jasper whose loss would affect her most deeply. She might feel she was alone in the world with no one really close and Prudence knew how desolate a feeling that could be.

Every individual, every family was in some way touched by death in that first sombre winter. Sick men, women and children were housed ashore in the common house or in the one completed domestic dwelling and every day and every night someone died. Aboard the *Mayflower* conditions were little better. Among the crew many fell sick and seven men died including the bo'sun and the cook. Civility and good humour evaporated and friends blamed friends for each other's misfortune. Shipmates, who were soulmates when bent on a bout of hard drinking, callously ignored their comrades' needs and loudly declared they were not going to risk their lives by courting infection.

Yet the churchmen, the often ridiculed 'Bible punchers', the quiet men so many of the sailors had reviled and despised as pious weaklings, came to their aid. They brought food from the galleys, took soiled clothing away to be washed, emptied slop buckets and performed other unpleasant tasks without hesitation, working tirelessly to make conditions bearable in the crew's cramped quarters. And many of the tough-minded seamen found a new respect and admiration for the passengers they had previously dismissed as troublesome, whining landlubbers.

Of the passengers only seven were untouched by the rampant epidemic. Miles Standish was one who stayed on his feet and, though still responsible for the defence of the settlement, he found time to work selflessly among the sick. Pat Ellis, Will Trefor and Daisy did all they could to help. But the governor, John Carver, and his unofficial deputy, William Bradford, were both laid low.

One of the oldest and most respected of the elders, William Brewster, managed to keep going and did much to help with the more unpleasant work in the overcrowded common house, removing stained sheets and clothing and helping to wash and feed his less fortunate fellow passengers. Few of the women escaped the sickness and those who did were left, along with any of the older children who were able, to form a desperately small nursing staff. Carver, who tried gallantly to direct operations from his sick bed, wanted Daisy, with her known nursing skills, to come ashore. But aboard the *Mayflower* Prudence still had a fever and Rose Standish was far from well.

Miles Standish had begged Daisy to stay with his wife and to keep him informed of her progress. He felt that in the privacy of her own cabin Rose would fare better than she might in the communal chaos of the common house. The ship's doctor, Dr Heale, agreed wih him and advised that Mrs Standish was, in any case, too ill to be moved. She should stay in her cabin and he would visit her daily as he tended the crew. The passengers' doctor, Dr Fuller, was ashore and showing every sign of succumbing to the same debilitating ailment as his patients. Neither doctor had much to prescribe apart from a limited supply of beer which they believed to be an anti-scorbutic, the only defence against the dreaded scurvy.

Aboard the ship the once crowded main cabin, where the air had been so stale and fetid the doctors had feared an outbreak of typhoid, was all but empty. Less than half a dozen passengers remained. Daisy's friend, Elizabeth Hopkins, had gone ashore with her husband and children. In fact, all the children had left the ship now except one, the two-year-old daughter of Alice Rigdale.

Alice, whose husband had recently died and been consigned to the waters of Cape Cod, sat all day long gently rocking her small daughter to and fro on her knee. The child seemed healthy enough, with her thumb thrust deep in her mouth and her bright, inquisitive eyes following anything that moved. But her mother stubbornly refused to take her ashore. She believed they were safe here, safe from the sickness that had taken her husband and safe from the 'wild Indian men' who were 'just waiting to pounce'.

'No good me goin' ashore,' she told Daisy. 'Me wi' no man to look out for me.'

'You'll have to go ashore eventually, Alice,' Daisy said. 'Unless you want to go back home.'

'Got no one in England now,' Alice said and she said it in such a calm, matter-of-fact way and with such an air of resignation that Daisy wondered if the loss of her husband and everything else combined had affected her mind. Sooner or later she would have to choose, go home or go ashore.

'You're not the only one without a man,' Daisy said. 'What about me? And Pru? Mr Carver says they will build a house for widow ladies and single women. You and little Alice will live with me and Pru.'

Alice smiled knowingly. 'You won't be on your own for long, dear. Not a girl like you.'

Daisy was in no hurry to go ashore. She wanted to be sure Prudence was well enough and she also wanted to honour her commitment to caring for Rose Standish. Both of her charges seemed to be responding well. But then, on the night of January the twenty-eighth, she began to fear the worst. Rose was a disturbing waxen colour and her eyelids drooped heavily. As Daisy entered the small cabin, Rose's pale lips moved and Daisy went down on one knee to hear what she wanted to say.

Rose's voice was weak but she spoke clearly and coherently and there was no doubt she was fully in control. She wanted, she said, to see Will. Will Trefor. Daisy said she believed Will Trefor was on duty at that moment, keeping watch from the poop deck. Rose begged her to ask him to come.

'Shouldn't I be sending for Miles?' Daisy prompted.

But Rose insisted. It was Will Trefor she wanted.

For once it was not raining and the wind had dropped. The ship creaked quietly at its three anchors but swayed only slightly and Daisy was grateful for the rare moments of stillness. The partly hidden moon cast a ribbon of silver across the black water and shed a welcome light on the bare-masted vessel. From the main deck, clutching a shawl about her shoulders, Daisy could see Will's dark outline against the night sky.

He was keeping a careful watch over the darkest stretch of water between the ship and the sandy shore. There had been talk that a flotilla of canoes might arrive under cover of darkness in an attempt to board the seriously undermanned *Mayflower*. It was unlikely and Captain Jones had dismissed the suggestion. But he had insisted that, in accordance with established practice, a watch must be kept at all times.

Below, in the crew's quarters, with two men dead and not yet disposed of, their bodies covered from head to toe by a tarpaulin, and with so many others sick there was chaos. Green-faced seamen lay in bunks or on the floor, anywhere, among them several of the supposedly toughest. The nearest to the wooden ladder from the deck above, a man who had been appointed master of the shallop, raised a hand in a feeble acknowledgment as Daisy stepped part of the way down. With a wan smile from his sick bed he told her he had changed his mind about the churchmen.

'When we fall sick,' he said, referring to himself and his fellow members of crew, 'we treat each other like dogs. They treat everyone like human beings, they church people – even us! They be kindness itself.'

She'd had no reason to like the man previously. He was an impatient, arrogant fellow. But she gave him a friendly smile. 'There's hope for you yet, Tom English.'

Daisy had ventured part of the way down the ladder in search of Pat Ellis. She found him doling out the only medication available, tumblers of beer, to the sick and the dying. She told him that Rose Standish was extremely ill and wanted to see Will. Daisy feared that Rose might not last until Will's watch was over. She didn't know what she should do, she said, and as always the Irishman came to her aid. 'I'll take over his watch for half an hour or so,' he said. 'You go back to Rose.'

Rose was lying despondently on her bed but she tried to smile brightly and raise herself on one arm as Daisy told her, 'Will is on duty, but I believe he will come.'

She gripped Daisy's hand and weak though she was her taut knuckles gleamed white in the poor light of the cabin. It was obviously urgent and of great importance to her to see Will. Had she had some kind of premonition? Daisy wondered. Perhaps she believed she was about to die and wanted to express her undying love for him from her deathbed.

Will appeared in the doorway, saw Daisy, looked at Rose and stepped inside. Daisy stood up. Will was clearly taken aback at Rose's frail condition. He came closer.

Daisy stepped aside. 'I will leave you,' she said.

But unexpectedly Rose said firmly, 'No, please. Daisy. I would like you to stay.'

Daisy looked at Will and he nodded as if that was what he wanted too, and together they knelt by the narrow bed.

Seeing Rose, seeing the brave smile that broke out of that chilling mask, Will Trefor saw also, in his mind's eye, the clear unlined face of the seventeen-year-old girl he had held in his arms as they lay together in the long Cheshire grass, close to the home he had also loved. It was a timeless face, a face that would never change, the face of a girl as fresh and as young in his memory as she once was. But he realized now it was the memory he loved, not the girl. He no longer knew the girl.

'I am so glad you could come, Will,' Rose said as if she was welcoming him to a soirée at her father's house. She offered him her hand.

The hand was as cold as a gravestone. He put it to his lips, clasped it tight to give it warmth. But Rose merely smiled and withdrew it.

'I fear,' she said, 'I am not long for this world.'

'That's nonsense,' Daisy told her spontaneously. 'You are going to get well. You must. The worst is over.'

'Is it?' Rose asked doubtfully.

'Daisy is right,' Will said. 'You have come this far. You must see it through.'

A faint smile again passed over Rose's drawn, sallow features. She seemed resigned, ready to accept her fate, as if she knew she was soon to die and was simply humouring them. From the depths of their dark hollows her eyes looked up at her two friends with warmth and a clear, unstinting affection. 'Daisy,' she murmured. 'Will.'

They strained closer as her voice sank to a whisper.

'I'm so glad you came, Will,' she said. 'I want to tell you and I want Daisy to hear it, as my witness, that I was deeply moved by what you did. To follow me here ... to risk all you had in this mad attempt to bring back the past – it was the gesture of a true romantic. There was something extraordinary, something beautiful in it. A wild, irrational beauty ....'

Will opened his mouth but she raised her hand weakly.

'I was thrilled to know you felt the way you did. But what we had is in the past, our past, yours and mine. It belongs to us. No one else. But time moves on and life with it. Things change. People change.'

'It's all right, Rose,' Will whispered. 'I understand.'

'I want you to know, Will, I married Miles because I loved him. I still love him and I will ....' Rose smiled ruefully. 'I was about to say "until the day I die" but such declarations are usually made when that day seems far distant ....' She paused, closed her eyes.

Then she went on, 'I will love him now and for as long as I'm here. He's a good man, Will. And what I would like most of all is for you and he to be friends. I would like Daisy to tell him I told you this.' She paused again. 'I want him to believe me when I say I love him and there is no other. I have great ... *affection* for you, Will. And we have our own special memories. But I love Miles now, as a woman loves a man. Not simply because he's my husband or because I made certain vows in church. I just love him for what he is, Will.'

Will put his fingers to her lips. 'I know,' he said gently, 'and I respect that. And now you are going to get well and make your life in this new world. You are a young woman, Rose. I want to see you set up a home here, have your children here ....'

'Dear, dear Will.'

'But look,' Will said suddenly, 'this is all wrong. Your husband should be here, by your side. I will bring him.'

'No,' Rose said. 'You can't. His duty lies ashore. I understand they fear an attack at any time. Miles is needed at the settlement.'

Will stood up. 'Get well, Rose Standish,' he said, pointedly using her married name. 'I insist that you get well.'

'*We* insist,' Daisy added.

'I must return to my watch.'

'Mr Ellis is standing in for Will,' Daisy told Rose.

'Smile!' Will ordered and Rose smiled bravely.

He turned at the door to look back at her once more then he left and Daisy hurried after him. He held her briefly by the shoulders and there was a light in his eye, as if something had finally been resolved. Then seriously, he said, 'I must go for Standish.'

'What about your watch?'

'Pat will cover for me,' he said. 'Things look bad for Rose. She doesn't seem to have the will to live.'

'You can't go for Miles alone.'

'I'll take a small boat and row ashore. If I can find him I'll bring him right back. Tomorrow could be too late.'

'Take someone with you.'

'There are no oarsmen left. They are all laid low with this damned fever. And anyhow, it's better that I go alone. That way there is only me breaking the rules. I should inform the captain but he would refuse to allow me to take a boat out on my own. I'll tell him when the job is done.'

Daisy followed him to the lower deck. Three of the small boats were tethered alongside and as he swung down into the nearest she called to him to take care. He put a finger to his lips to silence her.

He didn't want anyone, at that moment, to know he was taking a boat without permission.

Will cast off in the choppy water, turning the small boat with his right-hand oar. It was a cold, clear night with the moon high and bright and the air sharp to the nose and throat. He settled back and with the wind in his face he levelled the oars and began to row hard for the shore.

The white figure of Daisy, watching from the deck in her dark shawl soon merged with the shadows of the ship as he made good progress and it occurred to him then how thoughtless he had been. He was glad that Rose had said what she had said. It was what he wanted her to say – that she loved Miles and always would. It afforded him an honourable exit, the freedom to turn his attention to where he knew his true interest lay, and he wished he'd given Daisy some sign, some clear signal. A hug, a squeeze, a gentle word perhaps. He cursed his lapse. You might be capable of romantic gestures, he told himself, but you can also be incredibly insensitive.

Miles Standish was not in the common house. He was at the smaller building with Mr Brewster, helping to remove the body of a woman who had died earlier that evening. At the sight of Will Trefor the colour drained from his red face. He looked at Mr Brewster and the old man nodded. Anticipating the worst, Standish came forward slowly to meet the bearer of what he guessed could only be bad news.

'Is it Rose?'

'Rose is all right,' Will told him, aware at once of what was in Standish's mind. 'Or, at least ....'

'What is it, man?'

'She is in good hands. Miss Mason is with her.' He glanced around the small crowded room. 'I think you were right to keep her aboard ship. But I think, if you can, you should come back with me now.'

'Is it bad?'

'She could have taken a turn for the worse.'

'Have you spoken to her?'

'Yes,' Will admitted, 'and I know she would be very relieved to see you. She won't ask for you because she believes you are needed here.'

'I'll come now,' he said. 'Right away.'

Will nodded in approval. 'Then I'll row you there.'

Standish spoke briefly to Brewster then followed Will out and down the hill to the beach in silence.

'You came alone?' he asked as they reached the small boat drawn up on the sand.

'Yes,' Will said.

'Then perhaps I should row back,' he offered.

Will shook his head. 'I'm more used to it than you.'

Standish shrugged. 'Very well. Thank you. And thank you for coming. I must thank Captain Jones, too, for allowing you to come.'

'He doesn't know,' Will said, facing Standish and pulling on the oars, his back now to the black silhouette of the anchored ship.

Standish smiled in the light from the moon. 'You are not one for rules and regulations, are you, Mr Trefor?'

'There are times,' Will said, 'when rules must be broken.'

They were silent then and when Will eased the boat alongside the ship and tethered it back into position, Standish didn't wait. He gripped the rope ladder and swung upwards into the darkness.

In the small cabin Daisy had kept a vigil at Rose's bedside, sitting uncomfortably on a low stool, with Rose drifting in and out of consciousness.

'Miles,' Rose murmured once when she opened her eyes, but before Daisy could speak she had drifted back into her restless sleep.

'Hush now,' Daisy comforted her and as she watched Rose, the small oval face perfectly still, the pale temples tinged with a faint ice blue, she thought of the Duchess on her deathbed. In life the two could not have been more different but now … now there was something about the skull behind the face, the suddenly lank and lifeless hair and for a moment Daisy thought that Rose was dead.

Twice Daisy went to the door, thinking she heard their approach, and on the third occasion it *was* them. Miles Standish hurried inside, Will Trefor close behind him, and as if sensing her husband's presence Rose opened her eyes.

'Miles.' Her voice was weak and distant.

Standish was unable to speak. He knelt on one knee, held her frail body in his arms.

But there was something more than frailty now. There was a limpness, an air of finality, and when he lay her back against the pillow all three knew that she was dead.

31

Pat Ellis was saddened but not surprised at the news of Rose's death. 'From what I've seen,' he told Will as they stood side by side at the watch, 'there are plenty more to go yet.'

'I suppose you think what I did was a waste of time.'

The Irishman lit his gnarled old pipe and a gust of wind blew it out. 'In what way?'

'Jumping ship, coming out here ....'

'No,' Ellis said, 'as a matter of fact, I do not. I happen to think this was the best thing you could have done under the circumstances. If the girl had died and you had only heard about it when you were many miles away it would have all seemed very different.'

Will turned to look at him.

'Bein' here, seein' her with her husband, livin' happily with the man she married, made you realize that what you had was just a juvenile thing, that nothin' would have come of it even if the lady had lived. Comin' on this voyage has set you free.'

'And made me a fugitive.'

'From the King, yes.' He puffed at his pipe. 'But you are no longer a fugitive from yourself.'

'You're a wise old bird,' Will said. 'I'll grant you that, Patrick Ellis.'

'A bird, is it now?'

'A wise old Irish gentleman.'

'Not wise, Will,' he said. 'But old, yes. I'm just older than you, that's all.'

When the first mate came up to take over the watch, Will Trefor and Pat Ellis went below just as two members of the crew were bringing out yet another body for burial at sea. In the crew's quarters it was not always easy to make out who was sick, who was merely sleeping or even who had died. But ignoring their surroundings they lay back on their bunks, closed their eyes and tried to sleep.

Less than an hour later Prudence came to the hatch and called

Will's name. 'Mr Trefor! Mr Trefor there, please?'

'Stow yer racket!' a seaman yelled.

'Ye'll waken the dead!' cried another.

But someone roused Will and he came blinking up to the cold open deck. Miss Daisy was worried about Captain Standish, Prudence told him. Could he come, please? Will went back for a jerkin then followed her to her mistress in the main cabin.

'Miles is still in there,' Daisy said, 'with Rose. He told me to go away and leave them alone and when I went back later he'd locked the door and wouldn't answer when I called out to him. I just wanted to give him something to eat. He must be hungry.'

'Probably fallen asleep,' Will said. 'He was already fit to drop when I brought him aboard.'

'You don't think he'd do anything ... silly?'

He shook his head. Standish was a professional soldier, too honourable a man to commit suicide when his services were so essential to others. 'He'll be asleep, that's all.'

Will was right. He put his shoulder to the door of the small cabin and the worn wooden bolt snapped easily. Miles Standish was in a deep sleep, slumped across the body of his wife. Will touched him lightly on the shoulder and he came awake with a start. Then he saw his wife – the lovely face had a glazed look now – and he realized where he was and why. He struggled to his feet and covered her carefully with the bed sheet.

'Better come along,' Will said. 'Get something to eat.'

Standish hesitated.

'You must keep your strength up,' Will advised. 'People out there are relying on you.'

He nodded and followed Will into the passage and Daisy closed the cabin door. On the deck were two more bodies, each one rolled in rough sacking. They awaited a prayer from the captain prior to their disposal. Another was expected that morning. One of the crew was slowly losing his hold on life and the two seamen who were to row the bodies out for burial were waiting for him to die.

In the early afternoon Captain Jones would say the Lord's Prayer over the bodies and perhaps a few lines from his Bible. The bodies would then be weighted with stones brought in from the beach, lowered into one of the small boats and taken out to sea.

The sight of the bodies on the deck and the ritual that was to follow seemed to worry Standish. 'I intend to stay here in this new country,' he told Will, 'and make my future here. I intend to bury Rose ashore in a proper grave. I will dig it myself and I will bury her myself. I don't want her thrown into the sea.'

'There is nothing wrong with being buried at sea,' Will said.

Standish looked at him quickly, the soldier facing the sailor. 'No, no, of course not,' Standish agreed. 'It's just that I want to know where she is. I want to be able to visit her last resting place.'

'There will be objections.'

Standish nodded.

'And you will not be allowed to mark the grave in any way. At least, not at first.'

So many of the settlers had died and were likely to die that winter that the governor had decreed that no graves should be marked and the land should be restored after a burial which must always take place at night. He didn't want the Indians to know just how depleted their numbers had become.

'I will bury Rose myself,' Standish said quietly, 'in accordance with the rules we have all accepted. I will bury her under cover of darkness and I will leave no trace. But I will know where she is buried and, perhaps, one day when we have built our settlement and made it safe I will mark the spot in a suitable manner.'

'You will require Captain Jones's permission to take her ashore,' Will said.

'I will take her ashore with or without permission.'

'The boats are his,' Will reminded him.

'Then I will commandeer one.'

Will smiled. 'It may not come to that. But whatever happens, I will gladly help. And, if I may, I will also help you with the burial.'

'Thank you,' Standish said. 'I am already in your debt.'

They had quickly finished the bowls of hot soup which Daisy had brought from the galley. Now, as they stood on the main deck looking back to the shore, she returned with tots of brandy which they tossed back in unison.

Will felt the warmth flowing through him. He turned to Standish. 'Wait here.'

The captain was in his cabin, writing up the previous day's log. Some of the remaining passengers wanted to go ashore, Will told him. With the captain's permission he would take one of the small boats. It was not Will's responsibility to ferry people ashore and the suggestion was a little presumptuous. But the captain looked pale and ill himself that morning and he took little interest in Will's request. He merely nodded his approval.

In the main cabin Will told Daisy she should stay aboard with Prudence until a suitable place was available for them ashore. Then he went down below and told Pat Ellis he would probably be away for the rest of the day.

Miles Standish was waiting on the lower deck, the body of his wife in his arms. With his red hair blown over one eye, his broad shoulders shielding her body from the wind, he looked lost and alone and Will suddenly felt desperately sorry for him.

'We can go now,' Will said. 'Same boat.'

'I must thank Captain Jones.'

'No,' Will said. 'The captain doesn't know you're aboard. He doesn't know I came for you last night. If he did I'd be in trouble for taking the boat without permission.'

'He doesn't know ... about Rose?'

Will shook his head. 'I will tell him on my return.'

He climbed down the rope ladder, manoeuvred the small boat they had used previously into position, then saw that Standish was unwilling to use the ropes to lower Rose's body. He tried to hold the swaying ladder still as he stood, legs apart, in the bobbing boat. It was a hazardous descent but the squarely built Standish was a strong man with thick muscled arms and he negotiated the rungs carefully with the wasted body of his wife over his shoulder.

Reverently he handed his burden to Will who laid the sheet-wrapped body in the well of the boat. His face devoid of expression, Standish then stepped down himself and again offered to do the rowing. Again Will declined. The captain, he said, would not approve. It was a sailor's job.

When they were almost at the beach Standish waded the last few yards ashore with Rose in his arms and carried her body up the slope to where the settlement began. Will tied the small boat alongside the shallop which was under close guard and followed Standish.

A short distance from the common house a shrine had been erected, a wooden sheltered structure, where two of the older women kept a quiet vigil. Bodies lay awaiting burial and the body of Rose Standish was laid beside them. Standish spoke to the two women, instructing them that no one was to remove his wife's body. It was his intention, he told them, to bury her himself. Then as Will Trefor joined him he added, 'No one, that is, but myself or this gentleman.'

When he entered the common house Will was shocked to see so many of the settlers on their sick beds. It was bad enough aboard the *Mayflower* with half the crew laid low but this was worse. Roughly hewn beds had been pushed close together, leaving only a narrow central aisle. Less than a dozen helpers were on hand. Even Governor Carver was in bed and the frail-looking William Brewster appeared to be in charge. Mr Brewster was visibly pleased to see Standish and genuinely distressed at the news of Rose's death.

Out on the hillside two of the remaining able-bodied men were digging a narrow trench as if to make an added fortification against Indian attack. In fact they were preparing a communal grave. Mr Brewster explained what was happening and Will saw that Standish was not happy with the arrangement – at least, not for Rose. But Mr Brewster had other priorities for him. Standish, he said, was urgently needed at the makeshift fort. Only two men were there, keeping watch and guarding the musketry. If the Indians attacked now the result could only be a massive defeat for the settlers, probably a massacre.

Will took Standish aside. 'Show me where you want to bury Rose and I will prepare the ground.'

'I wanted to do that myself,' Standish said.

'You have your responsibility to these people.'

Standish led him out and along the hillside to where a cleft in the ground offered a spot sheltered from the harsh north-east wind. With the heel of his boot he marked out the place where he wanted to bury his wife.

'It will be ready by midday,' Will promised, aware that darkness fell early on that wintry shore.

Relieving one of the men at the fort Standish told him to get as much rest as he could for he would be back on duty in a few hours' time. Will found a pick and a spade in the compound set aside for building tools and out on the hill began the task of fulfilling his promise. First he had to clear the hardening snow, then he had to break into the already hard ground. The day broke with a cheerless light and the wind was bitterly cold, but the work warmed Will and he toiled all morning.

It was a job he could have completed in a couple of hours on a summer's day but the weather was against him and when the steady rain turned to sleet he began to realize that even his considerable strength was not limitless. Poor diet and strenuous work with little rest over a long period had taken a toll. Yet somehow, before the dark heavy clouds prepared to yield to an early dusk, the grave was ready.

Rose's body was not very long, no more than five feet two inches, but Standish had specified her grave must be at least six feet in depth. He wanted to be certain she was safe from the scratchings of wolves and wild dogs.

Resting against a boulder, in shelter from the wind and sleet, Will closed his eyes and thought of Rose and what strange twists and turns of fate had brought them here, to this unknown hillside in this alien land. He gazed upwards in search of some bright reassuring star but a large cloud hung low, like a pall of blackened smoke, in the darkening sky. Sleet fell across his brow and was caught in his long eyelashes but he didn't want to close his eyes.

When he closed his eyes he saw too much. The sylph-like figure of a young girl running through the woods at Merlin's Well, crouching with him in the bracken at the Edge where they saw the woman they said was a witch. They were children then, poised on the threshold of life. And he could only picture Rose now as she was then. The worn grey face of the past few days eluded him. All he could see were the fine, delicately carved features, the cheeks touched with a bloom of pink in the bright Cheshire air, the small oval face with the bowed lips and the deep dark eyes.

Was it any wonder she was dead? She had been too fine, too fragile to survive this harsh, unrelenting turmoil. Not for her this wilderness. She had no more resilience than a snowflake. Will brushed the sleet from his eyebrows and shook his head and water ran down his neck and inside his shirt.

Standish came striding out of the swirling mist, clutching a spade and some sackcloth. Will straightened up ready to greet him but Standish merely nodded and went to examine the waiting grave. Will guessed that Standish had his feelings tightly reined in and didn't want to speak. Perhaps if he had to engage in conversation he might not be able to do what he had come here to do. Will leaned on his spade, his head turned away from Standish and the slanting rain. Standish arranged the sackcloth on the floor of the grave then trudged back into the mist. This time he returned with Rose in his arms.

At the graveside Standish held his wife's body tightly to his chest as if trying desperately to hold on to something of what he had lost. She seemed smaller now to Will. Death had diminished her still further, returned her to the size and shape of a child. With one arm Standish held her close and with his free hand he folded back the cover from her face. Will turned and walked a short distance away. It was time to leave them alone.

On his knees in the snow and with the aid of two ropes Standish carefully lowered the body into the grave, then he sat back on his haunches, looking down. Through the darkness someone approached. Will came back, ready to protect Standish from any intrusion. But it was only the governor, John Carver, who had dragged himself from his sick-bed to say a prayer at Rose's graveside.

This done and at a nod from Standish, Will began to spade in the soil, gently and without haste, over the cloth that covered Rose. Standish struggled to his feet now and joined in the spadework but soon he had to turn away and avert his eyes. Will carried on until the ground was level. and then, together, they shovelled snow over the newly turned earth to obliterate any sign of the grave.

'Thank you,' Standish said without emotion. 'Thank you, Mr Trefor. Your help is much appreciated.'

'Perhaps one day,' John Carver said, 'you will mark this spot in a way that is appropriate.'

Standish looked down at the ground where snowflakes fell rapidly now and melted just as fast. 'I would like,' he said, 'to have a small rose bush sent out from England.'

The epidemic raged on. Six of the settlers had died in December. In January another eight, including Rose Standish. February took the heaviest toll with seventeen dead. March took another thirteen.

In some cases whole families were lost. Of the Mullins family, father was first, swiftly followed by Mrs Mullins. Then Joseph, the small boy who, despite all the difficulties aboard the *Mayflower*, had been so high-spirited, fell ill and died. Only his sister, Priscilla, remained.

Any constraints she had felt impelled to impose on her feelings for John Alden were no longer necessary but Priscilla was too busy helping to nurse the sick and John was too deeply involved in the urgent building of houses for any personal considerations. She had long ago said yes to his proposal of marriage and they would marry when the time was right, perhaps when the worst was over, in the joy of the spring that would surely come.

Of the twenty-four families of settlers, four were completely lost and sixteen suffered at least one death. Of the 102 passengers who sailed out of Plymouth, England, in search of this New World, exactly half died that winter.

32

Aboard the *Mayflower* conditions were no better. There was certainly more room now that so many passengers had gone ashore but the sickness had just as strong a hold. Half the crew had been lost and by mid-February Captain Jones began to fear he might have too few men to make the return voyage. Tempers were more than a little frayed and several of the seamen were eager to cast off and head for home. But the weather would not allow it for now the worst of the winter was upon them.

Even within its anchorage and sheltered as it was, high winds buffeted the ship and incessant rain pounded the decks. For three days the bodies of two members of the crew, rolled in sackcloth and awaiting burial, had been strapped to stanchions on the lower deck to prevent them from sliding overboard. Captain Jones wanted them disposed of as soon as possible but the sea was running too high for the small boats to be taken out. It was even too strong for them to be rowed ashore.

From the slanting poop deck the open sea resembled a bubbling cauldron where tall, arching waves suddenly rose to confront each other, like combatant cats, only to subside in a crash of foam. Roped alongside two of the small boats had overturned and the other, just visible under the slate grey water, had sunk. With the reduction in the number of passengers and the removal of most of its cargo the ship was now much lighter and but for its three anchors would surely have itself capsized. Captain Jones knew, long before he admitted it, even to himself, that a home crossing was out of the question now and, at least, until the early spring.

Cold was the worst enemy. The need to keep warm was paramount and on shore the gathering of wood for fuel and reeds for thatching were of prime importance. Two of the settlers, Peter Browne and John Goodman, both single men, were out collecting reeds with two of the dogs at their heels when the dogs scented a deer and took up the chase. Images of fresh succulent meat roasting on spits urged the men on and they followed the dogs. But soon they were lost and they began to wander about, going around in circles in the steadily darkening forest. At nightfall, bitterly cold and frightened they huddled together, scared by the baying of wolves and the sinister rustlings in shadowy trees.

A search party was despatched from the settlers' camp but no trace of the men or the dogs was found and it was feared they had been taken by Indians. Then the following morning, frozen almost solid and led by their shivering dogs, the two men staggered back. Dr Fuller did what he could to help thaw them out, warming them with hot soup and brandy, but both were badly frost-bitten. They'd had no means of catching the deer and they were scolded now for chasing an illusion. Better to stay together with what we have, warned the elders and the lesson was not lost. Peter Browne responded slowly and eventually recovered, but John Goodman was in too bad a state. His frostbite was severe and his shoes had to be cut from his feet. Within two days he was dead.

Yet despite the shadow of death that lay so heavily over those early months there was as much faith and hope among the settlers as there was despair. The power of prayer to fortify and sustain the believers was never more evident and, remarkably, nobody asked to be allowed to return with Captain Jones to England.

Of the younger survivors Priscilla Mullins was the most bereaved. Having lost both of her parents and her young brother, she was alone in the world. On the instructions of Governor Carver she was excused duties in the common house and told she might spend a period of mourning in prayer and meditation. But Priscilla was by nature a spirited girl and such solitary activity only made her more miserable. When Daisy and Prudence finally came ashore, Daisy told the governor that Priscilla felt wasted. She wanted to work with her and Prudence, assisting Dr Fuller in his ministrations, and Carver agreed.

Along with the six or seven settlers, including Mr Brewster and Miles Standish, who appeared unaffected by the epidemic, the three girls worked selflessly with the sick. Making beds, changing and washing soiled bedding and clothing – an unpleasant task in the overcrowded sick-bay – and coping with the difficult job of keeping the common house clean taxed them to the limit. But there were diversions.

The carpenter John Alden, who had joined the *Mayflower* as a cooper, had elected to stay with the settlers and had informed Captain Jones he would not be returning with the ship to England. When the time was right, by which he meant when his house was built and ready for occupation, he would marry Miss Priscilla Mullins, the young lady who had caught his eye the day she strolled the quayside with her father in Southampton.

Alden was a tall, solidly built young man with a pleasant open face and Priscilla, demurely and as far as propriety would allow, had not been slow to respond to his covert glances and admiring looks. John had made friends with Joseph and the boy had carried secret messages between the two – though when it suited his purpose Joseph was not above blackmailing his sister with threats of revealing details of the liaison to their parents.

Mr Mullins had for a long time disapproved of the young carpenter but before he died he had told his wife that he would be well pleased to welcome John into his family as his son-in-law. John was a craftsman and a conscientious worker, polite and sober and steady as a rock. He was also well thought of by his shipmates and by the church elders, and Captain Jones had said publicly he would be sorry to lose him. He was not, perhaps, the most *intellectual* of men. But Mr Mullins had come to the conclusion, he told his wife, that intellectuals are of little use in what he called 'the real world'.

Now, though all barriers had been removed, John and Priscilla had little time to spend together. John laboured hard and long each day, so hard that on one occasion, on his one day of rest, he fell asleep at Priscilla's side at the Sunday service. The elder conducting the service, Mr Brewster, turned the lapse into a virtue by asking the congregation in a great stage whisper to witness their brother who 'has so tired himself in honest toil he has closed his eyes in well earned rest under the benevolent gaze of the Lord.'

The bond beween John and Priscilla had for some time enchanted Prudence and at sixteen she was herself eager for romance. The epidemic had taken fourteen of the young wives and several of the recently widowed men had not failed to notice her. She was a woman now, no longer a child, and with her dark hair and her large dark eyes she was far from unattractive. But to Prudence most of the men seemed old. Only with Maurice Tinker, with whom she had maintained a friendship throughout the voyage, before and since the loss of her baby, did she feel comfortable and relaxed.

'When do you think John and Priscilla will be married, Miss Daisy?' she asked one Sunday after service as they walked to the spot where Rose was buried.

It was a question Prudence knew her mistress could no more answer than she could, but its true purpose was to raise the topics uppermost in her young girl's mind: boys, men, love, marriage.

'When they have their own house, I expect,' Daisy said tolerantly.

'An' will you marry Mr Trefor?'

Daisy stopped in her tracks and laughed aloud as if the possibility had never occurred to her. 'Marry Will Trefor? Whatever gave you that idea?'

'Well, you like him, don't you?'

Daisy hadn't realized it was so obvious.

'An' he likes you.'

She looked down into the wide eyes and found not a trace of teasing or mischief-making there. 'How can you say such a thing? Mr Trefor has never given any indication ...'

'He doesn't 'ave to, Miss Daisy. It's there. It's plain for all to see.'

'Is it?' Daisy asked doubtfully, though she was secretly delighted.

'Mr Trefor may not even know it 'imself, but I'd say 'e's in love with you – no doubt about it.'

Daisy laughed again, as if to scoff at her young protégé's temerity but really to cover her embarrassment. 'And what, may I ask, makes you such an expert all of a sudden?'

'Well, I'm not,' Prudence said. 'It's just that I've bin thinkin' about that sort o' thing a lot ....'

'Oh?'

'It's just that Morry thinks 'e should get married. At least, 'is family think 'e should.'

Maurice Tinker was not held in very high regard by the other male settlers. He was considered something of a weakling, only fit for the less strenuous jobs, such as carrying food from the galleys. He was a slender youth. Sensitive, his mother called him. And he was more interested in a book of poems one of the churchmen, a Mr Allerton, had given him than musketry or the building of houses.

'An' I think 'e means married to me,' Prudence added.

Daisy looked less than thrilled at the prospect.

'His family are 'ighly thought of, Miss Daisy. Mr Tinker 'as an estate in 'olland and 'e owns property in Lincolnshire. Morry told me so. They are not a poor family and that's important. You told me so yourself. You told me I should never consider marriage to a man who 'as nothin' much to offer.'

Daisy vaguely remembered saying something of the sort. It was an adage her mentor, the Duchess, had drummed into her. 'Men will take what you've got,' the Duchess was fond of saying, 'an' they'll give you little in return. You must 'old back as much as you can an' make 'em pay for it dearly, darling. An' if it comes to marriage, make sure it's worth it. Marry a gentleman an' not one as is down on 'is uppers either.' There had been a fair amount of good sense in much of the Duchess's worldly advice, but Daisy hadn't mean Prudence to take it quite so seriously.

'Do you love him?' she asked.

'I *like* 'im, miss,' Prudence said. 'Him an' me, we're good friends. But I don't know about love, if you know what I mean.'

'No,' Daisy said. 'I don't know what you mean.'

'Well.' It was Pru's turn to be embarrassed. 'Morry's sort of ... not like the other men. I mean, some o' the sailors make fun of 'im.'

'You mean, he's not an uncouth lout?'

'Well, not just that, miss.' Prudence was anxious to continue the conversation but finding the right words did not come easy to her. 'Morry likes readin' an' poetry an' stuff.' She paused. 'An' 'e's got a lute.'

'Oh? I didn't know that.'

'Yes,' Prudence said. 'But 'e thought if 'e played it on the ship they'd make fun of 'im.'

'There's nothing wrong with liking music and poetry. It just means you have some finer feelings.'

'Yes, miss.'

Daisy could see there was still something troubling her. 'What is it, Pru?'

'Well ... it's love, miss.'

Her eyes were so large and round now and had such a look of apprehension Daisy was tempted to laugh, but she didn't.

'Love?' she asked gently.

Prudence nodded. 'He says 'e likes me more than any other girl 'e's ever known an' 'e always will an' I think 'e wants to marry me. Well, I've thought about it. It would mean we'd 'ave an 'ome of our own. I've never 'ad an 'ome of me own. An' I'd be part of a family, Morry's family. I mean, as things are, I don't know what the future might 'old.'

'I know,' Daisy said. 'I know what you mean.'

'You are the only person I 'ave in the whole world, Miss Daisy. I love you an' I know you would only tell me what's best for me.'

Daisy squeezed her hand. It occurred to her that Prudence was the only person *she* had in the whole world. 'I love you, too, Pru. You know that. And until you find the right man I'll take good care of you.'

'Don't you think Morry is the right man?'

Daisy smiled. 'You haven't told me that you love him, have you? If you had I'd have said yes, right away. But if you're not sure I think you should wait. There's no hurry.'

On the hillside Miles Standish was standing, head bowed, near the spot where he had buried his wife. Daisy steered Prudence away.

'We'll come back later,' she said, 'when Captain Standish isn't here. I expect he'll want to be left alone.'

It was still cold that Sunday morning but it was not raining and the icy wind had dropped. Daisy and Prudence walked back towards the common house.

'Do you think Captain Standish will get married again?' Prudence asked innocently.

Daisy laughed in mild exasperation at the girl's propensity for asking pointed questions. 'Really!' she said. 'I expect he will in time but Rose is scarcely in the ground.'

'I don't like 'im much,' Prudence said. 'He scares me.'

Miles Standish had seen Daisy and her maidservant and even as he stood by Rose's newly turned grave the thought that Miss Mason, an unattached woman as yet, was a fine-looking girl and devilishly attractive, not for the first time, crossed his mind. For some lucky fellow she would make an excellent wife. He looked down at the hard ground. The light covering of snow had melted away but the sprig of juniper he had left to mark the spot remained.

He couldn't bear to think for long about Rose. He blamed himself for bringing her here to this early death. All the way they had been dogged by ill-fortune. If only the ship had sailed in midsummer as planned they would not have encountered such dreadful weather at sea. They would be established by now with shelters built and food stockpiled against the winter. They would probably not even be here. In a calmer sea they would have succeeded in landing further south where they would almost certainly have found the help and support of earlier settlers. All they had here was the bitterly cold landscape and the sometimes alarming glimpses of primitive natives.

He turned away and walked slowly back down the hill, forcing himself to concentrate his mind on matters of security. The church elders looked to him to recruit the assistance he required to create a force capable of repelling an attack. They were naturally anxious to make the settlement safe, though, apart from the minor skirmishes they had met with in their early expeditions ashore, they had seen little of the Indians.

The elders, in particular Governor Carver and Mr Brewster, insisted that no effort should be spared to make peace with the indigenous population who were, after all, there first. But strong in the minds of many was the mystery of Roanoke, the lost colony, and they were wary and mistrustful of making friends with the natives.

From time to time Indians had been spotted, but always at a distance. One of the settlers, concealed in some reeds and hoping to land a wild duck, had seen a file of them moving slowly, in a kind of silent dance, through the woods in the direction of the settlement. He had succeeded in making his way back by a roundabout route and alerting men who were felling trees in a clearing. The settlers had dropped their tools and raced back to their base camp to pick up their guns. But when they returned the Indians had gone – and so had the tools.

Standish himself and another man, when out felling trees, had left their equipment at lunchtime to return briefly to their base only to find when they returned that their tools had also gone. After these incidents it was decided that no tools or equipment would be left unattended and when the men were out working weapons would be to hand at all times. Obviously now it was necessary for the settlers to make contact and, if possible, make friends with the Indians.

The manner of tackling the problem was left with Standish. His resources were small. At the height of the epidemic the number of settlers and more crucially the number of able-bodied men had dwindled daily. There were simply not enough men to form a permanent, full-time guard. With so much work to be done on the construction of the settlement and the need for a rapid building programme the men were only available on a part-time, casual basis.

In addition to all this Standish had plans for a palisade that would enclose the entire settlement and make it easier to defend. About ten feet high and almost a mile in circumference it would be strong and solidly built with two or three strategically placed gates that could be locked and bolted. Sentries would be posted every night and, if necessary, in the daytime, too.

Yes, Standish conceded, it might well be possible to establish some kind of happy accord with the natives. But again, it might not. Doggedly, in between his own spells of labour on the building sites or felling trees, Standish had succeeded in identifying and establishing a small group of men he had come to regard as his own settlement guard. They were men on whom he could rely and at every opportunity he assembled them and kept them aware of their duties in the event of an attack.

The guard was divided into four platoons, each with a leader:

Isaac Allerton, William Bradford, Stephen Hopkins and Edward Winslow. Each platoon was assigned to a rallying point where the men must assemble and form up immediately an alarm was sounded. There was also a small group of firefighters detailed to deal with any fires the Indians might attempt to start.

On February the thirteenth Standish was addressing all four platoons assembled by the gun platform when Maurice Tinker, on look-out duty, signalled frantically from his hilltop post. Less than a quarter of a mile away, across the river, two Indians had appeared.

The Indians were making signs and Standish realized, out on the hillside now, that they were actually signalling to the settlers. They were inviting the settlers to come forward and meet them. The members of the four platoons laid down their arms and Standish indicated that the Indians should come to them. But there was no response.

Anxious not to miss the opportunity Standish took Stephen Hopkins with him and together they waded across the narrow, fast-flowing river and strode fearlessly up the other side towards them. But as Standish and Hopkins approached there was a series of whoops and shouts, accompanied by the roll of a tomtom, from the surrounding wood. The two Indians were obviously supported by many more. Daunted somewhat Standish and Hopkins continued bravely up the sloping river bank but unexpectedly the two Indians turned and fled.

Standish knew he was not dealing with a small local tribe and that there were many Indians in the region, both to the north and to the south. He decided it was time to bring his heavy weapons ashore and put them on display. Within a few days, with little prompting and perhaps happy to be rid of the remaining artillery, Captain Jones enlisted members of his crew to assist the settlers in landing all five guns. Two minions, a saker and two smaller cannon were quickly mounted and made ready to face, if necessary, the so far hidden enemy.

The first week in March the weather improved. The wind came not from the cold north-east but from the south and there was the distinct feeling that the winter was waning fast and spring was coming in. The settlers lost no time in sowing their seeds, mostly peas and beans. And then an extraordinary thing happened.

It was not long after the first two Indians had appeared when Miles Standish and his guards were again alerted by the man on look-out duty. Wading across the river and marching boldly up the bank towards them came a lone Indian.

33

The Indian was tall and straight-backed. His shiny black hair was cut short at the front and left long at the back. Armed with a bow and two arrows he was not in any way hesitant, as the others had been. His face expressionless, he marched between the two rows of partly finished houses.

Strong and muscular, he was naked but for a leather girdle with a brief fringe which the breeze and the momentum of his stride lifted lightly as he approached. For the sake of propriety the men moved forward to shield him from the eyes of the ladies present and he was confronted by Standish and Edward Winslow. Unabashed he raised his right hand in salute, greeting them in English with the word 'Welcome!'

His name, he said, was Samoset and he was a stranger to the area. He was the chief, he announced proudly, of a tribe settled in a place called Pemmaquid, some distance to the north. He was an Algonquin sagamore, a chief of chiefs, and he had learned his limited English from the fishermen who came in summer in English fishing vessels to fish off Monhegan Island. It was a day's sail away, he told them, four or five days on foot. Then he asked if they had any beer.

When the Indian first appeared most of the women had backed away, calling their children to the common house or one of the houses, out of sight. Now, as he relaxed with their menfolk, curiosity brought them out again.

He was enjoying a meal – gin, biscuits, cheese, a pudding and a choice piece of mallard – as they edged closer to get a good look at their uninvited guest. Some of the men were embarrassed at the presence of the ladies as the playful breeze, blowing up the narrow street, kept lifting the fringe of his leather girdle to reveal that he wore nothing underneath and was clearly well endowed. The dilemma was solved when a long, gold-braided horseman's coat was produced and offered to him as a gesture of goodwill. He accepted the coat with alacrity and wore it with pride.

Though his English was barely adequate Samoset was able to

tell his eager questioners that the place where they had chosen to
settle had until recently been the home of a tribe known as the
Patuxet. About four years earlier, he said, a plague had all but
wiped them out. The nearest tribe now, he assured them, would be
friendly. They were peace-loving, not in any way war-like and
would never steal from the settlers. The Indians who had
attempted to harass the settlers and had stolen their work tools, he
went on, were probably the Nausets.

The Nausets had killed three white men the previous summer,
injured two more who had managed to escape and were prepared
to kill any white man they laid eyes on. They hated white men,
Samoset said, and with good cause. The trouble had begun, he
explained, when a Captain Hunt, an Englishman, had arrived to
trade for furs along the coast. Hunt had deceived them.
Pretending to be friendly towards them he had taken about two
dozen aboard his ship, some Patuxet men and some Nausets, and
he had sailed away with them as prisoners to be sold into slavery in
Spain.

As the day wore on it became obvious that Samoset assumed he
was welcome to stay the night. Standish was not happy with this.
Suspicious by nature he was more wary of an Indian trap than the
trusting elders and he suggested Samoset might like to stay aboard
the *Mayflower* as a guest of Captain Jones. Standish hoped the
suggestion, in view of the incident concerning this Captain Hunt,
might send Samoset on his way. But the Indian seemed
undeterred. As it happened the tide was out and the wind was high
in the bay and though Samoset was willing to fall in with the
arrangement they decided not to send the shallop out.

The home of Stephen Hopkins, one of the first houses to be
finished, seemed the most suitable, divided as it was to provide
separate sleeping quarters for Hopkins and his wife, their son and
their two daughters. Samoset was invited to bed down in a section
with Stephen and his young son Giles. Snoring loud and long he
slept well but father and son found little sleep, dozing fitfully for
most of the night with half an eye on their new friend. Elizabeth
Hopkins later complained to Daisy that the smell peculiar to the
Indians pervaded her house for days.

The following morning, a Saturday, Samoset was sent off with
presents of a bracelet and a ring. In return he promised to try to
arrange trading with the tribe with whom he had been staying – the
Massasoits. On the Sunday he returned with five other Indians. As
agreed with Standish they had left their weapons a quarter of a
mile away on the river bank and carried nothing but furs on their

arms. They also brought back the work tools they had stolen – a gesture of goodwill but one which gave the lie to Samoset's assertion that the tools had probably been stolen by the less friendly Nausets.

The Indians were tall and sturdy with complexions like the gypsies the settlers had seen at home in England. They wore leather chaps and aprons, and feathers in their long black hair and all had painted their faces. The settlers greeted them cordially and gave them food and the Indians entertained their hosts with chants and dances. But it was a Sunday and the settlers explained that Sunday was their holy day, a day on which they could neither work nor trade.

When the five left late that afternoon they left the furs and promised to return with more. They also promised to take back the greetings and good wishes of the settlers to their chief. Samoset stayed on until Wednesday when, with a hat, shoes and stockings and wearing the coat which had been provided to cover his lower regions he, too, went off.

The weather in those early days of March had continued to improve with wintry sunshine filtering through the grey clouds and the building programme had progressed well. Edward Winslow, who kept a record of the settlers' experiences, noted that Wednesday, March the seventh, was a fine day and the sowing of seed continued. The day opened misty and the sun came out. Birds sang in the woods all around and it even felt faintly warm.

Friendly contact had been made with the natives. Fewer of the settlers were falling sick and things were definitely improving. But Miles Standish, anxious not to show how small in number his force had become, had been careful not to call his guard to assembly in full view of their Indian guests. He had fewer than thirty men and youths at his disposal where one small tribe, by all accounts, could muster at least a hundred braves. He was also less than pleased with the ingenuous Mr Brewster who, in an excess of friendship and warmth, had explained to Samoset that the seventh day was always a holy day, a day on which the settlers could neither work nor trade. The canny Indians, thought Standish, might construe this to mean they would also refrain from fighting or defending themselves on such a day.

In the quiet evenings the future of the settlement was now the main subject for discussion. And Governor Carver and his closest associates – Brewster, Bradford, Winslow, Hopkins, Allerton, Dr Fuller and Miles Standish – had much to discuss. They had already arranged for the single men to share a home with a family until more houses could be built. The Hopkins girls, Constance and Damaris, and the Allerton girls, Remember aged six and Mary aged four, naturally lived with their parents. But there were still the unattached, unmarried girls and, as a priority, a house, to be supervised by Daisy Mason, was built especially for them. Daisy and her maid Prudence, the bereaved Priscilla Mullins aged eighteen, and the other two girls newly orphaned, Mary Chilton aged fifteen and Elizabeth Tilley, thirteen, moved in.

The girls' house was, of course, like a magnet to the young men of the settlement but Daisy ensured a high degree of discipline and all the proprieties were strictly observed. Except to carry out essential work none of the men were allowed inside the house. Even the governor was permitted to enter only by invitation. The girls worked hard and long, coping with laundry, cooking, sewing and a good deal of fetching and carrying for the whole community. And at nightfall they were happy to return to their haven, usually exhausted by the day's work. Only on Sundays, after morning service, did the opportunity arise to walk to the hillside or down to the shore and to talk endlessly of eligible young men.

The governor's wife, Mrs Carver, had not been slow to voice her misgivings about Miss Daisy Mason and her influence on the young, impressionable girls in her charge. But her husband had told her quite bluntly that she was wrong. Miss Mason was held, he said, in the highest regard by the church elders for the way in which she conducted herself and especially after her tireless work with the sick. Indeed, he added as if to confirm her respectability, he would not be surprised if, in due course, she became the second Mrs Standish.

Mrs Carver was impressed. There had already been quiet speculation about the future marital status of Captain Standish. When his period of mourning was over he would surely be in need of a wife, a good woman to share his new life. Miss Mason, her husband assured her, was an exceptionally good woman. Mrs Carver and her companion had discussed the possibility in lowered tones and with lips pursed. They had considered most of the widowed and single young women as prospective spouses for the fiery captain. But Daisy Mason's name had simply not occurred to them.

There was a problem with Mrs Carver's companion, Miss Minter. She was a timid girl in her early twenties, dominated by her mistress, plain-looking and not considered, even by herself, a candidate for any man's choice of partner. She was not strong and she had not come through the voyage well. Though not seriously ill she had been sick most of the time. At first it was seasickness, then it was diarrhoea, then she was unable to eat and for weeks she had been miserable and depressed. She was clearly unhappy with the unwelcoming shore and was sadly disappointed with the prospect of life in the settlement.

She would probably, John Carver said, have liked to return home with Captain Jones but couldn't face another voyage. Mrs Carver disagreed. Miss Minter had no family to return to in England. They, the Carvers, were her family now and she was as much a part of the settlement as anyone else. She would surely want to remain with them. In that case, Carver said, she should look around for a suitable husband. They should encourage her, he said, in God's name, to set up her own family.

Miss Minter, his wife told him, was a born spinster. But John Carver, mild though he normally was, would not hear of it. There is no such thing, he said, as a born spinster. Men and women were put on this earth to marry and in the name of God to produce children. And if not all marriages were so blessed it should not be for the want of trying. What the settlement was going to need in the future was children, a new generation. Miss Minter should look for a husband. Mrs Carver, a little shocked by her husband's forthright pronouncement, said she would speak to her.

That Sunday Mrs Carver sent her servant boy, William, to the girls' house with a message for Daisy. Mrs Carver, the note read, would like to see Miss Mason privately and would be at home all day after morning service. Daisy sent a message back to say that she, too, would be at home for most of the day and Mrs Carver was welcome to visit.

Swallowing her pride, Mrs Carver arrived alone and unannounced at the house at the far end of the newly constructed street. When she knocked at the door and the youngest of the girls, Elizabeth, opened it all of the others, except Daisy, came to their feet. True, thought Daisy who was on her knees at an open trunk, she was the governor's wife. But respect had to be earned and, in Daisy's opinion, Mrs Carver had done little so far to earn it. She smiled in greeting, though clearly surprised that Mrs Carver had accepted the reversed invitation.

Priscilla Mullins had been sitting patiently on a stool in the centre of the room as Prudence, standing behind her, braided her long brown hair. That afternoon Priscilla had an appointment with John down by the sea-shore and naturally wanted to look her best. Mary and Elizabeth had been dressing a doll John had carved for Elizabeth's thirteenth birthday. Daisy had been searching for a shawl to wear against the wind.

'Mrs Carver!' Daisy said pleasantly as she pulled the shawl from the trunk. 'Do come in.'

Mrs Carver stood in the narrow doorway, surveying the neat little household. 'I see you are about to go out.'

They both knew that Daisy had not expected her invitation to be taken up and felt no obligation, therefore, to honour her commitment to 'be at home for most of the day'.

'Only a stroll to the beach,' Daisy said. 'Perhaps you would care to accompany me?'

'Thank you.' Mrs Carver nodded in agreement. It would be better this way, she thought and she sensed that Daisy thought so, too.

The two women, unlikely companions, began to stroll along the path towards the narrow strip of beach. It was a bright afternoon, the sun peeping occasionally from behind billowing white clouds and the wind far less piercing than of late. The shallop and two of the small boats were tied up at the water's edge. Off shore the *Mayflower* lay at anchor. Daisy wondered where Will Trefor was and what he was doing.

'I take it your intention is to remain with the settlement, Miss Mason, when the *Mayflower* sails for home.'

'Yes,' Daisy said without hesitation. 'Oh yes. This is my home now. Though there is much to be done.'

'My husband thinks highly of you.'

'And I of him. We all do.'

Mrs Carver came to a halt as the sun came out. In the clear light of day she looked old and tired and Daisy suddenly felt sorry for her. Mrs Carver had followed her husband faithfully, fleeing with him from prejudice and injustice in England to a period of relative peace in Holland. And from Holland, as the political climate began to change, she had followed him here in search of a freedom to live and to worship as they thought fit.

Many of her values had been called into question and Daisy guessed rightly that her head was in a turmoil. She was assailed by doubt. Doubt about the future and her own place in that future. She was an exile now as she had been for much of her life and the pull of England and home, the memories of those long gone times, of childhood, her young girlhood, her time as a newly wed, could still grip and tug at her heart-strings. As Daisy looked out, apparently not fearing the departure of the *Mayflower*, eager to live her life to the full, Mrs Carver could only look behind her at the dark, unknown wood.

'I envy you, Miss Mason,' she said suddenly. 'You seem so ... so fearless.'

Daisy looked at her with compassion. 'I'm not fearless, Mrs Carver. Only a fool would be fearless. But I believe we have much to be thankful for.'

'God has been good to us,' Mrs Carver said, nodding and falling back on a safe platitude.

Daisy wanted to say, I wish I could believe in your God. But she didn't want to upset Mrs Carver. She knew that seeking her out had taken quite an effort on Mrs Carver's part and she was curious to know what the lady wanted from her.

'My husband believes there will have to be several marriages if we are to survive as a community. The young women must choose from the eligible young men – and a new generation must be born.'

Daisy smiled. 'I don't think Mr Carver need worry too much about that. I'm sure nature will take its course. John Alden and Priscilla plan to marry in the spring and a fine couple they will make. My Prudence has at least one suitor. And even Mary and little Elizabeth, young as they are, show more than a passing interest in young men.'

'I'm sure you're right, dear.'

Daisy felt that Mrs Carver was holding something back, that there was something more she wanted to say. 'What is it, Mrs Carver?'

Mrs Carver came to a halt again and turned to Daisy with a look of embarrassment and contrition. 'I want to say ....' She hesitated, then blurted out an apology. 'I want to say I'm sorry. I'm so sorry, Miss Mason, and I want to ask for your forgiveness.'

'For what?' Daisy asked, in genuine surprise.

'I believe I was wrong about you when we first met. I'm afraid I behaved very badly towards you. I ... I would like us to be friends.'

Daisy put a hand on hers. 'Of course.'

They strolled on towards the sea and Mrs Carver said, 'My husband, as I said, thinks very highly of you. The way you have helped with the sick and the bereaved. The way you have taken care of Prudence.' She glanced sidelong at Daisy. 'I am ashamed of the way I treated that girl.'

'Mrs Carver,' Daisy said, 'there really is no need ...'

'Ah, but there is, dear,' she insisted. 'I am the member of the Church. I am the one who should show humility and a love of others.'

'Church or not,' Daisy said, 'for an adventure such as ours to succeed we all need each other. I believe that's something we've learned.'

They were silent for a while then, as they stood just above the beach, looking out to the bare-poled *Mayflower*, Mrs Carver said, 'There is something else. About my companion. Miss Minter.'

Miss Minter, thought Daisy, the prim and proper young woman who had been so unhappy throughout the voyage and had now become a nervous wreck, jumping and twitching at the slightest unfamiliar sound, terrified of the natives and of almost everything else.

'My husband thinks Miss Minter should return to England,' Mrs Carver went on. 'But I have told him she has no family there, no one to return to. I think, perhaps, if she were to find a husband ....'

'Miss Minter?'

'I wondered if you might be of assistance. Perhaps suggest someone suitable.'

A man for Miss Minter? It had never occurred to Daisy that Miss Minter might be interested in a man, *any* man. Perhaps she wasn't. Perhaps it was Mrs Carver's idea. Daisy had assumed Miss Minter was a dedicated spinster. She was about Daisy's age but she was so straitlaced and proper she was certain to deter any possible suitor.

'I will give it some thought,' Daisy promised and when Mrs Carver looked doubtful she hastened to reassure her. 'I will. Really. I'll think about it.'

'With discretion, Miss Mason. I would like this to be just between ourelves. At least, for now.'

'Of course.' Daisy was inwardly amused at being cast in the role of matchmaker. 'With the utmost discretion.'

'And what about you, my dear?' Mrs Carver enquired with a smile as they walked back along the ridge.

'Me, Mrs Carver? What *about* me?'

'A young woman like you,' Mrs Carver said. 'I'm sure you must have many suitors.'

'Er ... no. No, I don't, as a matter of fact.'

'I'm sorry. I have no wish to pry. It's just that ....'

Daisy waited.

'Well, there's Captain Standish for one.'

'Captain Standish?'

'Well, I realize he has only recently lost his dear wife. But he is not an old man. He will surely marry again in due course. Why, any girl would jump at the opportunity to marry a man like Captain Standish, a man of such bearing and such impeccable background.'

'I agree Captain Standish is a fine man,' Daisy said. 'But I don't think ...'

'I'm so sorry. I understood the captain had already declared an interest.'

Daisy shook her head. 'Not to me, he hasn't.'

34

When Samoset returned he did not come alone. He brought with him an Indian named Tisquantum – who quickly became known to the settlers as 'Squanto'. The smiling, friendly Squanto, Samoset explained, could speak far better English than himself. He would in future prove a far better interpreter. It emerged later that Squanto, who claimed to be the sole survivor of the ill-fated Patuxet tribe, was one of the Indians kidnapped by the treacherous Captain Hunt and sold into slavery in Spain.

Squanto had escaped from his bondage and made his way to London where he had found employment with a merchant in Cornhill. He had taught himself English and eventually his employer had loaned him to an explorer as a guide/interpreter on a trading ship to Newfoundland. Back home in the so-called New World, Squanto had run away to go in search of his family only to find the Patuxet tribe was no more. He had then joined the neighbouring tribe of Massasoits.

According to Squanto, Chief Massasoit was willing to talk with the settlers and was waiting in the nearby woods. At a sign from Squanto he would appear on the opposite bank of the river. The settlers were quick to agree – such a meeting would be made so much easier now with the services of a capable interpreter – and the statesmanlike Edward Winslow was chosen to represent the governor.

Flanked by Miles Standish and all the remaining elders, John Carver waited on the hillside close to the newly constructed gun platform. The settlers' numbers were seriously depleted now: only thirty men and youths and many far from well. As they gathered to watch, with the women and children hidden indoors, they were curious and not a little apprehensive.

Squanto turned to face the woods, raised his arms and Chief Massasoit emerged, his younger brother Quadequima and more than fifty braves in support. All had painted their faces, some black, some red, some yellow and white, all of ornate design. Chief Massasoit made an imposing figure, his face painted a pale mulberry colour in sober contrast to the others and reflecting his great dignity. Across one shoulder he wore a deerskin. A long chain of white beads made from bone hung around his broad neck.

As sole emissary, Edward Winslow, accompanied by Squanto, crossed the shallow river and with a low bow and an extravagant flourish presented the governor's compliments. He bore several gifts: a set of knives, a ring, biscuits and a pot of what Squanto called 'strong water'. To Quadequima he presented a knife and what he described as 'a jewel to hang in his ear'.

The chief wanted to give something in exchange for Winslow's impressive-looking sword but the young ambassador managed to talk his way out of this difficult and potentially dangerous situation with a long speech. His King, he proclaimed, King James of England, was eager to form a friendly alliance with the great and powerful Chief Massasoit. Though the chief had probably never heard of King James, Squanto translated for Winslow and whatever he said was well received. The chief agreed to go forward to greet and speak wih Governor Carver, the head of the settlement. With twenty of his braves he crossed the stony river-bed and marched up the hill, leaving Winslow as hostage to his safe return.

The settlers met the chief with smiles, bowing low as he approached and conducting him to one of the almost completed houses where a rug had been spread with cushions for him to sit down. To augment the ritual Standish had hastily summoned a squad of musketeers, flanked by a drummer and a trumpeter, to herald the meeting.

With great courtesy both John Carver and the chief bowed low, then Carver kissed the chief's hand. Chief Massasoit responded by embracing and almost crushing Carver in a kind of bear hug. The governor called for 'strong water' and toasted Massasoit's health and Squanto passed on Carver's good wishes. In response the chief took an enormous swig of the brandy, enough to make his eyes water and for him to break out in a sweat. What followed was the drawing up of a treaty that was to ensure a mutual respect and a peaceful co-existence for many years to come.

The main points of the agreement were carefully and patiently worked out. No Massasoit should in any way harm a settler. No settler should harm a Massasoit. If any did so then the offender should be delivered to the other side for suitable punishment.

Anything that was stolen from either side should be returned or replaced. If under attack from any outside source each side would come to the aid of the other. Any of the braves visiting the settlers would do so unarmed and vice versa. Chief Massasoit, in addition, undertook to inform all neighbouring tribes of the treaty and to testify to his friendship with the settlers.

From then on Squanto spent much of his time at the settlement. He wanted, he said, to extend and improve his command of English. But in the days ahead he was to prove in many ways invaluable. Where the settlers had made their new home Squanto had spent most of his childhood and he was able to point out the places where the best and biggest fish were to be caught and how to catch them. He showed the settlers how best to prepare the land for sowing Indian corn, how to plant it and how to fertilize it with the remains of small fish taken in shoals from the brook. And there is little doubt it was purely his expertise that saw John Carver and his diminished band of settlers through those early days. Without Squanto they would almost certainly have perished.

The agreement calmed the fears of many, especially among the womenfolk, but sadly the sickness was still with them. The day after his successful mission as ambassador to the Massasoits, Edward Winslow's young wife, Elizabeth, died.

With the slow, steady establishment of the new colony – buildings well on the way to completion, friendly contact made with the native Indians, seeds sown – and the coming of spring, Captain Jones prepared to sail for home. He was to carry no passengers. Despite all the discomforts and uncertainties of life in the New World, not even Miss Minter asked to be taken back to England.

Daisy and Priscilla Mullins, with the blessing of the governor, had arranged for a social evening to be held on the ground floor of one of the new houses. It was the first gathering of its kind, the first attempt at communal relaxation and for many it brought the first spontaneous laughter they had enjoyed in many months. Most of the recently widowed women and the men who had lost their wives assembled with the young single men and girls to dance and to partake of refreshment.

Some of the ladies, experimenting with wild berries, had produced a strong sweet wine and, with sober warnings of the perils of over-indulgence, John Carver had released a cask of beer. Entertainment was provided by a sailor who danced a kind of hornpipe, another who played a penny whistle, another who sang what seemed like an endless shanty and one of the younger girls who sang a rather sad West Country song. Prudence then persuaded Maurice to play his lute and his surprisingly accomplished performance was greeted with delight and vociferous requests for more.

From among the members of the crew Daisy had purposely invited a sailor who, according to Pat Ellis, had expressed an interest in remaining with the settlement and taking a wife. This was something Captain Jones would almost certainly frown upon but Daisy felt sure he could be persuaded to release the man if a suitable lady could be found.

The sailor, a little Cockney, was introduced to Miss Minter, who held herself rigid as if in a state of terror throughout the evening. It was pleasant outside, not wet and quite mild, and around ten o'clock the party began to disperse. Several of the gentlemen waited to escort ladies back to their homes and without undue coyness the ladies took the arms offered. But Miss Minter chose to walk stiff and erect at the side of the sailor who was a good four inches shorter than her and paunchy where she was almost painfully thin. They had been gone only a few minutes when those still at the house heard a piercing scream and rushed outside to find the bewildered sailor shocked and alone. 'I on'y touched 'er 'and,' he said, 'an' she took orf!'

Others were more successful. Edward Winslow, a good-looking, serious minded young man, highly regarded in the community and so recently widowed, had excited the attention of more than one eligible young lady. But that evening he had eyes only for Susannah White. And for Susannah, whose husband William had died a month before and whose infant son Peregrine had been born that December aboard the *Mayflower*, the attraction was mutual. From then on, when not engaged in house building or liaising with the Indians, Winslow spent most of his free time in Susannah's company.

Daisy had hoped that Prudence would take an interest in one of several young men who flocked around her but she seemed only to relax and enjoy the evening when Maurice arrived. Priscilla and John Alden were revelling in their freedom to hold hands in public and to talk freely of their forthcoming marriage. And Mary and Elizabeth, young as they were, were pink-cheeked with excitement throughout.

Towards the end of the evening Miles Standish joined the party and, after partaking of what was left of the food and tasting the wild berry wine, he asked Daisy if he might walk her home. Daisy, with Pat Ellis standing nearby, thanked Standish for his kind offer but gently declined. Mr Ellis, she said untruthfully, had already volunteered.

Showing no surprise, Pat Ellis went off to fetch her shawl. Then, as they walked out of the house and looked up at the stars, hard and bright now in a clear sky, Daisy took his arm. 'What,' she said, 'will I do without you?'

'You'll survive, Daisy,' he said confidently.

'And help to make Mr Carver's new generation?'

'Girls like you are just what this place needs,' Ellis told her. 'An' if I wasn't so old and decrepit I might even offer to marry ye meself.'

Daisy squeezed his arm and leaned against him as they walked. 'And I might even accept, Patrick Ellis! Then where would you be?'

He laughed. 'In a lot of trouble, I should think.'

Daisy had always felt safe and comfortable with Pat Ellis, from the first time they met on the quay at Southwark. She loved the way he teased her and the way, when he felt it was necessary, he would gently put her in her place. And she especially loved the endearing way he would broaden his accent to avoid sounding pompous when he had something serious to say. She reached up and kissed him on the cheek. 'Will I ever see you again, Pat?'

'Who knows?' he said. 'Maybe one day – though it has to be faced, it's not very likely. But I'll always be here wit' you in spirit. An' when I'm a *very* old man I'll sit by the fire an' remember this night an' that lovely face an' those lovely sparklin' eyes.'

Daisy fell silent now and he left her alone with her thoughts. They both knew that for Daisy and for all the settlers something was coming to an end. The *Mayflower* was going home and a new phase was about to begin.

Above the narrow stretch of beach they came to a halt and looked out to the anchored vessel. 'What will you do, Daisy?' he asked at last. 'Not marry that Standish fellow, I hope?'

'Why?' Daisy was shocked that he, of all people, should ask such a question. 'Why should you think that?'

'Well, you know how the gossip goes. The matchmakers are out in force right now. The governor has given them the go ahead. You said yourself he wants all the eligible men to marry an' start producin'. Certainly Captain Miles Standish is one of the most eligible an' he'll be lookin' to choose the best there is. An' that's you, my love. No doubt about that. Why, I've heard your name linked already with the militant Miles.'

'You should not make fun of Captain Standish. He is a difficult man, yes, and sometimes hot-tempered. But he's a good man and his heart is in the right place.'

'An' where is your heart, Miss Daisy Mason?' he persisted.

Daisy looked out to a light aboard the *Mayflower*.

'Captain Jones thinks Will should return with him to England,' Ellis said. 'He wants to help clear Will's name with the Admiralty. He says he's prepared to appear before them personally to speak for Will an' ask for a pardon. An' Mr Carver has promised to write a letter to the King on Will's behalf. These people have a lot to thank Will for an' the governor is aware of that.'

'But do you trust Captain Jones? He's lost half his crew. He might simply want to use Will for the voyage home.'

'I don't think so, Daisy. Jones is genuine. I'm sure of that an' I believe what he says. He knows Will is a fine sailor an' he knows, too, that but for Will's seamanship we would have lost the shallop when the rudder broke. An' prob'ly all hands with her. I'm sure he'll do everythin' in his power to help.'

'But they'll arrest Will.'

'Yes. But then he'd be brought to trial and, the hope is, he'd be cleared.'

'If he stays here he'll be free anyway.'

'No.' Ellis shook his head. 'As Captain Jones says – an' I believe he's absolutely right – Will would never be free. He would be a fugitive for the rest of his life an' the stigma would dog his family. These shores are goin' to see a lot of ships from now on. He'd be unable to trade openly with English merchants. Hidin' when a ship of the British Navy comes in, wonderin' who an' what each merchant ship might bring – he'd never really be free. He must clear his name at home. Then when he's free to leave the old world, he'll be free to live here in the new.'

'But if he does go back and he clears his name he might choose to stay in England. He might be given back his commission. He might even rejoin his ship.'

The Irishman smiled. 'Will's heart is here – with you. He just doesn't know it yet. He came with his head filled with an urge to right an injustice. He believed he'd been wronged, deprived of his heritage. They'd taken everythin' from him. His home, his family, even his childhood sweetheart. But it was anger that brought him to the *Mayflower*. Anger, not love. Anger in his head, not in his heart. He didn't know it but his heart was not involved.'

He took her hands and made her look at him. 'An' then he met you. Will Trefor is a fine fellow. I wouldn't have any time for him if he wasn't worth it. But he's confused, Daisy. He knows he should go home an' put things right, but what he really wants is to stay here with you. He wants to tell you that but the death of Mrs Standish has made it difficult for him. In a way it would be easier if she was still alive. But believe me it's you he wants – no one else.'

'If that's true,' Daisy said, 'he might want me to return with him to England and I can't. I can never go back.'

Smiling Indians, often with their wives and children, were now frequent visitors to the settlement. They would parade in noisy groups up and down the central street and they and their children would run in and out of half-finished buildings and over sites where work was in progress. So interested were they in the settlers' way of life they would wander in and out of even the finished houses often surprising the occupants.

One inquisitive brave was chased out of a house by the large Cockney lady named Mrs Billington whom he had disturbed as she was in the act of dressing. Brandishing a heavy ladle Mrs Billington had chased him out, hurling insults at his fast retreating back and leaving him quaking in hiding behind a pile of logs. The diplomatic linguist, Squanto, had calmed Mrs Billington by explaining that the brave in question was 'a little simple in the head'. He had then told the worried brave that 'the fat lady', Mrs Billington, was a mad woman and not entirely responsible for her actions. But the curiosity of the natives was entirely peaceful and innocent. The concept of private houses was unknown to the wigwam dwellers and they saw no reason why they shouldn't wander in and out at will.

Determined to maintain friendly relations the settlers stoically accepted these and other often disconcerting habits, such as casually and without asking permission sampling food off a neighbour's plate or carrying on a conversation in full view of all and sundry whilst urinating against a tree. More serious was the problem of entertaining these uninvited guests. The Indians expected to be fed as a sign of goodwill and, as word spread that the settlers were a kind and generous people, more and more came to visit. The settlers' store of food began to diminish alarmingly and it soon became obvious that something would have to be done.

Edward Winslow and Stephen Hopkins, with Squanto as guide and interpreter, set out to see Chief Massasoit in his headquarters some thirty miles away. Everywhere the little party was made welcome and the two settlers realized the offering of food and water was merely part of a time-honoured ritual in the greeting of visitors. All along their route they were met with a warm and unstinting hospitality.

In one small camp they were able to perform a valuable service. The Indians, they found, were plagued by a flock of crows that were eating up their crops. With a few musket shots they killed three of the crows and scared away the rest and the Indians were deeply grateful. The Indians admired the skill of the two marksmen. They were impressed with the noise and the smoke. But they were wary of touching the weapons:

It was soon after leaving this small village that Winslow and Hopkins came upon a wide area of desolation where the plague of a few years earlier that so devastated Squanto's Patuxet tribe had left so many dead. Skulls and bones were scattered all around, picked lean by scavengers. So many had died, Squanto explained, that the few survivors had been unable to bury them all and had fled the area in fear of their lives.

When they finally reached the home of Chief Massasoit, Winslow and Hopkins presented him with a fine red coat and the chief put it on at once with obvious delight. With great tact Edward Winslow, who had become adept at maintaining good relations with his new neighbours, said he wished to greet the Great Chief with all the deference his position warranted. Chief Massasoit listened to Squanto's interpretation then smiled benignly. Though he had little food to spare he offered his visitors what he could.

Winslow then informed the chief he was empowered by his governor to make recompense for the corn the settlers had taken when they first arrived. If the chief could trace the families to whom it had belonged he would gladly agree some form of payment. The chief nodded his approval. Winslow then brought up the delicate matter of the many visitors to the settlement. Chief Massasoit's people were always welcome, he stressed, but there was a problem.

The settlers had so little food in reserve, Winslow said, they might soon be unable to feed themselves. It was with great reluctance he was compelled to ask if the chief would save the settlers further embarrassment by requesting his people to limit their visits. The chief understood at once. He nodded sagely and, through Squanto, promised his people would be instructed not to pester his new friends.

The two Englishmen were invited to spend the night in the chief's tent and they accepted graciously. Their bed consisted of a few planks laid close to the ground and they soon discovered they were to share this with the chief, his wife and two of his henchmen. All six lay huddled together covered only by some well-used matting. They also discovered the strange and disturbing habit the Indians had of singing themselves to sleep. Nor were they alone in the bed with their hosts. The entire wigwam was infested with fleas and lice. Sleep, they found, was impossible and throughout the night the grunts and wheezes of their bedmates were punctuated by the unrestrained emission of farts.

The most disturbing news the two men brought back to the settlement and confirmed by Squanto was that, although the people of Chief Massasoit were friendly and harboured no ill intent towards the settlers, there were other tribes not too far away who were less well disposed. An old woman of the nearby Cummaquid tribe claimed to have lost three of her sons to the treacherous slave trader, Captain Hunt. She was out for revenge and ever ready to incite her people to hatred against any and all white men.

Winslow and Hopkins had wanted to travel on to meet the Cummaquids and apologize for Hunt's behaviour, but Squanto had advised against it. The Cummaquids, he told them, were part of the Narragansett Indians who had attacked them when they first ventured ashore. The job of Miles Standish as military commander was again seen as one of paramount importance and much thought was again given to security.

Dealings with the Indians and their disruptive visits had by now taken up much of the time the settlers needed to spend on finishing the houses, tending their crops, hunting or fishing for food and creating a store of wood for the next winter. Yet the work had gone well. Everyone now had a roof over his head, no one was living in the temporary dug-outs and there was a feeling of optimism, a feeling that good progress was being made.

But once again tragedy was poised to strike.

35

Among the settlers who were still housed in the common house were the recently widowed Alice Rigdale and her two-year-old daughter, also named Alice. They had been almost the last of the passengers to leave the *Mayflower*. As she told Daisy, having no husband and no family other than little Alice, Mrs Rigdale had been reluctant to go ashore. Mother and baby had been offered a home with the Brewsters but she wanted, she said, to be 'where there are lots of people'. She was afraid of finding herself alone in one of the new houses and the Brewsters were out all day attending to a variety of duties.

In the common house she could work at sewing and mending and help with the washing and laundering and there would always be people about. Perhaps, she said, there would be something to occupy Alice, too. And there was. Most of the women and girls would pick up Alice – a bright-eyed, responsive child – and they would carry her around for a while and keep her entertained. It had been the same aboard ship, even before her father died, and she was well used to such attention. But Mrs Rigdale, a nervous, apprehensive woman at the best of times, kept her eye on her only child almost all day long. To Alice Rigdale, still grieving for a dead husband, little Alice was all she had in the world.

What happened took place one bright clear morning towards the end of March. There was no sign of rain and the sun was stronger than it had been in months, affording the women an opportunity to hang out their washing. From the trees on the edge of the woods to nails in the side of the common house long clothes' lines had been drawn up and the washing hanging there flapped and rose from time to time in the sudden flurry of a breeze that came off the metallic grey sea. Little Alice was sitting on a stool in the sunshine.

The Allerton children, Mary who was four years old and Remember who was six, were playing only a few feet away. John Crackston, a boy of fourteen whose father had died in the epidemic, was working on the roof of a house nearby. Mrs Rigdale, a wicker basket at her feet, was hanging washing on a line. There seemed to be people all around as she went indoors to refill her basket.

The little girl knew she must not wander off and must not go into the woods. But she was happy to sit on the stool and play with the bunch of daisies Prudence had picked for her. Prudence had made several small daisy chains and Alice, who was wearing one in the form of a bracelet about her tiny wrist, was attempting to make another.

At the moment her mother went indoors there was a movement in the bushes on the edge of the wood. The little girl looked up, her attention caught. Someone was hiding there and Alice thought it was a game. She laughed and clapped her hands. There it was again. Alice laughed again and rocked back and forth on her stool.

On the roof John Crackston moved down a little way to create a new working space. He paused briefly and looked out across the hillside to where the tide slowly advanced on the pebbled shore only to be drawn back like an army in retreat. He wondered what time it was and how soon he could break for lunch.

At the end of the common house he could see two small girls, the Allerton sisters, chasing each other in and out of the lines of washing. And coming up the street to check on his progress was his supervisor John Alden. Young Crackston stood up on the sloping roof to wave to his mentor but as he did so, beyond the washing lines, he saw a tall slim Indian, his face painted red and black, move furtively through the trees.

The boy Crackston was used to seeing Indians in the settlement by now but this one was acting strangely. This Indian was alone and the young apprentice sensed that he was up to no good. He opened his mouth to call a greeting to John Alden but at that moment he saw the Indian glide swiftly and silently from the wood, scoop up the baby Alice from her stool and dash back with her into the bushes.

In his effort to attract John Alden's attention, young Crackston almost fell from the roof. But Alden merely waved back. Then, when he dropped down, Alden picked him up by the collar and demanded, 'What is it, lad?'

As the boy spluttered out his story John Alden, reacting quickly, told him to alert all the men he could find. Alden then ran into the woods in pursuit.

Mrs Rigdale came out of the common house with a basket of washing crooked in her arm, puzzled by the sudden uproar of shouting and running and several other women appeared behind her. 'What is it?' they asked. 'What's happened?'

She saw the upturned stool. 'Alice?' Anxiety creased Mrs Rigdale's face, crept into her voice. Then she panicked. 'Alice! Alice!'

Since the death of their mother in the epidemic Mrs Brewster had taken the role of grandmother to the two Allerton girls. She ran in search of them now, found them looking bewildered in the flapping washing and clutched them to her apron as everyone asked the same questions: 'What is it? What's happened?'

Every man within hailing distance had come running to the common house where Mrs Brewster had already relayed young Crackston's story several times. Within minutes they formed a long line and set out to search through the woods.

Miles Standish, who had been scooping buckets of small herring from the brook with the Indian Squanto, was in a quandary. He saw that every man in the settlement was eager to help in the search but his military instinct counselled caution. This could be a clever ploy, a diversion to draw the men away, a cunning prelude to a surprise attack. If all the men went on the search who would defend the women and children? He gripped young Crackston by the collar. 'Are you sure about this, boy?'

'Yes, sir. Honest, sir. I saw it with me own eyes,' the boy said and at Squanto's request he described the Indian he had seen.

Squanto frowned at Standish. 'Not Massasoit.'

'Then who?'

'Maybe Cummaquid.'

'Are we under attack?' Standish demanded.

Squanto shook his head. 'No braves in wood.'

Dr Fuller, who had been in the common house tending the remaining sick, was with Alice Rigdale. Mrs Rigdale had fainted when she realized her baby was missing and then, on hearing young Crackston's account of what had happened, she had become hysterical. She was more frightened of the natives than anything – hunger, sickness – and now she was distraught. The doctor wanted her to go indoors and sit down but she refused to move. She had become rigid, her eyes fixed on the edge of the woods into which little Alice had been spirited away, out of her mind as she silently screamed for the return of her baby.

The search that morning took several hours. The line of men, well spaced out in the trees, moved slowly forward, missing nothing as three or four of the younger men ran on ahead. Once, when they heard the shouts of John Alden, their hopes were raised. But Alden had searched far and wide and found nothing. Squanto, starting from where John Crackston pointed out he had seen the Indian on the edge of the woods, tried to pick up tracks. But too many men were involved in the search, too many footsteps had obscured the ground and he had no success.

As the search progressed Squanto drew Standish aside. In the direction the searchers were heading, he pointed out, lived the Narragansetts. If they went too far that way they would run into trouble. Standish agreed but those leading the search would not be deterred.

All morning the women waited, those with children clutching them close to their sides. A chair had been brought and Alice Rigdale had been guided to it. She was like a person under hypnosis now, a look of terror in her eyes as she sat upright, staring fixedly at the woods.

When the men did at last return, frowning and dejected, it was obvious at once they'd had no luck. Alice Rigdale, a look of eager anticipation on her face as the first two appeared, stood up from her chair. But as more came back, all of them downcast, the truth hit her hard. And when the last man trudged in she made a run for the woods and had to be caught and held then forcibly restrained.

'Alice!' she screamed. 'I want my baby!'

All the searchers had found, and they had decided not to tell Alice Rigdale this, were the ridge marks of a canoe where it had been drawn up on a stretch of soft sand along the coast and near to the marks a daisy chain in the form of a tiny bracelet.

If unfriendly natives had known it they could have taken the *Mayflower* that Monday morning. They would have encountered little opposition. Only Captain Jones and two of his crew had remained aboard. The rest, about nine men including the second mate, Mr Coppin, Will Trefor and Pat Ellis, had joined in the search for the missing girl.

The seamen came ashore in the shallop and strode up the path from the beach. Prudence was at the door of the girls' house. Will Trefor stopped to speak to her. 'Pru!' he called and she ran to meet him. 'Where's Miss Daisy?'

'I'm not sure,' Pru said, shy as always in Will's presence. He was one of her heroes, her favourite men. 'I think she might be with Mrs Rigdale.'

'I haven't seen you all for days,' he said warmly. 'How are you?'

'We're all right, Mr Will,' Pru told him. 'Or we were until the little baby went missing.'

He nodded.

'Why would the Indians take a little baby, Mr Will? Mrs Rigdale is out of her mind with worry. Miss Daisy says Mrs Rigdale will go funny permanent if Alice isn't found.'

He nodded again.

'Mrs Carver's friend, Miss Minter, says the Injuns are just like the gypsies back home. Gypsies steal babies.'

Will's companions were calling him. 'I'll have to go, Pru. Tell Miss Daisy I'll be back as soon as I can.'

'The governor wants us all to get married,' Pru said, delaying him further.

'What?' Will gripped her arm, half-smiling at her look of wide-eyed innocence.

'We're supposed to find a partner and be joined in matrimony. It's for the good of the settlement.' She blushed. 'We're to have babies and make families for the future.'

'And are you going to be married, Pru?' he asked. 'I always thought you were saving yourself for me.'

'Oh, Mr Will. I'm serious.'

'Well,' Will said, 'whoever he is he'll need my approval. Better be a fine young fellow. Only the best is good enough for my favourite girl.'

With a hint of defiance Pru looked him in the eye and said, 'Maurice. I'm going to marry Maurice. Maurice Tinker.'

Will hesitated. He wanted to congratulate her but he couldn't enthuse over Maurice Tinker. He believed she deserved better and he wanted to know more, but Pat Ellis had joined the others and was signalling that they were about to set off. 'And what does Miss Daisy think about this?'

'She knows we have to have someone,' Pru said. 'All of us. Even Miss Daisy.'

'Miss Daisy? Does she have someone?'

'I don't know,' Pru said. 'But that Captain Standish comes to call.'

Will was backing away. 'Tell Miss Daisy I'll call to see her – *soon*.'

Prudence smiled and raised a hand as he left. She was not a devious girl but she felt quietly pleased with herself. She'd managed to get precisely the response she wanted.

Half-running, Will hurried up the dirt road to the spot where Governor Carver was addressing the group of volunteers. ' ... can't all go,' he heard Carver say as he joined the listeners. 'Captain Standish insists, and rightly I'm sure, we must keep the settlement safe with sufficient men to guard against any surprise attack. But he himself is prepared to lead a small party to meet with Chief Massasoit and ask for his assistance. An Indian has stolen one of our children: I am certain the chief will do all in his power to help.

'We must find the Rigdale baby, gentlemen. Not just for poor Alice Rigdale's sake but for the sake of all our womenfolk. If we don't they will believe their children, *our* children, will never again be able to play in safety. In fact, they already believe that. Well, we must find the baby and we must bring the perpetrator of this dreadful deed to justice. And our best chance of success is to enlist the help of the Massasoits. Now, if you are all volunteers, Captain Standish will select half a dozen of you to go along with him and with Squanto as interpreter.'

There was a general murmur of approval. All were willing to go but Miles Standish appeared to have chosen four of his men already: Edward Winslow, Winslow's brother Gilbert, Stephen Hopkins and Isaac Allerton. A lean, wiry young man named Richard Gardiner caught his eye and he nodded. Though rather quiet, Gardiner was a reliable, resourceful fellow of whom Standish approved. Then he saw Will Trefor. Will held his gaze for a long moment. Standish nodded once and Will made up the six. With Squanto leading the way, Standish said, they would leave at once and make directly for the headquarters of Chief Massasoit.

The party of eight, with good wishes and cries of 'Good luck!' ringing in their ears, joined up and went down to the beach. As they marched, two abreast, with Standish and Squanto in the forefront, they passed the common house where the women around Alice Rigdale stopped what they were doing to watch them go. From the doorway, partly hidden by other women, Daisy also watched and she was surprised to see Will Trefor in the group. She had not seen Will for several days. He'd been aboard the *Mayflower* and now a date had been set for the *Mayflower*'s return to England she wondered if he was avoiding her. If he was then perhaps it was just as well. She had no good reason to suppose he was really interested in her. Anything she had heard had come from other people, not the man himself.

She could see the sun on his light brown hair in the row of volunteers as they went down the hill and she suddenly felt heart-sick. She wanted him. Mentally and physically, she wanted him more than she had ever wanted anything. She wanted to live with him and be with him for the rest of her life. She wanted to lie with him in a bed of their own, to be ravished by him and to be loved by him. Daisy looked around quickly, guiltily, as if people nearby might have read her thoughts. And when she looked again the double file of men had gone on to the beach and out of sight.

When Will returned to England Daisy knew her heart would ache as it was aching now. She was going to have to live with these feelings for a very long time, perhaps until she died. Will was the only man she had ever wanted and she knew he was the only man she would ever want. She thought of the Duchess and her Duke and now she understood.

'If it 'appens,' the Duchess had said, 'you know it. It only 'appens once and there's never any doubt.' Daisy had listened intently. 'But not everyone believes that, do they?' she'd asked and the Duchess had given her one of those gentle yet penetrating looks. 'Those who don't believe,' she said, 'are those it never 'appened to.'

*

According to Squanto the fastest way of reaching their destination and probably the safest was to sail up the coast and then travel inland. The men chosen by Standish sailed away in the shallop, keeping close in to the shore. It was almost dark when they saw two Indians who were examining traps for lobster. Squanto and two others went ashore in the small boat to question them.

The Indians knew nothing, they said, of the missing girl but they did have some worrying news to impart. They were men of the Massasoit tribe, they told Squanto, and only that morning they had heard that their chief had been attacked at his main camp and might well be dead, killed by the Narragansetts. Squanto did not believe this. If it was true, he said, the news would have spread like a fire in the forest. But he was prepared to believe the Narragansetts were attempting to depose the chief and force his followers to join them.

Leaving two of the men to guard the shallop and to sail away if they had to, Standish and Squanto led the others the rest of the way on foot. As they came across more and more of the local Indians, Squanto was able to piece together a picture of what had happened. It seemed a disloyal Massasoit named Corbitant had organized a coup against his chief and was openly boasting he would kill Squanto. The settlers, Corbitant said, would then have lost their tongue. No one seemed to know if the coup had been successful or where they might find Chief Massasoit.

Standish knew he must first determine if all this was true and assess the threat, if any, to the settlers. The search for the baby, sadly, became a second priority. The rebel leader, Corbitant, was said to be at the Indian camp known as Namasket. Armed with swords and muskets, Standish and his men arrived there with the declared intention of cutting off Corbitant's head and putting it on display as a deterrent to others. It was an image stark and vivid enough to frighten the impressionable villagers, though it was unlikely that even the generally uncompromising Standish would have sanctioned so barbarous an act.

At Namasket they soon located Corbitant's house and surrounding it they fired their muskets in the air. The Indians in the village were cowed by the gunfire but Corbitant was not at home. The villagers were assembled like children in a wide semi-circle and, through Squanto, Standish informed them that, though Corbitant had on this occasion escaped, sooner or later they would capture him. The villagers were to pass on the message that if Chief Massasoit had been imprisoned he must be set free at once. And if Corbitant had harmed the chief in any way the white men would hound him to the ends of the earth.

Standish then told the villagers of the missing baby. Appealing mainly to the Indian women, he told them of the distress of the baby's mother and the great sadness the disappearance had brought upon the settlers. If you are to be our friends, he told them, I beg you to help us find this unfortunate little child. He asked them to spread the word far and wide, and assured them that for any information leading to the baby's return a generous reward would gladly be paid.

The task of finding little Alice on that unpredictable and sometimes impenetrable shore was beyond the scope of so small a party of searchers. In the absence of any information or clues as to her whereabouts they needed a tremendous stroke of luck to find her and luck was not with them. Reluctantly they returned, empty-handed, to the settlement. They had ventured a day and a half away. They arrived back to be told that a messenger with a smattering of English had brought the news that Chief Massasoit was alive and well.

The chief had been impressed by the response of the settlers to the news that he might be in difficulty. Without hesitation they had honoured the treaty by attempting to come to his aid and he would not forget it. The chief had expressed his deep concern at the disappearance of the baby and had promised to do everything in his power to help. He had assembled his braves and instructed them to spread the word to all the tribes, friendly or otherwise, that this infant must be found. He, too, had offered a substantial reward.

36

When the shallop came into view around the headland a crowd gathered on the beach. There was hope and an eager anticipation on the faces of those waiting on the shore. But as the boat drew near the watchers knew the search had failed. If the men in the shallop had recovered the baby they would surely have held her aloft for all to see. The men were subdued and it soon became clear there was no cause for joy or celebration. John Carver, waiting at the common house, could not hide his disappointment.

Things had been going well for the settlers. Carver's gentle suggestion at a Sunday Service that those survivors of the voyage and the epidemic who found themselves without a spouse might choose to make a future with a new partner – 'from our own people', as he put it – had been well received. A number of potentially promising partnerships had quickly developed.

Edward Winslow and Susannah White, a widowed mother of two small children, had found a mutual respect and common interests that soon blossomed into love. They had asked the governor to set a date for their wedding. It was an expression of faith and hope in the future and a fine example to the other bereaved, a development for which John Carver was deeply thankful. And now all this had been blighted by the loss of little Alice.

The abduction of a small child had rekindled all the fear of the natives the women had until then successfully overcome. This one heart-stopping act had put the whole of the small community in a state of near panic. Men and women alike were suspicious of all comers and as unsettled as when they first arrived. An involuntary curfew had imposed itself on the tiny settlement and after nightfall only men with swords or muskets ventured out.

Children were only allowed to play under watchful eyes and most of the time indoors. Women and girls were fearful of finding themselves alone where some phantom-like Indian with a painted face and a hatchet they called a 'tomahawk' might silently steal up on them. All of the goodwill they had so patiently cultivated was lost and John Carver, as governor, was doubly concerned to hear of the troubles in the Indian camps. There were many problems to be faced. But first he must break the news of the searchers' sad return to Alice Rigdale.

Mrs Rigdale was in a bed in the common house, sedated as best he could by Dr Fuller who carried a small personal supply of laudanum. At first she had been given brandy, a little too much brandy. But now, from time to time, the doctor gave her a taste of the opiate. When she was not tossing and turning in a restless sleep, Alice lay awake with wild eyes and a look of terror akin to madness on her white face. Dr Fuller suggested she should only be told that the men were still searching and Carver agreed. But Alice caught a glimpse of Miles Standish and she knew the men were back.

Surprising everyone, she ran from her bed in her nightdress and gripped him by the shirt, her eyes pleading, willing him to give her the news she wanted to hear. Standish could only say softly, at the doctor's prompting, that the men were 'still out there, still looking'. Alice didn't believe him. Even in her demented state she knew who the searchers were and when she saw them outside the common house she ran from one to another, pleading for news.

Then she saw the Indian, Squanto, with his strip of fringed leather, his rugged gypsy face and his black shiny hair tied at the back of his head. She threw her frail body at him, pounding her fists on his wide brown chest and blaming him for her baby's disappearance. The tall Indian remained dignified and composed, holding her thin arms in his large hands and restraining her gently until others led her away.

When Carver apologized Squanto said he understood the lady's feelings perfectly. In his own words he said that Indian women were no less devoted to their children and the loss of a child in this way would be just as heartbreaking to a squaw. He would go alone, he said, to the Narragansetts to see if the child was with them. But it was suggested he should remain with the settlement until contact had been re-established with Chief Massasoit.

'I'll go,' Will Trefor spoke up. 'If you want to send a deputation, Standish, you can count on me.'

'You can't go,' Pat Ellis told him. 'You need Captain Jones's permission.'

'I don't need anyone's permission,' Will said.

'Cut yourself off from Captain Jones an' you're finished, me lad,' Ellis said and lowering his voice he added, for Will's ears only, 'Desert your post on yet another ship, Will, an' you can never go home.'

Edward Winslow said calmly, 'We must sit down and consider our options. We must not act hastily. For one thing, we can only assume the Narragansetts have taken the baby. We have no proof.'

'The description we have was that of a Narragansett,' Standish said, looking at Squanto who nodded in confirmation.

'The description given by a boy standing on a roof some distance away,' Winslow said. 'No, I admit it may well be a Narragansett who is responsible, but if we are wrong the suggestion would insult them. They would quite rightly feel offended. What then?'

John Carver did not want these matters of policy discussed in public. Any open disagreement among the leadership would only result in more unrest among the others, especially the women.

'Edward is right,' he said and he asked for a meeting of elders to
be held at his house. 'I hope that you two gentlemen,' he told Ellis
and Will Trefor, 'will also attend.'

They nodded that they would but when they were alone Pat
said, 'This is their problem, Will, not yours.'

'If I decide to stay it will be my problem.'

'You know you can't stay. You can go home an' then return,
yes. But first you must go home.'

Will was not so sure. Apart from the need to clear his name with
the navy he saw no good reason to go home. And clearing his
name would not be easy. So *why* must he go home? And where
was home? Not Cheshire. Not any more. And certainly not
London.

In London one was consumed by crowds. Crowded streets,
crowded squares – and indifference. Pavements lined with
unfamiliar, unsmiling faces. Every man pursuing his own private
goal. Here, there were no unfamiliar faces. Every face was known
to all. Every settler had a personality of his or her own and
everyone had an acknowledged share in the recent past. By
training Will was a sailor but a life at sea was not of his choosing.
The choice had been made for him and he knew now it was not
what he wanted. What he wanted could well be here in this return
to a small beginning. They really had come to a new world.

Miles Standish figured large in this bare landscape. He was not a
big man physically but like Carver and Bradford and Winslow he
had grown in stature in the minds of the others. He was a leader,
not a follower, and on the visit to the Massasoits Will Trefor had
observed him closely. Standish was clearly committed to the
colony, sure of his own place in its future. The death of his wife
had not changed that. Where another man might have felt
constrained to abandon the venture and return home Standish had
become even more determined to succeed. What was left of his life
would, in the main, be spent here. If he returned to England it
would only be as a visitor or for business reasons. This was his
home now.

Despite his early misgivings Will Trefor had come to admire
Standish. He admired them all, all the leaders. In so short a time
and labouring under such difficulties they had built the embryo of
a town. Already it was possible, in just a few weeks, to see the
emerging main street, the place where a church, a schoolroom, a
store would be built. And in the midst of all this they had found
the strength and the will to establish a rapport, a mutual respect,
with the native Indians. The key, they would say, lay in their

beliefs. But Will had never been less than sceptical in religious matters. All religions seemed to him to be built on dubious doctrines of fear. Yet there was little doubt that what the settlers had achieved so far had been guided and sustained by their belief in God.

Now that Edward Winslow was spoken for, Miles Standish was probably the most eligible of the unattached men. And certainly, Will thought, Daisy is the best-looking and most desirable of the eligible women. It would seem right and proper to the rest if the two were to get together. According to Prudence, Standish had already made a preliminary move. Will felt affronted by this, though without reasonable cause. Hadn't he had the audacity to approach Rose, not a single lady like Daisy, but a married woman? Now he knew how it felt to have a rival.

Even before Rose died, Daisy Mason was uppermost in Will's thoughts. He just hadn't realized it. But he realized it now. The emergence of Miles Standish as a potential suitor had concentrated his mind. Standish had taken Rose: he could now take Daisy. If Will went home he would be leaving the field clear for Standish. Yet he knew in his heart that Captain Jones and Pat Ellis were right.

If he was to have any kind of worthwhile future here he must first return to England, win a King's pardon. But what if he lost? What if a pardon was refused? He would certainly be gaoled. He might even face execution. His father had been executed as a traitor, an enemy of King and country. Already his family name was tarnished. Had his desertion not stained it further? And wouldn't all this weigh heavily against him?

They had been waiting in a small group to join Carver and Mr Brewster in John Carver's house. A small boy servant came to summon them. Mrs Carver had prepared a bowl of elderberry wine. A box of biscuits was offered round as each man filled a tumbler and took his place at the governor's table.

At the front door Will turned, looked back and saw Daisy leave the common house. He waved both hands to catch her attention. He hadn't seen her for several days and he thought she looked tired and a little downcast. Daisy smiled and raised a hand in return and he felt a sudden urge to rush to her side and sweep her into his arms. But what right had he to do that? Why should Daisy care anything about him? He had never told her of his feelings for her. Even though he had felt from the start they had a special relationship he had never mentioned it, never told her *how* special. All he had ever done was confide in her his feelings for Rose Standish.

'Mr Trefor?' John Carver said politely as the others settled about the table and Will went inside.

Daisy walked back down the dirt road to the girls' house. She was tired. She'd been awake most of the night, watching over Alice Rigdale. She tried not to think about baby Alice now. It was unbearable to imagine what might have happened to her. Most of the Indians she had observed so far seemed amiable, simple folk. Some of the men seemed silly, even childish, but harmless enough. She suspected it was the women, as always, who held the tribes together. And all of them, men *and* women, seemed to love their children.

There had been a suggestion that Alice might not have been abducted by an Indian. She could have wandered off, become lost. But surely the searchers, out so soon after her disappearance would have found her. It had even been hinted that wolves might have taken her. But in the face of all the questioning young John Crackston had steadfastly maintained that he had seen an Indian, a tall man, scoop up little Alice and race away with her into the woods. Daisy thought again of the baby's mother. That poor, poor woman! She must know, as they all knew, that hope of finding her baby was fading with every hour that passed.

When she arrived at her house Daisy found she had a visitor. Sitting on a log by the door was Maurice Tinker. Daisy was surprised to see him. She had just left Prudence at the common house. 'Did you want Pru?'

Maurice stood up uneasily. 'Er ... no, Miss Mason. It's you I came to see.'

'Oh?' Daisy was curious. 'If you would wait a moment, Maurice, I'll see if anyone is home.' There was no one in the house. All the girls were busy elsewhere. 'Come in,' she said, 'and sit down.'

The youngest girl had left her dolls' house on a chair. Daisy picked it up and put it on the floor. Obviously nervous, Maurice sat down.

'You wanted to see me?' Daisy prompted, not hiding her curiosity.

'Er ... yes.' He hesitated, as if he didn't know where to start. 'It's about Pru.'

Daisy waited, her face without expression.

'You are Pru's employer, Miss Mason, and as Pru has no family of her own I assume you are also her ... her guardian.'

'Yes,' Daisy said firmly.

'My father said I ought to approach you ....' He hesitated again.

'I … er, I want to marry Pru. And I would like you to give us your blessing.'

'Oh.' Daisy's reaction gave little away.

'We get on very well, Miss Mason. Mr Carver thinks people should marry if they get on well. My father thinks I should marry Pru.'

'And what about you, Maurice? What do *you* think?'

'Oh yes, I mean, I think so, too. We like each other a lot.'

'*Like* each other?'

Maurice faltered. 'Well ….'

'Don't you *love* each other?'

'Well, I suppose we do really. But not, perhaps, in that way.'

'In *what* way?'

'You know.' He shifted uneasily on the stiff-backed chair. Then he blurted out, 'But I would always take good care of her. You can be sure of that.'

Daisy looked unconvinced.

'My father is not a poor man,' Maurice said, a little pompously. 'We have property in England and there will be provision from home even when we are established here. I am my father's only son and heir. Pru would be marrying into a good family and, after all, she is only …'

'A servant girl?'

'I didn't mean that.'

'Oh yes you did, Maurice. Well, I'll tell you this. Pru may only be a servant girl but she is a good girl and she is my responsibility. When she does marry it will be on equal terms with her partner – no matter who or what he is or whatever property he owns in England.'

'Of course.' Maurice was totally flustered. 'I didn't mean it to sound that way. Please, Miss Mason. I want to marry Pru and Pru wants to marry me. I would never do anything to make her unhappy.'

'But you don't love her?'

Daisy's forthright question embarrassed him further.

'And if you don't love her,' she went on, 'in *that* way, then you won't really be married.'

'No, no,' Maurice protested. 'You don't understand. We *would* be married. We might even have children. It's just that … I'm not … it's not something that matters much to me.'

'Pru is a young woman, Maurice. Contrary to what you may have been taught to believe, I'm sure it would matter a great deal to her.'

Maurice hung his head. He had not expected opposition. He had assumed he was doing Daisy some kind of honour in offering to marry her maidservant. But he was unprepared for Daisy's questions and the questions still waiting to be asked. She was forcing him to face something he had evaded facing throughout his youth.

Watching him, feeling sorry for him now, Daisy wondered if she had been too hard on him. And, if so, with what justification. But again she remembered the Duchess and her many warnings.

English society, it seemed, was riddled with men who lived a lie, keeping up a façade with wives and children whilst supporting a mistress or visiting prostitutes. And according to the Duchess there was also an even darker side. Many 'gentlemen', some in high places, preferred to pay young *men* and *boys* for their favours.

It was humiliating for a wife and Daisy didn't want any of that for Pru. Maurice, she guessed, might well develop into this kind of man and she had willed him to answer her truthfully, to deny any such proclivities, preferably with great indignation. But he hadn't.

Strangely calm, as if he had nothing more to hide and therefore nothing more to lose, he asked, 'Then you refuse to give your blessing?'

'I'm sorry, Maurice,' Daisy said. 'I think you should put any idea of marrying Prudence out of your mind. Such a marriage could only end in misery – for you both.'

He stood up, was about to say something more but decided against it. Daisy followed him to the door and watched him walk up the already well-trodden path to the dirt road.

Later that morning Daisy had a second visitor.

'Welcome to my humble home,' she said as Will Trefor hovered in the weak sunlight at her doorstep.

'Not so humble as my bunk aboard the *Mayflower*,' Will said, looking over her shoulder. 'This place has the woman's touch.'

'The touch of three women,' Daisy laughed. 'Five if you count the girls.'

'Daisy,' he said, advancing only slightly. 'I ...'

It was all there, in his eyes, but he was clearly uncertain how to proceed and it was this very diffidence that touched Daisy far more than if he had attempted to sweep her off her feet.

He looked around quickly. 'Are we alone?'

'Completely,' Daisy said with a smile. 'Isn't it disgraceful? Alone and unchaperoned.'

'Don't make fun of me, Daisy.'

She regarded him solemnly, but the smile was not far away and she could scarcely contain her joy.

'What can I say except "I've been a fool"? I've known from the day I first saw you, when you stood at the window of the Ship Inn on Southwark Dock ...'

She waited, wanting him to say it.

'And now I'm told I must return to England with the *Mayflower* to explain myself to the King's Navy. But I don't want to, Daisy. Not because they would arrest me and perhaps sentence me to a term of imprisonment. No. I don't want to go back because I want to stay here and make my future here and ... and marry you.'

'You want to marry *me*?'

'More than anything else in the world.'

'Why?' she demanded. 'Why do you want to marry me?'

'Because,' he said, 'because ... I love you.'

She had made him say it and it was easy for him now. He said it over and over again as she opened her arms and this time he did sweep her off her feet.

'I've always loved you!' He swung her round and she laughed as he kissed her neck, her face and finally her lips. 'I never loved anyone but you.'

'Not even Rose?'

'Not even Rose.' He looked Daisy in the eyes. 'Rose was a lovely girl. But I didn't love her. I only thought I did. To me she was something I'd lost along with my home, my family, my youth.' He looked down at her, his forehead almost touching hers. 'It's you that I want, Daisy. Nobody else.'

Daisy stepped back, withdrew from his embrace. 'You don't know anything about me.'

'I know all I need to know.'

Gently she warded him off. 'Will, please. There are things about me you don't know, things you would have to know. And, I'm afraid, you might change your mind.'

He smiled and shook his head as if there was no possibility of that.

'You must listen carefully to what I have to say.'

He was still smiling, shaking his head.

'At home ... in England ... I killed a man,' she said, and her hand went to her mouth as if the statement had shocked even her.

37

Will drew her towards him. 'I know,' he said. 'I know you did and I know why.'

'How?' she asked in surprise. 'How do you know?'

'Pat told me. Pat Ellis. He told me all about you, a long time ago.'

'Pat? But why? I thought he was my friend.'

'He is your friend,' Will said. 'One of the best friends you will ever have.' He made her look at him. 'I've known Pat for a long time now, from my Dartmouth days when I was a raw recruit. He taught me most of what I know about ships and the sea. And when I needed help, when I was in London, it was Pat I turned to. I wanted to join the *Mayflower*. Pat was looking for a ship himself so he contacted Captain Jones. The captain knew Pat of old. He snapped him up, even though he'd already engaged two pilots. But the rest of the crew had been signed on and there was no room for me, even as an ordinary seaman.

'I stowed in the hold as far as Southampton. Then I paid one of the men to cry off and Pat persuaded the captain to take me on as a replacement. I only got the job on Pat's recommendation. He told me I was a damned fool to desert my ship and that I'd never be free until I went back and gave myself up. But when he saw how determined I was he agreed to help me. And I'll be eternally grateful to him. If he hadn't I might never have met you.'

Will looked tired, thinner now. Daisy wanted to feed him, nurse him, watch him rest and recuperate.

'Last night,' he said, 'I told him how I feel about you.'

'What did he say?'

'He said sure and he wondered why it had taken me so long to realize it.'

They smiled at Will's attempt at an Irish accent.

'He said he was very pleased,' Will went on, 'because he knew you felt the same way.' He looked down into her eyes and she didn't deny it. 'He said he always knew that sooner or later you and I would be together. I just had to get Rose out of my head first. He said he always knew I would and he wanted to clear the way for when I did. You had already told him about the man in St Giles. So he decided to tell me all he knew about you.'

'I'm glad,' Daisy said. 'I'm glad he did. But, the fact remains, I ran away from England. I can never go back.'

'You could go back as my wife. No one would know you or connect you with some missing girl ....'

'Will,' she said quietly, 'when I joined the *Mayflower* I didn't know any of these people. I didn't know anything about them. I was just a frightened girl, running away – then I discovered they were running away, too. They were running away from persecution. They were looking for freedom to practise their religion in the only way they knew how. I understood that and I came to see that they were good, honest people. People you could respect and trust.

'Since I came on this voyage and landed here in this strange new country my whole outlook has changed. My imagination has been stretched. I'm not putting this very well, I know, but what I want to say is I've grown to appreciate things, things I never gave a thought to in England.' She laughed. 'At least, not where I lived in St Giles. The great joy in a tumbler of fresh clear water after a whole day with a parched throat. The comfort of a really deep sleep. And how welcome a few rays of sunshine can be after day after day with the wind howling in your ears and the rain lashing your face.

'And all the sadness, too. With sickness and death all around. And yet hope and determination. The urge to live and win through – in spite of everything. What I'm saying, I suppose, is that since the start of this mad adventure, for the first time in my life, I have learned to live each day to the full. This is where the future lies, Will. I don't want to go back to England. This is where I want to be. I'm a part of these people now and they are a part of me. They are *my* people. I belong here, with them. You don't. You are a sailor and a good one. Your life is at sea.'

'Oh no!' Will was absolutely sure. 'That is not so. My life is not at sea, not any more.' He gripped her by the shoulders. 'My life is here with you, Daisy. We'll be married. We'll build a house. We'll make a home of our own and we'll help to build a new country, a country fit for our children.'

Aboard the *Mayflower* Captain Jones assembled the remaining members of his crew. Over half of his men had died in the epidemic that spring, but with no passengers and very little cargo the captain believed he had enough hands and sufficient provisions to make the voyage home. They would sail, he told them, on Thursday, April the fifth.

One of his men had applied formally to stay with the settlers. He had proposed marriage, he said, to a 'widder lady' and he'd been accepted. Members of the crew had signed on 'voyage and return' and, technically, the request could be refused. But Captain Jones had agreed and given the couple his blessing. In the case of Will Trefor he took a different view.

Captain Jones liked the young naval officer, valued his seafaring skills and genuinely believed it would be a sad mistake for him to stay behind. He must first go home, explain his actions and ask for the indulgence of the court. When Will returned to the ship the captain summoned him to his cabin and told him so.

'I understand your desire to stay with the settlement,' Captain Jones said, 'of course I do. Your choice of a marriage partner is admirable. I have come to know Miss Mason well and I admire her many excellent qualities.'

'So?' Will demanded, his old belligerence returning.

'If you were to marry her without first clearing your name you would be doing her a great disservice. There is much to be done here and it's men like you who'll do it. But you must be able to deal with your visiting countrymen on equal terms. There will be many ships, many visitors in the years to come. Traders, navy men, government officials, representatives of the King – they will all appear on these shores. And you would be at a disadvantage in all of your dealings. You would not, for instance, be in a position to accept office.

'John Carver is a good man but he will not live forever. I'm sure that in due course your name would be put forward for the office of governor of the colony. Oh, I know there are a number of good men ahead of you – Bradford, Winslow and others – but your time would come and with that young lady at your side you would certainly make a fine leader. But the governor of the colony, as you well know, represents the King of England and if you are in enforced exile you cannot very well represent the King.'

Will knew the captain was right. 'But if I return to England now I will be made to stand trial. I could be sentenced to a term of imprisonment. I might never get back.'

'That is a possibility,' the captain conceded. 'But you may rest assured, voices will be raised in your favour. Mine for one. Governor Carver's for another.'

Will looked doubtful.

'Governor Carver is aware of your predicament. And he has told me of his gratitude towards you. He believes your contribution to the settlement has been considerable. Your seamanship saved the shallop and all aboard her from disaster. You have helped Standish with his forays inland. You have even done a share of the house building though, of course, you were under no obligation to do anything. The governor tells me he would like you to marry Miss Mason and become a pillar of the community. Neither of you are members of his church yet he assures me he would be more than happy to officiate at your wedding. However, he agrees with me that you should first settle your affairs at home.'

'Easier said ...' Will began.

'Governor Carver has promised to write a personal letter to His Majesty on your behalf.'

'And what weight would that carry? I understood these people were running away from persecution ....'

'Governor Carver has asked me to deliver his report on the establishment of the colony in the King's name. His report contains several items of interest and importance – among them a vow of allegiance from Chief Massasoit and a copy of the agreement drawn up between the settlers and the native population. All of which will no doubt please His Majesty.

'The governor asks very little of the Crown in return. But one of the small requests he does make is that you should be pardoned and permitted to reurn here to help him with his work. There is a glowing testimonial to your conduct to date and a statement that you have long regretted your foolish indiscretion. It was not, the governor points out, a wanton act of disloyalty. It was the impulsive act of a headstrong and immature young man.'

'I don't know,' Will said, casting about for a way to express both his gratitude and his reservations. 'It's kind of Governor Carver but the truth is my father was executed, on the King's warrant, for treason. The King will not look kindly on any rebellion on my part.'

'You must have faith,' Captain Jones told him. 'The governor's letter and report will not be your only references. I intend to approach the Admiral of the King's Fleet on my return. He is not an unkind man and I have assisted him and his officers in the past. I shall personally put your case before him so that if and when he is consulted he will know the background.'

The stockily built Welsh sea captain wanted to help Will as he would have helped any one of his own four sons. He opened a small cabinet and brought out a brandy decanter and two tumblers. He poured a drink for himself and one for Will which Will accepted gratefully. 'I have invited your friend, Mr Ellis, to submit a report on your work aboard the *Mayflower* during our very difficult passage out and a note on your promotion to the watch. My pilots, Mr Clarke and Mr Coppin, will endorse both.'

'These things,' Will said, 'as you well know, Captain, take time. I might not see Miss Mason for at least a year.'

'Would she not wish to return with you to England?'

Will frowned. 'I can't ask her to do that. She has her responsibilities here now and I know she wants to stay. If I were to be imprisoned for – who knows? Five? Ten? Fifteen years? She might not feel able to return. I have no wish to ruin her future along with my own.'

'Then the choice is yours,' the captain said. 'Stay if you must. I will not attempt to prevent you – although, strictly speaking, I should.' He smiled. 'I should clap you in irons and hand you over to the navy at the first opportunity.' He stood up, his craggy, weather-beaten face kind and concerned. 'If you are to sail with me on the fifth I would like to know by sunset on the third.'

The imminent departure of the *Mayflower* meant that little work was done in the settlement. There was so much to be said to the departing seamen and there were so many requests for small favours. Many of the settlers wanted relatives they had left behind to follow them and their messages spoke optimistically of the future. A man named Warren, who had left his wife and five daughters behind in London, was now eager for them to join him. Another, Francis Cooke, wanted his wife and two children to 'come out on the very next boat'. But there was also much sad news to be imparted, a report of the many deaths incurred, in some cases the loss of a whole family.

So great was the press of settlers when a member of his crew appeared that Captain Jones, with the governor's approval, decided to set up a desk in the common house where all day one of his pilots, John Clarke or Robert Coppin and for a spell Pat Ellis, would receive notes and messages for delivery to relatives or friends in England or Holland. Just how all these requests were to be fulfilled the captain was not sure, but his instructions to his officers were to take them all and on the long journey home he would work out how best to deliver them.

Despite the constant stream of visitors to and from the common house desk and the general air of excitement, Miles Standish maintained his regular complement of men on guard duty, stepping up the vigilance to a round-the-clock watch on the surrounding woods. The Massasoits seemed to have gone quiet, their manner and approach more subdued since their chief expressed his deep sorrow at the failure to find the missing baby, and far fewer of them came to the settlement. His people and their associated tribesmen, the chief promised, would not rest until the little one had been found and safely returned to her mother.

But then, through the stupidity and insensitive actions of one of the older settlers, John Billington, and two youths, relations with the Indians suffered a set-back. In the woods where the river ran shallow, Billington and the youths had come across a group of young Indian women, several of whom carried babies strapped to their backs. Hidden in the bushes they had watched for a time in the hope that the women were about to disrobe and bathe, but the women were merely there to wash clothing. Disappointed, the three had confronted the women and brandishing knives had forced them to produce their babies for inspection.

'They could've 'ad the Rigdale mite,' was Billington's feeble justification. But his concern for the missing baby had not shown itself previously and the governor believed he and the two youths had been indulging in what Miles Standish called 'an ill-advised bout of squaw-baiting'. The women had been understandably alarmed, believing the white men intended to take their babies in some form of retaliation. They had run off, screaming through the woods, to alert their menfolk. The ensuing indignation and loss of trust required all the diplomacy Edward Winslow and Squanto could muster, and Billington and the two youths were made to apologize on their knees to Chief Massasoit.

Inevitably as day after day there was no news, no fresh information, the chance of finding little Alice seemed increasingly remote. A feeling of helplessness had descended on most of the settlers. Already in the minds of many she was lost and would probably never be found. It was this growing, unspoken acceptance that so horrified Prudence.

'We can't go on as if nothin' 'as 'appened!' she suddenly exclaimed one evening in the girls' house. 'We can't jus' give up! We 'ave to find 'er!'

'But how?' Priscilla Mullins demanded. 'What can we do? Where would we begin to look?'

'Do you think she's dead?' asked the youngest girl, Elizabeth, who in her innocence had a way of asking most of the questions the others tended to avoid.

'Perhaps it would be a blessing ...' Priscilla began.

'We just don't know,' Daisy said. 'She could be with a good Indian family who'll love her and take care of her.'

'But if they were good,' Elizabeth argued reasonably, 'they wouldn't have taken her in the first place.'

'We mus' think of 'er mother,' Prudence said. 'We can't give up. We mus' go on searchin' until we know exactly what's become of 'er.' Then quietly and with authority, she said, 'I know what it's like to lose a baby.'

The others looked at her with new respect.

'But, at least,' she added, 'I know where my baby is.'

Relations with the Massasoits were soon to be further complicated. One of Standish's most reliable men, Richard Gardiner, had been housed with the Billington family: the ill-tempered John Billington, his noisy Cockney wife Ellen and their two small sons aged six and four. The arrangement was temporary. Only until more houses were available, Richard was assured. But John Billington behaved as though Richard had been assigned to him as his personal manservant and treated him accordingly. Richard had complained to John Carver and the governor had promised he would be rehoused at the first opportunity. Then, one morning, when Richard was out chopping wood, an incident occurred that was to change his life completely.

A small party of Massasoit women were making their way through the woods to the settlement with an assortment of wooden bowls and basins and basketware for barter when they passed near to where Richard was working. There were the usual friendly greetings and some apparently suggestive remarks from the Indian women directed at the shirtless Richard and his strong wiry body that caused them to cackle among themselves and make Richard blush. Then he saw her, saw her for the first time and he watched, as if mesmerized, as she passed close by.

The young Indian girl was about sixteen with hair as black as a raven's wing cut short against her olive skin. She had bright black eyes, the whites startlingly white, and as she passed Richard her lips parted in a shy, white-toothed smile. Richard could only stare and this embarrassed the girl and one of the older women said something that made the others laugh. Richard stood perfectly still, his mouth open, his long-handled axe held limply at his side, as he gazed after the procession of women. Briefly the girl looked back and smiled again and Richard was spellbound.

From then on Richard stopped to look at every group of Indian women in the hope of seeing her again and one day he did. But this time she was alone. He was walking to his work with the warm gold of the sun filtering through the tops of the trees and the ground no longer wet and muddy underfoot and there, in the clearing where he chopped wood, was the slender maiden of his dreams. He was dumbstruck. He didn't pause to question why she was there or how she knew he would be there, accepting the chance encounter as a stroke of divine providence, the answer to his prayers. But, of course, it was not a chance encounter. If an Indian girl is interested, he discovered later, she doesn't wait for things to happen. She makes them happen.

He tried to speak to her. 'Hello,' he said, with a smile. 'My name ... my name is Richard.'

The girl laughed and ran away into the woods and Richard followed, chasing her through the trees as in a children's game, until she came to a halt against the smooth bark of a birch. He put a hand on the tree just above her head and looked down into her eyes. 'Richard,' he said again. 'My name is Richard.'

She gazed up at him and this time she didn't run away.

He prodded himself in the chest. 'Richard.'

She nodded.

'And you?' He pointed a finger at her. 'You?'

For a moment the girl looked puzzled.

'Richard,' he said again. 'You?'

'Richard,' she said softly.

He put his hand on her bare shoulder and his young heart seemed to swell up inside him. She raised her head, the dark pupils of her eyes dilated and her lips parted slightly. Then suddenly she broke the spell. As if with an effort she took his hand from her shoulder and led him back to the narrow path to the settlement.

Visiting Indians and several of the settlers, men working on buildings and women going about their business, stopped to watch in surprise and with not a little curiosity as the girl led Richard down the main street. Richard was proud to hold her hand and he walked beside her with his head held high. She was looking for Squanto, leading Richard to him.

When they found him, Richard said, 'Tell 'er, please, my name is Richard. An' ask 'er name.'

'Squanto know her name,' the Indian said. 'Squanto know her father. What you want with this woman?'

Richard was not sure what he wanted, except that he wanted to know more about her. 'I want to see 'er again. I want to get to know 'er.'

'Why?' Squanto's limited vocabulary often sounded brusque and sometimes downright offensive.

'Why?' Richard bristled. 'Because I like 'er, that's why.'

Squanto spoke rapidly to the girl in her own tongue and her eager expression changed. She looked anxiously at Richard, withdrew her hand from his, then turned and ran.

'Wait!' Richard wanted to run after her but Squanto laid a restraining hand on his arm.

'No!' the Indian said. 'She must return to her father.'

'I will go to 'er,' Richard said defiantly. 'She likes me an' I like 'er.'

'You must not go to her,' Squanto warned. 'That is not our way. I will speak with governor and with father of girl.'

Miles Standish was now constantly on the look-out for any sign of large scale movements of tribesmen. His scouts were sent out daily to reconnoitre the surrounding terrain, the gun platform was manned day and night and he was at all times aware of the danger of a surprise attack. He was not, he insisted, being either alarmist or over-cautious. The Massasoits, he believed, were genuine. But he did not trust the Narragansetts. Perhaps, he suggested, they were quietly waiting for the ship to sail away and leave a weakened force to defend the settlement. If they were, he told his men, he fully intended to be ready for them.

Those last few days before the *Mayflower* sailed Standish had few moments to himself. But he did make time to seek out and offer his best wishes to Will Trefor.

'You and I should be friends,' he said. 'These past months and especially these past weeks we have come through a great deal, quite a variety of experiences.'

He held out a hand and Will took it graciously.

'Have you decided what you will do?' Standish asked.

'I know I should go back,' Will admitted. 'But it rather depends on Daisy.'

'Miss Mason told me of your betrothal,' Standish said. 'My congratulations – I'm very pleased for you both.'

Will regarded him frankly.

'You're a very lucky fellow,' he went on. 'She's a fine lady, a woman any man would be proud to call his wife.'

Will nodded. 'But there's a problem. Captain Jones believes I should return ....'

' ...And he's right,' Standish told him. 'You must make your peace with the navy. Then you can come back here and marry the lady. We intend to make a land fit for future generations of Englishmen. You can be part of that. You must be part of it. Your friends are here. Your whole life is here now.'

'I've heard all the arguments,' Will said, 'but there are still doubts, reservations. I have no wish to rot in some navy prison.'

'I think there will be enough influential voices raised in your favour to avoid that happening. Go home and come back a free man. That's my advice.'

The accumulation of such advice was difficult to ignore. If he stayed he would inevitably be relegated to a secondary role in the affairs of the settlement, unable to take his full place in the community, unable to represent the colony in negotiations with visiting traders. And always when a ship came in he would have to hide or, at least, keep out of sight. He had no wish to inflict such a restricted way of life on Daisy.

The future of the new colony was clearly to be built on the sanctity of marriage and the values of family life. Already, within the settlement, Daisy had assumed a position of some prominence. Her voice was heard and listened to and many of the younger women looked to her for guidance. If she married a deserter, a man on the run from King and country, all this might change. If they were to have children the children, too, might suffer. They might feel restricted, their young lives and prospects tainted, as Will's had been, through no fault of their own. It was a matter of honour, Will decided. He had to go back.

38

Daisy listened to the arguments and, though it pained her to say so, she finally accepted Will's decision. He would return, he told her, with the *Mayflower*. Captain Jones had offered to accompany him, on their arrival in London, to the naval headquarters on Tower Hill. Whatever the outcome it would mean a long separation. Even if granted an immediate pardon he might not be in a position to return for at least a year. But Daisy knew and had known all along he would never be truly happy in any enforced exile. He might stay now and come to regret his decision with every passing day. She knew she couldn't bear to watch him grow bitter with age. And it was her agreement, her acceptance, that at last convinced him he must go.

He returned to the *Mayflower* in the shallop and informed Captain Jones he was prepared to fulfil his contract and work as a senior member of crew on the voyage home. Captain Jones welcomed his decision and assured him, with the testimonials to hand, he would not regret it. There was also now, and perhaps the most promising of all, a personal letter from Miles Standish to Her Majesty the Queen.

Standish, apparently, claimed to know Her Majesty well and to be in good favour. He had taken the trouble to write a detailed account of Will's reasons for leaving his ship, his romantic notion of pursuing *the lost love of his youth* and now he had at last *awoken from his fanciful dream* to regret his folly, to see the error of his ways and to work *with courage and dedication* to make reparation. *He has played a considerable role* Standish wrote, *in securing the allegiance of the Sagamores, the Indian Chieftains, in New England to His Majesty the King*.

'This letter to the Queen,' Captain Jones told Will, 'is probably just what we need. A personal approach from someone in favour. According to Mr Carver, Standish and his family are held in high regard, great favourites with the Crown, and two of his ancestors, it seems, were knighted.'

Will was not so sure. 'The King might take exception ....'

'We can only be guided by Standish. He appears to have completely reversed his opinion of you, Mr Trefor. He's been impressed with your conduct throughout this whole business – and this after he accused you of attempting to murder him!' The captain smiled. 'A dramatic sort of fellow, I'd say. But if he can use his contacts, then why not let him? He says that if anyone can be relied upon to influence the King it's the Queen and he's probably right.'

Back on land Will sought out Miles Standish to thank him. 'I hope,' Will said, 'it works.'

'Trust me,' Standish reassured him. 'I'm confident and as a mark of my confidence I have a request to make of you.'

Will smiled. 'I should have known there'd be a catch.'

'When you are pardoned,' Standish went on, ignoring the interruption, 'I would like you to grant me a favour. I could, of course, ask someone else. Your friend Mr Ellis – he's a reliable fellow. Or Mr Clarke. Or Captain Jones himself. But as a mark of my confidence, my certainty that you will be a free man, I make my request of you.'

Will listened, curious now.

'It's about Rose,' Standish told him. 'In some ways it's better I ask you, rather than someone else, because you know the family. You know their new home in Lancashire. You went there once, I understand. Well, the fact of the matter is, I would like them to hear of her death from someone who can answer their questions from his own, first-hand knowledge. I would not want them to see her name on some impersonal list issued by the London Company of Merchant Adventurers, as they call themselves, or from the office of that reprobate Weston. I would like them to hear of Rose's death in a kind and compassionate manner. And I would be immensely grateful if, when you are free to do so, you would visit them and perform that task on my behalf.'

'I am not exactly the most popular person in their social circle. You realize that?'

'Yes,' Standish said. 'Yes, I do, and I have no wish to embarrass you. I thought, therefore, you might prefer to approach Rose's sister rather than her parents.'

'I remember Barbara,' Will said. 'She was only a little younger than Rose. She had a touch of that same delicate beauty, but when I knew her she was more ... more robust, a stronger version of her sister.'

Standish nodded in agreement. 'She's a fine girl. The more I think about it the more I am convinced she would be the best person to inform. I'm sure she would be strong enough to break the news gently to the rest of the family. Rose's parents, I fear, will take it very badly, especially her mother. Rose's mother has been in poor health for some years now.'

'If I am free to do this,' Will said, 'I shall do it. And if I am not free I shall find someone I can trust to do it for me.'

The two men shook hands.

'If I return ...' Will began.

'*When* you return,' Standish corrected him.

'When I return I will bring a rose bush for you to plant at the place where Rose lies.'

Standish managed a smile. 'A red rose, if you will. For Lancashire.'

Richard Gardiner would not allow the question of his Indian girl to go unanswered. She had not been back to the settlement since their encounter with Squanto and Richard had no idea from which village she came. But he was determined to find her and so persistent were his enquiries he was called to a meeting with the governor. Edward Winslow and Miles Standish were also present.

'Why do you wish to see this young woman, Richard?' the governor asked in a kindly, sympathetic manner.

'I loves 'er, that's why,' Richard said.

The three men looked at each other and the governor said reasonably, 'How can you say you love her? You don't know the girl. You don't know anything about her.'

'I knows enough.'

'Do you know what love is?' Standish asked.

'No.' Richard shook his head. 'Mebbe I don't. I never loved anyone afore. Never 'ad no family, nothin' like that. So 'ow would I know? But what I do know is I 'ave feelin's for 'er. An' she 'as feelin's for me.'

The governor looked concerned. 'You haven't done anything wrong, I hope?'

'No, sir,' Richard said. 'We ain't done nothin' wrong.'

'Then,' Winslow asked, 'what do you think should be done about these ... feelings?'

'I wants to marry 'er.'

The three men again exchanged glances and for several seconds silence reigned.

'You want to marry her,' the governor said at last.

'How old are you, Richard?' Winslow asked.

'Eighteen,' Richard said.

'Have you thought this through, son?' the governor asked. 'I mean, if it were possible for you to marry this girl, where would you live? What would you do? Would you want to bring her here, to us?'

'That may not be possible,' Winslow intervened. 'It would depend on the attitude of the girl's father.'

'According to Squanto,' Standish said, 'her father is an important man. Head of his village. He may not allow her to leave.'

'If 'er father will not allow 'er to come to me,' Richard said stubbornly, 'then I shall go to 'er.'

'You would go native?' Winslow asked.

'Yes.'

'You can't do that,' Standish said. 'Go and live with the Indians? Live in a tent, learn their ways?'

'Why not?' Richard demanded. 'If she came to me she would 'ave to learn *our* ways.'

'She's a woman,' Standish said. 'Women can adjust. They have to. It's different for men.'

'You would be giving up so much,' Winslow said quietly.

'What?' Richard scoffed. 'What would I be givin' up? I came 'ere because I was promised we were comin' to a new world. Well, far as I can see, it's no different to the old world. We still 'ave masters an' servants an' there's no way out on it. That madman Billington thinks I'm 'is manservant. Well, I'm not. I want to be somebody, not jus' somebody's servant an' 'specially not 'is. I know what I want an' if I 'ave to go native, as you call it, to get it – then so be it.'

Winslow was touched by Richard's passionate sincerity. 'We must consider this matter carefully, gentlemen. I may have been wrong to use the term "go native", with all that implies. It may well be that in the future our sons and ... and our daughters may indeed, to some extent, integrate with the sons and daughters of our Indian friends.'

Governor Carver and Miles Standish frowned. Winslow's emancipated view was something they had not previously considered and both were a little shocked. They had heard, of course, of Pocahontas, the daughter of Powhaton, an Indian chief of Virginia, who had married an English planter and been presented at court to His Majesty the King four or five years earlier. But Pocahontas was a lady of noble blood, her marriage to an Englishman exceptional.

'The first barrier, Richard,' Winslow continued, 'is the language. You would have to learn to speak the girl's language. Or, perhaps, the girl would have to learn ours.'

'I will do whatever is necessary,' Richard said.

'Then,' Winslow said, turning to Carver, 'I suggest, if the governor will leave this with me, I make enquiries, find out what Chief Massasoit's feelings are ....'

Carver nodded in agreement, more than willing to leave it to Winslow.

A subdued air now descended on the settlers. It came with the feeling that an irrevocable step was soon to be taken. The only link with home was soon to be severed, the last exit closed. It might only be for a short time. By chance some other ship might appear on the horizon. But this was unlikely. Not until the *Mayflower* had safely berthed in an English port would plans be made to send out another ship. And what if the *Mayflower* with her skeleton crew failed to reach England? For all of those men and women who were to remain there were mixed feelings. Much that was unknown lay ahead and inevitably thoughts of Roanoke surfaced yet again, the legend of the lost colony a chilling parallel. Yet they were thrilled that news of their arrival and establishment might soon reach home.

It was both an end and a beginning, a time of much talk and little work and in the midst of all this the news of the betrothal of Will Trefor and Daisy Mason soon spread. No one was surprised when Daisy accompanied Will on all his farewell calls. He shook hands with the Carvers and the governor thanked him for his work with and on behalf of the settlers. In return Will thanked him for his letter of support and both Mr and Mrs Carver wished him well and a speedy return. He said goodbye to Bradford, Winslow, Hopkins and others he had come to know well and finally to old Mr Brewster. Then he sought out Squanto, the Indian guide, a man he held in high esteem and whose respect and friendship he had earned. They embraced and Squanto gave him a lucky bone that would ensure, the Indian said, that they would one day meet again.

When Will and Daisy were alone at last the wind dropped and as they made their way up the hillside the sun found gaps in the clouds. Without a word, in a place where they could not be seen from the settlement, they sat down, their fingers entwined in the sparse grass.

'This is madness!' Will exclaimed to the world at large. 'It's taken us all this time to find out what we should have known from the start.'

'I *have* known from the start,' Daisy said with a smile. Then sadly she added, 'And now you have to go.'

He put a hand to her lips. 'Don't say it, Daisy. Don't even mention it. I can only go if I don't think about it.'

Spring was here to dispel the scent of death. Life was exploding in green shoots in the woods and along the shore and in the glow of Daisy's cheeks. That he must leave was cruel and unfair.

'I'll be here,' she promised quietly, 'waiting. If I have to, I'll wait forever.'

They looked out to where the *Mayflower*, still bare-masted but soon to be fully dressed, lay at anchor. Already men could be seen, ant-like creatures from this distance, moving about the decks and in the rigging.

Daisy turned back to Will and there was a look in her eyes he hadn't seen there before. Her voice sounded strange, urgent. 'Stay, Will,' she begged, though she knew she shouldn't. 'Stay with me. We'll survive. We'll have each other. We won't need anyone else.'

Will was confused, his head in a turmoil. He had resigned

himself to the prospect of leaving and he hadn't expected this. Daisy had always been so strong. If she weakened now he knew his own resolve would crumble. He kissed her lips to halt the torrent of words and she responded with an abandon that surprised him.

'If you go now I'll have nothing.'

Will tasted the salt of her tears.

'We could be apart for years ....'

He held her face in his hands. 'I don't have to ....'

But then Daisy drew back. She seemed calmer, more composed, as if she was winning the battle to contain her feelings. 'I'm sorry,' she said. 'I should not have said what I said. It isn't fair.'

He held her tightly to his chest. He wanted to hold her like this and never let go. He wanted to be bound to her in some way. Then suddenly, as if he had stumbled on some startling revelation, he said, 'We could be married now, before I leave.'

Daisy looked at him blankly. Then she laughed, taken by surprise. The thought had not occurred to her. But why not? Why shouldn't they be married now, before he left?

'We don't have to wait,' Will said, his enthusiasm mounting. 'We can be married right away.'

Daisy didn't dare to believe it possible.

'It would take just a few minutes,' Will said. 'A few words, that's all.'

'But what would we do?' There was so little time. 'Who would we ask?'

Will shrugged. 'I don't know. Mr Carver, I expect.'

'But we are not of his faith.'

'Does that matter?' Will asked. 'Is it important?'

Will was right. It didn't matter. The church elders did not regard marriage as a sacrament. In their eyes a marriage was a civil ceremony and should be carried out by an appointed magistrate in accordance with the Dutch law they had observed while resident in Holland. It was simple and straightforward. But preparations for the marriage of John Alden and Priscilla Mullins had been going on for weeks. Priscilla wanted a church service with bridesmaids and a specially made dress – all the trimmings.

'We couldn't just get married,' Daisy said.

'Why not?'

'We'd need time to prepare.'

'We are prepared, aren't we? I'm prepared to marry you and you are prepared to marry me.'

Daisy laughed again. All the trimmings were fine. Most girls would enjoy the fuss. But none of it was essential. 'Could it really be so simple?'

'We can soon find out,' Will said and he pulled her to her feet, held on to her hand and ran with her over the rise and down towards the settlement.

At the water's edge Pat Ellis was drawing a small boat up on to the sand. He raised a hand and they ran towards him.

'Pat! Pat!' they cried and when they reached him they were breathless and for a moment unable to speak.

'What in the name of ...' Pat began in surprise.

'Pat!' Will gripped his arm. 'We want to get married.'

'Well now,' Pat said with a grin. 'You do surprise me.'

'No!' Will almost shook him. 'You don't understand. We mean now. Right now.'

Pat laughed. 'I see. It's that urgent, is it?'

'What do you think, Pat?' Daisy asked soberly. 'Could we?'

'Well, I don't see why not,' the Irishman said and Daisy threw her arms about his neck.

'Hey! Hold on,' he said. 'An' who's goin' to perform the dreadful deed?'

'We thought we might ask Mr Carver,' Will told him. 'We know Daisy is not exactly a member of his congregation but we thought he might oblige.'

Pat looked thoughtful. 'You're serious about this? You want to be married before we sail?'

'Yes,' they said in unison.

'And we haven't much time,' Will added.

'An' you're still goin' back, Will?' Pat asked.

'Yes,' Will said sadly. 'I'm still going back.'

'Then, if Daisy doesn't mind,' Pat suggested, 'I think, if I were you, I'd ask the captain.'

'Captain Jones?'

'You're a sailor, Will. Your home at present is aboard that ship.' He jerked his head towards the *Mayflower*. 'The captain of a ship is empowered to conduct a marriage ceremony – you know that. An' I'm sure Captain Jones would be delighted to do the job.'

'You're a genius,' Will told him.

'I know,' Pat said.

'What do you think, Daisy?'

'I think it's a lovely idea.' She reached up and kissed Pat on the cheek. 'But is there time?'

'Get in,' Pat said, indicating the small boat. 'We'll go across there now an' see the man himself.'

*

Captain Jones agreed at once. Both Will and Daisy were free to
marry and he was free to marry them. Strictly speaking, he pointed
out, he ought to announce a forthcoming marriage at a shipboard
prayer meeting in lieu of banns and allow a day and a night for any
objections to surface. But there was no time for that, he said, and
he agreed to perform the ceremony that evening at seven. The one
stipulation he made was that only a limited number of guests could
attend. His ship was ready to sail and he didn't want the disruption
of a wedding party and all the possible complications of rowdy
behaviour and a drunken crew, not to mention a run on rations, on
this last night. Nor did Will and Daisy. They just wanted to be
married.

The best and biggest of the private cabins was the one previously
occupied by the Mullins family. The captain told them he would be
happy for them to spend their wedding night there. And so the
race was on.

Daisy was bewildered by the speed of events but this was what
she wanted and her only problem now was in limiting the number
of her guests. The governor, Mr Carver, agreed to play a paternal
role and give her away. With Mrs Carver he boarded the shallop
along with Prudence, who would be the chief bridesmaid, and
three girl attendants: Priscilla, Mary and Elizabeth. The only other
guests were Stephen and Elizabeth Hopkins and Miles Standish.
Pat Ellis was the best man.

A little before seven o'clock on that Wednesday evening, April
the fourth, the wedding party, arranged in a semi-circle before
Captain Jones on the main deck of the *Mayflower*, awaited the
arrival of the bride. Will Trefor, freshly scrubbed, his hair brushed
and shining in the mauve and bronze glow of the setting sun, wore
a rust-coloured doublet with shoulder caps and broad stripes down
each sleeve, a borrowed garment that didn't quite fit his wide
shoulders. Beside him, Pat Ellis wore his best leather jerkin over a
dark green shirt and for once Pat had removed his cap and combed
forward his sparse black hair. Ready to conduct the proceedings
Captain Jones was resplendent in his royal-blue, gold-braided
longcoat and his navy-blue felt hat, flat at the front and cocked at
the rear.

From the passage leading from the bridal cabin Daisy emerged
on the arm of Mr Carver, closely followed by Prudence and the
others. The ship's boy, who had led Daisy aboard that day so long
ago in Southwark, was ready and waiting for a nod from his
captain. He wanted to be a piper in the King's Navy and on cue he
made a commendable job of piping the bride into position. As

Daisy reached Will's side the single plaintive notes died away and Captain Jones, holding forth his Book of Common Prayer, intoned, 'Dearly beloved, we are gathered here in the sight of God, and in the face of this congregation, to join this man and this woman in holy matrimony ....'

Daisy looked radiant in a white robe Elizabeth Hopkins had produced from the depths of her trunk, the gown she had worn at her own wedding four years earlier. A crown of fresh spring flowers hastily prepared by Priscilla adorned Daisy's hair and in her left hand she carried a nosegay of large ox-eyed daisies. The ship rocked gently, the last rays of the sun sent fingers of red and gold across the calm waters of the bay and the watchers listened enchanted as the solemnization progressed.

' ...till death us do part,' repeated Daisy, her right hand clasped in Will's right hand, 'according to God's holy ordinance, and thereto I plight thee my troth.'

Captain Jones loosed their hands and held out the open prayer book. Daisy and Will looked at each other in dismay, only then realizing they didn't have a ring. They needed a ring and they didn't have one. It simply hadn't occurred to them. It hadn't occurred to Pat Ellis, the best man, either. Pat looked round at the rapt faces in the semi-circle of onlookers and Mrs Carver came to the rescue.

Without hesitation the governor's wife removed her own wedding ring and passed it to Pat, an action so swift and unobtrusive that those furthest away didn't even know it had taken place. Mr Carver nodded and smiled and squeezed his wife's hand as Pat placed the ring carefully on the captain's book.

There were no further hitches. Captain Jones pronounced Will and Daisy 'man and wife' and finished with the blessing ' ...that ye may so live together in this life, that in the world to come ye may have life everlasting.' Then a cheer went up and there was a surge forward to congratulate the groom and to kiss the bride.

From his limited stock the captain had released a cask of beer, some wine, some Holland gin and some French brandy, and this was soon consumed. By nine o'clock the shallop had left to take the guests ashore and the groom and his bride were alone at last.

The cabin was small but at least the bed was a little wider than the average cabin bed and the bolt on the door ensured they would not be disturbed. Will and Daisy fell into each other's arms. Every moment was precious now for they were both aware that this would be the one and only night they would spend together for many nights to come.

*

Next morning the strains of a hymn drifted up from the settlement on the shore. The farewell service had begun. Governor Carver was offering prayers in gratitude for those seamen who had helped and made friends with his people. He wished them well and a safe passage home. Captain Jones had come ashore with his first mate and Pat Ellis. Will and Daisy had followed later. Only Robert Coppin and a handful of men had remained behind to mind the ship.

The governor invited Captain Jones to read the lesson and the captain delivered a short passage from his King James' Bible. Then he spoke personally to the congregation. There had been times, he said, when he must have seemed to them a tyrant, times when he appeared unfeeling and lacking in compassion, times when they had tired of him and he of them. He knew that. But this venture had been unlike any other he had undertaken and he had been forced to learn and to adapt as he went along. It was an experience he had not wanted but now it was one he would not have missed for the world.

The farewells began again and Will released Daisy for a few moments into the arms of Pat Ellis. Pat held her tightly and told her she would live in his heart until the end of his days. He would return, he said, to his beloved Ireland. And if he should make just one more trip to sea before he 'turned up his toes' he would certainly sail west that he might once again gaze upon the lovely face of his 'adopted daughter'. Tears filled Daisy's eyes and she held him close, but Pat made her promise she would keep a brave face for Will and not send him away with a heavy heart. Then he joined the others in their single file troop down to the beach and the waiting boats.

All around the sailors were tearing themselves away, words of goodwill ringing in their ears. Daisy fought to fend off her tears. 'Come back, Will,' she said. 'That's all I ask. No matter how long it takes. Just come back, that's all.'

Governor Carver walked down to the water's edge with Captain Jones. Most of the men had gone now. Will held his new wife's face in his hands and placed a long, lingering kiss on her lips. The watchers in the assembled congregation smiled and nodded in approval. And at last, with an effort, he turned and walked towards the waiting boat. But then he stopped and looked back.

He was dressed for work in a brown sleeveless jerkin, a dark-blue shirt and rough serge breeches and with the morning sun behind him, the breeze ruffled his thick fair hair. He held out his arms, his clear blue eyes smiling through the heartache. Daisy caught her breath and in that instant the image of him standing there with his arms extended was stamped indelibly in her mind's eye. This was how she would always remember him.

She ran to him and again he clasped her tightly, whispering urgently in her ear, kissing her eyes, her nose, her lips. Then he turned on his heel and joined the captain.

As the last of the boats pulled away into deeper water the congregation pressed forward along the shore. Daisy, her hand raised, kept her eyes on Will until his face was no more than a blur on the slate-grey water. Then she went a little way up the hillside and sat down on the sparse grass as out in the bay the small boats were hauled aboard the *Mayflower*. Behind her, a few yards away but there if needed, Prudence sat down to watch over her mistress.

There was a chill in the air, much of the bright blue of the morning had clouded over and the watchers had drifted away. But later, when the *Mayflower* slipped anchors and began to edge towards the open sea, they were out again in force. Topsails and foresails filled out in the strong breeze. The main sail slid up its mast, billowed then flapped into position and the sight sent a *frisson* through the watchers on the shore. From the gun platform Miles Standish fired a salute, a dull boom from his biggest cannon. Moments later came a small yellow flash from the ship's poop and a distant boom in response.

For the older members of the new community it was a moment of truth. Apart from the Indian tribes, some friendly, some hostile, their nearest neighbours were the English in Virginia and the French in Nova Scotia, 500 miles or more either way. The option that had always been there – the chance to go home – had gone with the *Mayflower*.

On that Thursday morning, April the fifth, 1621, the ship they had come to know so well faded from view and they were left to rely on their own resources for food, drink, shelter and the ability to defend themselves.

Aboard the *Mayflower* Will Trefor had already begun to regret his decision. What on earth had possessed him, he asked himself, to leave his lovely wife, his wife of only one day on that untamed, unknown shore?

39

First priority now was the planting of corn and the settlers lost little time. Under the patient guidance of Squanto, who demonstrated the tried and proven Indian method, they made good progress, planting wheat and peas in addition. The house-building programme was also going well and the settlement was gradually taking shape. Not surprisingly, with all this industry and the steadily improving weather, a fresh optimism began to emerge. Soon, Squanto assured an eager band of workers, the river would be brimful of fish – and so it was.

That spring, on every tide, thousands of herring flooded the mouth of the river and poured into the traps the settlers had laid under Squanto's supervision. The herring were then used to manure the freshly planted corn. Indian tradition decreed that 'when the leaves of the white oak are as large as a mouse's ear' corn must be planted in little mounds of earth about three feet apart, three herrings must be set to each mound, heads to the centre, and in time the seeds must be thinned to the strongest plant.

Twenty acres of ground were cleared and prepared, over forty tons of herring were set to more than ninety thousand mounds – and survival that first season was assured. But without this Indian corn and therefore without Squanto, who showed them how to sow the seeds, the settlers would probably have perished. Sadly, in the midst of all this hard work and good progress, tragedy struck yet again.

The *Mayflower* had been gone less than a week when the governor, John Carver, returned from a long day's work in the corn fields complaining of a headache. Wearily he took to his bed, fully intending to resume work the following morning. Mrs Carver and Miss Minter were constantly on hand to minister to his needs but almost at once he fell into a deep sleep and subsequently into a coma. Dr Fuller was summoned but there was little he could do and within just a few hours the settlement's first governor was dead. He was fifty-four.

John Carver was buried with some ceremony on the hillside overlooking the bay and several volleys of shot were fired as a mark of respect. William Bradford, who had lost his wife Dorothy and had since immersed himself in working for the community, was elected governor in Carver's place and Isaac Allerton was elected deputy. Miles Standish remained in charge of defence and military matters and Edward Winslow, the acknowledged diplomat, was officially appointed ambassador to the Indians. These four and Stephen Hopkins, who was responsible for a number of projects, were effectively the governing body in the new colony and their authority was not challenged. The oldest of the churchmen, Mr Brewster, was more than happy to leave the day-to-day administration in the capable hands of these younger men. Concerning himself mainly with spiritual matters he became the settlers' recognized religious leader.

The death of John Carver was a serious blow. Not to morale – for death was no stranger – but in the sense of loss most of the settlers felt. To many Carver had been a father figure, one of the rocks on which the colony had been founded. To Mrs Carver the death of her husband came as a deep shock, a shock from which she was never to recover. Within a few days she took to her bed, despondent and despairing. And at this, deprived so summarily of her guardians, the unfortunate Miss Minter went about with a look of dumb terror on her thin, sharp-featured face. What would she do now? Who would take care of her? So obviously fearful was she that the new governor asked Daisy Mason to keep an eye on both her and her rapidly failing mistress.

Though in the early days of the voyage she had displayed a haughty, 'holier than thou' manner and a wickedly sharp tongue, Mrs Carver had mellowed. She had become, as so many of the settlers had, more tolerant and more aware of the needs of others. She had never been a robust woman and without a determined effort on her part there was little chance she would survive. She called Daisy to her bedside and held her as firmly as she could by the hand. Daisy leaned closer to catch her faltering words. If there was no suitable husband to be found for her companion, Miss Minter, she hoped Daisy would persuade the poor woman to return home on the first ship that came from England. As for herself, Mrs Carver told Daisy, all she wanted now was to join her husband. And within a few weeks she was dead. Mrs Carver, Dr Fuller concluded, had lost the will to live, a verdict interpreted by many of the settlers as 'she died of a broken heart'.

Matters of life and death and love and marriage followed in

rapid succession. No sooner were the Carvers dead and buried than a wedding was announced. On May the twelfth Edward Winslow, whose wife Elizabeth had been dead only six weeks, married Susannah White. Susannah, a sister of Dr Fuller, had two small children. The spring epidemic had taken her husband and their two menservants. The marriage now between Edward and Susannah was a civil ceremony performed by the new governor. Edward's younger brother, Gilbert, was the best man and Dr Fuller gave the bride away.

The marriage raised no eyebrows. Quick remarriages were normal and necessary, and for both Edward and Susannah their marriage was an act of faith in the future. The celebrations were quietly happy and a congenial gathering, including a number of Massasoit Indians, joined in the festivities. The balmy weather and the appearance of the first apple blossom no doubt encouraged the general feeling that this wedding, with due respect to their previous partners, was the result of a love match. Edward was a fine young man – certainly, as John Carver had several times asserted, a 'pillar of the new community' – and his bride Susannah was exceptionally pretty. Romance was palpably in the air that day in May and none of it was lost on Prudence.

Thrilled by Daisy's shipboard wedding to Will and spurred on by almost daily progress reports from Priscilla on preparations for her marriage to John, Prudence was eager to advance her own plans. Everyone's getting married, she told herself. Why not me? And before the night was out she had again beseeched Daisy to give her blessing to her betrothal to Maurice Tinker.

'Maurice wants to marry me,' Prudence argued. 'His father wants 'im to marry me. Please, Miss Daisy.'

'Mr Tinker wants Maurice to marry you?'

'Oh yes,' Prudence assured her. 'There's only you.'

'If you go to the governor,' Daisy said, 'you'll find you don't need my blessing. You can marry whoever you like.'

'But I wouldn't be 'appy if you didn't approve.'

'I'll see,' Daisy said at last and the look of delight on Pru's face caused her to add at once, 'I only said, "I'll see". That's all.'

'Mr Tinker said 'e would like to see you.'

'Good,' Daisy said, 'and I would like to see Mr Tinker.'

Daisy's resolve was weakening. Perhaps she was wrong about Maurice. But, at least, she would make certain that Tinker was not simply solving two problems for himself at Pru's expense by finding a wife for his less than adequate son and an unpaid skivvy for the Tinker family household.

Soon after the Winslow wedding two unfortunate incidents concerning Alice Rigdale and her missing baby occurred. Alice appeared to have calmed somewhat but there was still the wild, haunted look in her eyes and no one underestimated her torment. Dr Fuller still feared she was slowly losing her mind. But the search for the baby had not been called off. And all of the Indian newcomers to the settlement were asked if they had any knowledge of the whereabouts of the missing child and made aware of the reward offered for the baby's safe return.

The first incident occurred when an old squaw claimed the baby was living with Narragansett Indians in a village to the north of the Cape and went on to describe the child and the clothing she wore. Alice was ecstatic and begged to be taken there at once but Edward Winslow, not trusting the squaw, pointed out that a general description of the child and the clothing she was wearing at the time of her disappearance could be obtained from a number of sources. The tribe the woman mentioned, Winslow said, were one of the least aggressive of the Narragansett. They knew the baby was missing and living as they did in an isolated spot, closer to the Massasoit than to their own people, they would be unlikely to want to cause offence. The new governor called a meeting and after some discussion his closest advisers, including Winslow, agreed that every lead, no matter how tenuous, must be followed up. It was resolved that Squanto be asked to make the forty-mile journey and, taking with him goodwill gifts from the settlers and greetings from the King of England, find out if there was any truth in what the squaw alleged.

Squanto received a less than friendly welcome from the Narragansetts – he was widely regarded as a white man's tool – but he returned convinced that the child was not and never had been with them. The squaw, who had persistently claimed the reward, pestering the governor at his every appearance, was finally warned that if she did not desist from telling her lies the white man's God would descend from the skies and wreak a terrible vengeance upon her. She responded by putting a curse on the whole settlement and shuffling off into the woods, muttering and wailing as she went. Later it emerged, from information received from the Massasoits, the squaw was a well-known local trickster and she was wholly discredited.

None of this helped Alice Rigdale who was trying to hold on to her sanity. Not physically ill she was able to help with minor jobs around the common house although someone was always on hand to keep a watchful eye on her. It was one morning soon after Squanto's return that the second incident occurred. Alice had pinned her hopes on the tall Indian bringing home her baby and she had refused to accept or even acknowledge his failure. Now, unfortunately, a lone Indian, a tall, physically well-proportioned man not unlike Squanto emerged from the edge of the wood. He was cradling a small bundle in his arms.

From the rear of the common house Alice saw him first and she let out a little yelp of joy. With no one near enough to stop her she raced to meet him and taking him by surprise she attempted to wrest the bundle from him. Naturally the Indian resisted and in the struggle that followed the bundle unravelled and a variety of small carved objects fell to the ground. The Indian was bringing his handiwork for sale to the settlers and his first thought was that Alice was trying to steal his goods. When he saw the look on her face and the gleam in her eye he concluded she was mad and at that moment she probably was. When she saw there was no baby in the bundle her joy turned to a massive disappointment and frustration and she rained blows on the Indian's painted chest.

It took three women to restrain Alice and several men, who had been at work on a house nearby, to calm the innocent brave. Winslow insisted on dining the man well and Squanto spent more than an hour explaining who Alice was and why she had behaved as she had. And from then on Alice Rigdale was regarded as unstable, a person who, sad though her circumstances were, would in future have to be kept under much closer surveillance.

As early as the end of May Daisy knew she had a baby inside her and she was overjoyed. At least she had something of Will. Even if she had to wait for years for his return, if all went well she would have something, a part of him to cherish and to love. At first she told no one, then one morning when she felt an uncharacteristic nausea she told Prudence. Pru who was wildly excited at the prospect, told Priscilla and the others and soon it was common knowledge. Miles Standish, with an armful of flowers, was one of the first to offer his congratulations. Dr Fuller called to see her and the Winslows, the Hopkins, the Allertons all came to pay their respects. The governor, Mr Bradford, who said he was delighted at the news, also came to wish her well.

Most of Daisy's visitors stayed to partake of her sweet white wine, made from the local grape. Some of the older ones discussed Will's prospects in England but invariably the conversation would turn to names for the baby. There were many suggestions, though most assumed she would call a male child 'Will'. Daisy never entered the discussions. Already she had made up her mind. A male child she would call Patrick in tribute to their mutual friend Pat Ellis and she knew Will would approve. If the baby was a girl she would call her Rose in memory of Rose Standish who, in a strange way, had brought her and Will together.

Those early summer months, warm and pleasant, did much to restore the good health and well-being of those settlers who had survived. For some time now food had not been in short supply. Cod and bass were there for the taking and occasionally, in the woods, a deer was stalked and shot. Even their original store of food was not yet exhausted and due to the reduction in their numbers there was still about ten pounds of oatmeal per week for each settler, man, woman and child. But throughout that summer and into autumn there were rumbles of trouble and veiled threats from various sources, usually retailed through Squanto who had become aware of his unique position and power as sole interpreter.

Miles Standish began purposely to distance himself from Squanto and quietly cultivated a Massasoit who held the rank of *pinese*, a title which denotes a brave who has undergone a long and arduous training. Superstition had it that a *pinese* lived under the protection of the gods and could never be wounded in battle. Standish's *pinese* was called Hobomok and he was chosen because he had somehow acquired a little English and was eager to learn more. Not surprisingly Squanto was jealous, but more and more, using Hobomok, Standish was able to check the validity of any threats.

Now was the time for the settlers to give thanks and to count their blessings. They had survived for almost a year, reduced in number, racked by sickness and disease, lacking until recently adequate food and shelter. But they were beginning to realize they had overcome the first major hurdles and were well on their way to establishing themselves in their new surroundings.

The yield from the English seed had been disappointingly poor but the Indian corn, sown under Squanto's direction, had done exceptionally well. Fish and fowl were plentiful and from the wild grapes several varieties of wine could be made. Flights of duck were there for the shooting and large numbers of wild turkeys had suddenly appeared.

With the harvest in, Governor Bradford sent four marksmen fowling and they returned with enough birds to feed the settlers for a week. The governor promptly invited Chief Massasoit and a large number of his tribesmen to a party of rejoicing, a kind of harvest festival. The chief accepted happily and arrived bearing five deer to add to the feast.

Miles Standish arranged a military review and his small band of auxiliaries put on a display of musketry and shooting skills. Games were played, the evening wore on and the Indians, in the glow of several bonfires, danced and chanted well into the warm night.

The great party went on for three days and both settlers and Indians enjoyed helpings of duck and goose, eels, clams and other shellfish, leeks, watercress, a variety of herb salads, wild plums and dried berries, lots of corn bread, and white or red wine. High on the menu was the succulent venison but so, too, at that first Thanksgiving party, was an abundant supply of roast turkey.

That they permitted so many of their squaws and their children to join in the governor's party was a tribute to the trust and goodwill of the Massasoits. But two young people who might have symbolized the increasing ties between the two sides were noticeably absent.

In the matter of Richard Gardiner and his love for the Indian girl, Edward Winslow had conferred with Squanto. Both men were of the opinion that the girl's father would not allow her to leave her village. Squanto knew the man, a proud and well-respected sachem. He also knew the man's four sons, all of them strong and worthy braves. If the English boy was to marry the girl he would have to be accepted by her brothers as well as by her father. But this should not be a problem, thought Winslow. Richard was a strong, wiry young man. He had come through the epidemic and his health was good. He learned fast and he cut a fine figure chopping wood or working outdoors, stripped to the waist.

News of Richard's romance with the Indian girl had spread fast and though many of the women, especially the younger women, were intrigued, some of the settlers, both men and women, had mixed feelings. It was what they saw as an irreconcilable clash of cultures. There were just, they felt, too many obstacles. Though what these obstacles were no one could put into words.

When John Billington heard of his young lodger's involvement the two almost came to blows. 'You want to marry a native?' Billington exclaimed loudly and in a derisory way. 'A redskin? I wouldn't 'ave one o' my boys bringin' one o' them lot 'ome, I can tell you. Wouldn't want my missus mixin' in with the likes o' them, either.'

'It may well be,' Richard told him bluntly, 'they wouldn't want any of their people mixin' with the likes of you.'

Billington was incensed. 'What do you mean by that?'

A scuffle had developed and it had taken four or five men to restore order. But, although John Billington was disliked by most of the settlers, there were undoubtedly some who shared his sentiments.

Winslow, as always, was true to his word. He consulted Chief Massasoit who summoned the sachem. The girl's father showed no sign of knowing of his daughter's interest in Richard, listened carefully to what the chief and Winslow had to say and went away. A few days later a message came for Winslow to the effect that the sachem would not allow his daughter to become 'a white woman'. The white boy must come to him and speak with him in his village. If the sachem approved of him and his proposal of marriage then, to marry his daughter, Richard would have to become a Massasoit.

Richard had gone to the girls' house to seek out Daisy Mason. Will Trefor, he told her, would have advised him. He had accompanied Will on most of his shore excursions and he had come to admire and respect Will's judgement.

'What would he have said, Miss Daisy?' he asked. 'What would Will have done?'

Daisy didn't know. She couldn't say for certain what Will would have advised.

'Then what would you do,' he asked, 'if you were me?'

Daisy knew now that, in her own case, if she had the choice again she would do everything in her power to prevent Will from leaving. The risk that he might not return, that she might lose him, was too great.

'If I were you,' she told Richard, 'I would follow my heart. Go to her, Richard. If you lose her now you may regret it for the rest of your life.'

Richard had gone at once and Squanto had gone with him. Squanto had returned alone. The sachem, he explained, had given his consent and the marriage would be arranged by the sachem's eldest son. All of the settlers would be invited to the wedding. According to Squanto, marriages were solemnized by an exchange of gifts between the families of the bride and groom. Richard had no family, Winslow said, and this could prove a problem. But Governor Bradford said, 'We are Richard's family, all of us. We will provide suitable gifts and we will be happy to attend the celebration.'

Richard had agreed to marry the girl and go to live with her tribe. But he did not want all of the settlers to attend the celebration, Squanto said. He did not want any of them to attend. Richard had told Squanto he wanted to cut himself off from the settlers and his white-man's past completely and forever. The sachem could not understand this, Squanto said, and it was finally agreed, if this was acceptable to the settlers, that Mr Winslow, Captain Standish and Richard's only two friends Gilbert Winslow, Edward's younger brother, and another young man, Peter Browne, would represent the governor. Governor Bradford could only shrug his shoulders and agree.

The sachem took the four men to be Richard's brothers and greeted them cordially. Each presented him with a gift and received a gift in return. Then Winslow gave the sachem a small jewelled dagger in a leather sheath, a present from the governor. The sachem responded with an exquisitely carved wooden figure of a moose.

When the proceedings began Richard stepped forward with his radiant young bride and bowed first to her father and then to her eldest brother. He was wearing bleached breeches and a rough grey shirt. Standing before the chief he removed the shirt and his sun-tanned arms and shoulders looked pale against those of the braves. He kicked off his buckled shoes and slowly removed his breeches. Wearing only a waist-cloth now he knelt before the sachem. Standing upright the sachem placed a band with a single feather on Richard's head. Then Richard stepped back and, hand in hand, he and his bride turned away.

With one last glance at his four English 'brothers', Richard followed the girl who led him to a wigwam festooned with flowers. Then, as they entered and the flap closed behind them, the bride's attendants and other young females formed a ring around the marital tent and the dancing and the chanting began.

The men from the settlement didn't see Richard again that evening and he was never again seen in European clothing.

Some days after the governor's party of thanksgiving, when the settlement had been restored to something like its previous order and work in the fields and on the houses had resumed, the thoughts of many turned to home and there were those who were homesick. For the first time since their hazardous arrival the settlers found a period of relative calm. Now, with the prospect once again of bleak months ahead, they could look back and consider the ravages of the voyage, the ensuing epidemic and the losses sustained by almost every family. And it was one morning during this quiet period of hard work and hoarding for the winter that a momentous event occurred and the news ran through the settlement in seconds.

The five-year-old son of Susannah White, now Winslow, saw it first and he ran to tell his mother who nodded, busy with her washing, and murmured, 'Yes, yes.' But the child was insistent, tugging at her skirts until the excitement in his voice and the word 'ship' got through to her. By the time they had run outside and down to the beach others had seen it, too. On the horizon a small ship had appeared.

What would it bring? What news from home? It was well over a year since they left England. But as the excitement grew among the settlers gathered on the shore their leaders warned that the ship might not be English. It was too far out to identify its flags but it could be French or Spanish. It could even be a pirate ship.

A shot was fired from one of the cannons and Standish and his men – and in times of danger this meant most of the adult males – took to their arms and formed up on the beach.

But they need not have worried. The ship was the *Fortune*, a fifty-five ton English vessel out of the port of London.

40

For several days without success those aboard the *Fortune* had scoured the coastline for signs of a settlement. They had begun to fear the settlers from England had somehow perished. Perhaps the dreadful epidemic Captain Jones had recorded in his log of the voyage and landfall had finally wiped them out. Perhaps they had simply starved to death in the wake of a failed harvest. Perhaps they had been slaughtered by the Indians. Such fears had resulted in the newcomers refusing to go ashore in search parties.

They feared the unknown but they also feared that the master of the *Fortune*, a Captain Thomas Barton, might sail away without them. The captain assured them he had no such intention. There were sufficient reserves of food and water, he said, for them to stay for a while and search the coast. If they had no success they could then sail on to Virginia. But few had faith in Captain Barton. He was an impatient and often imperious man, not to be trusted. And so the slow search continued offshore until, that November morning, the *Fortune* arrived in the bay at New Plymouth.

Flying the flag of St George of England, the long awaited ship from home dropped anchor and the settlers gathered on the shore welcomed her with cheers and tears of joy. But the joy, at least for the governing body of the new colony, was short-lived. Though there were letters and packages and small parcels for many and news of relatives and friends, Governor Bradford and his advisors soon realized the *Fortune* had brought more liabilities than assets. There was little in the way of practical equipment or items of use to the new community. The settlers had hoped for so much: tools, seeds, even livestock. But there was nothing. Instead of bringing more food and urgently needed medical supplies the *Fortune* had brought another thirty or so mouths to feed. And despite their good first harvest and the stores they were busily laying in it was immediately obvious the settlers would be hard put to feed themselves *and* the newcomers in the months to come.

There were about thirty-five passengers on board but when they came ashore not all of them wanted to stay. Five or six decided to return home. Of those eager to remain there were some strong workmen, but they brought with them barely any food, no pots or pans or other utensils and very little clothing. Aboard the *Fortune*, remaindered from some earlier voyage, was a consignment of cheap, ready-made garments. These were hastily unpacked and distributed. But there was little else.

To many the most precious of the few items the *Fortune* brought was the bag of mail containing letters from relatives and friends in both London and Holland. The bag was carried carefully, almost ceremoniously, up the sloping road to the common house. The original settlers crowded into the main hall as Governor Bradford drew out the letters and small packages one at a time and always with an exaggerated flourish that seemed to delight the children watching. The name of each lucky recipient was greeted with a small cheer and sometimes a squeal of excitement.

There was a bulky letter for Miles Standish which he put inside his tunic to be read in private. There were two letters for Daisy Mason, both from Will, which she tore open. But these had been written aboard the *Mayflower* on the voyage home. There was even a letter for Prudence, which both thrilled and puzzled her. She had neither family nor friends in England – 'none as could read or write, anyways,' as she put it – and this, too, turned out to be a letter from Will, also written on the voyage home. In it, Will thanked Pru for attending his wedding, asked her to thank the other girls, wished her luck and hoped she would 'take good care of Miss Daisy' for him. But in all three letters there was, of course, no new news of Will.

It was almost a week after his ship's arrival that the master of the *Fortune*, Captain Barton, who had until then been busily engaged in discussions with Governor Bradford and others, began to make enquiries about a Mrs Trefor. At first his questions were met with blank stares then someone recalled that Daisy Mason was now Mrs Will Trefor. Daisy, who by this time was seven months pregnant, had given up heavy work in the communal wash-house and was content to sew and repair clothing at home in the girls' house.

Captain Barton arrived unannounced and introduced himself on Daisy's doorstep. Daisy didn't much like the look of him but courtesy prevailed and she invited him in. The podgy captain took a seat and Daisy offered him a glass of her elderberry wine which he accepted with alacrity. He noted that she was in an advanced state of pregnancy and enquired when the baby was due. Early January, she told him. Excellent, he said. Then, licking his lips of elderberry wine, he said he had news of her husband. Daisy jumped from her chair in excitement but he held up a fat hand to calm her.

'It's little enough, dear lady,' he warned.

Daisy resumed her seat and sat facing him, her hands in her lap. 'What is it?' she asked. 'What news?'

'Captain Jones of the *Mayflower* asked me, if I should ever reach this place, to seek you out. He told me he performed a ceremony of marriage for you and Mr Trefor aboard his ship the day before he sailed for home. He also told me of your husband's predicament.'

'Yes,' Daisy said, eager to hurry the long-winded and pompous ship's captain but not wanting to alienate him.

'The master of the *Mayflower* asked me to inform you that all of the documents relevant to your husband's case and also his plea for mitigation have been submitted to the appropriate authorities.'

She nodded.

'And that he – Captain Jones, that is – has arranged to make himself available to bear witness at any trial ....'

'What news have you of my husband, Captain Barton?'

'Mr Trefor was taken into custody in the Port of London, ma'am. He awaits trial by His Majesty's court-martial.'

'Where did they take him?'

'I understand, as there is no naval prison in the city ... though there is one, of course ... quite a large one, in Dartmouth ....'

Daisy's patience was running out.

'I understand Mr Trefor is at present held in the Tower.'

Daisy shaded her eyes. The thought of Will incarcerated in that bleak hell chilled her heart. She saw the clay-coloured Tower, the King's colours flapping above the battlements and Will's face, his blue eyes, his stubborn jaw ... his chains. Would he be left to wait alone in some foul dungeon? Or would he be cast among thieves and murderers in a stinking, overcrowded communal cell? Oh, my darling, she murmured silently. Have faith. Hold on. Pray for the day ....

A pleasant, warm smell from the kitchen pervaded the house. Captain Barton raised his squashed pink nose and sniffed. 'You are baking, are you not, Mrs Trefor?'

With a clear, dry eye Daisy regarded the insensitive captain. 'Baking?'

'Baking.'

'I have nothing ready,' she said, though she knew there was a large bilberry pie already done.

The *Fortune* stayed less than a month. The settlers had put together a cargo of oak staves and beaver skins estimated to be worth about £500. This was stored in the ship's hold to be traded in London. The governor and his advisers hoped for a quick exchange and that supplies and equipment they sorely needed would be shipped out to them at the earliest possible date. But for now they were faced with more immediate matters, not least how to sustain the enlarged community throughout the winter. It was agreed that the whole settlement should be put on half rations – enough of a reduction, they hoped, to see them through.

Unfortunately, on the return voyage, the *Fortune* was waylaid, either by pirates or French sailors masquerading as pirates, at the entrance to the English Channel. The thieves took most of the cargo along with anything else of obvious value including even the ship's instruments. But they were not interested in the papers and documents in the captain's locker and these were preserved, among them a letter written by Edward Winslow which was later printed and published in London along with other items of news and information about the New England settlement.

Winslow's letter was clearly designed to encourage emigration to the New World. He described the events of that first Thanksgiving celebration and praised the Indians for their friendship, good faith and generosity. *We have found the Indians very faithful in their covenant of peace with us*, he wrote. *We often go to them and they come to us* .... He compared the weather to that in England. *If there be any difference at all, this is somewhat hotter in summer. Some think it to be colder in winter, but I cannot out of experience so say. The air is very clear.*

As for the fruits of the earth, Winslow wrote: *For fish and fowl, we have great abundance; fresh cod in the summer is but coarse meat with us; our bay is full of lobsters. In September we can take a hogshead of eels in the night, with small labour, and can dig them out of their beds all the winter. All the springtime the earth sendeth forth naturally very good sallet herbs. Here are grapes, white and red, and very sweet and strong also; strawberries, gooseberries, plums of three sorts with black and red being almost as good as a damson; abundance of roses, white, red and damask .... The country wanteth only industrious men to employ, for it would grieve your hearts if, as I, you had seen so many miles together by goodly rivers uninhabited.*

Everything in his letter supported his assurance that *I make no question but men might live as contented here as in any part of the world.*

Soon after the *Fortune* left for home the Narragansett Indians, rivals of the settlers' friend Chief Massasoit and sworn enemies of all white men, issued a challenge. Like the other tribes along that north-east coast the Narragansett, who occupied most of what is now Rhode Island, had heard that the ship from England had brought no arms and few supplies, only more mouths to feed. Under the impression the settlers had been reduced to a bewildered band of mainly women and children struggling to survive, they sent a fearsome-looking brave to present the small community with what turned out to be a bundle of arrows wrapped in a snakeskin.

Squanto explained to Miles Standish that this was both a threat and a challenge: either fight us to the death or surrender. Standish recommended at once that the snakeskin should be filled with powder and shot and returned to the Narragansett chief with a message. The message, translated by Squanto and delivered in the presence of the other Indian interpreter, Standish's guide Hobomok, was to the effect that the settlers had done the Indians no harm and their consciences were clear. They were neither frightened of the Narragansett nor unprepared to do battle. If the Narragansett wanted war they could have it.

The brave returned to his tribe and soon both Squanto and Hobomok were of the opinion the Narragansett would not attack. They had heard that the settlers' response had scared the

Narragansett chief who believed the powder in the skin represented a curse and the threat of a deadly plague. The chief had refused to touch it and would not have it near him. But despite these assurances drums and chants could be heard in the surrounding woods. Taking no chances Standish posted extra guards and look-out men, though he was anxious to show the settlers were not living in fear of attack and Indian visitors to the settlement were as welcome as ever.

Towards the end of January, in the midst of all this uncertainty, Daisy Mason Trefor gave birth to a son. *A fine baby boy*, Dr Fuller recorded. *Both mother and son in rude good health.*

There was great excitement in the girls' house and Daisy was not short of willing helpers. Prudence and Priscilla and the two younger girls all wanted to take care of the baby. Nor was she short of visitors. Miles Standish brought a gift of a gold sovereign for the boy and stayed to tea. He had received an encouraging letter from his dead wife's sister, Barbara. Apparently, at Will's request, Pat Ellis had called on Barbara at the home of her aunt in Richmond. Barbara had, of course, been deeply saddened by the news of Rose's death and had arranged to return at once to Lancashire to inform her parents. But she had also expressed an interest in coming out on a visit or, perhaps, to stay. Miles was obviously excited at the prospect.

The elderly Mr Brewster presented the newborn babe with a book of the Old Testament, a volume he had treasured since his own childhood. Edward Winslow's new wife, Susannah, brought baby clothes which her children had outgrown. So, too, did Elizabeth Hopkins whose own baby, born aboard the *Mayflower* and christened Oceanus, had not survived the epidemic. Mary Chilton, now aged sixteen, had secretly made a sampler with the baby's name and date and place of birth embroidered in gold thread: Patrick William Trefor, 24 January, 1622, New Plymouth.

With so many smiling visitors and with so much goodwill in their comings and goings, Daisy had little time to pause and reflect. But when she was alone with her child and she felt the bond that would bind her now for the rest of her life, Daisy realized, for the first time and as only a mother can, just how desolate Pru must have felt when she lost her baby and, perhaps even more difficult to bear, how Alice Rigdale must feel in not knowing what happened to her little Alice.

Protected by all, Alice Rigdale roamed the settlement now with a vacant but serene look in her eyes, murmuring quietly to herself as if privately she lived in a happier past. Her mind had finally gone one morning when she looked out to the hillside where so many dead were buried and saw her baby daughter sitting on a grassy mound. Little Alice was laughing and raising her arms as if asking to be picked up. Alice dropped her work basket and ran towards her. Others followed, thinking she might be about to do herself an injury. But her eagerness gave Alice added speed and she reached the mound first – only to find there was no one there. No baby; nothing. It was all in her imagination.

Alice had fallen to her knees and as people gathered round she knelt with her head in her hands and wept. Elizabeth Hopkins' husband, Stephen, had been the first to reach her and it seemed sensible to him to allow her to cry and to recover in her own time. But she never did recover. When her thin, narrow shoulders at last stopped shaking and she looked up at Dr Fuller with that strange, detached expression the doctor knew the worst had happened. At his request the women had led her quietly back to the common house and without a word between them they knew, too. Alice had lost her mind.

Ironically, some of the new people from the *Fortune* unaware of her circumstances, tended to glance anxiously at their own children whenever the slightly deranged-looking Alice appeared. Some of their older children even started to tease and torment her and refer to her, in their childish play, as 'Mad Alice'. But the governor sternly put a stop to this, reprimanding the offenders and informing their parents.

And so the life of the settlement went on. John and Priscilla were married and a week later Prudence married her Maurice. Susannah White Winslow called on Daisy with an apologetic laugh and a hint that when Daisy's little boy had outgrown the baby clothes she might need to borrow them back. With any luck, as Governor Bradford frequently predicted, there were going to be lots of babies.

As for Daisy Mason, that second year was a time of hope and patient waiting. Whether at work in the common house, her baby strapped to her breast, or at home in the girls' house her heart and mind were with Will. Was he cold and hungry? Was he alone in the dark, a bleak and wintry London beyond those high walls? Was he allowed visitors? Pat, perhaps. Or Captain Jones. Daisy was desperate for news, a letter, a message, anything.

Friends rallied round. Elizabeth Hopkins and her husband, Susannah and Edward Winslow, the governor himself – all called regularly to encourage and reassure her. The next boat, they said, would bring more letters, more news from home. It might even bring Will, a man free to take the place of honour and high esteem that awaited him. Old Mr Brewster urged her to pray, to ask God for 'the early deliverance and speedy return of her fine young husband to this community devised and created in the name of God and to which he has so much to offer.'

The year wore on and sometimes, when the weather was fair, Daisy would take a blanket and sit on the grassy hillside overlooking the bay, her baby by her side. Often she would reflect on the strange sequence of events that had led her to this place, just a few feet from where her friend Rose lay buried and almost 3,000 miles from where her husband languished in the dreaded Tower. And sometimes, as she scanned the horizon, she would see the smiling face of her Duchess. Not as it was in that tiny bedroom in that dingy hovel in St Giles the night she died. No, not like that. She saw the Duchess as she was in the days when together they strolled like ladies in St James's Park, just as she wanted to remember her.

Thanks to the Duchess, Daisy had what the Duchess herself had always wanted and could not have: a new life in a new world. And this *was* a new world and a part of it belonged to Daisy. It was her home, the first real home she had ever had, and it was her child's home, too. With a feeling of joy, Daisy would look to the north and then to the south along that unfledged shore. It was new, as new and unspoilt as her baby son. This was her land now, her son's land, their homeland. All she needed to make her life complete, she told herself, was Will. And sometimes, in her sleep or in her mind's eye, she would see the ship, all flags flying, that one day would appear on the horizon and bring him back, bring him home to where he truly belonged.

It was the end of May when Daisy, at the girls' house with her baby, heard from Prudence that a shallop carrying seven Englishmen had arrived in the bay. The shallop was from a ship called *Sparrow* believed to be fishing off the coast of Maine, a vessel owned by Thomas Weston of the London Company of Merchant Adventurers. The men in the shallop, according to Pru, had brought a bag filled with letters from home. Mr Bradford was about to distribute them.

Along Leyden Street doors and windows were open to welcome the morning's warmth. It was a lovely day, the sun coaxing out the early summer buds and shoots, that feeling of life about to begin anew in the air. Daisy wanted to go up to the common house to see if there was a letter for her but her baby was sleeping so peacefully she didn't want to disturb him. Not yet. And so she waited and as she waited she began to accept that there was nothing for her – not this time. If there had been a letter Pru would probably have come running to tell her.

She wondered later at what precise moment she knew the truth. It was before she saw the look on his face. It was probably the moment she saw him at her door, Elizabeth Hopkins at his side.

'I have received a ... a communication,' the governor said. 'From Mr Ellis ... the Irish gentleman.'

'Sit down, Daisy,' Elizabeth said softly. 'Please.'

Daisy looked from one to the other.

'Mr Trefor ... your husband Will ...' the governor began.

'What?' Her eyes dared him to say it.

'I am most dreadfully sorry to have to tell you this, my dear, but ... Will is dead.'

Daisy sat down.

'Mr Ellis asked me to tell you personally,' the governor rushed on. 'He didn't want you to hear it in ... in some casual way.'

There were no tears. Not yet.

'It would appear that all efforts to save him failed,' Bradford told her. 'Many people, I believe, spoke on his behalf but the King was adamant. Will pleaded guilty to a charge of desertion and asked for the court's indulgence. But this was refused.' He frowned and looked perplexed. 'I would not have thought that leaving one's ship, except in a time of war, was a capital offence ....' His voice trailed. 'There was an appeal for clemency but this, too, was denied.'

Daisy barely heard the governor's words.

'And this ... this is for you, my dear.'

It was a letter from Pat. Daisy took the letter and lifted her sleeping baby from his crib.

'Daisy,' Elizabeth said anxiously.

But Daisy seemed perfectly composed as she turned and went out into the sun. Cradling her baby in her arms, Pat's letter clutched in her fist, she walked slowly towards the hillside.

Prudence came running from the street. She had heard the rumour. But no, it couldn't be. It was a lovely summer's day. A day to rejoice in the sheer joy of being alive. Then Elizabeth met her at the door and she knew it was true. She saw Daisy and turned to run after her but the governor laid a gently restraining hand on her arm and shook his head.

Daisy sat down in the short dry grass at the spot where so often she had scanned the distant horizon. She fixed her gaze on the line where the sea met the sky. It had become a habit and it was strange to think there was no longer any reason to watch for ships from home. A ship might sail, all flags flying, into the bay. But none now would carry Will.

The baby was sleeping soundly. Daisy held him in the crook of her arm and told him softly that his father, the father he had never seen and who had never seen him, was dead. Rocking to and fro she nursed the child and tried to focus her thoughts on the mind-numbing news. Then she opened the letter from Pat.

My dear Daisy, she read. *By now I trust Mr Bradford has told you the worst. There is little more for me to say and yet so much. As you would expect, Will died a brave and honourable death. He didn't complain or rant at the injustice. The rage was mine. For days I was unable to speak at the colossal waste of a fine young man, murdered – yes, murdered – on the orders of a lunatic King. Of this I shall say no more. Except that if this note should fall into other hands I would have it known that these words and this treason are mine, not yours.*

I was permitted to stay with Will for much of the night before that dreadful morning, the night that was to be his last on this earth, and all of the time I was with him he spoke only of you. He wanted to tell you of his feelings for you and he asked for the means to write. But his request was refused. A last letter to his beloved wife – that was all he asked. But the court had decreed he should be denied all means of communication with the world outside lest his words corrupt. He was seen as a danger, a member of an anti-monarchist family and condemned for whatever sins his father may or may not have committed. And all he wanted was to write a letter of farewell. A last letter, he said, to the only woman he had ever truly loved.

All through that last night his thoughts were only of you. He had always imagined, he said, that one day he would find God. But it had not happened. He found you and then, so soon, he lost you. How could he believe in a God who treated him so badly? But if there is a God, he said, he would like Him to know that already he has seen his own true heaven – for now nothing could compare with those few fleeting hours he spent alone, with you.

He said, too, that he wanted you to begin your life anew – without him. You are young, he said. Others will be drawn to you as he was. He hoped you would find love again, though no one could ever love you as he had.

At times he was confused, at others a model of clarity. I have tried to recall the very essence of what he said and one vow, one declaration, stands above all else. In his youth, he told me, he considered himself something of a poet. 'But now,' he said, 'even in the shadow of the axeman, the only words that will fall from my lips in those final moments will be Daisy. Daisy Mason.'

There was a space then Pat had written: *As for myself, I can truly say that had I been blessed with a son I could wish for none better than Will. I must live what's left of my life in the sad knowledge that I was among those who advised Will to return to England and so condemned him to so untimely and undeserved a fate. Much of the pain you will be feeling now, believe me, I feel with you. For, as you well know, to me you are a daughter, a daughter I love dearly.*

A tear fell on the page and Daisy looked up at the clear blue sky. She looked out to sea, towards that distant land where her heart lay buried. Her baby stirred, opened his eyes. She held him close. This was her land now and this child was her future – hers and Will's.

Postscript

Of the 102 passengers who made the celebrated voyage aboard the *Mayflower* just over fifty survived, twenty of them under the age of sixteen. The married women fared worst. After that first bleak winter only six out of eighteen were left. But most of those settlers who did survive steadily gained in health and strength. And John Carver's wish that they would marry and produce many children for the future of the settlement was certainly fulfilled.

From the girls' house Mary Chilton married John Winslow. John had come out from England to join his brothers Edward and Gilbert. He and Mary had nine children. When she was eighteen Elizabeth Tilley married John Howland, the young manservant who almost drowned when he was swept overboard in a storm. They had ten children. John Alden and Priscilla Mullins produced eleven.

The story of the seaman, Dyke, is substantially true. There *was* a seaman who threatened and tormented the passengers and he *did* die in the manner described but there is no record of his name.

(The name 'Dyke' is the invention of the author.) The man named John Billington, a Londoner who joined the *Mayflower* with his wife and family at Southwark, was in many ways of an equally unpleasant disposition and he, too, met with a sorry end. After many transgressions he was hanged, in October 1630, for the murder of a young man named John Newcome with whom he had quarrelled.

Over the years there were many tales of a white man who rode with the Indians and dressed as a brave. And there were almost as many alleged sightings of a young white girl who lived and travelled with the natives. Later still there were tales of a white squaw. But little Alice Rigdale was never found.

On a happier note, Miles Standish, who had lost his wife Rose, was delighted when her sister Barbara arrived on a visit in 1623. Barbara stayed and in due course she and Captain Standish were married. They had four sons. Prudence and her Maurice produced two children. The first a boy whom they named Will, the second a girl whom they named, not surprisingly, Daisy. There appears to be no record of what became of Daisy Mason.

These then are the people who crossed the wide, wild Atlantic in the late summer of the year 1620 in a small, overcrowded ship in search of a New World – and thus began the creation of what was to become the United States of America.